"With *The Crying Forest*, Venero Armanno delivers a tale of murder and magic, of dark desires and the even darker cost of their fulfillment. Swift-moving, brutal, with unexpected moments of tenderness, it compels the reader's attention all the way to the end, then lingers in the mind afterward."

—John Langan, author of *Children of the Fang and Other Genealogies*

"*The Crying Forest* is a compelling folk horror story that combines elements of crime fiction and the occult to create a unique vision of a world teeming with ghosts, shapeshifters, and a profoundly human evil. The writing is crisp the authorial voice assured, and the horror is real and gritty."

—Gary McMahon, author of *Glorious Beasts*, and the *Thomas Usher* and *Concrete Grove* series

T0118905

Venero Armanno is the author of ten critically acclaimed novels, including his recent book *Burning Down* (2017). His other well-known books include *Black Mountain* (2012), The *Dirty Beat* (2007) and *Candle Life* (2006). Further back, Veny's novel *Firehead* was shortlisted in the 1999 Queensland Premier's Literary Award; in 2002 *The Volcano* won the award with Best Fiction Book of the Year. His work has gone on to be published in the United States, France, Germany, Switzerland, Austria, Holland, Israel and South Korea.

DARK PHASES TITLES BY IFWG PUBLISHING AUSTRALIA

The Crying Forest

By Venero Armanno

The Crying Forest

All Rights Reserved

ISBN-13: 978-1-925956-66-5

Copyright ©2020, 2021 Venero Armanno
V1.0

Printed in Garamond and The Dolbak typefaces.

IFWG Publishing International
Melbourne

www.ifwgpublishing.com

Part One

In the Rooms
of the Red House

1940: A Country Killing

Soon as the truck engine was rattling outside, and he heard his papà hurry into the house calling for Antonio to get out of his bed, Giacomo Mosca—Little Jack to everyone in this new country Australia—slipped from under the sheets and hid himself inside his room's clothes closet. He waited, heart pounding, then in a minute he'd made a decent fist of changing out of his pyjamas into grimy work clothes and boots.

It was well past midnight; the house previously so quiet was now busy with scurrying feet.

Little Jack had expected something like this. A good farmer like his father didn't spend an entire afternoon sharpening the blades of a half-dozen axes for nothing. Jack guessed his brother Antonio, at eighteen twice Jack's age, would be dressed and collecting his rifle. Antonio would stand in front of that intriguingly locked timber cabinet off from the living room, the one holding exactly fifty square cardboard boxes of ammunition. Papà would have the key. Mamma in her nightgown would be fussing around, frightened and tense, cradling the baby. Six-year-old Anna would clutch her skirt. If Jack showed his face Mamma would pull him to her bed-warm body— "Giacomo, stay here"—because he was far too young to go out night-hunting and animal-culling with the adults. The men went for deer, animals which might appear very pretty but were in fact an introduced species of pest and disastrous for the region's natural habitat, most especially for all the region's crops. Everyone would defend those crops with everything they had; after all, what people still said was the longest and most destructive drought in recorded memory had only broken last season—like a miracle, a blessed miracle!—and now was the time for families and their farms to finally prosper.

Tonight Jack would not stay home. Home was the place for women.

"Look after the house," his father had told him, last time a chase was on. "Look after the family."

"But I want to come."

"There'll be no nightmares for you," his father spoke, a man little given to moments of tenderness. Yet he'd then added in a kindlier voice: "Not until there have to be, you understand?"

Hunting and shooting in the woods. Jack hadn't seen any reason to be thinking about nightmares; he simply didn't understand whatever secrets these adults were carrying.

So tonight, while the commotion carried on downstairs, he climbed out his bedroom window. He clambered down the side of the house, lost his footing and his grip, and fell the last five or six feet, banging heavily onto his backside. There was a quick shooting pain up into his skull, a momentary dazzling of stars.

Dusting off the seat of his pants, Jack hid in the cool dark, still with his heart beating fast. He judged the distance to his father's farm truck. The way was mostly unlit but the bright clear night shone with a searchlight of a moon.

Had to be very careful now. Voices at the front door.

"Antonio, you mind whatever your father tells you." That was Little Jack's mother speaking. "No stupidity."

He sprinted the short distance to the truck, just about willing himself into invisibility, then he clambered fast into its flatbed back. Moments later there was the cough of the engine kicking over, Antonio in the long bench seat beside his father. Little Jack risked a glance before ducking down again. Antonio's shotgun was in his hands, barrel broken. When they arrived at wherever they were going that barrel would snap into place and the safety catch would be tested; then, off in the forests somewhere the spotlighting and the shooting would begin. Little Jack would finally discover the secrets everyone made it their business to hide from children like him. Adults talked about deer, it was true, but like all the other youngsters of the region Little Jack suspected there was more to these hunts.

Because if it was all just a simple deer cull then why did everyone get so anxious? Little Jack and Paulie Munro, whose father's farm was three miles away, mulled the problem over often, usually during lunch at the local school.

How many shots do people fire? How many deer do they kill? What else could they be after?

The truck moved off. Maybe in a minute Mamma would go upstairs to check on Little Jack. Like the rest of the family he had his daily chores, collecting warm eggs, milking the cow, slopping the two pigs, and getting to and from school as sharpishly as he could: she'd expect he had slept through this whole ruckus. Maybe the baby would keep her attention. Well, if she did check on him it was too late. Jack was on his way.

The old Ford shook and rattled down the one-mile expanse of dirt from the Mosca farmhouse to the road, then it travelled along multiple dusty and ungraded laneways into the dark countryside of this region the Moscas had made their home, known as Grandview.

———◆———

Α nd now the truck skidded to a stop and Little Jack heard the sounds of men shouting. Other farmers' trucks were already there. Lanterns and powered bulbs darted through the trees like glowing, excited ghosts.

Still unseen, Little Jack climbed down from the flatback and followed his father and brother, the running men and their swaying lights. Here the trees were so dense, yet alive with activity. He couldn't tell where they'd ended up when usually he knew just about every corner of the Grandview countryside.

"They're trapped!"

"Lights on them, against a rock wall!"

"Nowhere to go!"

"Quick...before they have a chance..."

It was like some over-excited crowd moving into the local showgrounds for the annual fair, except there were no women, no small children, no grandparents. Only men and older teenage boys holding rifles of varying calibres instead of hot dogs and fairy floss. Little Jack recognised almost every single one of these folk, his farmland neighbours.

Mr Bell, tall and gaunt; unfriendly Mr Egan; there was squat Mr Margolin with Mr Bartlett, Mr Taylor, Mr Goddard and Mr Bretzki. Here another Italian, a man from the north, Mr Claudio Cima with his fat and furry drooping moustache everyone made fun of. To the left of him, Finn Westwood, Antonio's friend from a neighbouring property, now talking just as fast as he always did.

"They tore up three cows or something, killed the pets too, don't know

5

whose place. And I didn't have a clue what was happening until Jim and Joe Hadfield turned up at the front door…"

A handful of teenage boys running. More lights, voices raised.

"There! See them there?"

Now a clearing, moonlight above, lanterns held aloft and shining. Farm trucks had their headlights trained ahead—some enterprising souls had manoeuvred along a rough forest trail, far off the roads and laneways.

Not deer but a pack of wild dogs, worst scourge of all. So that's what it was about. Bad for farm animals, killers of anything they could get their teeth into. People said they might even set upon a person walking happy as can be first thing at dawn or on a balmy evening. Dangerous to corner them but there this pack was, gathered against a wall. Coiled and tense, ready to break and bolt, yet blinded in the glare.

"Jesus, Jack, just look at them!"

It was Paulie Munro, Little Jack's friend from school. He shouldn't have been there either; Jack guessed he might have hitched a secret ride as well.

"*Minchia…*" Jack breathed, "… shit…"

"Bloody hell," Paulie echoed.

For there were mangy dogs; big ones; small ones; dogs that snarled; dogs that hid behind other dogs; dogs that stared wide-eyed into blinding light and some that only had one eye. All of them, ears pricking at the voices, at the danger, at death. Some trembling with fear, some poised to attack, many more doing both.

"Must be thirty, forty of the bastards!"

"What'll we do?"

"Shoot!"

Instant volleys of pounding gunfire. Little Jack jumped and he felt Paulie grab his hand.

The two of them stepped forwards for a better look. Antonio was right at the front, firing without let-up, shooting and reloading for the glory of sound and fury. Little Jack's father was different—and so was Mr Munro, Paulie's father, also different. The two men stood shoulder to shoulder alternating calm shots.

Steady, aim.

That's the shot. Now, steady, aim again. Draw the bead.

A rifle's strong recoil.

Think, aim again. Squeeze the trigger.

Not fast but steady.

Not slow but deadly.

The fumes of gunpowder, the stench of cordite, blood and meat bursting, the terrible dances of death. Bodies torn to literal shreds by slugs and buckshot.

After the deafening roar, lasting less than a minute, a deafening silence. Small whimpers from dying throats then single shots silenced those as well.

A shout.

"Oh God!"

A silhouette staggered aimlessly. Not the shadow of a dog but of something more terrible, a wounded man. Coming closer, out of a dark nest of trees at the rock wall's edge.

Some farmers recoil; some gather for a better look, which is just what Little Jack and Paulie do, following at the heels of men too transfixed to notice them.

But who is it? What's happened?

Shirt drenched. Bleeding holes in a heavily gasping chest. One hole, two. Looks like three.

The man stretches out a hand. Little Jack knows him. Paulie knows him too. He owns that place they call the red house. His name, it means that colour too, red.

"It's Mr Rosso!"

"Shit no!"

"He must have been—"

"—in the line of fire."

"Got too excited?"

"Got himself shot!"

Little Jack notices men now backing away, thinking better of being there even as Mr Rosso stumbles closer. He's blinking fast as if trying to drive away sleep. He cries out once then drops to his knees.

And pitches forwards onto his face.

"What do we do?"

"The police—we'll get Barry from the station."

"Wait, just think for a second. Are we to blame?"

"It was an accident. The volley of gunfire."

Teddy Quinn in
Rosso House

Uneasy and waiting, Teddy Quinn checked today's Rosso House sales sheet one more time:

> Tuesday 25 January 1977
> Midday: Mr Paul Munro

No one else was booked; Teddy could get away fast.

The seller, Mrs Agata Rosso, today had a relative working on the property. The guy was wiry and mean-looking, and had worked there maybe a half-dozen times in the last few months, clearing fallen branches and vast clumps of every species of weed imaginable. A thick accent and broken English: some newcomer to these shores with a name that tied up your tongue, Donatello. Donatello's wife was also there, carrying her baby while her husband sweated in the sun. Previously she'd worked on the inside of the old empty house, dusting, sweeping, polishing, washing down walls and floors—anything and everything that needed doing so that someone might walk in and finally want to buy the place.

Tomorrow slashers and mowers and weed sprayers were coming to turn twelve acres of overgrown paddocks into something resembling the attractive country retreat in Gavin Realty's advertisements.

Far from neighbouring properties, at the crest of the type of long and acutely inclined hill that Teddy Quinn at twenty-six wouldn't like to hike, the house wasn't a null or even a laidback sort of place. Because if homes can have a particular character then this one was spoiled for choice. One day Rosso House was tranquil, the next a leaden threat hunched at the peak of a hill of wild weed and twisted trees. Other times Teddy fancied the house glowed in the sunlight as if its doors were ready to burst open and spill laughing children into hot summer days. Then there were the visits Teddy positively hated, those occasions Rosso House was like a mirror of the owner wanting to sell it—a nasty little hunk of crone all wizened angles and shadowed gazes.

Even the approach to Rosso House from the winding laneways below felt wrong. For the gradient was too steep and motor vehicles struggled and truck engines almost faltered before making it over the rise.

By rights the owner should have had the home completely renovated before placing it on the market, but the boss Mr Gavin had given Teddy some straight advice:

"Agata Rosso says she hasn't got any money so she won't spend any money. And she hasn't lived in the place at least thirty-five years. Big accident or something, did her husband in. The property's been empty all that time, not even rented out. The old bat's stubborn as a rock but I'll give you a tip: do *not* get on her bad side."

Teddy met Mrs Rosso just once, going to her current home for a hard-negotiated cheque to cover Gavin Realty's extra advertising and costs. He'd met a woman who on paper should have been in her fifties yet in the flesh looked a hundred and fifty. Not only that, but she'd spoken to him in a cackling and crackling voice that made him want to run.

Waiting on today's prospect Teddy again felt weirdly uneasy. The walls and floors, and even the ceilings, were in the sorts of dark colours that definitely didn't speak of any welcoming.

Well, Teddy would meet this Paul Munro, show him through, give the standard spiel about what a great and wonderful rural retreat this property was, then get the hell out.

———————————

A long way past the hour a bland white Holden finally appeared over the rise of the hill, smoke blowing from its exhaust. Teddy Quinn had moved outside to the shade under a jacaranda tree, one of no less than fifty on this property.

Teddy stepped forwards, perspiration on his face and his white poly-ester-cotton shirt damp all over. The car was a tired whale of a thing, pulling up in the circular parking area where Teddy's metallic-red Triumph Stag waited beside a ghastly bucket of bolts: the green-panelled, white-roofed, 1969 Torana HB SL sedan belonging to Mrs Rosso's two relatives.

The Holden's front doors opened: Munro was with his wife.

No, wrong.

The passenger was a teenager and, look at that, but she's just about black. Maybe light enough to be mixed race, but definitely not as thoroughly Caucasian as Paul Munro. The man was in grey trousers and a business shirt, collar open, looking like any middle management sort of guy. Maybe mid-forties. The tall, slender girl with him was his opposite. Brown hair to the shoulders and what was she? Aboriginal? African? Middle eastern or something? You didn't get any of that in Grandview. The original farmers had to have gotten rid of the blacks a hundred years back. Except for a few Chinese and a preponderance of wogs the area was as white bread as a shopping mall.

"Mr Munro? Good to meet you. Teddy Quinn."

"This is my daughter, Lía."

Daughter, so black against his white? Well, okay...

"Hi," she said, maybe fifteen or sixteen years of age. Teddy noticed her hair wasn't so much brown as a sort of caramel—maybe even cinnamon— though he was moving beyond his powers of description. He preferred things to be simpler, especially in relation to the opposite sex. Blonde, brunette, tall, short, available or not. And old enough—meaning a hell of a lot older than this exotic-looking kid. Her skin was dusky, a honey-toned complexion, and Teddy noticed with a small shock of surprise that her eyes were green as some kind of jewel.

Paul Munro seemed affable enough. Early that morning he and his daughter had flown up from Melbourne for two job interviews the man had. Apparently they'd used to live in Hong Kong and were now back, thinking about where to live.

Munro said something about the Grandview region and the bad roads leading in. At the same time his so-called daughter stepped to the open front door of the house and ran her fingertips over its panelled wood grain.

"The roads? There's been a lot of talk about a highway. One day it'll be a breeze to shoot to the city and back."

Even as he spoke Teddy noticed a subtle change in Munro's daughter, this kid named Lía. Her father noticed it too and moved beside her and took her hand—the one touching the front door's grain. She was in a simple yellow dress and sandals. A ribbon the colour of her eyes tied the back of her hair, and she appeared to want to say something.

Munro now soothed his daughter's hair. What was it about the pair

Teddy couldn't quite put his finger on?

"We took a little tour," Paul Munro said. "Sorry for being late. I wanted Lía to get an idea of where we are. I lived in Grandview a long time ago."

"Then I guess you saw how things are changing? Big developments are on the way."

It was what most people wanted to hear. They'd consider moving to the country, but only if it was semi-rural or not-so-rural after all, more of a quiet urban outpost where you didn't have to miss too much about living close to town.

"You've met the old families?" Paul Munro asked.

"Maybe a few."

"We were the Munros. Three miles from us was the Mosca farm."

"Hmm," Teddy spoke. The names didn't mean anything to him. "I've met the Egans."

"I remember them."

"It's a long way from Grandview to Hong Kong."

"It is."

"What were you doing?"

"I'm an engineer originally, then I moved into construction and project management. Hong Kong offered a lot of work, especially in what I was interested in."

"What was that?" Teddy could see that the man hesitated, as if he really didn't want to talk about himself, or not about the past, but Teddy's salesman's instincts told him to make as much of a connection with this prospect as possible.

"Green space. Stuff that stops people going mad in big cities."

"I get you. Was it successful?"

"You end up fighting a lot of corporate interests. Every square foot of land represents potential income."

"We've got nothing but green space here."

"True."

"But let me take you inside."

Instead, Munro turned to the distant panorama. There was a vast timber reserve and the smudged blue of endless mountain ranges.

"Over that way," Paul Munro pointed, though his daughter wasn't paying all that much attention. "It's coming back to me. The timbergetters. Maybe I'm imagining it, but can you see where there used to be a path cut through the woods? That blurry line in the green?" He let go of Lía's hand and stepped forward. "It might be a fire track now, for the local emergency services, all volunteers. There are lots of paths, or at least there used to be. Men used to drag tree trunks and logs to the river. They had this wonderful system of floating them downstream, putting the river currents to work. The logs floated all the way to the mill."

He went to the wider expanse of grass at the front of the house, studying the distant ranges and topography of the land. His daughter didn't follow. Instead she squinted into the gloomy interior of Rosso House.

"I really want to see inside," she told Teddy Quinn.

"Let's get your dad."

Paul Munro was out of earshot. The girl's eyes turned to Teddy. She was silent a moment, then Teddy had the oddest impression that she wasn't so much looking at him as she was studying the very air around him.

"What?" he heard himself say.

"There's a small bed, isn't there?" Her voice was softer, almost conspiratorial.

"Four bedrooms inside," Teddy Quinn replied. "And, uh, the main bedroom's very spacious."

"No, a small bed for a very sick woman. She dreams of reading her favourite books and smoking her favourite cigarettes."

Teddy felt a heavy wave of something a lot like dread move through him.

"She's not going one way or the other… She calls it 'floating'."

"There's n-no one inside," he managed to stammer. "Furniture, beds, nothing. Rosso House is completely empty."

"Not like mount…mount…"

She couldn't quite find the word, but, all the same, a cold fingertip travelled the back of Teddy Quinn's neck.

"Okay," Paul Munro said, stepping back to the house, "ready to look around?"

Lía Munro's face cleared and she was a dusky-skinned teenage girl again, standing in sunlight.

Teddy Quinn couldn't make his face or anything inside himself clear. "I'll wait over there," he said, indicating a wooden bench in a broad patch of shade. "Feel free."

Paul Munro gave him a curious look, then guided his daughter inside Rosso House, into that gloom. Teddy heard Munro's voice speak softly to his daughter, then all sense of the pair disappeared.

The Munros and Rosso House

They were upstairs and Paul Munro let Lía look into dusty rooms and lead him down the wide hallway with its dark walls and a high ceiling painted even darker. He didn't mind how much time they wasted; both that morning's job interviews hadn't gone particularly well and the return flight for Melbourne wasn't due until eight in the evening. Paul knew he'd impressed the business managers talking to him about the jobs they had open, but more to the point they hadn't impressed him. Electronic Data Processing was still so backwards in this country; it almost made him long to be home in Hong Kong with folk who understood what the future was going to be about.

Jesus, he had to stop thinking of Hong Kong as 'home'. That place wasn't that anymore and a new one hadn't taken shape, though it would. Brisbane was a long longshot, way down the list of possibilities, but there was no need to rush; he and Lía had barely been in the country three months and he had a good nest egg from the business he'd sold back in Kowloon.

"What do you remember about Australia?" Paul had asked her when they'd first discussed the idea of a return.

"I don't know," Lía had replied, her voice uncertain, the girl still upset at being expelled from the school she'd really loved. "Maybe beaches? And trees. I remember a camping trip. But I was five when we moved away, right?"

Right, Paul reflected, thinking back on the time. *I took you and your mother to Kowloon and I think we were happy, even if you did have some strange moments. Little things like knowing what I was going to say before I could say it or telling your ma what she'd planned for dinner before she'd even started. Your mother and me, we used to laugh about it, our smart little girl so good at reading people.*

This morning in their rental car Paul and Lía had stopped by the area where the Munro farm had once been. A sign said the entire locale was now Westwood Meadows and new homes were going in. When he was a boy the Munros' road had been a dusty track without a number on the farmhouse gate. Paul's mother used to send him on his bicycle to the postmaster's office once a week.

"And what about Ma's place?"

So then they'd driven to the Mosca farm and of course that was gone too. Not developed into anything just yet; they saw one great tract of bulldozed land rolling with long hills and deep valleys.

"My Uncle Giacomo disappeared here?"

"Little Jack, yes, somewhere around here. We never found him."

"Do you still think about it?"

"Sometimes."

"And then the family?"

"Terrible—it was the time of the war. Italy got involved in June 1940. So here, well, foreigners, migrants, they stopped being friends and suddenly became treated like the enemy. Your grandfather Angelo and your uncle Antonio got interred for the duration. A prison camp with hundreds of other men. When the war was over they just couldn't see this country the same way any more: Angelo sold up and moved the family back to Italy. They probably couldn't stand the memories about Little Jack too, I don't know. But I was lucky. I'd stayed in contact with Anna and the rest is history." That part always made Lía smile, adopted child or not. "We'll meet your mother's side of the family one day, hey?"

"They're not really my family."

"If I'm your father and your mother was your ma, then they're definitely family."

Lía Munro had said, "Okay."

"I mean it."

Driving away from the vast nothing of the Mosca farm, on their way to meet a real estate agent named Teddy Quinn, Lía had then asked, "Was it on one of these roads you saw the walking dead man, Dad?"

So much of what Little Paulie Munro had grown up with might have vanished, but the sharpest memory he possessed was of that night Mr Rosso was supposedly killed by rifle fire. Instead there was a miracle, something truly inexplicable.

"Yep."

"Come on. Tell me again."

"So it was one early morning months after the dog hunt. I was driving with your grandfather in his truck. We were coming down this way. My brothers Bill and Jimmy were already gone to war so it was just the two of us."

"What did you see?"

"Dead Mr Rosso, on the button. Walking plain as day. He was hiking the verge of a woody laneway with a staff in his hand."

"And?"

"And your grandfather muttered something."

"What?"

"'Turn your eyes away. Don't you look at that man.'"

"But you did look."

There'd been no smile from Mr Rosso, no neighbourly lifting of a hand. That day riding in the truck Little Paulie had felt a thrilling tingle of excitement and trepidation right down to his belly.

"He was a lot older than before and—and sort of dried up. Like the accident took everything out of him."

"So he wasn't dead after they shot him."

After Mr Rosso's recovery there were hushed tones to any conversation about the man and his wife. No one ever wanted to mention the night in question. The night-hunting had come to a stop. Wild dogs proliferated and sometimes farmers went out at dawn to find their animals slaughtered. If they did any more shooting it was only within the confines of their own properties.

"And then, Dad?"

"And then forget it."

Though Paul Munro never would—because that same terrible night the worst thing of all had happened, even worse than three smoking holes in a man's chest. His friend Little Jack Mosca went missing and locals laid odds that there were even more wild dogs out in the woods that had taken him. How could it have happened? Why on earth would Jack leave his home in the middle of the night? His brother Antonio took him home, his mother bathed him and put him to bed—and the next morning Jack's bed was empty and he was nowhere to be found.

The whole thing was a mystery never solved, no matter how extensive the investigation became. Some day a timbergetter, horse-rider or country hiker would come across what was left of the boy's bones, yet endless search parties never found a thing. Not a trace of skin, hair, clothing or blood. Paulie had gone on many of those searches as well.

He'd cried with Jack's kid sister Anna. Paulie and Anna grew close. Even after the Mosca family and the Munros moved away the pair of them kept in contact, pen pals.

A new story started. You called that *life*, right?

They entered the main bedroom. It was at the front of the house and a set of double doors opened to a small balcony, revealing a spectacular vista. From this vantage point Grandview was still a region of the farm paddocks and wild meadows Paul used to run through with Bill and Jimmy and their dogs.

"What do you think?"

"It makes Hong Kong look like a pretty stinked-up place."

For a moment Paul wondered what life would have been like if his family had decided to stay on the land. His parents abandoned their own connection to country life after what happened to poor Bill and Jimmy. The twins left home to join the Royal Australian Navy. Their first deployment was their last; the brothers were assigned to the light cruiser HMAS Sydney and a month before Christmas 1941 the Sydney went down off the coast of Western Australia, no survivors.

From then on Henry Munro was never the same and Margaret Munro found only brief moments of solace in her church. The farm went for a song and Paulie and his parents tried to settle into uneasy suburban life. Henry Munro drove his truck for deliveries and was often away. Margaret cleaned houses, ironed for strangers, and helped at the neighbourhood Catholic church. Paulie was sent to the closest state school, which he disliked for the absence of horses or common sense. It was a funny thing, but after leaving the farm Paul Munro felt he'd never had a real home again. Every place felt transitory and was even more so in this whole year since Anna died.

"Dad, you're squeezing again."

Gripping Lía's hand as they watched the panorama.

"Sorry."

Yes, a year back Anna's cancer won the battle against Anna's body and will and slowly he'd started drinking, more and more so that each new day was incomplete until he'd poured himself a first glass. Even here, right now, Paul wanted something to slake that endless thirst and stop his thoughts.

The perspiration of anxiety prickled his forehead.

"Dad?"

"Yes?"

"How about if we did live here?"

"It's just a visit to show you around, remember?"

"But if we did."

"We're back in Melbourne tonight." Paul used his handkerchief to wipe the dryness of his mouth, then the sweat at his brow. "I'll find a great job and we'll find you a great school. Country life isn't for us."

"We're never going back to Hong Kong?"

"That part of our lives is over."

"Then this is the place."

"What?"

"It's green and it's big and there's...there's everything."

"There's nothing. You couldn't live on a farm and neither could I, not again."

"This isn't a farm. It's a house with a lot of space."

"Just the two of us out here? You must be joking."

Lía shook her head; she wasn't.

What's got into you? Paul wanted to ask, but he decided to let her have this moment. It'd pass.

A few moments later, downstairs, he led her out the back door, circumventing the salesman so they could take in the jacaranda and bougainvillea trees, plus the bottle boabs, ferns and giant Chinese elms. Paul watched Lía's eyes fill with the sight of the many hoop pines, all of them so outrageously tall and straight. By their size he knew they had to be at least a hundred years of age apiece; then he remembered something about these particular trees:

"Those trunks, all so long? They used to be cut down and carved into tall masts for sailing ships."

"That's a crime," Lía spoke.

"No, only history," Paul replied, but in a way he thought she was right. At least in so much as all of this around here should now be protected, despite what the salesman Teddy Quinn had said about development.

He took a deep breath. They started down a decline. The Rosso property offered no neighbours and a sky full of clean air, a place as peaceful as some holy sect's mountain sanctuary. Even the three farm sheds Paul noticed further back appeared so unused as to be part of the scenery. One long straight finger of smoke drifted into the naked blue from some property hidden by the undulating hills. That smoke trail reminded Paul of his father firing up their ancient tractor, the wheezing, rasping cough and mechanical clash of gears somehow congruous with the quiet of the surrounding hills.

Then he heard gunfire too, and he smelled the cordite, sharp and almost sweet, superseded by gunpowder after World War II yet used in abundance that night back in 1940. He shook the thought away; the sounds, the smell, none of it was real except in his head. Being in Grandview once again, how it brought things back.

Paul noticed a figure working with a rake, too far away for him to discern the man's features. He was in rough clothes, a straw hat and his back was half turned so that he didn't notice them. They kept going. Lía spied a bird nest, in low branches. A distant, bottom paddock was covered by a vast cloud of cockatoos feasting on Bunya seeds, something Paul Munro hadn't seen in thirty-five years.

———◆————————◆———

So they hiked the property's acres, coming to long stretches of fence wire and even longer stretches where the fencing had collapsed. Neighbouring paddocks were dotted with cows and in others horses were grazing. None of these were very close. As they walked up a shaded hillside Paul's thighs burned and his breath rasped. Then as they were coming back up to the house they noticed a woman sitting on one of the long stone walls. She was in the shade, a pair of pale pink slip-on flats beside her, a bundle in her arms. A hardback book was turned face down.

"Making inspection?" she called.

"Taking a look around." Paul caught his breath and tried not to notice this woman's olive-skinned loveliness. "You too?"

"My husband, he works."

It had to be that guy with his straw hat and rake. "Hot day for it."

With a small smile Lía approached the woman. "Do you have a girl or a boy?"

"Boy, name Lorenzo. We are calling him Zo sometimes."

"Zo? That's cool. How old is he?"

"Three and one-half months. How many years do you have?"

"I'm nearly sixteen."

"Nearly sixteen." The woman nodded, and for a brief moment her dark eyes appeared to study Lía. Then she looked at Paul.

"And this is my father," Lía said.

"You like this house?" the woman asked him.

"It's a big place."

Lía asked the woman, maybe in her mid-twenties, "What about you?"

"This house? Too big and very dark."

"I think it's got something really interesting about it."

Again the woman seemed to take her in, brow slightly furrowed. "Then," she said, "maybe is gonna be good for you."

"Good for me?"

"Everyone they like a nice home, no?"

The woman's accent was strong, though Paul thought she worked hard to modulate her pronunciation and intonation. With her strong Italian, maybe Spanish looks, today her thick curling hair was pinned up for the heat, revealing a long neck. Her lips, Paul thought, seemed made for laughter, even if there was something about her that said laughter might be a very distant possibility.

"A long time ago I sort of knew the people who lived here," he offered. "Well I knew *of* them."

"How?"

As he told her a little of the background she gently caressed her baby's face. Paul wiped his mouth again, thinking about the airport and how he could buy a beer or glass of wine at the bar.

"Well, is funny. My husband he works here because he is—what you say, nephew, grandnephew—of her, the Agata Rosso."

"You mean you're related to the owner?"

"Donatello he is. Agata she call him to dis country so he can help her, she not got good health no more. So here we is."

"I was wondering—the salesman said Mrs Rosso left this house decades ago, but she's only selling it now?"

"Maybe was gonna live here again. Dunno. But now like everyone else she need the money."

Paul glanced around at the heavy chunking sound of an axe at work in the trees behind the house.

"Maybe one day your little one would like to live in all this nature."

"No." She shook her head, her attention returning to Lía. "Big place don't bother you?"

"I like that it's big," Lía replied. "We used to live in an apartment."

"The house don't make you scared?"

Lía smiled as if that would be impossible. Again, Paul couldn't understand why she seemed so taken with the place.

Lorenzo was now awake, blinking his eyes.

"You want to hold?"

Lía pushed herself up to sit on the wall, then cradled the baby. "Does he cry?"

"The opera when something he don't like."

"His eyes are amazing. So beautiful."

"Huh, true." The woman eased herself down and picked up her book. "While I wait I read. This one very hard."

"*Great Expectations.* I remember it from school."

"This book need more fire. But it helps make my English good."

"Where are you from originally?"

"Friuli. In Italia, the north-east."

"You think you'll stay?"

She gave a shrug, which wasn't a happy one, and there was a shadow to this woman Paul couldn't quite understand. Then the salesman Teddy Quinn came into view.

Lía passed the baby back. "Good to meet you, Zo," she said, which finally, finally, gave the Friulian woman a moment in which to hint at a smile.

Mount... Mount...

Teddy Quinn stumbled drunk into his flat. Every moment of his drinking had been meant to drown the memory of what that strange girl had said: "No, a small bed for a very sick woman. She dreams of reading her favourite books and smoking her favourite cigarettes."

Right there at the front of Rosso House he'd wanted to fall to his knees. He could have wept. He still wanted to.

Mount... Mount... Mountford. How could she *know* that?

Roxanne was sprawled on the couch watching a James Cagney movie. Must have let herself in with her key. It was almost eleven. Had he promised to cook her something special, just the two of them?

"Teddy... Finally Teddy rolls in..."

Roxanne was well into her own sinkhole of booze. On the glass table in front of her an empty bottle of white wine stood next to a second bottle that looked just about empty too. And still she hadn't dozed off. Or got herself out of there, swearing never to return, which in the four months they'd known each other she sometimes had. Teddy saw she'd helped herself to every packet of snacks his cupboards had to offer: the detritus littered the floor. Maybe she'd starved herself all day, anticipating some three-course indulgence he'd create in his kitchen. Teddy tried to tell her something like, "You know, I'm really sorry," but his stomach flipped and he only just made it to the bathroom. The wet retching was like pushing deadly poison out of his system.

Then, in the shower, he was conscious of Roxanne through the dimpled glass.

"What kind of a salesman can't even keep an appointment?"

Teddy rinsed his mouth and his hair and pressed his temples.

"You know what? You're not that great a salesman."

On the other side of the misting glass Roxanne's arms were folded hard and firm. Her father owned a chain of used car yards and the topic of her own sales skills was one she liked to expound upon. Issues of nepotism aside, Roxanne's ambition was to top the leader board at Mighty Max Mortensen's Motors. She knew it would be hard. She knew people hated buying cars from women.

"Come on, get out of there."

Roxanne was drunk, she was angry, and now she was doing a gawky bathroom striptease. Teddy scrubbed his face, expecting she might join him under the spray, but when he opened his eyes the bathroom door was ajar. He turned off the water and wrapped a towel around his waist. Roxanne wasn't in the bedroom. He tried to navigate a straight line to the kitchen and living room but his left shoulder kept bouncing off the wall.

On the television, James Cagney was snarling at two block-headed cronies. Roxanne was stretched out, naked and lovely, the last crumbs of a bowl of potato chips at her hip. Crumbs salted her breasts.

"You're a shit," Roxanne told him, and kept telling him in multiple variations as they had sex on the couch.

James Cagney meanwhile thundered his way into his own mad demise. Teddy had one eye on a TV screen blurred into triples. His vision blurred even further until nothing was discernible but lines and light.

Poor Nanny Viv stuck in Mountford, Teddy Quinn thought. How'd a girl just a kid know how bad it is for you?

Mr H and His Long, Wrong Road

For months now Karl Haberman had known he was dying and so this fortnight's trip to London would be his last. A nice sentimental journey for a man with little time for sentiment, if not an out-and-out repugnance for human emotions in general. London business finally concluded, this chilly and wet evening Karl Haberman was being driven to Mayfair in London's West End, and a brothel named Gorton's; high class, exclusive, one of Haberman's absolute favourites.

His trip had involved the mundane task of divesting himself of his international property holdings. With no children or family, and no causes or political convictions, Haberman was selling his investment portfolio and shares and making certain all ensuing funds were directed into his regular bank accounts. Forget the Caymans: he had no more use for secrecy and discretion. Instead he'd spend as much as he could as fast as he could on whatever disposable pleasures remained open to him. One thing he'd learned for absolute certain was that money couldn't buy him his health back; he'd tried and tried, of course, with innumerable doctors, specialists and a handful of genuine quacks.

It was months since he'd been the true version of himself, walking with a powerful stride, back straight and body strong, bald skull waxed to gleaming: a gentleman of stylish Fedoras and smart attire, a full six feet and two inches tall. Well, this rain-dampened London evening the *DS420* carried a far-diminished and still diminishing Karl Haberman to Gorton's. Suffering with aches, Haberman appreciated the smoothness of the handmade Daimler's journey. Its coachwork was Carlton Grey, the interior a combination of maroon leather and black and grey leather. Its overuse of vinyl was, at least, subtle, and very well matched to the extensive use of hide. From the back he listened to radio-voices chattering about a riot against the National Front, though he couldn't have cared less about any world affairs. For he'd just signed away a house in Greek Street, a row of terraced homes in Bexleyheath, a squat office building in Slough and a tavern in Bankside he'd really favoured. Dispiriting, all of it. Now all he wanted was his salve, his number one outlet.

The hotel and club overlooked the length of Berkeley Square and resided in a building constructed in the 1820s, once the private residence of a lord. As Haberman noticed their approach, he tapped on the glass for the division to be lowered.

"My flight's tomorrow." He peered through a rain-glistened window at clouds the colour of iron. "What do you think?"

"Ye'll be lookin' t' sunshine come marnin', sir." The driver spoke over his shoulder, English crucified by a thick Irish accent.

The vehicle slid into Gorton's tiled entryway. One each of the bellmen and liveried attendants stepped forwards and a pair of hands in black gloves opened his door while a large black umbrella was positioned to protect him from the elements. His luggage would be transported straight to his suite.

They knew him there and he wondered why he hadn't installed himself at Gorton's as soon as he'd arrived in London. No, he didn't wonder. The reason lay inside his increasingly decrepit body; even if he'd survived a fortnight's attempt at good fucking, his spirits might not have coped with failure after failure. Now he'd try just the once. He'd try with everything he had left, which, he suspected, was not very much.

At the reception counter Karl Haberman didn't need to flash a membership card, sign a form or provide some secret handshake. He was welcomed as a dear friend then escorted through. Ninety minutes after he'd settled into the *Suite of Angels*, washing down prescription pills with a bottle of medically forbidden Krug, bathing, shaving and changing, and dining on the best Langouste dinner he'd had in a year, two hostesses sent his dinner trolley away and ushered in the six-person troupe he'd asked for.

Possibly overkill, the half-dozen, but they met Haberman with polite *Good evening, sirs,* and *How do you dos?* Each angel possessed a distinct, different accent. They wore silk slips, glossy long hair flowing as in advertisements for expensive shampoos and conditioners, and diaphanous little wings attached to supple shoulders.

Now Haberman drank a *Chateau Mouton Rothschild '61* and patted the increased girth of his belly; he picked at a silver platter of fresh snacks and observed the short overture to the main act. There were four young white women, one brown and one black—the eldest might have been twenty-one.

They danced and twirled and made their wings wave. Haberman took a deep sigh as they started to undress and couple. Every shilling spent at Gorton's—and these were substantial shillings indeed—was worth it. He stretched out his legs and flexed his aching toes.

Two angels came to massage his soles. Another refilled his crystal wine glass and offered a herbed mussel straight to his tongue. None of them appeared to notice the size of his belly or the eczema tattooing his bald skull, covering his shoulders and scarring the backs of his arms. They nursed his swollen feet, his sore toes, and others opened his robe and covered his pink bloat in feathery kisses. Music played, something light and orchestral he couldn't place, and he found his mind turning towards it, trying to recall the name of the piece and its composer.

Wait. Not this again.

Distraction overcame him more than the ministrations. Haberman's penis lost blood, then in mid-paradise shrank completely.

Oh dear. Here we go.

None of the angels appeared to mind, though the women who'd worked in Gorton's during his last visit not eight months back had encountered a Karl Haberman corpulent as a bull: fleshy, aggressive and quick to excite. This evening, however, he removed his increased bulk to a plush lounge chair. From there he observed a ceremony thoroughly fake; the magic had vanished.

Haberman poured more of the Rothschild, a vain attempt to dull the erotic doubts he couldn't explain and certainly didn't want. Goddamn his heart; goddamn his stupid kidneys. Goddamn whatever else was going wrong with his insides. He should empty the room and drop into bed—a most sensible option—but some harder part of his psyche refused to relent. Why not die right here with these women? So he rang down for a second trolley. Before another polite knock came at the Suite of Angels' door he threw up into the toilet, defecated long and wetly, brushed his teeth, showered again, staggered out in a robe and ordered three young women to leave and the remaining three to allow him to be their master.

They understood what that meant but he had to remember the safe word. *What was it again? Angel-hurt? English-bird? Ankle-girt?*

The brown angel—Ceylonese, he'd decided—was repeating "Engelbert". Ah, that was it, as in Engelbert Humperdinck the chanteur.

She seemed to be bleeding from the mouth. Haberman had gone too far. Even the flecks of blood refused to excite him. Haberman pulled away as she pressed the back of a hand to her lips. She found her feet, wrapped herself in silk and retrieved her discarded wings. With a quiver of a smile she left, passing the arriving trolley. Roasted pork and root vegetables, a pitcher of thick brown gravy, white bread rolls and golden curls of butter. Haberman settled in like a hog, dull-eyed, shovelling food, slurping *Blanc de Blanc Brut '43*, and wondering if he might actually be already quite dead.

The remaining pair did their best to please his blurring vision. They were a piano keyboard of intertwining fingers and limbs: black, white; black, white; black, white. At check-out the next morning he'd hand over a cheque for the extra tips required. Haberman's blurring vision noticed a riding crop and nipple clamps and plugs. Through gobs of half-masticated pork and creamed potatoes Haberman applauded the lines of raised welts in soft skin.

And his blood *still* wouldn't rise. Not a thing. Not a bloody thing.

"You're playing. You're children being silly. You're not even trying—you think management won't hear about this?"

Haberman threw the useless pair of them out, threw up again, then slumped where he was, dozing fitfully, his stomach groaning, hatred of nothing and everything swelling within his belly.

And without the slightest clue how his life was already being changed.

London–Sydney–Brisbane, Haberman experienced a prolonged needle-sharp pain in his liver. He drank too much, criticised the third-rate food of the first class cabin, and cursed the pilot who came to speak to him in a half-pleading tone. Haberman told the fool to concentrate on not flying them into a mountain. The mirror in the bathroom where he doused his face and neck with cold wet cloths only made things worse; he saw a self-hating football-sized head with raw, scaly rashes in the scalp. He was certain he had halitosis. His heart felt like a rock in his chest and the needle sharpness moved, he thought, towards a kidney or some other delicate organ.

On arrival he was met by no one. A taxi transported him home; there was none of a Daimler's lovely smoothness. He told the new migrant driver with bad teeth and worse English he should go back to wherever the hell he'd come from.

Haberman slumped a good forty-eight hours before demanding to see his two specialists, one a cardiologist, the other a nephrologist specialising in renal disease. Both men altered his medications and dosages and yet again told him to stop drinking and improve his nutrition. That is, if he wanted to see Christmas. It took more days in his bed before he could force himself to investigate domestic business matters.

Things, surprisingly, had gone well without him. Haberman found that in the weeks of his absence his best lieutenants, Nasser and Lundy, had collected almost every cent of owing monies, while at the same time ditching their usual driver, a Greek immigrant they'd never quite trusted. Haberman suspected that if Spiro Poulitis was still breathing, he'd now be wishing he'd never accepted such well-paying work in the first place.

"You've taken on another dago, I suppose?"

They had.

Hassan Nasser, born in Lebanon, forty-three years of age, new to the country in 1956 and long since a naturalised Australian, and Ronald Lundy, ten years older, perfectly Australian to six generations, held a view that desperate new arrivals would always be more inclined to carry out the unsavoury tasks that so often needed doing. The majority of these tasks were simple enough: driving girls to clients and remaining on hand to ensure there were no physical excesses, or that if there were they were paid for; collecting weekly and monthly payments when needed and delivering carefully apportioned percentages of cash to an ever-varying array of drop-off points.

A driver working for Haberman would never actually see the police officer or political apparatchik who collected his brown envelope, and he would never be a part of the small circle of influence at whose centre Haberman sat. Yet discreet drivers and good bonebreakers were as useful to the overall Haberman enterprise as bent cops and greedy councillors. It also helped if these men were thick as bricks. Most were, and enjoyed being kept loyal and quiet via generous bonuses. Despite any of that

31

Haberman had mistrusted every single one he'd ever allowed Nasser and
Lundy to employ, to a man.

"This one's okay, Mr H. Three bad debts he cleaned up in a single day."

"Really? Let's take a look at him."

Mid-twenties, another damn wog, pretty much uneducated. More wiry
than muscular and strangely proportioned too. His arms might have benefitted
from an extra six inches either side, and that sorry, longish face, well, it was
as if the skull had been shaped by someone thinking of an entirely different
sort of creature to fit it onto. Yet Haberman thought he saw something oddly
sensual in the boy, a sort of atavistic charm in the full lips and languid eyes.
Haberman imagined the boy would indulge in the kind of sexual congress
that occurred in fields between beasts.

"Tell me your story."

"Mister?"

"What do you want out of life?"

"Position."

"And the money that goes with it?"

"A'course, mister."

"What a surprise, money and position. What's your name?"

"You know my name."

"I'd like to admire the proper pronunciation."

"Donatello Zappavigna."

"My god, eight syllables."

"Mister?"

"Difficult for the ordinary person."

"People in dis country they callen me Donny Zap."

"You must be joking." The languid eyes simply stared back at him. "All
right, Donny Zap, so you're a new arrival. Where do you hail from?"

"What?"

Nasser intervened. "He wants to know where you used to live."

"*Provincia di Friuli.*"

"I'm unfamiliar with that part of Italy." Haberman pondered a
moment. "Wait. I visited Klagenfurt."

"Yeah, close. Over da border."

"What's the name of your town?"

"Is small, you don't know it."

"Near the capital?"

"Trieste? No."

"Let me see: your family dealt in crime?"

"Never."

"I bet."

"My papà he makes shoes and my mamma she work in a rich house."

"For a rich family, you mean?"

"Si, era un politico—yeah, the owner, he was the politician. But my parents, they killed in their car when I got thirteen."

"You were involved in the accident?"

"Back seat."

"You saw them die?"

"No, mister. I sleep in hospital eight days and when I wake the nurse she tell me what 'appen."

"A child of tragedy. And then?"

"Gotta make a living."

"Not as a shoemaker or a houseboy."

No reply. Haberman saw his new driver seemed to lack a certain spark of intelligence, yet what was this thing so appealing about him?

"What's brought you to our fair shores?"

"Gotta relative and she callen me and my wife and the baby."

"So you're married. And you have a—?"

"Boy."

"Enchanting. Well, let's start this evening with two golden rules, Donny Zap."

"Yeah, mister?"

"One: never tell your good wife your business or mine. Nothing, ever. You're a driver for a wealthy businessman, and that's it. This businessman is generous to a fault, which explains your regular bonuses."

"I like this."

"If you let anything slip, in the slightest, please consider the lovely swimming pool in my courtyard. Because in its deep end is where you'll enjoy your last thoughts."

"Never gonna say nothin', mister."

"And two: another 'never' I'm afraid. As in I never want to meet your wife. You'll never bring her here or anywhere I might see her. Your wife will never meet Nasser and Lundy. Marriages sour and thankless partners create endless difficulties. So we keep our two worlds nicely separated. *Hai capito?*"

Donny Zap pricked his ears at the Italian expression.

"*Sì. Ho capito.* I understand."

"Excellent. So you said a relative called you from darkest Friuli?"

"*La mia prozia.*"

"I might have given you the wrong impression with my showing off. My Italian is limited. Please speak English."

"Here you say great-aunt, but I just callen her 'Zia'—'Aunt'. She gets too old and she need help. Her husband he sick long, long time. I got nothin' else so is okay."

"Another housemaid?"

"Huh?"

"Your great-aunt, what does she do, clean houses? Or has she entered comfortable retirement?"

"Zia she is helper."

"A nurse?"

"The *strega.*"

In fact, Karl Haberman had picked up quite a lot of the Italian language, gleaned from years of travel and of dealing with the local migrant businesses he did his best to bleed. Yet this word, 'strega', he wasn't quite sure he'd come across it. Or, wait—wasn't it supposed to be an insult? Something like a slut or a bitch?

"You'd best give me your translation."

"You say 'witch'. My aunt she is one a dem."

Haberman waited for a punchline that didn't come. "You'll elaborate?"

"She the woman got medicines when you sick and when you get hurt she can fix. Her friends, she fix fast. Their children too."

"Let me understand. Your great-aunt is a nurse of sorts, yet as a cultural phenomenon particular to your people, possibly because she's sometimes successful in curing individuals of their ailments, elements of the magical or supernatural are attributed to her."

"Dunno what you sayen, mister."

"My God," Haberman said, looking into Donny Zap's utterly stupid face, "we let you people in by the boatload."

"Got more to tell you."

Haberman waited.

"So, Zia, she see things through her fires. The fires in dem special candles she got. She can look for what it is that happen long time ago and what it is that one day is gonna come."

"She sees the past and the future."

"That's it."

Haberman took a moment to consider the pagan practices of a culture that ought to have known so much better. Art, history, music, such a privileged birthright in these Mediterraneans, yet Donny Zap and his ilk could skew their beliefs towards witchcraft. Maybe this Friuli was a stranger place than most, and its émigrés even more so.

All four of them moved outside to the pool area. Lundy mixed Haberman a cold vodka spritzer. Three men stood; one reclined, though it was with a pain in his chest, a pricking needle in his side and a need to speak more quietly than he liked.

"You make me curious—curious about this woman who's brought you to our shores. What's her name?"

"Agata Rosso. My Zia Agata."

"If Zia Agata can read the future, what does she say of your own prospects?"

"Is something I no can tell to you."

"Far too much money and position in your stars?"

The dullard shook his head.

And yet… And yet the boy remained appealing. What he possessed was not so much charm as magnetism. Haberman felt it: a purely visceral, almost sexual movement of his body towards the boy.

But I'm not a homosexual and have never needed to resist any tendencies. So what's this now?

"I understand you collected three recalcitrant debts?"

One word too difficult, yet Donny Zap understood the rest. "The two misters here they say what I gotta do and so I done it."

"Mr H," Nasser spoke up. "The kid got to the worst debt and snapped his left arm. Then he put him in a choke hold two seconds from breaking his neck."

The infelicitous details of this criminal world Haberman would soon be leaving.

"Where did you find this boy?"

"He found us."

"Meaning?"

"Lundy and me, we were drinking in the Federal and he came up to us saying he was looking for a job. And the job he wanted was working for you, Mr H."

Haberman felt blood and frustration rise in equal measures. Could his men be so truly reckless?

"Let me tell you something, Donny Zap. If you're undercover—" And he didn't complete the sentence, instead giving Nasser and Lundy the sort of brief nod they read in an instant.

Lundy pinned the boy's arms from behind. Nasser opened Donny Zap's shirt and felt around; he dug into his trousers as well.

"And you can be sure we checked him out every single time we went on a job. We don't take risks."

They let Donny Zap button his shirt and readjust his waistband.

"Think you're clever?" Haberman addressed him.

"I come lookin' for them two because Zia Agata she tell me something about you."

"What exactly?"

"She say you very sick. You on a road comin' to the end. But she gotta new road ready for you so all gonna be good."

Haberman blinked. He lingered over his drink so that he might have time to process these words, and did his best to breathe evenly, ignoring the pains inside his rotting body. How on earth did an old woman know about his health? Was word spreading?

"What does your great-aunt advise?"

"You gotta come see her and listen to what she say."

"You expect I'll make a pilgrimage to some witch's frightful door?"

Donny Zap's expression changed. So did the air around him, as if negative and positive atmospheric charges combined. Haberman felt a breath catch in his throat just as a fresh needle of pain now pricked at his heart. Nasser and Lundy sensed something as well. They didn't quite draw the .38s Haberman knew were under their coats, but each man did take a step backwards.

That impression of animal magnetism about Donny Zap became its negative; Haberman thought of a beast being provoked to attack. The boy hadn't liked Haberman's last comment and wasn't afraid to show it. He might not even, in truth, be afraid to act on it.

Then he turned on his heel.

"Don't you dare," Haberman breathed from the depth of a sharp new pain. "Don't you dare try to leave while I'm talking to you."

The young grunt did.

Moving

Sale contract and deed concluded, the salesman was more helpful than expected. Where Paul would have thought Teddy Quinn might vanish into thin air he instead made himself available for the essentials that needed attending to. Electricity, gas bottles for the stove, power, telephone, water. He even had advice about Grandview Produce, a store built like a warehouse, full of every type of farm and building tool imaginable, plus animals and animal feed, if the Munros ever wanted to go that far into country living.

While Teddy Quinn offered his help Paul wondered what he might want in return. Maybe he was attracted to Lía? Not impossible, despite the age difference. Paul didn't see anything—there were no covert glances—and Lía certainly didn't mention anything, but Paul made certain to keep one eye on the salesman.

It was just the two of them in Rosso House, and one of the much older hands down at the produce store recalled that the Rossos used to have a live-in maid and a live-in gardener, a married couple named the Celanos. There was plenty of room for private quarters; maybe the Munros wanted to hire a local couple to move in?

"Should we?" Paul asked his daughter.

"Nope," she replied, as if in her heart she'd never been meant to be around lots of people, and maybe not to live in big cities either.

Maybe neither of them were.

Paul took to all the new space and liked this freedom long forgotten, plus the memories. Of the old farmhouse with his family, the chores, of helping his father with a tractor or the fields. Then there was his mother trying not to make him the favourite and the twins lifting him in the air and just about hurling him one to the other in some teasing, good-natured game. Good days. He saw Little Jack and Anna—Anna most especially, with scuffed knees and long braids, and large brown eyes that said, *Will you come and sit with me a while?*

Not wanting to be around other people was one thing, but soon Lía was telling him how, more than anything, they needed dogs. Growing up she'd never owned as much as a cat—yet she kept talking about how she wanted four canines. Bemused, and maybe even a little astonished at how she seemed to be opening up, Paul said maybe *one*.

After the big city bustle and confusion of a teeming urban centre in Kowloon, they now lived in a habitat designed for lorikeets and cockatoos, for scrub turkeys. In overgrown grassland and among shrubbery and bushes closer to the house, Paul showed Lía the water dragons and bearded dragons that gathered then scurried away: other types of lizards as well. Of course, snakes were plentiful. He made sure she knew to wear closed shoes outside and avoid long grass, rock walls, the timber sheds which he always kept bolted shut. Grandview was home to venomous eastern browns and black snakes that might be taipans or red bellies or something else altogether; the dangers were leavened, of course, by carpet pythons eating rats and mice, and very pretty green tree snakes slender as electrical wire.

"You know what to do about snakes, right?"

"Back away. Live and let live."

There Lía would be, standing still or sitting in a garden chair, taking in these new wonders. Whenever Paul saw her like that he knew, absolutely knew, why he'd decided to take this unexpected plunge back into Grandview. Lía had lost her mother; she'd lost the school she'd been in since her primary years, plus the friends who'd been there with her. Gone forever was the only place she'd known as home. Yet now she said she was happy in Grandview. That was enough for Paul. No, it was more than enough; it was a miracle.

"Dad, so the timbergetters are gone?"

"Decades ago. Foresting changed to crop farming and dairying, but that's been dying out as well. Even back in my day. We had a drought that lasted ten years. I was born into that drought. I even remember it breaking. It was the first time I saw real rain. Our dogs went crazy like they thought the sky was falling. But all this bulldozing now, the clearing for housing estates… I guess that's how it's going to be."

"Who was here first?"

"We grew up with talk of tribes but even back then I didn't know them. The Jagera and Turrbal people, if I remember. There'll be ancient bora circles somewhere nearby."

"For ceremonies."

"Mostly proving grounds for boys growing into men."

"None of the tribes are left in the area."

"That's what I'm saying. A long, long time now."

"I must be the blackest person around."

"Could be."

"Where do I get that from, really?"

They'd discussed Lía's background so many times, but it was something she always came back to.

"Your colouring's common in Southern Italy. Remember your mother showing you the map?"

"The Strait of Sicily."

"Exactly. Cape Bon's just a hundred kilometres from the island so that's where your roots must go. Skin colour only became a problem when there was migration to other countries. In the American south Southern Italians got the same treatments as Negroes."

"You mean slavery and lynchings?"

"Don't let it bother you. Australia's completely different."

"Then where are our black people?"

"Not in Grandview," he had to agree.

Still, Lía's heritage, African, mixed race, whatever it was, didn't bother her. She only remained curious, and Paul knew that someday she'd make her own pilgrimage to the places he'd mentioned, go discover her roots for herself. Of course, Paul and Anna had never known who Lía's biological parents were; it was unlikely she ever would either.

At least she was already used to being unique, Paul told himself, to being a subject for staring eyes. At the produce store, at any store, Lía stood out. There she'd stand in a tool or grocery aisle, different as different could be, and with a father as ordinary for the locals as Grandview's trees and fields.

Then before he knew it April came and Lía turned sixteen, just seven weeks after they moved in. Paul bought her a new dress, two books and a record album she wanted. He got busy in the kitchen—a place he always liked anyway—and made a chocolate cake with local cherries on top. He tried to create something of a party atmosphere, but it was just the two of them in a big house they didn't much know yet, and one important person was missing. The first birthday for Lía without her mother. Lía blew her candles out without any tears and just the sight of that, knowing how brave his daughter could be, made Paul retire to his room with a fresh and full bottle of whisky that wasn't so full come morning.

Anna's voice missing when he'd sung *Happy Birthday*. So many small moments of absence to go with the overall emptiness of trying to live without her.

"Okay, so we'll find you a school. I visited one in Grandview the other day but it looks like a dump."

"There's a bus line. I can go wherever."

"Start in the new year?"

"Dad, you're such a great home-schooler. Why should we change?"

"Because I need to get a job and every now and then you need to get out of Rosso House."

"You mean stately *Munro Manor?*" she smiled at him, and that kept Paul away from the bottle three nights straight.

Lía Alone and Not So Alone

One morning after pancakes and freshly squeezed oranges grown in Grandview, Lía watched her father drive away in the used '72 Chrysler Valiant he'd purchased on moving in. Today he had a job interview at a company called NCR. She sensed a certain hopefulness in him. NCR manufactured cash registers but had also moved into new technology her father told her revolved around the silicon chip.

"We need the money but a new start doesn't mean a bad start. Let's see if this is the right thing or not."

She'd liked that, and she liked it too when he wore one of his suits, as he did that morning. Lía thought it made him look even more handsome than he usually was. Some of the girls at Good Hope used to tease her about him:

"That white man you call your father."

"Maybe he's some rich guy and you're his native girl, Lía?"

"If that's your real name."

"Hey, if you're supposed to be adopted, what *is* your real name?"

She didn't know the answer to that question, just as she hadn't been sure how to react to all the teasing. In the school yard Lía had done her best to join in with the day-to-day sorts of things schoolgirls were supposed to be so concerned about, silly stuff that kept them all chatting and whispering in and out of classes. After the horrible expulsion from her school it wasn't a surprise to Lía that she didn't miss any of those old friends. Events had proven they'd never been friends in the first place. Now, like the facts around what might be her real name and the possibilities of where she might have come from, the girls were something she kept pushed into the back of her mind. Her job in this new place called Grandview was to concentrate only on what she had right now.

That woman with the baby, she'd managed to ask the perfect question—

"The house don't make you scared?"

—with a one-hundred per cent correct answer:

A smile that meant *Nope, maybe it'll be my oasis.*

<hr />

Lía went upstairs after cleaning up in the kitchen. She had schoolwork to do—*home* schoolwork, set by her father, today a composition about an aspect of a book by Charles Dickens called *The Pickwick Papers*. She'd read the book twice in the past fortnight and knew she could answer the question he'd selected from an English literature teaching manual he'd picked up from the library in town. There he'd found useful textbooks for a variety of the subjects most students would be studying: English, geography, both ancient and modern, mathematics—her *bête noir*—and economics. Art he left to Lía on her own, something she had a natural talent for.

She'd write her composition, then later when her father had returned, they'd continue with something very different: the garden plantings they'd started. Paul always helped Lía and showed her what to do because in work that involved an outside world of dirt and garden tools and seeds and water, she was a complete novice. To her surprise, Lía learned her father wasn't. Over many days he had Lía getting used to digging and irrigating nice rows and furrows, carrying buckets to and fro from the rain tanks at the back of the house. Surprising to see her father so at ease with this stuff, planting and nurturing as if these elements of country life had always been a part of him. Even to the way he knew how to propagate seeds, which was so much like applied science. Or just plain magic.

"Well, I studied a lot more than engineering in my day."

"Where, Dad?"

"A polytechnic in Melbourne after I did my masters. Then in Maastricht long before I even thought about Hong Kong. Or you," he smiled, a streak of dirt on his cheek being cleaned by a line of perspiration.

"Maybe I could do the same type of study one day."

"Here's the best learning of all."

He was right about that. Lía was even more surprised to see blisters on her hands, and to feel how her legs and the small of her back could ache from a day's work in the garden.

Today on her way up to her room, however, Lía's lower belly started to feel full and tense; she knew what that meant. She'd need the hot water bottle, not a novel and a notepad, and maybe she'd put on a record and curl up in bed.

Her room was okay but still not quite arranged the way she wanted it. Lía looked at her small collection of LPs. No, she'd leave them alone and close the door, draw the curtain. The homework could wait. She curled up over the covers, the side of her face against the pillow, knees drawn a little way up to her chest.

Why don't you lie on your back?

The thought came so clearly it was as if someone was in the room with her. Quickly Lía sat up and looked around. The sensation of something gripping in her belly became stronger while at the same time she felt tiny beads of perspiration gather on her upper lip. Then instead of being afraid of where such a clear thought could have come from, Lía felt herself succumb to the warmth in her room and to the image of the way she might actually lie flat.

Which she did.

An easy lethargy overtook her, moving from her feet to her thighs to her chest and her head. She was comfortable and untroubled, as if she'd trudged across a hot plain to find an unexpected oasis—yes indeed, her oasis after all, right here. As soon as she closed her eyes she knew she'd fallen asleep.

It's not sleep, sweetheart: it's travel.

There was a kindness to that voice Lía hadn't heard for a long time, not in a full year. A *female* sort of kindness, touched with understanding, and so as she drifted Lía knew it must be her mother. Funny thing was, the voice didn't sound like a voice so much as like a drifting yet very clear thought, or image, meant solely for her. She wouldn't be able to explain it, understand it, but right now that hardly mattered.

Because, just like that, Lía felt herself in a room with her ma again, and she was six years of age, and her mother was reading to her from a book, a favourite for the both of them. Lía felt her mother's comforting arm around her slim shoulders; Lía was nestled into her and they were in Lía's small bed in her pretty bedroom, this home a nice high apartment with a view of city lights and a harbour.

Lía's mother, whom she'd missed and missed and missed.

"All men have the stars but they are not the same things for different people," Lía's ma read. "For some, who are travellers, the stars are guides. For others they are no more than little lights in the sky. For others, who are scholars, they are problems. For businessmen they are wealth. But all these stars are silent." Her mother squeezed her a little more tightly. "You—you alone—will have the stars as no one else has them—"

"What does that mean?" Lía remembered asking.

No, not remembered. Lía was there asking it right now. She was that little girl with a simple question, and her ma was closing the book with a smile, putting it aside.

"We'll find out tomorrow night when we read some more. For now let's turn out your light."

"But I—"

But I'm away from that place before I want to be.

Then a very different thought had a very different crystal-clarity to it.

Lía, that's enough for a first time. Travel back to your bedroom in Grandview now, and remember to never roll onto your side. Or to roll onto your front. If you do you won't be able to return. Your spirit will be trapped far away and you'll be like someone dead.

So she was on her back, and Lía did return.

Return from the strangest, clearest sort of dream she could ever remember having.

Lía caught herself blinking at the ceiling. She sat up and asked her room, "Ma, where did you go? What happened?" and the answer was nothing—but the gripping pain in her belly was gone and she felt, not so much lightheaded as light, as if she'd grown an inch taller or had found the answer to an equation she hadn't even realised existed.

More than that, it felt as if a door had opened. A door into her mind opened by someone not herself. Yes, it had to be Ma, opening Lía to something Lía had always suspected was there but had never quite been able to touch.

"But Ma what does it mean?" she asked the empty air.

The answer wasn't the sound of a disembodied voice, a drifting thought, or a footfall in the hallway or any sort of movement, yet somehow Lía knew something was passing her door. Whatever it was she sensed— maybe just the simplest breath of wind—travelled on towards her father's bedroom.

What do I do?
Lía didn't say it. She thought it; there was no thought in reply.
Except her own:
Open the door. Step into the hall.
The house don't make you scared?

———————◆———————

L ía opened her father's door to a room flooded with sunlight. The odd
thing was how the room didn't feel sunny; it didn't feel light, as if the
word sunlight itself lied to her.

In fact the air was just that little bit heavier and so her body felt heavier
too, as if Lía had stepped onto a different planet with atmosphere more
dense than her own. It took an effort to walk, even to lift her feet. Her
shoulders wanted to drag down. Alongside these negative feelings Lía
caught the scent of her father's aftershave, even of the leather shoes he
liked to keep polished.

Confused by what she was experiencing, wondering if she should back
away, close the bedroom door again, Lía stepped slowly to the panorama
through the windows and doors. She saw a shimmering heat haze. The
outside world was quiet and dry and brown with the utter absence of rain,
yet huge swathes of this landscape also managed to be mysteriously and
magnificently green.

Inside, her father's bed was unmade, the room messy. He'd told Lía in
their first days there, "We'll clean the house together but leave my room
alone. Dusting, vacuuming—don't worry, okay?" Now she noticed shirts
and other clothes bundled in a corner. A coat needed hanging and a pair
of trousers he wore while working outside looked like they'd benefit from
a good soak in soapy water. Then there was a dusky bottle on the floor by
the bedhead, and Lía knew this was the reason he wanted her to leave his
room alone.

Sometimes her father had red eyes that accentuated the tiredness in
his face. Those types of days his breath would be stale and his mood flat.
On better days, such as the way Lía had seen him that morning, having a
good breakfast, nicely dressed and heading to a job interview, his breath
was fresh and he was all good health and good cheer. What pushed him
one way? What sort of thing pulled him the other?

Lía moved closer. The bottle was one from an open cardboard carton
in the garage: Ballantine's Finest Blended Scotch Whisky. The most

important thing about that bottle was that when her mother was alive its like had never been around. So maybe she ought to get rid of it.

What stopped her was the shadow of a boy in a corner. Despite the sunlight, he'd found his own dusk.

"Hey," Lía said to this boy, the soft air that had passed her room.

His eyes were dark and so, so longing. He didn't make a sound but raised his right hand and with the tips of his fingers drew a slow line down from his throat to his belly, and lower.

"Wait," she spoke again, afraid he might leave.

He didn't turn and he didn't run. He didn't wait, either. There were no footfalls anywhere, soft or hard, and no sense of a breeze, but the boy left all the same.

Praying

At the end of the day Paul laid himself down, a little sore from the few hours of property and garden work he'd spent with Lía in the late afternoon, a little disappointed that the NCR job had turned out to be just another piece of crap. A paper shuffler in their maintenance division: he could do better than that. Yet soreness and disappointment didn't mean it hadn't been a good day. Any day spent planting seeds was a day worth living—and any day Paul saw Lía forgetting the things behind her was even better again.

When he'd come home he'd asked her how she'd been, all alone out here, still such a new experience for the girl.

"Fine, Dad. I slept a fair bit, but I wrote my essay too."

Those few hours' guilt had followed Paul: was it really such a good thing to leave a teenage girl alone, especially in a place as secluded as Grandview?

"That idea about dogs…"

Her face had already started lighting up. "What?"

"…I'm thinking you're right."

Paul had felt something just as happy light up inside himself.

Yes, a good day.

Of course there were negative glimmers still in the girl, glimmers he maybe should worry about, but Lía was being dutiful with her studies and helpful with every bit of their outside work. She genuinely liked it here and seemed so much less troubled than she'd eventually become in Hong Kong. Now she was interested in their new home, the property as a whole, and especially their evolving garden of lettuce, asparagus, sweet potato, spinach and, so far, five different herbs. She'd told him that tomorrow she wanted to help him set up tomato vines, another thought to make Paul feel good inside.

He reached for the bedside light and turned it off.

Yet as he settled into the darkness, he found himself imagining the day Lía wouldn't need him quite so much, not in the sense of her everyday life. Sixteen. A blink of an eye to university, to a place of her own, and boys of course—then what? Would Paul wander this country house with its rolling acres on his own? Maybe he'd go make some life for himself elsewhere, though he'd never dream of starting a new family. Thing was, though, should a widower have to live so alone?

Grandview was growing, just like the salesman Teddy Quinn had said. Probably in a few years Paul could sell Rosso House—"stately Munro Manor", according to his daughter—at a tidy profit. Then, just as the world was waiting for Lía, maybe it would welcome him as well.

No, stick with the now.

After dinner he'd taken the time to sit in a lounge chair and read Lía's essay. One thousand words about the personal growth of an ignorant soul name of Samuel Pickwick, Esquire. Her writing was as good as ever. Where his daughter got her ideas, her insights, was beyond Paul—yet this was Lía to a T. It was also Anna of course, who'd encouraged their daughter to be such a thoughtful reader.

Standing at her bedroom door, he'd found Lía spinning black vinyl on her record player. He placed the essay on her table.

"I don't know if you're a genius or I'm a genius teacher."

"The latter."

"The former."

"But it took too long. I could have spent more time outside."

"Tomorrow mathematics?"

"Ugh."

"One day it'll click."

"Did it ever for you, Dad?"

"Some of us have strengths elsewhere."

The music Lía played was no longer the poppy stuff she used to listen to just yesterday. The saccharine junk of a young girl had changed into the type of music even Paul might relate to. This was a Bob Marley album; waiting next to it was a new record she'd asked for last week, by *Talking Heads*, a band he'd never heard of.

"So," Paul said, considering the room, "got it the way you want?"

"Close."

"You used to have pink everywhere. And little dinosaurs."

"Dad," Lía spoke, hesitating a little, "do you ever think about Ma?"

A small chill touched Paul's neck, one he wanted to pretend wasn't there. "What's on your mind?"

"Do you feel like Ma's still with you?"

Ask the bottle by my bed. Ask the nights I toss and turn and can't sleep a wink.

"She'll always be with both of us."

Lía's eyes said she wanted to know something else.

"What's up?"

Paul saw his daughter hesitate, then she said, "Nothing. Good night, Papà."

"Papà?" She hadn't called him that in a couple of years. "I like it."

With a kiss on her forehead Paul had left Lía's room. And so now in the dark he told himself one more time that it had been a good day.

I never prayed a day in my life, Anna, not until you were sick. First I prayed you'd get better fast, then I prayed your suffering would end faster. After you were gone I prayed Lía would learn to live without you, then I prayed I'd never forget you.

I haven't and I won't.

He was still in the dark of his room, yes, but without quite realising it these thoughts so much like prayers had taken Paul out of his bed. He was standing at the doors to his balcony staring out into the moonlit night. The whisky bottle was in hand.

Paul drank neat, one swallow, three.

❖————————————❖

It was hours since her dad had closed her door behind him, hours since she'd played that last record album of the night. Lía kept her eyes shut and tried to sleep. On her mind was that strange sensation supposedly called travelling, and the boy. She didn't even want to think this:

Why don't you come back and talk to me?

Yet she did. And the reply she received was clear and quiet:

Don't be afraid whatever happens.

Ma, is that really you?

Be curious about anything you don't understand, and all will be well. I know you can do it.

Then there was nothing else. Only silence, her own drifting thoughts, and Lía opening her eyes to the dark of her room. Without realising it, dreams, or maybe her mother, or *whatever*, had actually taken her away. She hadn't been awake at all—now those very clear words remained in her mind and felt like the best advice imaginable.

But what's supposed to happen?

No answer.

She wondered which troubled her the most, a disembodied voice—or the way it felt so strangely unsurprising, as if she'd waited to hear it just about all her life. And the boy too, why didn't the idea of a ghost—because a ghost he had to be—not scare her the way it should have? Looked a lot like her ma's advice was already true: Lía was more curious than frightened. What Rosso House offered were questions, interesting questions, which she'd started to feel the first moment she'd run her hand over the panelling of its front door.

Touching the house had been the first step. Perceptions heightened, she'd seen things in the salesman Teddy Quinn: fears, anxieties and love for an old woman floating, whatever that was supposed to mean. Then inside the house she'd felt a presence, so much so that she'd had to hold her tongue from immediately telling her father. What would he have thought? Not of this place, but of her? So an instinct very much like self-preservation had told her to keep this part of her life in Rosso House—or the life of Rosso House itself, which invited her in—very much to herself.

The next step? That advice about lying flat, Lía's mother showing her how to travel. Grief had vanished; confusion too. Instead of wanting to fall to her knees for being so close to her ma again, Lía had instead experienced a wonderful moment like opening a door—a door inside Lía's own mind.

What it meant she couldn't say.

But she liked it.

Lía was out of her bed. Funny, she couldn't remember moving. She was by her study desk, the chair pushed in. She was there, barefoot, yet felt no cold. The air in her room was heavier; her head felt lighter. And here in the dark the little boy with dark eyes was beside her. She sensed more than saw his presence. Sadness seeped into her. It was his, and so now it was hers. The boy didn't move his fingertips from under his chin to his belly button. He didn't let her know that under those fingertips would be skin;

muscles; ligaments and tendons; organs and bone.

Instead there was a thin scraping sound. Lía looked down. The sound was of pencil on paper. The pencil was in her own right hand. On the desk was the hazy shape of an exercise book, a page was open.

Lía breathed shallow. The air returned to normal. Her eyes snapped open.

She was lying flat under her bed covers, all of it before some trick. She'd travelled. Now as she quickly pushed herself out of her bed she felt the night's chill. The house was silent, asleep. There was no boy.

Lía went to her study desk and reached for the desk lamp. Her eyes flinched hard from the glare. On the open page of the exercise book wasn't her usual lovely looped cursive script, but scratched in harsh letters:

Not your ma.

Mr H and His Long, Wrong Road

More tests informed him that his impotence was pathogenic, meaning he hadn't lost the desire for sex only the physical ability to do anything about it.

"Perfectly natural, Mr Haberman. With confirmed cardiovascular disease and the possibility of neurological problems and hormonal insufficiencies, as well as the effects of the drugs you're taking, we'd consider it remarkable if things were otherwise."

He had far worse problems, anyway. The renal specialist referred to CKD, Chronic Kidney Disease, and found Haberman to already be at Stage 4.

"Meaning?"

"You're approaching renal failure."

"A transplant, then?"

"With your heart you'd never survive, I'm afraid."

So, yet another regimen of medications. Nothing would reverse or cure the disease, so the best hope was to try slowing down the degeneration. Haberman had pills for his kidneys, pills for his heart functions, pills to thin the blood, pills to ease the palpitations that appeared without warning, and pills to stabilise his blood pressure. Instructions about what to eat and not to eat were repeated gravely. No alcohol. Clear fluids were good but in minimal quantities only. Forget milk or any dairy product. Per day he could enjoy maybe two small cups of weak tea, clear soup, and two tumblers of water only, sipped slowly. His kidneys simply couldn't process very much fluid. Haberman had never heard such madness, but as if to give him proof, for a week his legs swelled from the knees down until they actually started to leak through his pores, and ulcerate. His belly bloomed with bloating. His bed and socks, always wet, until he received new pills to negate so much water retention.

All his properties now, not only the international holdings, sold; Haberman started passing the criminal baton.

"Nasser, you'll take the red-lights. Lundy, you'll collect monies for our friends the police."

Nasser and Lundy almost shook with fear and joy.

"What'll your cut be, Mr H?" the newly appointed bosses wanted to know.

"While I remain on the surface of this stupid world I'll keep small businesses run by dagos, plus the grunt to drive me around. The rest is yours. If you need to use friend Donny Zap, make it sparingly."

So Haberman had Donatello Zappavigna collect the vig from a score of ethnic cafés, restaurants and corner stores. This was the simplest task: he visited each place, collected the cash, made sure it was right and took it to Max Eureka, Haberman's accountant. If business owners heard whispers the terrible Mr H was letting go his grip, the grunt could work some magic. Which he did.

"Scrub the blood from under your fingernails. Don't ever come into this house like that again."

Haberman managed his dying business affairs as he managed his own dying: with as clear a mind as he could muster, which wasn't easy. Many nights Haberman would come awake staring wildly into the darkness of his bedroom. He'd hear his own sleep-cries. He had nightmares and took to sleeping with a nightlight.

We get old; we regress to childhood. He hated it all.

Better nights he dreamed of women. Many he'd known and many he'd never met. In these dreams he imagined the rock-hard erections now beyond him. He suffered sexual desire as intensely as he ever had, and in the face of looming death it might have been even more so. His erotic mind was alive but his tortured body mocked that desire. It was unbearable. Another man might take the option of a quick bullet to the brain—Haberman's home did hide a Russian Pistolet Makarova—but if Haberman was to deliver his own demise he'd do it with French champagne plus a final moment of something at least approaching pleasure. Was he asking for the impossible?

Fate, you miserable piece of excrement, you'll cheat me out of even that, won't you?

Unexpectedly, it was Donatello Zappavigna and his great-aunt the witch who brought him his best chance.

———◆———

One early morning the Friulian grunt came to the house when he didn't need to, a serious expression in that long face. With him he had what looked like a sealed re-used jam jar.

"Zia say if you no come to see her then she send you a tonic. Here is. You gonna feel better."

If the container was a jam jar, its contents looked like horseshit streaked with beetroot, though the contents offered notes of orange blossom.

"You eat, mister."

"You must be joking." Haberman put the jar aside. "I need you Saturday. This is very important. Go see Max Eureka and get the details."

True to his intention Haberman had planned a final high. He would meet oblivion via pleasure: suicide by sex, or in its most vainglorious attempt. If he couldn't die in mid-coitus or post-coitus because he remained incapable of coitus, then he'd at least go with his mouth sucking a beautiful breast. And if the poetry of *that* final moment didn't work, then he had an ace up his sleeve, a single pill, one valuable artefact from British and American Intelligence, circa-World War II: an infamous L-Pill.

Break it between your teeth, experience instant death. Or close enough.

Haberman had found to whom the final breast would belong. Her preferred name was 'Svetlana'. The photographs he'd been shown revealed a long sleek body and hair like gold. She was—he'd heard from the assistant commissioner of police, who helped himself to five hundred illegal dollars a month—an ex-photographic model specialising in sports advertising. It was put around that in her former home of Ukraine she'd held several significant 'Miss' titles. Well, even if Haberman didn't believe that he understood how all stories need their sizzle. Svetlana's rates were ridiculously over the top line, yet she was said to be worth it.

A cultured intelligent woman might just inspire that last bit of juice out of him. *In flagrante* he'd die—and if there was to be no fucking, then he'd die on her anyway, the glass pill broken between his teeth.

Oh, you humour-filled god, let her be the magic I need.

"Mister, you eat?"

Haberman noted the frown in the young grunt's forehead. "You're of the sincere belief that I would put a scrap of that muck in my mouth?"

"Mister, is life."

Donny Zap found a teaspoon. Haberman watched with weary fasc-ination as the boy himself tasted the evil creation. He took a second and third taste, nodding as if assessing a delicacy.

"Is sweet too, like chocolate."

A poor choice of description, Haberman thought, seeing how wettish brown those contents were. Despite the pleasant orange scent drifting towards him, his belly filled with disgust. Then he noted the extraordinary light entering Donny Zap's face, a thing impossible to fake.

"Give me."

The grunt did, with a fresh teaspoon. Haberman tasted a speck the size of a lentil. Was there something that reminded him less of an orange grove and more the miniature petals of extraordinary flowers?

"Your great-aunt really thinks of herself as a helper of the needy?"

"If they pay."

"I'm not giving her a cent."

"This a gift 'cause of why you my boss."

"How much am I to take?"

"Swallow what you want. Zia Agata, she make you plenty more."

"She might make it look a little more palatable."

Karl Haberman helped himself to tiny shred by tiny shred, surprising himself by finishing the entire jar. It was the most food—or whatever this was—that he'd managed to put down his throat in a month of Sundays. He relaxed back in his armchair with a surprising feeling of wellness, even of energy, going through him.

"As I said before, make sure to talk to Max. You'll be here Saturday with a delectable visitor." Haberman sighed and patted his belly. "And you might bring more of your witch's muck."

———

Come Saturday evening Haberman was freshly shaved, showered and well dressed. Other than the blood-thinning agent streptokinase he'd dispensed with other medications. Since eating the witch's tonic he'd felt somewhat better and wanted his system as clear as possible for this evening with Svetlana, his last evening on earth. The terminus had been reached; there was no need to argue the facts. If Svetlana's body didn't kill him, in the coin pocket of his trousers he carried the L-Pill.

Two flute glasses of proscribed *Dom Pérignon '59* enlivened the thoughts in his head. His heart, his kidneys, all other tortured organs, blessed him by not rebelling immediately against the alcohol. New batches of the strega's tonic had also given him a boost: the young grunt had come in with three jars at lunchtime.

"Zia Agata she no forget you."

Throughout the day Haberman hadn't been able to resist dipping a teaspoon into the first jar, then he'd nibbled at the second. By evening's fall only the third was left, and he quietly spooned titbits from it as he waited with the Dom. Then Donny Zap returned, ushering Svetlana into the house as Haberman pressed a white linen napkin to the corners of his mouth.

While Karl Haberman took Svetlana's warm hand and bowed his head over it, Donny Zap withdrew.

She was in low heels and a silk crépon evening dress. The swing to her hips was either a pure force of nature or something well-practised. That dress was light, almost gauzy, purple-black in colour. Buttons down the front led to pleats at the waist. The sleeves were silk. Perfect for this summer's night. Her hair wasn't golden as in the pictures the police commissioner had shown him. She'd changed the style; it was blonde-brown and touched with ash, falling in waves to her shoulders. Somehow she looked perfectly natural: elegant but in no way overdone. The air of rude health about her was something for Haberman to envy.

"Welcome," he said.

She moved close. He caught the scent of her hair.

"Very nice to meet you."

The huskiness of her voice made the words thrilling. She said she liked that they weren't going out and accepted the Pérignon he poured her. They made small talk. Svetlana sipped her champagne, taking Haberman in, and the living room.

"You have record albums."

"Feel free."

At the stereogram she placed the turntable's needle down onto the record already on the platter. A crooner of the forties crooned. When she sat on the couch next to him Svetlana said, "I don't know if I want to call you Haberman or Mr H."

"Mr H," he said. "Where would you have heard that?"

"I like a little research."

"I shouldn't blame Max Eureka's big mouth?"

"He didn't tell me anything I didn't need to know. Instead I went looking for information about tonight's mysterious assignation."

"Is it so different for you?"

"I understand you are."

"Really?"

"A man's name spoken in whispers."

Haberman had been with smart call girls in the past; few could deliver their lines with such panache. Even in Svetlana's gentle teasing, that slight mockery, there was a sort of unaffected warmth. A near-perfect routine. So far, artifice seemed very distant indeed.

"There's one thing I'd very much like," he said to her.

"Please, Mr Haberman."

"May I call you by your real name?"

"You'll never know it, I'm afraid."

"What if I'm the type who also enjoys simple research?"

"You didn't." Then she realised he had. "*Mr Haberman.*"

"A pleasure to meet you, Miss Khamitova."

"My name is Virna."

"So much prettier."

"On the other side of the coin, Haberman is your real name?"

"At your service."

"Where is it from?"

"Czechoslovakia. My father was a refugee."

"Will you tell me about him?"

"He arrived in this country a bachelor and worked to make a life."

"You've been to your mother country?"

"Though not to discover my roots. I couldn't care less about family background. My father was a drunk and a thief and he was killed by a business partner who proved to be a business rival. My mother died early as well, succumbing to her own personal weaknesses. As a young man I took over my father's portion of a nightclub. And his rival's portion, as it turned out."

"Will you tell me about that?"

"Why would I?"

"Because it would be a change to know a man with a history like yours. The people I spoke to painted a picture, though necessarily incomplete."

"You're wired."

She straightened her spine. "Why not be sure?"

Haberman leaned into Virna Khamitova and pressed his lips to the fragrant nape of her neck. As he did he ran a hand down her back, along her sides, over her flat belly and firm thighs.

Nothing was hidden; the touch of her made him want to quiver.

He said, "The rival's name was Andrei Klimov."

"And what became of Mr Klimov?"

Something was going through Haberman, that quiver, still, but more: his hand had to grip his glass as if to keep himself secured to the present. A wave shook his senses and Virna Khamitova's face actually shimmered.

Oh, this feeling of wellness, it was the one truly counterfeit thing in the room. Haberman was sick all right, no witch's muck would change that. His plan for dying might unfold just as he'd imagined, the L-Pill superfluous.

"Mr Haberman?"

"A moment's small reflection."

Virna Khamitova frowned, waiting.

"Well," he started as the moment began to pass, "if you want this conversation…"

"I do."

"I had no great love for my father, but there are times of course when circumstances demand action. So I made myself comfortable in the garage of Klimov's home. An hour, two hours. He arrived and climbed out of his car. When he closed the garage door I walked to him and waited for him to recognise me. Which he did. The son of the man he'd ordered weighted with chains and thrown into Moreton Bay. Thrown in alive, I suspect. An effective way of ending a business partnership, though one should always give thought to unforeseen complications, such as a son. What I had with me was a simple galvanised steel tent peg, the sort of spike useful on a camping trip. Andrei Klimov died nicely, thrashing on the garage floor, while his wife cooked his dinner and his children played in the house."

"You're not embellishing your story?"

"Hardly."

"So," Virna Khamitova settled into the thought, "where did this remarkable action lead you?"

"In those early days this town was pregnant with an untapped fortune in gambling and girls. The rest is the rest. Is it enough to say that all of it has led me toward this most companionable evening with you, Miss Khamitova?"

Virna Khamitova kept watching him. Haberman tried to assess if he'd really just betrayed himself with the law. No, he couldn't believe he had. A large part of this young woman wasn't an act. She liked being here. She liked his story, that small piece in the bloody tapestry of Haberman's life.

Virna took his hands. Slowly she kissed them.

"Mr H," she said in her husky burr, "whatever you want tonight, it will be an honour."

"Another glass?"

She shook her head.

"Might you disrobe to another record?"

Dimming the living room's lights to dusky shadows, Virna Khamitova did. The stereogram now offered a mellow-as-aged-whisky voice singing some jazz standard Haberman couldn't quite place.

Mind, of course, on more pressing matters.

From which he'd allow no distraction.

"And will you dance for me?"

He pressed a firm hand to his chest for the ache that threatened to intensify. Oh, to be dying when this Virna Khamitova turned and turned so slowly, arms raised, elegant hands snake-entwining over her head and all of her looking no less than life itself. God but he needed something, anything to help him endure his slow demise.

"That jar," he spoke, "do you see it? Feed what's left to me."

On her knees, skin golden, she did feed him, teaspoon by teaspoon. Haberman felt the strega's magic on his tongue. Soon that magic neared his tortured heart. Notes of chypre filled him head to toe; the surprising rapture of a witch's goodness overturned his senses. He heard himself cry out. Haberman pushed his thrumming body from the couch and pulled Virna Khamitova onto the floor. She slid beneath him, an invitation, and god-oh-god but she was pure warm velvet.

For moments then minutes he was young and bull-like, viciously strong.

Before the memento mori of a needle through his chest, a needle that told him he was none of these things, he was weak and needed to stop, or kill himself this way.

Good. I am Haberman. I choose my own road.

"Yes, yes, keep going," Virna kissed him deeply, a warm wet mouth, "you're a champion, so good…"

His plan; perfect timing; the end.

Yet for all the pain and exertion his heart wouldn't give out. So he struggled for the L-Pill, to find it, take it, crunch down on it then move his head to one of Virna's engorged nipples and clamp his mouth to her.

Then, before he could grind his teeth and break the glass, the pain in his heart flared into a full, shocking fire. His body tensed, his back arched. Haberman felt himself leave the moment. His twisting lips stuttered some non sequitur and his hands in Virna's hair couldn't feel her anymore.

Eyes so tightly squeezed shut, he tumbled into a void.

A velvet void, as inviting as Virna.

Haberman couldn't hear the crooner's song; he slipped away without conscious thought, the intact pill dropping onto the perspiration sheen of Virna Khamitova's skin.

A Visitor

They found the dogs at the local RSPCA, where the on-duty vet said both were well trained and came from the same family home, broken by a divorce.

Into Grandview and the Munro home the two dogs came.

Buster, a tan German Shepherd crossed with something else, about twenty months, and Dakota, a jet-black mixture of breeds, maybe a year older. Buster was skittish, batlike ears pricked, lean body always ready to run and get to work. At night when distant dogs howled he was tight all over. Lía imagined that inside his canine mind there was some hard-wired longing to join a pack in the wild. Dakota was Buster's opposite, content to lay on her side in hot grass in the endless sunshine. Any drifting cries from the hills and forests went unnoticed. The dogs complemented each other, one fire and the other milk, yet always nuzzling together, and both slept by Lía's bed.

Lía and her father were three months into Rosso House now, and how much better was this home with a pair of good dogs—but the dry cold winter made them need fresh water all day long.

Today as with so many days there was no breath of wind. Many trees had skeleton-fingers poking accusations at the sun. As she stood in the kitchen preparing lunch Lía lifted her eyes. Through the windows a distant wood-fire's smoke made curling spirals in the shattering blue. Standing, she ate her sandwich, still watching. Next she'd go to her room for study and her father's set exercises. Lía would concentrate on the beauty and vast expanse of this new world she was in; she'd concentrate on her father's tutelage; she wouldn't think about a voice or the presence of a small ghost-boy. She had her dogs now. They were friends. It was almost as if some greater intelligence understood this; weeks had passed without further incident. Rosso House was allowing itself to become Munro Home.

Lía knew all was quiet; inside herself *Lía* was quiet.

Now she saved her father's sandwiches on a plate wrapped in cellophane and led the dogs to her room. They curled up together in the cold early afternoon. Lía turned to her work.

More than an hour passed before she was finishing a rough draft for her father's latest English exercise, this one not about a specific book but about a specific writer, F. Scott Fitzgerald. She'd loved *Tender is the Night* but the unfinished *The Last Tycoon* had threatened to break her heart. So much beauty and longing in those pages, yet the writer hadn't been allowed to complete his story. Though Lía concentrated her essay on Fitzgerald's background and influences, his body of work, she couldn't quite take her mind away from his premature death: a heart attack at forty-four, no doubt brought on by a life of alcoholism and trouble. Lía was thinking of her father. He was at the same age; he drank; in recent times he'd known too much trouble. First with Ma dying, then with Lía herself. What would she do if like Fitzgerald one day her father simply dropped?

An ache grew in her lower belly; her head was light. What she imagined, the sadness and dread of it—

No, no. I don't want to travel. Not like this.

Lía's fingers tightened on her pen.

My dad won't die. It will never happen. I won't let it.

She dropped the pen and gripped the edge of her study desk as if to hold on to her room's reality.

You won't let it—then how?

That question came in Lía's own voice. It wasn't borne from some disembodied entity that might be her mother or *not her ma* at all. She knew this was her own doubt speaking, her fears for the person she loved most in this world.

I'll look after you, Dad. That's all there is to it.

The moment was passing. She wouldn't travel. Instead Lía would leave this essay and go find her father, remind him to eat. Maybe sit a while and chat about nothing. They might go water the garden and check their new bed of winter herbs: dill, parsley, sage and sorrel.

Lía rubbed her temples, then her eyes.

Her father's job hunting had died off. He'd been occupying his time by fixing up a few of the rooms. Lía sensed just how much these small jobs, always fiddly and detailed, gave him purpose—plus fewer mornings of reddened eyes and stale whisky breath. For now, he'd left the upstairs intact; however most ground floor rooms held stainless steel buckets and tin pails overflowing with slop and rubble. Rags and tools were scattered around. Tins of paint, ancient wooden horses he'd retrieved from one of the old farm sheds out back, and brushes and bottles of turpentine cluttered the living room. Already a small study and larger sunroom were fresh and sort of, well, more alive.

Just as Lía stretched back in her chair, Buster started barking. Loudly. The noise that came out of him was incredible, the first time. He'd jumped to his feet and was already worrying and scraping at the bedroom door.

"What? What is it?"

She tried to shush him, then realised a car was arriving.

———◆——————◆———

Lía's father had already let the visitor in through the back door. They stood in the kitchen. Though Dakota was merely interested in this stranger, Buster was wild.

"Jesus Christ, Lía, put the dogs outside."

In his white shirt, tie, brown trousers and *Hush Puppies*, Teddy Quinn got himself out of the way. Lía dragged Buster by the collar. Dakota followed more quietly. Lía closed the screen door on the dogs, then because Buster kept barking, the back door as well.

"Buster wouldn't bite," she heard herself mumble, though she had no evidence of that. For all she knew the young dog might have liked a piece of meat from a stranger's leg.

"It's okay. I like dogs."

Covered in white dust and speckles and splashes of paint, Lía's father's arms and hands filthy, even his hair and eyebrows were powder-dusted. "So what brings you all the way out here?"

"Just sort of wanted to see how you've settled in, but if you're busy—"

"That's okay." Lía's father frowned. "Just let me get cleaned up a minute." Lía knew he was wondering what the salesman really wanted. "What about tea?"

"I'll put the kettle on," Lía spoke, though it was without enthusiasm. "There's some orange cake."

Her father left the kitchen. An uncomfortable silence filled the room as the salesman decided between standing and sitting. Lía didn't tell him what to do. She poured water from the tap into the kettle.

"So… You were going to look for a school, right?"

"We haven't really started."

"Then you're the envy of every kid in Grandview."

Lía lit the gas and put the kettle over the burner. She opened the pantry for what was left of a cake she'd baked a couple of days ago.

"Your dad's a good teacher?"

"Yes."

"What's your favourite subject?"

"I don't know. History's good. Geography too, but probably English. I hate maths."

"That's the only thing ever made sense to me at school."

"Really?"

"When it comes to mathematics and mathematics alone, I'm a bit of a whiz. If you ever need any help…"

Lía set out two small plates and dessert forks, not three. She wouldn't stay. There was a dry creek a kilometre away she could go investigate with the dogs. The salesman didn't seem like a bad guy, but the experience of seeing into this man's thoughts, or *whatever* it was that had happened all those months back—

—well, it had already returned.

She tried to keep herself from opening her mouth again, and definitely didn't want to acknowledge what she was seeing.

There's cigarette smoke all around you, Mr Quinn. The elderly woman I saw before is dreaming of smoking.

"Lía, are you okay?"

"I have to go."

"Wait, I wanted to talk to you."

They both heard Lía's father's footsteps returning down the hall.

"You feel her, right? I know you do."

Of course Lía did. Soon as the barking had died down and Teddy Quinn's presence had filled her senses. Or *not* Teddy's presence; someone else's.

Today she—whoever she was—existed in the cigarette smoke floating around this man's head. Lía even had the bitter taste of the woman's cigarettes in the back of her mouth.

"Poor More," she said with absolutely no idea of what she was saying or what she meant.

The salesman's eyes widened, then her father was there in a clean shirt. He'd washed his face and hands but paint was still on him and white dust was still caught in his hair.

The kettle started to whistle. Lía turned to it.

"I'm not looking to buy any new properties, you get that, right? And we're doing just fine here."

"I—well, to tell you the truth, Mr Munro, I remember you saying you'd be looking for work."

"That's on the back burner."

"There's a possibility at the office."

"What?"

"An interesting job's going."

There was a pause before Lía's father said, "I guess it's very kind of you to think of me, but why would I want to get into real estate? That's hardly my background."

"Well, in a way it is, isn't it?"

Lía's father pulled up a chair, becoming curious. "Sit, please."

They both did. Lía let the tea draw in the pot, then her father poured it, no sugar or milk for him or Teddy Quinn. She served the slices of cake and was about to leave them to their discussion.

"Wait," her father told her. "Let's see what you make of this."

"It's real estate, Mr Munro, but not the way you're thinking of it. When we did up your contract at the office, Mr Gavin—that's the boss—well, he was interested in your background. That project management company in Hong Kong? We took a look into it. Pretty big stuff, from a standing start as we understood it. Correct?"

"Sure, it was my baby. Until I sold it. Engineering, construction, even town planning."

"That's what I'm talking about. You mentioned it the very first day you came to see the house."

"Did I?"

"And your special interest in what you called *green space?*"

Lía could see just how dubious her father remained.

"Well, yes, I was an engineer in my early career, then I got interested in land use in urban environments."

"The country in the man."

"Huh." Lía's father frowned more deeply, as if he'd never thought of it that way. "I guess."

"So this is what's going," Teddy spoke up. "You might have guessed Mr Gavin's a real estate kingpin, but now he's interested in developing what he can lay his hands on."

"What's that, supermarkets or something?"

"New communities from scratch, here in Grandview. Meaning all of Grandview. Every farm. The open spaces. Hillsides. Whatever's not protected, and believe me, only the state forest is. Mr Gavin says he needs project managers with practical good sense and maybe even some knowledge of the area. That made me think of you and when I brought up your name, he didn't say no."

"Well, I am."

"What, really?"

"Come on." Lía watched her father sip his tea then take a small bite of the cake. "Why come all the way out here to try and get me interested?"

"Mr Gavin's helped me a lot. A lot more than just a boss. I wouldn't mind paying that back."

"And?"

"And I spent a lot of time selling farms out here. I guess I got to liking the place."

Lía's father nodded towards her:

"What do you think?"

"I like Grandview the way it is."

"So do I. Sorry, Teddy. I won't have anything to do with tearing this place up."

"But the original character could—"

"That's enough."

Teddy Quinn turned his teacup in its saucer; first one way, then the other. "Then I guess I wasted my trip."

"Thanks anyway." Lía's father stood. "Lía, better make sure Buster doesn't take his leg off."

❖

They were outside, the red Stag parked in the courtyard by her father's Chrysler. At first Buster did need more coaxing to calm down, but soon he and Dakota were only interested in getting as close to this visitor as they could. They'd decided they liked him; Lía only wanted to get back inside as fast as she could.

With his back to the house, stopping to crouch and pat the heads of her dogs, Teddy Quinn spoke low: "Why don't you tell me?"

"There's nothing to tell."

"Poor More is Pall Mall. Those are the cigarettes my grandmother loves. How could you know that?"

"It was just a mistake."

"How could you know about a sick woman dreaming about her favourite books and smoking her favourite cigarettes? That's what you said. Right over there at that front door."

"I don't remember."

"You remember."

The sudden ferocity in his voice frightened her, but still he spoke low, hands caressing both dogs' heads. She was conscious of how he tried to control himself.

"You and I need to talk. Properly. The Grandview produce store? I'll wait for you there in an hour."

Lía thought he'd stride purposefully to that stupid sports car of his. Angrily slam his door. Her heart was hammering. She wouldn't go anywhere, not for him. Yet Teddy Quinn didn't stride away. She sensed he wasn't so much keeping in control as trying to keep himself together. He hesitated where he was, taking comfort from the dogs. Dakota licked his hand. Buster positively rubbed himself against the young man.

Then Lía saw the way Teddy Quinn's Adam's apple worked. In a moment barely restrained tears glistened in his eyes.

"It's my grandmother… She's sick. She's so sick, Lía ."

Lía felt that ache in her belly return. Her mind wanted to drift away from this moment, to let light-headedness take her away from here and to—

—to the sad and ailing old woman she saw quite clearly, lying still and flat in a hospital bed.

It was hardly Lía's own voice saying, "I can't make it to the produce store, I don't drive."

"Then how about—Jesus, I don't know. Where?"

"There's…there's a dry creek bed a kilometre from here. Down the bottom of that highest ridge."

"They call it Post's Gully. Big Chinese Elm where the creek forks?"

"Yes."

Teddy Quinn got himself together.

Now Lía needed to hold the dogs back. They wanted to follow Teddy Quinn to his car. Buster wanted to chase the throaty rumbling of the Stag's slow departure. Lía watched the salesman go, wondering why she'd agreed to meet him, then when she turned back to the house she was sure the shadow of her father was moving away from the kitchen window.

Post's Gully

Then when he was away from Rosso House he was driving too fast, his head wanting to explode. Teddy Quinn pushed down on the accelerator for the teeming thoughts that kept him up at night, that kept him always *worrying*.

He sped into verdant laneways and dirt, into gravel sidetracks he knew too well thanks to all those months trying to sell Rosso House. He swerved the Stag into a sharp left, only just avoiding a tractor hauling a great mechanical slasher. It was Jake Minter, his heavy-duty equipment taking up the entire lane. Teddy Quinn's sports car skidded then slewed sideways before coming to a crunching halt. Jake's tractor rumbled past. Teddy saw the driver, all nutty hair and black bushy eyebrows, turn back to check he was all right. Teddy waved a disconsolate hand. Jake didn't wave back.

The Stag was in a deep, natural cul-de-sac of overgrown shrub and towering trees. Lucky to have not gone off the road. The engine was dead, stalled. Dust settled around the open top and hot metal ticked. So, driving like a madman didn't help his mood. What a surprise. Nothing helped. Maybe the girl would. Or maybe he was just plain crazy and her as well. Just about the only thing certain in his life was the shallow rise and fall of breath in Vivien's chest. Teddy's *Nanny Viv*, what she'd always liked him to call her, no matter how childish it sounded.

Viv was alive inside herself somewhere and she was talking to him through a teenage girl with skin a colour he'd never quite seen before. Teddy wanted to weep some more; it was something that never left him, just like the endless, excruciating process of Nanny Viv *not* leaving her exhausted body behind.

Mount... Mount...

Just what the girl had said: Mountford. As in *Mountford Rest Home and Hospice*. Lía almost had it. So what was Lía Munro then, some kind of conduit into things no sane person ought to believe in?

Post's Gully, one hour. He checked his watch.

Teddy twisted the key in the ignition. *Hrrng, hrrng, hrrng:* his engine made the sound of a sick goat. Jesus but he was supposed to be elsewhere, at the Egans' property the way Mr Gavin had instructed him.

"Get out there and make the old bastard's sons listen to reason. Do not take *no* for an answer."

Easy to say when you're the boss.

Over that way, the Volkmann farm, pineapples and assorted vegetables and debt destroying another family. German immigrants from before the first war, nice people and friendly as hell. Looking forward to the good price Mike Gavin and Teddy Quinn promised they could get them. But just a country hike up and down the next hill and you came to Jim Egan's dairy farm. Not so friendly. In fact a sour shit of a farmer fighting foreclosure and any proposal for subdividing, much less selling out completely. Not at all inclined to be gracious about it. Bankruptcy, the worst curse word you could use around here. Teddy had to call on the Egan farmhouse three times before that wood-faced patriarch with the long gnarled limbs and a pate burned crisp by the sun had agreed to speak to him. They stood at the gate, which stayed latched, Egan one side, Teddy the other.

"Not interested."

Teddy called two weeks later with the boss himself. The Egans were a little more polite this time, grudgingly inviting both men into a timber cottage with little ventilation and the windows sealed shut. A hothouse. A fucking sauna. Mrs Egan, as ugly and hard as her husband, had poured glasses of tepid homemade non-alcoholic cider. She offered the two of them in their white shirts and ties perfect little fruit mince pies warm from her wood fired oven. Which made the whole place even more stifling. Teddy had felt like he needed to gag for air.

Jim Egan had his heels dug in hard and counted off thirty-eight souls who relied on his farm for their living and their homes. There were seven cottages on the property, plus the main farmhouse: a veritable family village. Grandchildren and great-grandchildren were everywhere. It took a good twenty minutes before it sank into Teddy and his boss that they were talking to the patriarch of one great Mormon clan.

Mr Gavin, a very strict Baptist, had narrowed his eyes, maybe with greater respect. He was a hard man himself, a God-fearing father of three, notoriously unyielding in his beliefs, straitlaced if not out-and-out puritanical. How Teddy managed to keep his drinking and sexual adventures hidden from him, he didn't quite know. Staff had been sent home for taking an illicit drink during working hours; more than one had been sacked on the spot for a hint of in-office prurience.

"So, Mr Gavin, you begin to understand my responsibilities? Then why would you expect me to give up my land?"

"The bank could decide for you."

"We look after our own and we bring them up to obey the Lord's will, whatever it may be."

"I don't argue with that—"

"Before your time, however, during the great drought, so many did give up hope, Mr Gavin. They did it far too early and I watched them go. Yet those of us who preferred to stay prayed with all our hearts. And the Lord provided. He gave us the means to endure. The rain finally came and our land prospered. Now our region's in economic difficulties and it's happening again. Families are selling instead of praying and men like you prosper from their weakness. I know better than that. So, we'll wait. Guidance always comes."

"Maybe I'm the guidance that shows you how to prosper elsewhere."

"A silver tongue reveals you're not."

"Mr Egan, let me put it to you this way. My company's forming a consortium—"

"Carpetbaggers."

"—a consortium to redevelop Grandview into prime real estate. A real township, not just scattered houses all over the place. How does 'Egan Village' sound?"

"You have children, Mr Gavin?"

"Three girls."

"You expect they'll always come back."

"What?"

"Once your daughters leave and make their own way in the world, like any good father you'll pray they'll return to see you some day. Especially if they're in need. They'll come back for the arms and the home they know."

"Of course."

"Children return to their family home no matter how long they're forced to be away. When mine do, they'll find the safety they expect."

"This area will develop with or without you, I'm afraid."

"Satan thrives on commerce. And one more thing before you go. You're not my blood, Mr Gavin, and neither is your young friend. Only blood returns to blood, so don't darken this doorway again."

Behind the wheel, driving away, Mike Gavin had exploded. "What a bloody nut! Those glorious 'children' of his will be selling up soon as Jim Egan's body lies a'moulderin' in its grave."

"Because the children always come back." Quinn had laughed.

"No," Gavin told him. "You're going back. Start working on the sons."

Jesus, today Teddy would have to pretend that he had, because talking to Lía Munro was more important. He tried the ignition again. Still flooded. Teddy climbed out and pulled up the soft top, locked the Stag, then started what he knew was the hike across country to Post's Gully.

<hr>

The dogs ran ahead and Lía watched them loving these wooded hills as if they'd lived their entire lives in Grandview. They'd been like this from the day of their very first excursion. Today, a little after Teddy Quinn left the house, her father liked the way she wanted an afternoon hike. It seemed to make him happy whenever he saw her leave the house and take to the countryside, as if he believed nature itself was a cure for all ills. Maybe it was. Hiking with the dogs was something Lía was doing every day now that she had the dogs. If he hadn't been working on a room her father would have come too; he'd stayed behind, what Lía had expected.

What, for at least one day, this day, Lía wanted.

"What do you think of our salesman friend?"

She'd shrugged in the best offhand manner she could muster, pretending to look for her walking shoes.

Now Lía picked her way down from the tallest rise across a slope of dry long grass. She saw Teddy Quinn waiting. He was under the Chinese elm, an old giant, tall and wide with multiple huge limbs thick with leaves. No one else was around. Lía's anxiety about meeting a virtual stranger in the middle of nowhere intensified. She tried to assuage her fears by looking at the way both black and brown dogs now streaked toward him. They'd taken an instant liking to this young man.

She wondered what they sensed. She wondered what *she* would sense when she was next to him again.

He'd taken off his shoes and socks. They were to one side on a flat rock. The long winding creek remained as dry as ever, full of pebbles and rocks; it traversed this gully to a long plain then travelled on into the woods. She'd followed it several times now, two, three kilometres into the forest before the vegetation thickened and there was no way to go on. Why was Teddy Quinn bare-foot? There was no water to splash his feet into. Not to mention that he seemed so much a city type. Just like Lía—or the Lía of Hong Kong.

"Do you know if it ever runs?" she asked him.

The dogs pressed to Teddy Quinn as he looked one way then the other.

"I guess, if it ever rains again. I noticed you and your dad are growing things in some new garden beds. Water's not a problem?"

"Those tanks behind the house? They're full. From whenever the last rain season was."

She watched Teddy Quinn think about that, or about something else entirely. Then he said, "It's good you came."

Again Lía tried to put her edginess aside. Her dogs, who she thought of as the most elemental creatures, liked this person. They trusted him. Maybe she could too.

"You said she's your grandmother?"

"Yes." Teddy Quinn glanced up into the elm. "Do you climb?"

"What?"

"When I used to have to come out here for my boss, and the days got too long and boring, I got into the habit of leaving my car somewhere and exploring cross-country. Sometimes I walked across those empty paddocks to here. I always like these big trees."

Teddy Quinn was loosening his tie.

"This one's sort of perfect. I've been up it a couple of times. Easy, and look how far you can go."

Lía looked; she didn't climb.

But maybe she could start.

———————◆———————

Lía copied where Teddy Quinn put his hands and feet. He wasn't much taller than her so she didn't have to stretch too far. And he hadn't lied: she found the climb easy enough. The Chinese Elm's branches were thick and strong, and so plentiful that with a little exertion they really could climb quite high. This tree would have been the perfect place for a cubby house, Lía thought. There was one almost its twin at Rosso House. Wouldn't it be something to ask her father to use his building skills high up in the seclusion of a tree?

She'd taken off her walking shoes and was barefoot like Teddy Quinn. The summer dress helped the climb. Then when they'd gone up as high as possible she watched Teddy shimmy without fear out onto one of the largest branches. Now she knew he really had been doing this before, and in a way it made her want to laugh, a city salesman throwing off his shoes and socks to get so much closer to the places he was supposed to be selling.

Lía followed him along the branch. He reached out a helping hand but she didn't need it. Then they were safe and high, looking out over one of the most remarkable views Lía had ever seen.

"Sort of goes on forever, right?"

"So you really do like Grandview."

"I never thought I would. Maybe it got under my skin. The city's so boring. It's got nothing. There's nothing out here but that's the best thing about it."

"True."

Lía reached for a leaf, touched it but didn't pick it. She ran the back of her hand over the tough skin of the branch they were on and made herself more comfortable. She watched a worm nearby inch its way along.

"So do you want to tell me what you see? I mean about my grandmother?"

"I...I don't know if you can call it seeing. It's more like a feeling."

"What about now?"

Lía shook her head.

"But you saw her around me."

"Sort of."

"And?"

"And she knows she's drifting."

"That's what you said."

"Floating, yes." She had to fight the urge to clam up and say nothing else. "But one thing... She wishes she could smoke again, but she knows she won't. She wants to drink her favourite drink but can't."

"What else?"

"That's it."

"No, try."

Lía wanted to tell him, *How can I?*—yet at the same time she already knew she had at least one more answer.

"She wants to read but you do that. She likes it a lot, the way you read to her."

Teddy Quinn's face softened yet again, just the way it had back at the house. He could seem so much like a different person, as if the salesman part of him was manufactured, a mask honed to fit a role. What she saw now was someone with the type of raw feelings that made tears well up in his eyes.

A part of her wanted to reach out and touch Teddy's arm. His expression reminded her of the nice new hospital in Kwai Chung she'd come to hate; how she'd felt visiting her ma; the long moments she'd held her still-warm hand while the hospital staff waited to perform the final stage of their duties.

"Can you tell me," he asked, passing the back of a hand over his eyes, then watching softly outlined mountain ranges, "can you tell me exactly what my grandmother says?"

"She doesn't say anything. At least not directly. It's more that I can feel what she's feeling."

"Does it hurt?"

"For her? No. That's the drifting part."

"What about for you?"

Lía shook her head, but it was a good question. She could hurt, but not in the way of a physical pain. The old woman's presence made Lía feel— lost. Sort of hopeless. But she wouldn't tell Teddy Quinn that.

"What?" he asked.

"Don't worry, she definitely doesn't feel any pain. But she wants to go. She really wants to go."

"She wants—" A muscle in Teddy Quinn's jaw hardened, outlined like a stone.

"So she's your grandmother."

"Her name's Viv. Vivien. But the truth is she's been more like a mother all my life... She *has* been my mother. And of course, she's dying. She's been dying forever, in this nursing home, their acute care ward. They feed her through tubes and wash her where she is. It's just a long, long coma. Alive without being alive. They have this pulley system that they use sometimes, when they give her a full bath. She's just floating, drifting, just what you

79

said. And she used to love drinking vermouth and getting lost in library books. Her special brand of cigarettes. Pall Malls. When she was okay she was never without one." He wiped at his eyes again. "Jesus, Lía, how do you do this?"

Lía didn't reply.

"Who knows about you?"

"What?"

"This thing—this thing you've got. How many people know?"

"No one."

"Come on, your father, your friends? They must—"

"No. No one. I keep it to myself."

"Viv must know. She must want to see you. Why else all this?"

"No, that's not it." Lía shook her head. Then, surprising herself, she said, "Yes she does. You're right. She wants me to come to…Mount… Mount…"

"Mountford Rest Home and Hospice," Teddy sighed.

Lía felt a wave pass over her. No, it was through her. A wave that said she'd been right all along, she wasn't imagining any of this about the old woman. It was real as real can be.

Mountford, the name always so close, only just eluding her.

"So, when will you come?"

"To see her?" The idea startled Lía . She'd never for a moment imagined she'd want to see this person. Quickly she said, "I can't. My father—"

"He doesn't have to know if you don't want him to."

"Wait, wait. This is wrong. I don't want to see her. This hasn't got anything to do with me."

She returned Teddy's gaze. His expression was so easy to read. He didn't say the words, but she felt them as clearly:

How can you even say that? My Nanny Viv is calling you.

"Nanny Viv?" she asked.

Teddy Quinn froze. He was watching her with awe. Even a moment of fear.

"I never said that name to you."

Lía swallowed hard.

"See? You have to come. How much more of an invitation does my Nanny Viv have to send you?"

Despite herself, Lía felt her defences crumbling.

"I've been using the lending library in town," she started.

Teddy Quinn waited.

"My father and I, both of us. We get our books and stuff. But I've been meaning to go to the State Library for the type of reference books I need for my home schooling. Encyclopaedias. History. We don't have anything at home. You can't loan anything from that library. I think they have study areas or something. I guess when I have to, I could be there just about all day."

"Yes?"

"On my own I mean."

"Then that's where I'll meet you. We can go to Mountford, then I'll bring you straight back."

"But I don't want to lie to my father."

"Then tell him. What are you afraid of? Just tell him you want to visit my grandmother with me. I can talk him round. I'm good at that. It's my job."

All the trouble her dad had been through; then to try to explain something like visions, or if she wouldn't go that far, then to simply make up some story about becoming great friends with a salesman at least ten years older than her. Did she really just expect her father to nod sagely and say, "Have a good time"?

"I'm not telling him."

Teddy Quinn nodded. "All right." He started to move, ready to climb down.

"Wait."

He waited.

"Today when you came over, all that stuff about a job at your office, that was just a trick so you could ask me about all this."

"Only a bit. I did mention your dad to Mr Gavin."

"Why?"

"Like I said. They're all going to turn this place into one big city. Someone like your dad might be able to offer something different than a scorched earth policy."

Lía had to take this Teddy Quinn in. Sitting in this giant tree, such a vista all around them, talking about such things.

"And you know what?"

She shook her head, trying not to imagine all of Grandview gone.

"If your dad was involved, you might have a quiet say too, right, at the end of each day?"

Teddy Quinn gave her a half-smile; the tears weren't very far distant; but he was smiling.

Mr H and His Long, Wrong Road

After his Saturday evening with Virna Khamitova he hovered at death's door a week yet wouldn't cross the black threshold. In a private ward and private room the doctors gave Karl Haberman new, increased doses of medications; along with only slightly more positive outcomes these managed, amongst other infantilising difficulties, to make his bowels lock up entirely.

Lord, why take another breath? Haberman would ask himself during infrequent stretches of acuity. Best to have Nasser or Donatello retrieve the L-Pill from wherever it fell, be done with things entirely.

Two things stopped him issuing the order: the strega's fragrant muck, which Donny Zap brought him and even fed him daily, plus erotic dreams so intense and violent they felt sent from some black spirit not Haberman's own.

Always it was this: the crisp uniform of a good school, worn by a girl, her hair clean and her body washed and pampered.

This pretty gem isn't some piece of suburban trash destined for supermarkets and squalling brats at the hip. Instead she's smart and full of potential, a young woman already admired by those around her. Definitely no part of any cruel girl, rich girl or deviant-teenage-girl group. Not some frumpy opposite either. She'll do something like peace studies one day, or look forward to a medical degree so she can join do-gooders in an international humanitarian organisation.

Destined to be an intelligent asset to society—if not for one Karl Haberman. In these dreams he doesn't know how he's captured her, but he finds himself facing the girl already tied into a chair. He always ignores her questions about what it will take for him to let her go, allowing her to talk until the moment his desire becomes too much. He makes her bleed; he's a shark maddened by blood. The innocent's life turns too easily to vapour, yet he's strangely satisfied by the encounter, even uplifted, and whenever he wakes it's not blood he tastes in his gorge but the dazzling flavours of the strega's muck, somehow giving him life.

———◆———

"Why am I still alive?" he asked the visiting surgeon.

"The body is resilient, Mr Haberman, and most forgiving."

"It doesn't feel very forgiving."

Max Eureka visited, meeting Haberman's voice all whispery as he asked if his affairs were concluded.

"Every one of them, Mr H. You're as honest as a pope."

Or as bereft as a fallen king giving away the last pieces of a worthless empire. In a subsequent blur of days Donny Zap arrived with two fresh jars and a sheaf of papers.

"Mister Max he say you gotta sign these."

Haberman signed, though he could imagine a court of law taking reasonable issue with the indecipherable scratches his hand made. Then he struggled for enough wind to make himself heard.

"What's next for Donatello Zappavigna?"

"I stand by Mr H."

He saw himself reflected in the boy's eyes. How utterly reduced the terrible Mr H must seem. How ridiculous to dream about finding more pleasures. Where was that damn L-Pill? The grunt was unscrewing the lid from a new jar; fragrances like welcome hands passed over Haberman's aching bones.

"My *zia* she want to see you."

"I doubt I'll be out of this place except in a body bag."

"You gonna be good. And she callen you."

"I'd rather the bag."

"You don't unnerstan' nothin'," Donny Zap said, offering Haberman a teaspoon.

"I understand the staff expect I'll die in this bed."

"Then why you don't go die where you want?"

The one piece of real wisdom Haberman had heard in a month of Sundays. Funny it should come from such a dullard.

"Come back in the morning. If I'm breathing, get me out."

A nurse of indefinite age and bristly chin dressed him. Before his trousers were on she slipped and slid him into an adult nappy.

"I've slept with beautiful women. I've dined in the finest salons. I've had men hurt and killed."

"Oh you terrible man." The nurse buttoned his shirt. "Yet you've managed to be such a sweetie. Now here's your medication bag with the printed list and scripts inside."

Eleven a.m. and he was tidy and waiting in a damnable wheelchair. Donny Zap arrived with a baby in a sling against his chest.

"Dis Lorenzo."

"What is it doing with you?"

"Gotta little trouble at home."

Karl Haberman didn't refer to the swaddled thing again, even though its waking moments revealed eyes that seemed to shine through Haberman. A baby was the last thing he wanted to know about. The parallels were too great: he was already dampening himself.

Donny Zap had him down the elevator, the hospital's front stairs, then into Haberman's dark 450SEL. The boy folded the collapsible wheelchair into its spacious trunk and put the baby into the type of backseat travelling capsule Haberman would never have tolerated before.

"Got you a hat, mister."

It was a white Panama. Expensive, a little jaunty, but not bad.

"We're going somewhere?"

"Yep."

"Take me home."

"Old friends they want to say hello."

"What? Don't let me be seen like this."

Yet the streets they soon travelled into were so familiar; Haberman had always imagined he owned them, which, in a way, he had. The laneways, crossroads, alleys and anonymous storefronts were the places where he'd run his little clubs and backroom casinos. Where he'd supplied women to punters, crooked politicos and cops alike. The secret spots he'd arranged payoffs and paybacks.

All right, then, why not visit the only spots deserving of a Haberman farewell? Newer men and women would make their marks there, create

85

their own successes and downfalls, make fresher faces light up with joy or collapse in tears.

I'm wrong about Donatello. He's no brainless lug. He's an angel direct from Hell, sent to show me my life.

Donny Zap parked and negotiated Haberman into the wheelchair. He secured the baby to his chest.

"We go in here, mister."

"Wait, no. Why?"

"'Cause of it time you start understandin' tings."

The grunt pushed the wheelchair; what was Haberman to do, rise up and break the boy in two? He could barely break wind.

They entered a hole-in-the-wall coffee shop and pizzeria, run by one Alf Tomaso: a definite touchstone of Haberman's bygone days, always smelling of hand-rolled cigarettes, roasting coffee beans, fennel and crystalised sugar. The place was frequented daily by scores of migrants—a small business venture profitable as hell. Tomaso came forward, hands extended, clearly having expected this arrival. He grinned as if at an old friend.

Some old friend.

Back in the early days didn't I have a much younger you beaten up, Alf? How many times was it before we finally managed to bring you to heel? I remember the occasions. In those days I liked to be present. You barely cried out but you did curse me with every name under the sun. I thought you brave and stupid, until that stubborn will of yours collapsed. You were never quite so interesting again. I remember telling you, Signor Tomaso, not to feel especially persecuted. The percentage applied to this place your lifeblood was equal to that I imposed across all dago cafés and bistros.

"Mr H, good to see you."

Once you learned the rules you were always civil. This café of yours became my favourite place to drink coffee and hear the latest whispers. Many times I was more at home here than in the arms of a woman: did you ever suspect such a thing?

"… and so that's what the stone witch was able to do for me, Mr H."

What? Haberman had been lost in some kind of pharmaceutical reverie, not listening at all.

Alf Tomaso brewed Haberman his usual dark and fragrant espresso. Donny Zap held the small cup and saucer for him. The baby against the grunt's chest slept and drooled. At the same time his father helped Haberman sip the espresso as he might have helped his baby suck from its bottle of milk. For all the punishing sentiment of the morning's journey, Haberman appreciated the taste of this full-strength Italian coffee. Hardly good for an ailing heart but was that something to care about any more?

Then, just that little more alive, Haberman's damnably quivering fingers picked through a Marsala-scented *cannolo siciliano*, made by Tomaso's wife. The woman was ugly as sin: her desserts, exquisite.

"And then I had to pay her more than I pay all my cooks combined just for one weekend of numbers at the horses. I win three straight, I lose three, then, bang, I take two big ones. Four times what my business makes in a month, one hit! Good luck you never found out, eh, Mr H, or else you claim your share, true?"

With dusted, broken pieces of vanilla cannolo caught on his lips, Haberman didn't have a clue what this man's enthusiasm was about.

"Next time I visit she tells me I got enough. 'Don't be so greedy,' the witch says. No more numbers no matter how much I offer to pay her. She got her rules."

Alf Tomaso looked around, summoning one of the cooks working in what never failed to resemble a steam bath at the back.

"Claudio, come here. Tell Mr H your story."

Claudio Cima, a long-termer in this place. Once a farm hand when fresh off the boat, he must have been working in the café twenty-five years at least. Heavy, heavy moustache, and eyes so deep and wounded it was as if they'd seen all the pain life could offer.

"Go on, Claudio, talk," Alf urged him. "Donatello wants you to tell him."

Claudio sat down, chair reversed, leaning his arms against the back and staring hard into Haberman's face.

"This was a curse of love. A very bad one. Placed by the family of a jealous ex-girlfriend on my eldest boy. My son went from being a star at school, a top athlete, to nothing but trouble. Accidents here, disappointments there, police coming to the door. I paid five thousand dollars, Mr Haberman. Five thousand, in pieces over three years. But the money—every cent was worth it. The witch broke the curse. Today my boy's a banker, married to a girl with money of her own. A well-connected family. Two little daughters pretty as heaven. My son walks on gold. No more trouble."

"So glad to hear it," Haberman mumbled.

"No—you don't hear. You let yourself be too blind and too stupid and like a coward you'll let yourself die." Claudio Cima sniffed and cleared his throat in disgust, wanting to get away. "Then die. Go ahead."

Haberman tried to focus on that sad, earnest face. In another life he would have had Claudio Cima's eyes gouged out. What was this ignorant wog trying to say?

Cima stayed where he was.

"Only for Donatello we give you this information. For Donatello we let you know a secret business between us, the old-country people."

"What exactly am I supposed to be hearing?"

"Donatello told you about the stone witch."

"The what?"

"*La strega pietra*. His *zia*, Agata Rosso. We call her the stone witch because that's her face. You need to see her."

"Why would I want to do that?"

"Is there anyone left who can help you?"

Haberman tried to weigh the trick in all this. They had to be after his money. Moments passed as he caught his breath. "You expect me to believe you care about my fate?" He included Donny Zap in his baleful stare.

Alf Tomaso put the fact of it into words: "Aren't we all part of this life we made, Mr H? It's been a long time and a long road. The new ones coming in, they're young and too greedy."

"There's no money to leave you."

"We got what we want," Alf spoke.

Haberman motioned for Donny Zap to wheel him out of there.

"Mr H."

Claudio Cima, this doleful cook, wasn't done.

"The most beautiful and terrible thing I ever saw with my own eyes?"

Haberman was forced to wait.

"Nearly forty years ago a man was killed. I knew this man. I worked on his property for him."

Haberman breathed shallow.

"Dead—a doctor's pronouncement. I heard it and saw it. Many did. Three holes in his chest by three different rifles." He held up a single finger. "One hole was enough to kill him."

"And so?"

"And so cold hands folded over his chest. Like this. Eyes taped shut. Cotton stuffed into him. But..."

"But what?"

"The stone witch made her sacrifice and she raised him."

"A sacrifice?"

"To save her husband she used everything she knew. She even used herself. And then her husband's own fingers stripped the tape off his eyes. Took the cotton out of his mouth. And I guarantee you even today this man still lives."

Haberman jerked his chin towards the door. "Lies and tricks," he breathed, rediscovering his abhorrence for these men, hating himself for his moment of ghastly sentimentality.

Disappointed, disheartened, that baby with the extraordinarily haunting eyes still against his chest, the great Italian grunt finally wheeled him out.

———◆———

And now of course Haberman's waited too long to find that innocent schoolgirl to pleasure himself with; he's waited too long to have Virna Khamitova one more time; he's waited too long to add up the worth of his life and see if it could come to more than zero.

It's a new dream, a thoroughly less enticing one.

He's in his bed or on a slab or in a coffin. Maybe he's been set out in a field for birds, worms and ants to come take their fill. He's naked or dressed; under a roof or a moon. There's a keening howl in the distance belonging to a dog or a wolf. And there's a presence too; someone is watching him.

Warm fingertips prise the death-tape off Haberman's left eye. They prise the death-tape off his right eye. Haberman blinks rapidly at the man looking down on him. He's handsome, possessing jet-black hair only touched by silver at the temples, and dark eyes that know heaven and hell combined.

His chest oozes black blood. Black blood from three holes.

"But who are you?"

Then Karl Haberman's alone, in a cheap black suit, wearing a cardboard collar and a rag for a tie. He sees the chapel around him. He's been laid out in a coffin with no flowers to sweeten his death. He clambers out of the cheap casket's brittle timber. By the chapel's cold entrance there's a stone font. Instead of holy water it bubbles black muck. Haberman swallows great mouthfuls. The gunk tastes like lentils cooked with lamb in cinnamon, ginger and marigolds. He eats more greedily than he would Virna Khamitova's throat or an innocent's white flesh.

He hears more howling, coming closer, and so he half falls, half runs. To where? To where?

———————

"Donatello, where are you?" he hears his own voice whimper into a dead night. The Haberman bedroom undulates with horrors. "Take me to someone who can save me. Take me to her."

Mountford

Bad news calls at 1:57am, first thought in Teddy Quinn's head. It was Matron Barrett from the rest home.

"Miss Badger has been, um, quite lucid."

Lucid? Unlike Teddy Quinn, forced awake by the braying of his telephone.

"You sure you've got the right patient?"

"Miss Badger has been asking for things."

Real-life crime stories, gossip magazines, a radio for her favourite old-time music stations? Or maybe she'd found a way to get herself alive and ask for a nice new pack of Pall Malls.

"Like what?"

"Miss Badger is asking us for poison."

Teddy Quinn was on his way.

———————◆———————

Vivien Badger, Teddy's mother's mother, lover of cigarettes, spring, sentimental movies, crime novels, *Doctor Who*, and, apparently, all living things. She'd brought young Teddy up after her already widowed daughter Georgina took her own life. Hanged herself in a locked bathroom while her boy in their rented cottage slept alone. Neighbours found the six-year-old wandering the street and took him home. Police worked out he'd been on his own at least three days. Georgina didn't leave a note.

Vivien April Badger, closest next of kin, a sliver-thin sexagenarian widow with no work and one eye lost in a childhood accident. She took the boy in and cooked and cared for him. She read to him from her most favourite book in the world, *The Little Prince* by Antoine de Saint-Exupéry, over and over until little Theodore thought he must know every word by heart. At his eighteenth birthday she sat him down.

"A boy needs to make his own way so he can learn to be a man."

While he was busy learning-but-not-quite, Teddy lived in a squalid share house where he alternated complete moral dissipation with the multitude of part-time jobs that helped pay his rent, feed him and provide money to Vivien. In time his grandmother suffered a series of strokes, worsening diabetes, then treatments for mouth and tongue cancer. No surprise her lungs were a disaster. She survived the removal of the left plus a quarter of the right. Next came ailments that were like divine punishments for who could say what, followed by the creep of dementia, which brought with it the added insult of incontinence.

Teddy found her a high maintenance rest-care facility, paid for via illegally-concurrent six-hour shifts in a meat-packing plant plus extra work in every dump that offered money under the counter. In between shifts he was at Mountford, foregoing his louche life so that he might share every step of one sick old woman's decline. She never got to hear about his big new step, a career in sales, and how he turned out to be so thoroughly good at it.

For if Vivien Badger had been a slip of a woman before her sicknesses, the more time that passed it was as if all Teddy could find of his grandma was a tissue facsimile of the person she used to be. A tissue that might easily be collected by the breeze and sent up into the blue.

"It's the strangest feeling. I'm just floating, dear."

Some of the last words she was ever able to speak.

Heard only by Teddy Quinn, until the fact of the Munro girl.

———————

He left the Stag at an angle, not bothering to snap the soft top in place. Matron was still doing her rounds.

"How is she?"

"Doctor's added a sedative to her drip."

"Is what you told me true?"

"Miss Badger spoke, yes."

"And?"

"She wondered what poisons we had on hand."

"Anything else?"

"She begged for an end to her floating. Then she was gone again."

Teddy entered the ward and approached the little cot that was Vivien's bed. Her left arm was bandaged from some recent small procedure and that limp scrap of tissue and bone constituting her right arm absorbed what the tubes fed her. A grim tight line for a mouth revealed just how horrible her successive operations had been. She was all meatless bones and scarred skin. There was no indication whatsoever that she'd been awake and talking, or ever would again.

"What can I do for you?" Teddy whispered in her ear, though there was no sign of life other than her slow, shallow breath, same as always.

She wants to read but you do that. She likes it a lot, the way you read to her.

Remembering Lía Munro's words, Teddy sat into the chair by Nanny Viv's bed. On her side table was a monolithic Agatha Christie anthology marked at page one thousand, three hundred and sixty-four, where Teddy had last left off. It was the end of *The Mystery of the Blue Train* and next came *The Body in the Library*.

Just as he angled himself so he'd have enough light to read by, with a small squall of panic Teddy noticed that grim, tight line of his grandmother's mouth move. He heard a breath:

"Puh…puh…puh…"

Matron Barrett had spoken the truth. Nanny Viv was actually trying to speak. Here it came again:

"Puh…puh…puh…"

He took her right hand in both his own. What she was saying had to be gibberish, just a slight sleep-mumbling.

"Puh…puh…puh…"

No, wait. He knew his grandmother. Teddy Quinn knew her better than any person alive.

"Puh…puh…puh…"

It was a code that made sense to him. He could hear exactly what the fullness of it was supposed to be. Vivien was trying to say:

Please.

Nanny Viv didn't want help with a glass of water. She didn't want to be moved into a more comfortable position. This woman didn't want to hear what was going to happen on page one thousand, three hundred and sixty-five.

Puh-puh-please, Teddy: I need someone's kindness to help me finish, because, well, look at me.

One more time: "Puh…puh…puh…"
Now she was begging.

A Smoker Calls

At first Lía dreamed her mother was still alive, and the girls at the Christ-ian-based Good Hope Girls' School in Kowloon still liked her, and the missionary sisters didn't watch her nervously from the corners of their eyes.

By her bed Dakota and Buster slept on their rug. She sensed their breath-ing. She also sensed her own. Then, unconsciously, she moved herself flat on her back, only to hear a clear entreaty:

Puh...puh...please...

Lía feels herself move into a very different place than her bedroom. It's a little timber home in a quiet street of timber homes that are just like it. Inside this home there's a boy's room and a very slender older woman with greying hair. A smoking cigarette is at the corner of her thin lips. The boy with her has downy hair, and he's in his pyjamas, lying in bed.

"Please?"

"Please what, Theodore?"

Lía wants to smile at the good humour with which the woman speaks that name.

"Please Nanny will you read to me?"

Nanny Viv has one eye that sees nothing and so the other needs to focus hard on the elegant, small hardback book she takes from a side table busy with small plastic dinosaurs.

"Let's begin where we left off last night, Teddy."

She reads in a mellow voice and the boy's eyes reveal how entranced he is. Lía thinks him not much more than six or seven years of age—and he seems so small, vulnerable as a teardrop. Lía feels something move inside herself, something almost like pain, yet a lot like beauty.

She notices the book's cover. Oh wow, she even recognises the edition.

Lía's read this story herself, many times, because it's one she loves. The boy listens with soul-eyed attention.

"The Little Prince went to look at the roses again. 'You're not at all like my rose. You're nothing at all yet,' he told them."

The woman crushes the Pall Mall into an ashtray brimming with butts. Tendrils of smoke float from her mouth.

"'No one has tamed you and you haven't tamed anyone. You're the way my fox was. He was just a fox like a hundred thousand others. But I've made him my friend, and now he's the only fox in all the world.' And the roses were humbled."

By the lonely look in his face Lía thinks that maybe the boy would like a fox for a friend. Or anything or anyone, for that matter. She gives thanks for her dogs, so much like a hundred thousand others, but she's made them her friends and now they are the only dogs in the world.

Lía blinks and the boy with downy hair is a young man and it's his turn to read, this time from a far heavier book. She sees the familiar name of Agatha Christie on the cover. The listener is a skeleton-woman hardly a person at all, more like human remains.

Then, as he reads, beneath the mellow sound of his voice the old woman's own voice comes, soft yet clear. Yet the grim tight line of her mouth doesn't move at all.

…puh, puh, puh…

Lía doesn't have to decipher the code. She understands.

Please, please, please.

"Please, won't you listen to me? I see you, dark girl. You see me. Then aren't you the one to help me?"

❧

Morning takes its time coming. Lía's all nerves, waiting until she's sure her father's in his shower and can't hear her using the telephone downstairs. She hides the business card Teddy Quinn gave her back up her sleeve. He'd written his home number on it; now his voice is on the line.

"Today," she says, "all right?"

"I was with her last night. I mean this morning."

"Teddy—"

"Yes?"

"So was I."

The Blue Bird Café

Showered and shaved for his interview, Paul Munro walked to his car with Lía and the dogs seeing him off.

"Don't forget you talked me into this."

"Because it might be just what you need."

"Real estate," Paul Munro shook his head. "How did you change your mind?"

"Don't worry about that."

"How did you change my mind?"

"Grandview needs saving."

"You know, if this works out today," he spoke, moving behind the wheel and now looking up at his daughter, "or when I start any job really, we're going to have to get people in to stay."

Paul saw Lía's expression change. It happened so quickly, just like the arrival of threatening storm clouds.

"A live-in housekeeper, maybe a live-in gardener or handyman," he went on. "There's the separate quarters. Like they told us about at the produce store, remember? Maybe an older couple."

"No."

"With me gone all day, there's no way you're staying out here on your own."

"I've got the dogs."

"That's not enough."

"Of course it is."

"We'll talk about it tonight," Paul said, his voice firming.

Lía's was firmer, and possessed a much sharper edge. "We won't."

And there was actual anger in her face as well, if not barely restrained fury. Her already dark skin had darkened even further; a suffusion of blood.

So over the top. *What the hell?*

Bad things coming back, or just a momentary lapse? Paul hadn't taken a drink all week, but he wanted one now. Best to calm the situation. After dinner, say, things might seem more reasonable. *Lía* might seem more reasonable.

"Sure you don't want a lift into town?" Paul spoke. "Or at least to the bus stop? It's such a hike."

"Which will do me good. Then I'll be at the State Library most of the day. So I won't be home early."

"And I'll try not to be late."

Had the moment passed? Paul drove off trying to clear his mind of his daughter's sudden display of temper and think only about the meeting ahead with a man named Mike Gavin, principal of Gavin Realty. Maybe it was natural that Lía should feel like extra people on the property—intruders, total strangers—would spoil what they had.

But to react so?

He shook his head, driving country laneways that snaked and turned on his way to larger roads. Grandview needs saving: only Lía could say something like that and make it sound reasonable. More to the point, the renovating was becoming more irritating than diverting; with a decent income Paul could afford to bring a gang in. They'd be done in a fortnight. The way he was going the house would still be a shambles this time next year. Then he'd need to think about the outside, which really needed attention. That sort of work would cost good money.

Not to mention school for Lía. The big private ones he wanted for her weren't cheap.

Funny how Lía had changed her mind about this job the salesman had mentioned. Funny that Paul had thought it over as well. Then, after talking it through with her he'd finally called Teddy Quinn, who arranged today's meeting.

Paul drove on, and a good hour later easily found the address he needed. At the reception desk of a modest one-storey building in the inner-city suburb of West End, he was shown through to a private office. Waiting for him was the towering figure of Mike Gavin and the crush of Mike Gavin's handshake. This was a power thing, Paul understood, a big man's authority reinforced.

Mike Gavin's opening gambit: "Mundell?"

"Munro. Paul Munro."

"No experience in my line of business and you're over forty years of age."

"My resumé tells you what I do have experience in."

"Just now in our parking lot I observed you climb out of a lemon I wouldn't buy my seventeen-year-old."

"A vehicle doesn't define a man, does it, Mr Gavin?"

"What about middle age?"

"Isn't that experience?"

"Which ought to have taught him his limitations."

Paul nodded, considered the shit-eating grin in the bigger man's face, thought a moment longer then stood from the chair.

"Thank you for your sixty seconds, Mr Gavin."

He walked to the door with the back of his neck burning. As his hand touched the door's handle, he heard a deep chuckle behind him.

"Desperation's the first thing I check for. The second is arrogance. A firm but courteous exit… Very nice. Your shoes are very good too."

Paul let himself turn.

"Come back and sit down. There's a lot I want to talk to you about."

"I won't be spoken to that way."

"Clients and associates will do worse."

"Them I can handle."

"What this office lacks, Munro? A certain amount of style." Mike Gavin was a bear in a business suit, literally looking him up and down. "You cut a figure. Sure a nice gentleman like you wants to work in a cut-throat business like this?"

Paul returned to the chair but didn't quite make himself comfortable. "Why don't you convince me of the benefits?"

"First let's talk about Teddy Quinn. He tells me you have a sentimental attachment to Grandview."

"I do."

"How's that going to help me turn it into a nice new satellite town?"

"There's two things in what you say. One, you mean a lot of money's waiting to be made, which I don't have a problem with. Two, you can have both, new communities plus beautiful fields and pastures, not to mention woodlands, all protected."

"The government doesn't have any laws to stop me."

"But good sense might. People go mad in urban jungles."

"Farmers facing bankruptcy shoot themselves."

"Then let's make things better for both sides."

"You lived in Hong Kong until recently."

"I did."

"That influences your thinking?"

"You breathe enough smog, you start looking for alternatives. But let me ask you a question, Mr Gavin. How greedy do you think you really are, deep down? Your answer will tell us what we'll do and won't do."

"Consortiums are nothing but greedy."

"That depends on who sets the thinking from the start."

"You know the story of King Canute? He showed his people that no man can stop the tide, and no tree hugger's going to stop land development once it's going."

"God sets the tides, Mr Gavin. Men drive bulldozers."

"God?"

Mike Gavin considered Paul. And kept considering him.

———◆———

The meeting was a long one; rather than being an interview it had changed into something like an exchange of ideas. Paul couldn't quite believe it: for all his capitalist bluster and background Mike Gavin didn't *want* to create an urban jungle of concrete, he said investors did—and he needed help to sway them to a better way of thinking.

"God gave us open spaces to use properly, Mr Munro. And that's what we're going to do."

Jesus, the guy was serious. Some weird idea of God actually came into this.

Mike Gavin saw him to the front door past a busy reception desk and switchboard.

"I've got a conference call now, but you and I aren't done for the day. Be back in an hour."

"Okay."

"Take this job and in a month you'll be the one taking calls and running meetings."

Paul checked his watch. "Two o'clock?"

"And remember this: keep straight with me, Munro, it's my number one rule."

Paul gave a nod and crooked grin, then went to kill an hour.

❖────────────❖

He knew he had no childhood recollection of this suburb yet wanted to look it over; Paul didn't understand why. It was as if he should search for something familiar. In his powder blue suit and burgundy tie he wandered around observing heavy-set, moustachioed greengrocers and fishmongers selling fresh pickings. Women wore scarves around their hair and carried string bags. Some wore thick brown stockings. Paul stopped at a corner and considered the mix of ethnicities, so many pieces of Europe embedded into one suburb.

The warm currents of cooking and frying with spices were in the air. He wasted some time in an expansive second-hand bookstore and left with a decent copy of Truman Capote's *In Cold Blood*, seventy-five cents. Still distracted, something turned—not unpleasantly—in the pit of his stomach. It wasn't hunger; again he felt he needed to look for something.

As he entered a small Greek snack bar, and an older woman greeted him with a loud "*Kaloston*," Paul made a quick apology and left. He didn't know why.

Then he took in the glass frontage of a place three doors down, the *Blue Bird Café*, and whatever was in the pit of his stomach settled and he knew this was the place he wanted.

Shaking his head at his impulse, he found a seat in a booth at the back. Multiple booths in front of him were busy, people pressed together eating and drinking. There were talkative groups in little cubicles at the centre of the place as well. Others on their own sat on stools at the milk bar and sometimes gazed at themselves reflected in a huge polished mirror featuring an engraved bluebird, wings extended. Behind the main counters, shelves positively shone with white ceramics and polished silverware.

A waitress came for his order. Without looking up he told her what he wanted, already reading the first pages of his book. In what seemed like no time at all hands with smooth olive skin placed his small lunch plates onto the table.

"Thank you."

There was an accent too: "This is good as everyone says?"

The chatter in the café, and piped music, made him unsure of what he'd heard, but it was almost as if he recognised the voice, so musical.

"Excuse me?" Paul asked, eyes darting up from the page, and as soon as he saw her dark eyes and wide lips he knew who she was.

"I have watched this movie last year. It makes me wonder for the book."

He kept his place with his finger. "I've only just started."

"The movie hurts very much, especially the end," she spoke, her bearing straight and restrained, yet somehow still very welcoming. "But I will not say how it turns out."

"It's a famous story so I already know."

"Not my favourite, when things finish so bad." Her curling, jet-black hair was pulled into a fat bun, held by a net. There were tiny bluebird studs in her ears.

"Probably wouldn't be the book for you then."

"I am halfway in *Tender is the Night*."

"Yes, I liked that one."

"I worry how it will turn too." Despite a small smile now, there was that seriousness he recalled in her expression. "Please do not reveal."

"So are you still reading to learn the language?"

Waitresses in the same outfits and aprons as hers served at other tables; she could have kept herself extremely busy if she'd left his booth and kept on with her job.

"You remember."

"Of course. *Great Expectations*."

"And your daughter of fifteen years."

"Now sixteen."

"The house you thought you would never purchase?"

"Well, I did."

The young woman didn't quite react to that, as if she'd expected he might, and again he felt that curious sensation in his belly, of looking for something. No, of finding something. Someone: *her*. Paul did his best not to stare.

"So then 'never' is a word to never use."

"And look how your English has improved."

"You think?"

"I do."

With a smile she moved between the tables and booths to the bar. Paul watched the swing of her hips, the way she swept up a waiting order while balancing four plates. He tried to return to his book, but the coincidence of this meeting, and of the feeling that he'd wanted to come there all along, made it impossible to concentrate on a single sentence, much less an entire page. He was pleased when she was back to clear his table.

"You know, we should have a talk," he offered.

"Of what subject?"

"The big house, I guess. I'd love to hear what you know about its history. What the Rossos are up to these days."

"Well... I don't know."

"Just for ten minutes."

"I am owed my lunch break in thirty."

Paul checked his watch. "Meeting at two."

"Then come later." She shrugged, as if it didn't matter if he did or didn't. "Federico is the owner and he will make you the best coffee you never had."

Paul did his best not to smile at the easy mistake, then watched her concentrate on writing out the bill. When she left it he saw her handwriting was looping and bold. The word for each item ended with a small stroke, a sort of curlicue that made him think of generosity, of a nature made for giving. There was a quick sketch next to the total. She'd made a quick drawing of a bluebird that matched the large engraving in the mirror and the small studs in her ears.

Jesus but it felt like an invitation.

Lía and Mrs Badger

The nurses performed their lunchtime rounds. One named Summers checked Mrs Badger's lines and did her best to have her swallow several drops of water through what she called a Pasteur pipette. Lía watched the Adam's apple in that emaciated neck twitch three times. She understood these were involuntary actions, a human body doing what it had to do. Mrs Badger herself made no sound at all. She barely drew breath and Lía felt nothing from her. No thought, wish or word. There was no cigarette smoke to smell. Around Teddy there was blank space. Now Lía was so close the whole thing felt a clumsy fantasy.

Which kept Lía fixed on that upswell of blood that hit her as soon as her father had mentioned the idea of people moving into the house with them. She needed to talk to her father tonight. She needed to apologise. The way he'd blanched at her reaction left her feeling sick to her stomach. Why had she reacted so strongly?

Nurse Summers was through. Teddy thanked her. It was obvious he knew these steps by heart. So now they were alone what was supposed to happen?

Mrs Badger, why did you want me here?

Teddy Quinn picked up his grandmother's left hand, his eyes dark, sunken and brooding. Mrs Badger remained exactly as she was. Lía heard laboured breathing from other beds, several quietly rumbling snores. She wanted to tell Teddy how useless it was to have just about coerced her to come. Or for this poor woman Mrs Badger to have coerced her.

Teddy took a vinyl-bound collection from his grandmother's bedside and turned pages to a bookmark.

Agatha Christie, just as Lía had already seen. She didn't move, back straight, wondering what any of this could mean.

"'Followed by Dr Constantine, Poirot made his way to the next coach and the compartment occupied by the murdered man,'" Teddy started, but then turned to Lía. "Why don't you do it?"

Lía took the book, heavy as an encyclopaedia. With a little hesitation, keeping her voice low, she started at the same place.

"'Followed by Dr Constantine, Poirot made his way to the next coach—'"

And as she did the words of a crime story more than forty years old folded in on themselves and her own voice became an indistinct, almost disembodied hum.

Are you really so blind, Mrs Badger?

"'The first thing that struck the senses was the intense cold. The window was pushed down as far as it would go and the blind was drawn up. "Brrr," observed Poirot.'"

But you hear your own heartbeat. And you know I'm reading to you.

"Save me, child."

How? What can I possibly do for you when you're like this?

"Stop me."

Stop you? What does that mean?

"Stop this never-ending hell."

Lía's throat froze. She couldn't read another word. She understood Mrs Badger and what she was being asked to do. Teddy Quinn stared at her. Lía closed the book.

"I want to go home."

"We only just got here."

Lía was up and striding out of the ward; she knew she was running away.

———◆———

There was no breathing space, even in the passenger seat of the Stag. Lía still felt Mrs Badger and what she wanted; it might even have been more strongly, as if the old woman had finally attached herself to Lía and not her grandson. Teddy started the car but when Lía leaned forwards, putting her head down and pressing her temples, he let the rumbling engine die.

"What's going on, tell me."

He saw the whites of Lía's eyes.

"Jesus, what's the matter?"

Teddy put out his arms maybe to hold her, maybe to steady her; he didn't have a clue what to do. Lía seemed weak, just about nerveless, yet her skin was hot, so hot.

For Lía, Teddy Quinn and his Stag, and the stretch of car park before them had vanished. She travelled; no, it was far more correct to say that this time she floated, just as Mrs Badger did. She noted that fact herself. Somewhere in the confusing swirls of her own mind she felt so close to Mrs Badger they might as well be one.

And in being one, she truly understood what the woman wanted.

Needed.

The best thing.

So, without hesitation Lía reached out her hand.

Beside her in the car, Teddy watched her hand stretch out for nothing.

Lía grasped a weakly beating heart.

Teddy watched the girl's fingers close, ever so gently.

Lía felt that heart struggle against her palm, but only briefly.

Teddy saw Lía's hand drop, as if robbed of all strength.

She leaned her head back against the vinyl of the passenger seat's head rest and slowly opened her eyes.

"You bastard," she told him. "You tricked me."

"What are you talking about?"

"You knew exactly what would happen."

"How—how could I know—"

Lía didn't care how real his confusion seemed; she didn't care how concerned he appeared to be.

"You've got your wish," she spoke, bitterness turning her voice to gravel.

Lía let out a sigh that came from deep, deep inside. *No more tears,* she told herself. *There's no more need for them at all. Mrs Badger is free and I need to rest.*

It was true: she'd never felt so drained of life before. She might also have had a slight fever. In her heart Lía now only wanted to be away from Mountford; to be out of this tiny car and away from Teddy Quinn; solace was in her bedroom, with the dogs curled on the rug and her door locked tight.

A house with no need for anyone else at all.

Teddy Quinn's eyes, wounded and hollow, shifted away from Lía. Through the Stag's windscreen they both observed a figure coming across the car park. It was Nurse Summers hurrying in her flat sensible soles, crunching gravel underfoot.

"Teddy, please, could you come back?"

In a moment Teddy Quinn was rushing ahead of the nurse. He disappeared inside Mountford Rest Home and Hospice. Lía sat alone.

I should hate myself for what I am.

I should hate myself for how far I let myself go.

I do.

Candela and Trouble

After lunch at the Blue Bird Café, Paul was back at Gavin Realty. In the boardroom Mike Gavin's financial men talked about a Grandview supermarket complex, stage one of three stages that would see a massive expansion probably less than ten years hence. The afternoon passed with spreadsheets, topographic maps, and endless artists' impressions of the type of housing bounties to come. The afternoon stretched on. Every so often Paul glanced around the offices for Teddy Quinn, who didn't make an appearance.

Finally finished for the day, Paul agreed to be back at eight the next morning. As he left the building an awful pang of doubt struck him, despite all the handshakes and welcomes. So this was now a job; he was no longer free; he wouldn't be home with his daughter just about every hour of every day. He'd have to find a good housekeeper, and fast, despite what Lía might want. It would need to be someone good at home schooling, which was a lot to ask. Maybe too much; all right, he'd forget that part, but he wouldn't settle for anyone he wasn't sure he could trust. The idea of a nice older couple used to Grandview and farms was sounding better and better. He'd have to visit the produce store; they'd know who might be around.

Paul should have climbed into his car so that he could get home and tell Lía the news; instead he left Gavin Realty and walked back down to the Blue Bird Café, that strange sensation of earlier gone. It was as if his belly was letting him know he was taking the right steps—steps to the woman who worked there.

Paul shook the sensation off. The café was at closing time, a last group of customers exiting. He saw her up the back wiping an empty table, talking to an older man, the owner. She was in profile, her features strong, her nose, as he'd recalled, just about straight.

"The machine is going still," she told Paul. "Federico, two?"

Federico nodded, "*Va bene*," and in his soiled white apron and little white cap he moved behind the counter to his espresso machine. The café was darker than earlier in the day. The woman wiped her hands with her cloth, pulling the gauze net from her head; black hair tumbled past her shoulders. She slid into the booth she'd been wiping down.

"Come," she said. Paul slid into the opposite side, facing her. "So I cannot believe that a house like that you have wanted for your home."

"Somehow it suits us."

"And your daughter?"

"Probably likes it more than me. Why do you ask?"

She hesitated, then smiled. "You have said you want to talk about this house, know about the Rossos. Well, when we think of Agata Rosso, *oof*."

He suppressed a laugh. "What's that mean?"

"I do not want to scare you."

"Why would you scare me?"

"Agata she will say she spoke to the spirits in those rooms."

"Decades ago."

"So none left?" She smiled again.

"We've been there for months. There's nothing in that place that's bad and I don't believe in spirits anyway. We're perfectly happy with whatever isn't going on."

She looked at him more carefully now. "Your daughter is comfortable?"

What made his chest tighten? That particular question, or the way she watched him as if with a sort of expectation?

"Like I said, Lía loves living there."

"Ah, I remember this name. Very pretty."

"And I'm Paul."

"My name is Candela."

Her eyes shifted past his shoulder. Federico was bringing their coffee. The older man placed them down and as he did Paul caught the stale perspiration of a long day's work. There was a plate of little biscuits.

"Amaretti," Candela told him. "Honey and almond." She picked one up and took a bite. Paul followed her lead.

"That's certainly something."

"New to you, things that come from somewhere else?"

"Mostly…but my wife was Italian." Paul hesitated, then went on a little too quickly, "Born here but her family was from the Aeolian Islands, in the south."

"And so your daughter's looks."

"Sort of."

She gave him a curious smile, uncertain.

"We adopted Lía."

"Really? This is a beautiful thing. How does it come to happen?"

It was something he never really spoke about, and no one had ever asked him quite so directly. Yet with this Candela, to answer seemed the most natural thing in the world.

"We were travelling from Lipari to Catania, visiting orphanages, but only for my wife's research. Her name was Anna. Studying for her doctorate in sociology. Her subject involved the physical influences on child development. Her interest was in foundlings."

"Foundlings, yes. I know this word. What has happened to Anna?"

"Breast cancer."

"I am so sorry."

Paul needed to take a deep breath before speaking again. Beneath the table, his hands gripped together. He told himself they *did not* want to be holding a dusky bottle of whisky.

"We met Lía in a nursery run by Carmelite nuns. She was just a baby. She didn't even have a name. Someone had left her for them to find without a note. And that was that."

"But I love this story."

"When I say 'that was that', the process itself took over a year."

Candela sipped her coffee, then glanced at the wall clock beside the great bluebird mirror.

"You have to go?"

"My Lorenzo he should be delivered to me thirty minutes ago."

"While you're at work, is it your husband who looks after him?"

"Sometimes," Candela nodded, "true. Donatello has him today."

Now Paul remembered the shadow he'd seen in her face that day at Rosso House. Donatello was the husband's name. Was that shadow back when she mentioned him? Then Paul saw the way Candela almost seemed to pick that thought up from him, maybe read it in his face.

"Do you know of our great book *Il Gattopardo—The Leopard*?"

"I think I saw the movie," Paul replied, "but years ago."

"In the story, Prince Don Fabrizio Salina he speaks these words: 'Yes, love, of course! Fire and flames for a year, ashes for thirty.'" She gave a rueful smile. "Not thirty years for me, but ashes all the same."

"If that's what I think it means, it's very sad."

"Sadder to stay in a life that is wrong. So this work for Federico, it is my start. I am making a new life with a new place to live. And if the father of Zo will ever agree, I will return to my little village in Italy. Or maybe go to Spain, where I have many friends. This country is beautiful but it has not been good to me." Candela stopped, as if to consider how much she'd say. "The law it makes us be separated for twelve months before we can divorce. So we share our baby equal, until the end it comes. From there what happens who really knows?"

In a moment of silence, the café's front door opened.

A man entered, saw Candela at the back and started to walk down. Then he slowed, eyes narrowing, and he stopped halfway. The husband, of course, Donatello, in biker's leathers all black and grey. In one arm he held his swaddled baby, Lorenzo's head nestled comfortably against his shoulder. Candela moved out of the booth. She went straight to the man and took Lorenzo. Paul stayed where he was. The pair spoke, voices terse and low, unhappiness and resentment as obvious as the great bluebird mirror. Yet as they spoke the husband kept staring toward Paul. Candela returned; the baby was waking, yawning, mouth wet.

Even though Candela walked away from him Donatello didn't leave. In fact, with a great frown in his face he slowly started forward. Candela had slipped back into the booth. Paul guessed she wanted to give Zo her breast; in a moment he'd head home. The baby's eyes widened with delight at what must have been a first sight of his mother, and reached out for her. Candela let one finger be held in his tiny fist. Then, unexpectedly, Zo stretched his other hand toward Paul—and seemed to fix his eyes upon him. Paul thought he caught the hint of another smile.

So did the father.

Who now stood above them and said something to Candela in Italian.

Candela answered him in English: "Don't be so stupid."

Donatello turned his attention to Paul.

"My son he does know you?"

"What?"

"You have held him?"

"What are you talking about?"

Yet Paul did understand, the absolute, immediate stupidity of what this fool suspected—and as if to anger his father even more little Zo now stretched both hands to Paul and twisted his body towards him.

There were even the makings of a babyish gurgle, a laugh.

Paul didn't move. His eyes met Donatello's, now burning with anger.

"What you think you do with her my wife?"

Before he could answer Donatello grabbed Paul by the lapels of his suit jacket. Paul felt himself hauled upwards, his tie twisting askew.

"Dis piece of English *merda* you break a family for?"

"Donatello, are you crazy?"

"He the true reason why you leave?"

"Get out. Go on, we don't need—" and now Candela spat words in Italian Paul couldn't follow.

Her husband shouted over her, also in Italian: "*Sei una puttana—una grande puttana*," and Paul knew just enough of the worst words of that language to understand he was calling her a prostitute. A prostitute, and Paul the reason for their separation.

It was madness. He tried to pull himself out of that iron grip. Donatello's hands were too strong and the fabric of Paul's jacket gave way, tearing. Candela kept shouting for Donatello to leave, and the baby started to wail at all the noise, and even Federico emerged from the kitchen to yell his fill.

Finally Paul managed to shove himself away from Donatello's hands, losing the rest of his jacket as he did. But he wouldn't be made so helpless.

"Get the fuck out of here." His fists were tight; Paul knew he wouldn't be afraid to swing them. "You've got it all wrong—"

The first blow, he never saw. He thought he was hit again, so fast he couldn't comprehend what was happening. Paul slipped into a momentary black, then as his vision came stuttering back he realised he was on the floor. Donatello slammed the café's door so hard behind him its timbers cracked, and three rectangular panes burst into glass splinters.

A Stone Witch

In that horrible dream Haberman half-fell and half-ran, to where, to where, and in a panic had cried out for Donatello to bring him to someone who could save him, and so today the grunt was wheeling Karl Haberman to Zia Agata's dilapidated home in the suburbs and a door already ajar.

"Why," Haberman breathed, "why do you seem so disconsolate?"

"Dis-what, mister?"

"Troubled."

"Yeah, trouble. Too much trouble. With my Candela."

"Marriage. Spare me the unsavoury details."

Grim-faced, Donny Zap pushed Haberman down a creaking, polished-wood hallway with a long runner over it. Their destination was a small anteroom carrying scents Haberman had come to know very well: crushed fennel seeds and rosemary, lilac and ginger, many more and all of them so bracing. Yet from brief glimpses this home appeared tacky and cheaply decorated, Italianate and artless.

Haberman had noted the discreet hand-painted sign outside—*Magia Bianca*—yet the Virgin Mary and Jesus Christ stood cheek by jowl with horned nymphs and bare-breasted women wearing devils' masks. In this quiet Colonial-style home, Karl Haberman muses, even as his breath catches and fails, several types of madness collide. And so isn't there an even worse madness to him being here?

He has to concentrate on his breathing. The beat of his heart—well that's a law of its own. A pulsing headache drills one temple and a kidney aches as if pierced by a witch's needle.

ootfalls coming. When he turns his head he sees the boy has disappeared. A stoutly diminutive woman arrives. Her hair is a bad fright wig of curls and she has a face that knows no warmth.

"You're the witch?"

"My name is Signora Celano. You are ready?"

He manages a nod before she wheels him through an opposing door.

"Your visitor." With a sense of the dramatic Signora Celano adds, "I introduce…Mistah Carlo Hubbamante."

"Haberman," he speaks, voice husky and weak. "Karl Haberman."

In this wide, overstuffed living room he takes the time to glance at imitation gold and silver brocade, and ancient furnishings he won't be seduced into thinking are genuinely antique. It's all an affront: a clutter of bargain-basement paraphernalia mirroring, he expects, the bargain-basement witch in front of him. Who stares straight ahead, maybe at the wall behind his head. Haberman notices four disconcertingly lifelike dolls the size of small children. They're arranged in a semi-circle, as if called to apprehensive attention in a schoolroom. There's no trace of happiness in their pretty, startling, waxen faces.

And none at all in the truly stone-like face of the crone. Yet, even as he understands her sideshow act Haberman feels a deep tremor that for once isn't due to illness. He actually wishes Donatello was at his side. The witch doesn't speak or even look at him. So in his whispery voice Haberman addresses Signora Celano.

"What are those dolls supposed to be?"

"The seasons of our earth."

Or just four stupid dolls. Haberman imagines there'll be a hundred more absurdities in this place—absurdities he doesn't wish to meet while sitting in this wheeled, steel-sided monstrosity. With considerable effort he pushes himself up and moves from the wheelchair to one of the over-decorated living room's armchairs. It's nicely comfortable and comforting, and his nappy dampens beneath his trousers.

"Would you take that thing outside with you?"

"A course, sir."

"And is your witch planning to say anything?"

Signora Celano doesn't reply; she pushes his wheelchair out and shuts the door behind her.

They're alone. Despite the beneficence of tonics and potions, Agata

Rosso—mid-to-late eighties maybe—still betrays no welcome. He notices a tray at her elbow holding a dainty glass cup. There's a light-green liquid in it, maybe infused with some sort of herb. On the tray is also a knife with an inlaid-pearl handle, one-quarter of a red apple beside it.

"Well, madam," he speaks, trying to keep the impatience out of his voice, "here I am."

And if the four lifelike dolls were children then the witch has the right sort of face to frighten the living daylights out of them. Add wispy hair the colour of iron, and fingers skeletal as stick insects, and any adult would be forgiven for feeling just the same way.

"Quindi stai morendo e come tutti gli uomini non vuoi morire."

"Might you repeat that in English?"

It appears she wouldn't.

Haberman notices that the tight line of the woman's mouth ends in an acute droop at the left corner. He guesses a stroke or strokes. The lips, though pursed and severe, are full and thick, almost colourless. They remind him of week-old liver. Now she's yawning, ostensibly bored, revealing a small number of yellow-stained, spoiled teeth. Skeleton-thin, a pastiche of cartoon witchery, with fingernails the colour of wood and each at least an inch long, finely pointed. She's a nice fairy-tale hag, and, of course, she's a hag without the slightest miracle in her.

"Come si senti?"

This is a question; Haberman's modicum of Italian doesn't go this far. Again he needs to catch his breath.

"Ho capito...che si parla Inglese," Haberman says, enunciating each unfamiliar word, too quickly running out of air. "I understood we'd speak English."

"All right."

"Good. So what did you just ask me?"

"How do you feel?"

"Terribly fine, thank you for enquiring." He tries to ignore the pain under his breastbone, the ache beneath his ribs. At least the stabbing in his temple has passed. "And that first thing you said? Quindi-stai-something-something?"

"So you're dying and like all men you don't want to die."

"Ah."

For the first time she locks eyes with him.

"It's not a bad thing, to die." Agata Rosso's voice is quiet, yet it has the quality of sandpaper scratching a rough surface. "We all have to take our turn."

Accented, grating, yet her English is perfect. This surprises him; he'd expected something like Donny Zap's broken sentences, the argot of greengrocers and imported fishwives.

"Isn't this true?" she asks, now wanting an answer.

"Yes…but if there really was some way of avoiding being pushed to the head of the queue?"

"Where you find yourself."

"I'm all right."

"Except for the air you can't keep in your lungs."

"What do you propose?"

"If you want to be sent to the back of death's line, think about what a man like you can offer in return."

"I assume you mean money."

A wicked, teasing grin enters her otherwise deathly visage. In the perfect pretence of some cackling ethnic witch she says, "Gonna costa lotta, Hubbamante. Gonna costa lotta."

"Haberman," he reminds her.

"You've purchased yourself the best doctors and clinics but all your beautiful dollars, what are they worth now?"

"So I might as well send it your way?"

"I'll take everything."

Yet she says this with a shrug of one thin shoulder. In a way Haberman finds himself believing the indifference in that shrug. What's this mad old crone really after?

"Why don't you tell me what you have in mind?" he says.

"You could die today. You could die tomorrow. But Hubbamante—"

"Karl Haberman."

"—you should be dead already. Only my creations have saved you."

"Several highly paid medicos might have opinions on that."

As he says it, Haberman notices something new. There's perspiration on her brow. One fat bead rolls down the left side of her stone face. Is she suffering somehow?

"I think you understand how things are." Even the very reduced voice he produces can't hide his irritation. "I have no more time to waste."

"Tell me what you want."

"You're supposed to be some kind of witch. White magic and so forth. Most clear-minded individuals would share my incredulity." He pauses, breathing. "But I have experienced your tonics. So, the back of death's queue... Maybe you have other things that could move me there?"

"You want to live. You're not done yet."

"Yes."

"You're asking for a miracle?"

"The money you want, that can be arranged."

"Money is such a small part of this world."

"Then?"

"Will you believe in me?"

"If that's what you ask."

The stone witch shakes her head at the easy lie. It strikes him she moves like a skeleton with only faint life in it. Maybe she's the one at death's door. Maybe she's the one who needs a miracle. Another bead of perspiration rolls down from her temple.

"Haberman," she says, "what you've heard is true. I've raised a man from the dead."

"Are you suggesting you could do it again?"

"Not alone."

"Then—?"

Her drooping top lip lifts above a couple of yellow rotting teeth, spaced far apart. It's her smile. "There's a girl, Haberman, and she's what we need. I've seen it in my fires and the spirits know she's near. When she helps me with what I want, I can help you with what you want. Do you understand?"

"Not a word."

"Then understand this: today you can walk out of my home a healthier man, if you agree to find her."

"Surely Donatello could do something as simple as that for you? There are a thousand girls just outside your door."

"Not like this one, Haberman. And to capture her then do what needs doing requires a man without problems of conscience." The stone witch leans forwards in her chair. "A man who will enjoy doing this."

"Why would I enjoy it?"

"What would you like to do to a special young girl, Haberman, if I sent you to capture her?"

"Capture—so you're talking about a kidnapping?"

"To start."

"Me, a man in a wheelchair?"

"You'll dance out of that chair."

"Why don't you try your very best to make me believe that's possible?"

Agata Rosso eases to her feet, taking enough time that Haberman now understands just how greatly she possesses her own aches, her own pains. When she crosses the room she touches Haberman's head almost fondly, though he twitches away. The woman opens a window, then another. A summery breeze makes it seem they're about to travel somewhere unknown yet lovely.

"My aim is to make my husband well. You—you're easy."

"What do you mean by that?"

As she raises two darkly veined fingers to her flat, empty breast Haberman feels unexpected warmth suffuse his own chest. It's the sort of warmth and enlivening that her tonics sometimes bestow—though ten times better.

Not looking at him, she makes a slow smile. One that's different from any that came before.

That smile lifts a veil.

But I can see it. She was beautiful once. For all the ravaging of age, inside this crazy old hag there's a girl, a glorious young woman.

The witch now flattens a palm against her sternum. She makes a cooing sound. The new warmth that sinks inside Haberman is a spreading ecstasy. He's reminded of Virna Khamitova and her sensual caresses; it's inexplicable and just about maddening.

"Tell me, what do you dream?"

What does he dream? Even in this unexpected physical bliss, he'd never say. He'd never utter the words. Those girls at Gorton's with their bloodied mouths coalescing into the innocent schoolgirl he's dreamed of snatching away for his pleasure...

"The horrors are in your mind now, Haberman. Good. Haven't you wondered why you've seen such things?"

"Not you—"

"No, *you*, Haberman. If the black seed wasn't inside you there'd be nothing for me to grow. Donatello's a lamb compared to what's in your heart. Your dreams can come true. First to be healthy again. Then to devour a very special young girl. And I promise you this one will be extraordinary. You can have her, Haberman, untroubled by inhibitions or conscience. Would you like that?"

"These are mad ideas—"

"No more pain, no more medicines and humiliations. I'll lift the illnesses I've placed on you."

The stone witch starts to tense all over, her hands curling into small fists the colour of putty. The old aches and weaknesses inside him return. They build. Haberman clutches his chest, then has to clutch at his throat for breath that won't come.

"See how easy it is to play with you?"

"*Stop it.*"

"Tell me you agree."

The pain's so great he twists violently from the armchair and falls thudding to the floor. Haberman gasps and coughs, his face in the rug. He chews lint and grit. The greatest agony of all, powerful as a gunshot, makes Haberman rip open his lilac-coloured business shirt to get to the burning in his chest. Buttons fly; the sound in his ears is his own keening cry.

"You'll hunt her, Haberman."

"I—I—"

"You'll slaughter the lamb and give me her blood—"

Haberman feels himself drowning.

"You can feast like a dog on her—"

A black door opens and he sees himself being drawn through.

"Will I save you, Haberman?"

He wants to scream one word.

"Will you believe in me, Haberman?" The stone witch is on her bony knees beside him. There's no white magic in her at all: she is black as the blackest sin. She grasps both his hands. "Say it."

The one word, his constricting throat finally produces it: "*Yes...*"

Those hands of hers, despite their skeletal boniness, despite the pain and death's door yawning wide, he feels how they now possess a sort of probing warmth.

Slowly Haberman's vision clears. The witch gulps for air. Her features— *Dear God!*—are falling inwards.

And those four dolls, have they come close in curiosity? In the swirling madness of death and life he almost believes their lips are moist and full of colour; there's light in their eyes.

And in the blossoming of his own light Karl Haberman's life finally changes.

The Boy and the Children

Lía laid in her bed and she knew she would never forget this house and the countryside where it resided no matter how many years passed or how far she travelled. And she would travel. Not in her mind but the real way. She'd leave, which meant she'd have to leave her father, which was sad but necessary, and go places new and strange, completely distant. She didn't know where these places might be, but she did know why she wanted it—to be someone else, not this thing she was.

"I told you I'm okay."

"I can't just drop you off."

"The State Library where you picked me up. I left my books in a locker."

"Lía, my grandmother's dead. I do have to make arrangements—"

"And so you must be happy."

"I'm not... But I'm...I'm glad she's not suffering anymore."

"Stop talking. Just drive me there. That's it."

Getting home from the library with her satchel of books on her back had taken so much effort there were times she'd thought she wouldn't even make it, especially on the long walk from the dusty country-road bus stop four kilometres of winding, hilly laneways back to Rosso House. But she'd been relieved to be away from Teddy Quinn. She'd never see him again; she'd never hear Mrs Badger's name again; or feel her.

Which she didn't, because the woman was gone.

At home the dogs were jumping with excitement at her arrival, first time on the property without her. Then, absorbing her mood, they'd quietened. Lía's father's car was in the courtyard and she'd wondered how she might avoid him. He'd want to know how things at the library had gone; he'd have news about the job interview.

No and *no*.

He was in his bedroom. When she offered a mumbled hello at his door he didn't emerge. She heard vague words from inside, something about taking a nap, she shouldn't worry about dinner for him. Lía went into her own room with the dogs taking to their places on her rug. They wouldn't move, as if sensing the awful weight of Lía's thoughts. What was left of the day faded. The bedroom darkened. Lía heard nothing from her father's bedroom and the very idea of doing something like making dinner and trying to live a normal life was stupid and unpleasant. Her eyes remained heavy and they ached. So did her body. Reaching out and holding Mrs Badger's heart had drained her in a way that didn't make sense; her mind too, it felt emptied of every worthwhile thing.

Someone's gone away forever and it's because of me.

Rosso House listened, and the answer it gave was to remain quiet as a dead thing.

Until Dakota and Buster were silhouetted at the side of her bed as if she'd called out to them. Their eyes were fixed upon her, but both dogs were calm. Soon Dakota took a snuffling breath and let herself lie back onto the floor. Buster's shadow moved to her bedroom door, where he waited, attuned to something Lía didn't or couldn't perceive.

She snapped on her bedside lamp and slid her feet into furry slippers, then opened the door. Buster didn't head towards the staircase to the ground floor. Instead he turned straight for Lía's father's room, and Lía pinched her arm to make sure she was awake. To make sure this wasn't some different style of leaving her body. She made Buster sit at her father's door. Buster licked her palm, rough and reassuring.

Yes, this is real. No dream, no travel.

Lía turned the burnished brass handle. Inside, vague streaks of moonlight shone through the opposite windows, glinting off the cupboard's full-length mirror and casting a shimmer across an opposite wall. Her father was a grey bump in his large bed, covered in a blanket. She couldn't quite make out his head on the pillow, though the glint of moonlight managed to send a pretty sparkle off the whisky bottle on the table, so close to his reach. Her father breathed heavily once, then made no more sound.

Why had he gone to bed so early? Why was he so thoroughly asleep?

Buster went to the very centre of the room, turned a circle and lay down as if that was all he'd wanted to do. Lía peered into dark corners. In one there was a bundle of clothes needing to be washed. Lía rubbed her eyes, exhaustion again creeping over her. A soft ripple disturbed the air. The shadowed bundle of clothes slipped across a wall and came forwards.

The boy stood with that familiar look of longing in his young face. Lía again thought him maybe nine or ten, and quite small for his age. His hair was jet black and unkempt, eyes dark but not dead, even though he certainly was.

"Why are you in this room?"

"I like the man who sleeps in that bed."

"My father? Why do you like him?"

"I can't remember."

"Does he ever see you?"

"No, only you can."

"Why did you warn me about my mother?"

"Because someone else is talking to you."

"Who is it?"

"I don't know."

Lía wondered if a boy so insubstantial might not be sure about anything. When he moved his head she saw straight through to starlight in the distant sky.

I'm not afraid, only curious.

The boy found her thought in the air. "Is that true?"

Lía said, "Yes."

"I'm afraid."

"Why?"

"Because we all are."

"We?"

The boy's glance away made her look at Buster curled on the floor. Shadows covered the dog with their sad, sad delight. They were children: three girls and one more boy.

"Do you all live here?"

His dark head inclined into a nod, and that was his answer.

"Why do you live here?"

The next answer was that slow gesture she'd seen before: he put his fingertips to a point beneath his chin and traced a very straight line all the way down. The shadow children stood with him then, and Lía watched the way they traced their own lines.

"You're very sad now," the boy told her. "You're very sad and you want to go away forever. But if you hate yourself then you can't help us."

"Help you in what way?"

"To leave."

"I can do that?"

"When you say."

"Then go, all of you, you're free."

They remained where they were, watching her, and without them saying it she knew she just wasn't right yet.

"Why not? What's wrong with me? Why can't I make you go?"

The boy the shadow, and the children the shadows, took her in.

No one has tamed you and you haven't tamed anyone. You're the way we were. We were children like a hundred thousand others. But we've made you our friend, and now you're our only friend in all the world.

The words sank into her. *And where are my friends,* Lía had to ask herself. *What if I'd let myself find a friend in Teddy Quinn?*

Teddy—do you hear me?

"When you need friends," the boy spoke, "you really need to call them."

"But," Lía said, "why?"

"Because you're in danger. Can't you feel it?"

"From what—that voice?"

The boy shook his head. "The thing you might become."

"Me? What does that mean?"

Lía felt the reply like another ripple through the air, coming to rest somewhere in her mind, or maybe it was her heart.

It means you might become as bad as a stone witch or you might be as good as a friend, the only one in our world.

Part Two

In a Crying Forest

1940: The Singing Woods

Little Jack Mosca sits in the warm bath his white-faced mother ran for him. He's still shaking, remembering the way Agata Rosso, kneeling by her dead husband in the forest, had looked at him.

Little Jack's almost too scared to move, happy when his mother returns to the bathroom after making certain six-year-old Anna and baby Maria are asleep. Without ceremony his mother gets to her knees and washes Jack's hair. She scrubs him so hard he knows she wants to eradicate this terrible night from his existence. In Italian she tells him he doesn't need to worry. He's safe.

"Other children go, but not you."

He knows what she means. Four children who used to be at the local school with him aren't there anymore. One by one there were no more playground games with them, no more running and catching one another outside Grandview's little church while the adults socialised after mass.

But where do they go? Even the many city police who've come in and out of Grandview haven't found answers.

Little Jack doesn't ask the question any more. He doesn't ask because people will always look so strange, so hurt, so sort of wounded whenever the topic comes up. There have been searches, endless searches that Jack's father and brother and all the region's men have been on. He remembers one thing clearly, spoken by one of the adults he likes a lot—Mr Claudio Cima with the big drooping moustache and perpetually sad face, always reminding Jack of the face of a bulldog.

"They're stupid, those children. They go wandering and playing in the woods when they shouldn't. Those bloody wild dogs grab them for dinner. That's where they are. One day we'll start finding bones…"

Now Jack's mother gets him dripping from the bath and dries him off. Her face is still very drawn as she dresses him into clean pyjamas as if he's not a big boy of nine but a baby of five. Then he's in his bed.

"Now anything that happened tonight, it was just a dream." There's a glimmer of a smile as his ma tucks the sheet and blanket in hard, as if to lock him into his bed. "This time go nowhere."

"Can Antonio sleep in my room?"

Some time later he hears her in the hall talking to the eldest boy. Antonio comes in without complaint. He makes a joke and lays a sleeping bag with pillows and blankets on the floor, then is asleep in minutes. Much later so is the house, with the patriarch returned from whatever business needed to be concluded off in the woods.

Little Jack hates the dark and prays dawn and daylight will come quickly.

———◆———

They don't.

Instead of a new day's sunlight illuminating all the corners of the world Jack dreams of the looming woods beyond his window. This time the forest doesn't contain terrified dogs or a dead man falling or the bitter, exciting smells of gun smoke. There's a wind moving through the trees that makes birds and animals twitch awake. Jack's never heard this type of wind before; it's something different—in fact it's a voice, and it sings sweet and clear. Little Jack dreams of a song so lovely that he should go find where it's coming from.

The bedroom remains silent, but for Antonio's breathing. The open window calls Little Jack and so he's climbing out of it, then climbing down until he feels grass against the soles of his feet, and prickles and thorns that don't hurt at all. The only thing he wants is the voice. When he looks up the stars are millions and the moon lights the sky.

He takes a moment to glance over his shoulder at the farmhouse receding, as if to bid a final goodbye, then when he looks ahead there she is, Agata Rosso with a smile and her hand outstretched, just at the start of the first line of trees. The woods are thick and full behind her, and yet they resonate with the purity of her song.

Into fragrant arms he goes.

Funny how Little Jack smells things that remind him of his mother's kitchen and cooking: rosemary and basil, fennel and marjoram, other things so familiar even if he isn't certain of their names.

In Agata's arms he sleeps with a pleasure so sensual it reminds him of the way their dog Ciocolata—named for her chocolate-coloured fur—lets her puppies suckle her teats. And so Little Jack suckles on the pretty signora's warm teat until she has him where she wants him, and steps away. The young wife of a dead man is now naked under the million stars and the sliver of moon, with golden hair falling to her shoulders and a long blade sparkling as if with a life of its own.

Little Jack sees she's not alone: there's the dead man himself, Giancarlo Rosso, naked on a stretcher set over the grass nearby; and there's a man Jack immediately recognises as stern-faced Mr Egan from the big dairy farm; and behind him are two of his sons wanting to hide their faces: Walter everyone calls Silly Wally and Nathan everyone calls Big Nate.

Now Little Jack feels as if his dream has turned into something more substantial. There are the wet, earthy smells of the forest, the darkness of the trees, ropes cutting into his wrists and the way he can wriggle but not move. His eyes fill with the sight of Agata Rosso's skin and breasts, one red nipple still wet and distended from the way his mouth had sucked to it. She's long-legged; her bush is thick. Shocking and heart-stopping to see any woman like this, but Little Jack's more astounded by the fact beautiful Agata has no shame, standing right out in the open, in front of Mr Egan and Wally and Nate, and even in front of himself, just a small, small boy.

One part of his mind thinks, *Wait until I tell Antonio about this,* and another part of his mind makes him cast his gaze down to see he's as naked as the signora.

His wonder—for that's all it's been so far—only turns to something else when Agata Rosso moves forwards. She brings that blade to the level of his eyes. Her singing continues, but the mysterious words and sounds aren't so sweet anymore. Instead they're rough and guttural as the worst of Little Jack's father's snoring, or of a cow bellowing wetly while its throat is being sawed open. Agata Rosso, or this thing she's become, or is, kisses the tip of the blade.

"Scream," she tells Little Jack. "Scream while you die."

Little Jack doesn't wet himself until he realises her eyes are like the eyes of goats on their farm after they've been slaughtered: rolled back, perfectly white and unseeing.

"Wait," he hears Mr Egan speak, "this means no more children," and when the signora inclines her blind head Little Jack understands that means *yes*—and so Mr Egan takes his sons by the shoulders and turns them away. They won't have to witness what happens next, which Little Jack himself doesn't see but does certainly feel, until the million stars and the shining moon lift him away, just away.

Rusted Parts

A butcherbird made his persistent dawn cry for a mate while Paul Munro lay in his bed staring out his windows and glass doors, eyes flinching. He dry-swallowed two more painkillers prescribed by the hospital's on-duty medico. The stitches ached and pulled under the gauze; the left side of his face was swollen.

"The police will put him behind bars and throw away the key."

"Paolo, you better listen to me."

"There's nothing to listen to."

He learned there was: a small matter of Candela's separation from her husband, due to the fact she'd discovered Donatello's employer was a criminal with police and politicians in his pocket.

"All the more reason," Paul had replied hotly. "All the more reason he should be in jail."

No, all the more reason Paul had to calm down. There wasn't only Candela and her baby to consider, but his own daughter.

"This is the kind of people they are."

Her words shocked him into silence; the very idea of this seemed unthinkable.

"I tell you the truth, Paolo. When I went to the police for help to keep Donatello away two officers have come to my door with a warning. 'Play nice, or pay the price.'" So I tried with detectives. They have followed me in their car, not to help but to tell Donatello what I am doing. And this was true, he knew my every move."

Under the garish fluorescent lights of the emergency waiting room Paul had understood what he was up against. Even in Hong Kong news of this state's alleged corruption made the newspapers. Paul had read about a barely hidden cabal of illegal activities, with police as enforcers and government officials as the lap dogs of cheap criminals. If you wanted to find a brothel, red lights shone as openly as department stores' window displays; if you wanted illegal gambling, just follow the crowd.

"Paolo, I hope you will believe me. I did not know about this Haberman and his deep friends. He was only a name, the man who gave my husband work."

"How did you find out?"

"Donatello has done something stupid." Paul watched her pull Lorenzo with his extraordinary eyes so much closer. "Stupid and dangerous for my baby."

The tightness around her mouth told him there was a lot more to this story; her downcast eyes told him she didn't want to be asked about it.

Later, cleaned up and with a line of twelve stitches in the side of his face, Candela drove him back to his car, still parked at Gavin Realty. They were in an old dark blue Toyota. Paul had a vague memory that the first time he'd met Candela there'd been a green Torana parked next to Teddy Quinn's red Stag. That was it: green with a white roof, a horrible-looking thing.

"Please... I can take you home."

"You've done far too much." His face hurt; it was difficult to speak. Then he'd turned around to look at the baby capsule. "Lorenzo's asleep."

"Many women suffer, but my baby is an angel."

"He looks it."

"Paulo," she'd said as he'd opened his door to leave, "we should meet again."

Spoken in just such a way that, despite the awful day, her words sent a thrill through him.

———◆———

Before seven Paul gave his face a quick glance in the mirror, then showered, moving gingerly. After he dressed and combed back his wet hair Paul knew he shouldn't put it off any longer: he tapped at his daughter's door. At her murmur he opened it. The dogs came to greet him.

Lía seemed exceptionally heavy with sleep, slow to move. As she sat up her hair was tousled, but her eyes were only half open, and very dark-rimmed. Still, she took him in.

"Don't worry how I look. It's really nothing."

"But Dad..." she spoke slowly, "you're so... hurt..."

And he didn't quite know how it happened, but it just seemed right: they hugged and she held him hard, then quietly cried, shoulders shaking.

Paul let her stay in bed. There was another thing he couldn't put off. He went downstairs and rang the Gavin Realty main reception number. He had to hold the receiver to his right ear. Even at this time of day, a very bright voice answered the call.

"If you could pass a message to Mr Gavin please."

Telling his lie, a stupid excuse, his head throbbed. Then there was a real throbbing—the rumbling and heavy throttling of machinery outside. Paul remembered: of all the days to have booked that local guy, Jake Minter, to come roll his slasher over their drily overgrown paddocks...

So Paul went out to meet Minter as the man climbed down from the truck's cabin, his giant field-slasher towed behind it.

"You'll want a raw steak on that eye."

"I hadn't considered that approach."

"You got done good."

Minter, all curly hair and wild black beard, looked around, considering the job at hand. In dusty work boots, a pair of shorts and a singlet that looked and smelled like he'd been wearing it a week, he seemed perfectly suited to operate his slasher, a thing like some bizarre prehistoric animal.

"My old man knew the old owners here."

"Everyone around here knew everyone else."

"The Munros too. You married one of the Mosca girls. What was her name?"

"Anna."

"Them Moscas left. Like a lot of others. They went after one of their boys disappeared. Jack?"

"Everyone called him 'Little Jack'."

"That's right," Jake Minter said. "Little Jack."

"So look...you know what to do today."

"This gunna be a regular job?"

"If you want the work."

"I do. Plenty a rain's coming."

Paul shaded his eyes from the cloudless blue. "Doubt it."

"It's coming all right. That means it'll take a lot of time and work keeping ya property in shape."

"We'll play it by ear."

"It's a good place up here, but no one never liked Johnny too much."

"Johnny?"

"Giancarlo Rosso. Gianni. So, Johnny."

"I think I remember that."

"When I was looking after this place for that real estate agent guy? I saw some of Johnny's old machinery still in one of them sheds. Maybe we can use it instead of me dragging this beast all the way up here."

Minter had already started walking across a paddock to the old barns, heat radiating off every flat surface, including the dry grass underfoot. A wilted carpet of bougainvillea flowers was like a red flood around the three very large desolate sheds, a part of the property Paul never had a need to go near.

These had no power or light. Two of the sheds were abandoned. Back in the Rossos' day they would have been full of farm equipment. Now there were a few long-forgotten bales of hay, some rolls of wire fencing, off-cuts of timber and useless bits of leftover bricks, blocks and roof tiles. Nice homes for spiders, bush rats and snakes. Paul had made sure Lía knew to stay away, and that included her dogs. To make certain he always kept the doors shut, though there were no locks, only bolts. Then there was the third barn, the biggest, and it held the machinery the Rossos hadn't bothered to get rid of.

Paul and Jake Minter entered its dusty gloom. There were two old slashers, vintage 1930s or 40s, and a backhoe just as old. Against a wall were some leftover tools: a pair of mattocks, an axe and a saw, a long-handled shovel and another with a shorter handle and a square mouth.

Seeing those tools leaning there, a fact hit Paul—something so obvious he simply hadn't thought of it before. Candela's husband, the thug Donatello, had been working on the property the day Paul first arrived with Lía. He'd probably used these very tools. It was the day Lía entered Rosso House and felt it her home; the day they met Teddy Quinn for the first time; the day Paul spoke to a stranger, Candela, nursing her baby. And so her husband had been there as well, though they hadn't even come close to one another.

All of it so much like a start. Like it was meant to be.

And wasn't there one more thing meant to be? That strange sensation in his belly that had let him to the Blue Bird Café and Candela?

No, no. He needed to shake that kind of thinking off.

"Man, look at these antiques. I might be able to make something of 'em after all."

The machines were rusted, maybe broken in parts, homes for crawling things. Paul watched Minter walk around.

"Nothing too serious wrong that I can see. This one here's had its fuel lines stripped. Probably used somewhere else. And see here? That's rats chewing the wires and eating the rubbers, 'cause rats, that's what they do."

"Any hope?"

"Got spare parts left lyin' around anywhere?"

"Not that I've seen."

"Reckon I could make one working slasher out of the two."

"That would help you?"

"And you. If I gotta keep dragging my own up here—it don't move at much of a clip. An hour just getting' here, then that hill's a killer. Add another hour home. You pay for every minute of that time, Mr Munro, and I ain't even started work yet." Minter tugged at levers, inspected gears. "Got the keys?"

"No."

"Probably hidden around here somewhere," Minter said, passing his gaze along the wooden walls, the cobwebbed rafters. "And this thing." He moved to the old backhoe.

"Ancient, all right," Paul replied. "You know, I don't remember Giancarlo Rosso as the farmer type. He always seemed so well dressed. Least, that's how I picture him. I can't see him riding this thing."

"For a while my old man was the one who did. Worked for Johnny on and off. Never liked him, but. And was happy not to have to come up here anymore."

Paul turned at a shadow. Lía was in the barn's great doorway, sunlight silhouetting her. For a moment her silhouette looked smaller and younger than she was, and he felt a regressive ache for a vision of pretty Anna stepping into some forgotten farm shed where he played cops and robbers with Little Jack.

"You shouldn't come in here."

"I tied the dogs up so they wouldn't."

"This is Mr Minter," he said.

"G'day," Jake Minter said without looking at her.

Paul noticed Lía's eyes were on the machinery. She came closer. As she took his hand it felt for all the world like Anna's, tentatively taking his hand and neither of them knowing the reason why.

"Dad," Lía said, "I don't like those things."

"Mr Minter might be able to get one going."

"Don't." She shook her head and looked away from the old machines. "Please."

He felt the grip on his hand tighten. She was real, Lía his daughter, and he had to put Anna with dirty knees and an impish smile back into a far corner of his mind. Now Lía wanted to lead him away from this dusty shed. Paul did want to get out of there; the left side of his face throbbed to the steady beat of his heart.

"When you're finished for the day," he told Jake Minter, "come up to the house and let me know what I owe you."

"Let me…just let me stay here a bit."

"You all right?"

"Checking this stuff out."

Paul wondered what was going through Jake Minter's mind. He was about to say something else, but the man appeared lost in some sort of reverie, and Lía had turned to go.

The New Mr H...

Saturday morning, three days past his collapse on the stone witch's floor, and every word the old witch had spoken appeared to be true. For Virna Khamitova's back arched and her lovely mouth sighed as a small fountain of Haberman's old-young sperm flowed into her. Haberman's lungs rasped with pleasure, no pain inside him at all, not even its echo. Meanwhile, distant thunder cracked and forks of blue-white lightning marked the sky past his windows.

Virna caught her breath and propped herself up with two pillows, thought a moment then reached over and poured their morning champagne.

"Tell me," Haberman said, making himself comfortable beside her, "where does a woman like you get her start?"

"First steps in Vienna, then Prague." She put the rim of his glass to his mouth and let him sip. "I was with a group of dancers—exotic dancers."

"May I guess at their real business?"

"Pleasuring low aristocrats and wealthy businessmen."

"And then?"

"You want my history?"

"Why not?"

"That part of my life didn't last very long. One of the men I met fell madly in love."

"With you, who wouldn't?"

"He had a poet's soul and wrote me romantic verses. Plus he happened to have a lot of money."

"So you let him spirit you away."

"Eventually." A curious frown came to Virna's brow. "What's so funny?"

"Funny?"

"You seem… How exactly do you seem?"

"I smile for the pleasure of your company."

"There's something else."

"I will admit to a polysyllabic name that has provided me some amusement."

"Polysyllabic?"

"Meaning many syllables, in this case seven. Can you think what might fit this description?"

"Karl Haberman."

"An inadequate four."

Virna Khamitova gave a smile of delight. "It's me."

"Six. We want seven."

"All right. How about your man, that driver…what's his name?"

"The eight-syllabled Donatello Zappavigna." Haberman paused. "Seven, please."

Virna had no idea what he was talking about—then goosebumps appeared along both her arms.

"Ah," Haberman spoke. "You have it." When she shook her head Haberman spoke the name for her: "Pavel Dolgopolov."

Virna had stopped drinking. She'd also stopped looking at him.

"Never fear, it's all to the good," he reassured her. "Let's not have impediments to our pleasures."

"What do you think you know?"

"Wouldn't you expect me to be careful with those who approach my inner circle?" Through the bedroom's large windows Haberman noticed the rain that was beginning to patter down. "So, your Pavel. He ran his own brothels in Budapest but the fact of you made him want to extract himself from that world. He kindly purchased your freedom from your masters, then to save the both of you from further entanglements he whisked you to these shores. An admirable act of love."

"He gave up everything."

"Only to recreate it more discreetly here. A word-of-mouth agency. You at its heart, as 'Svetlana', plus pretties who would like to be you."

"Mr H, why do you mention these things?"

"To let you know you no longer work for his enterprise."

"I'm sure," Virna started, a blush—not of pleasure, but of rising anger—coming to her skin, "I'm sure Pavel will have some thoughts on the matter."

"He won't."

"Why not?"

"Pavel no longer has the capacity for thought. Last night while you slept in this bed like the princess you are, I was making my visit."

"What?"

"Here."

He lifted his right hand to Virna's face so that she should smell his fingers. She did, hardly wanting to, then jerked her face away.

"Sex."

"And?" he asked.

"I don't know. Something smoky and half-sweet."

"Cordite. Your poet received a bullet to the base of his skull. I'm not sure why I felt personally compelled to pull the trigger. Usually I'd turn to some reliable other, but there you have it."

Haberman spoke truthfully. He really had wanted to fire the gun at that poor stranger, a man he didn't even know. The thrill that had travelled through him at the explosion of Pavel Dolgopolov's head, well, it had been enormous.

"In any case, a colleague by the name of Nasser will refurbish the scene of the crime and subsume Pavel's little operation of women into his own."

Virna Khamitova, Haberman saw, was stunned silent. He also saw that despite this very understandable shock, her heart might not quite be breaking over the news. One romantic poet meets a sad demise. The world moves on.

"Proceed, Virna, don't be shy. Ask what's on your mind."

"So I have to work for this man Nasser?"

Haberman turned Virna's face towards his. Had she gone cold? She was warm. Was her skin damp with anxiety? It wasn't.

"Or is it you I'll work for?"

"You don't work."

He watched her absorb the news.

"Where is Pavel now?"

"Never to be found and his affairs put in order. As I said, I have reliable others."

"The police will—"

"Already paid in full."

Virna Khamitova turned onto her side so she could better face him. The sheet was down to her waist, breasts artfully exposed. She took his arm by its meaty bicep and pressed her warmth to him.

"Poor Pavel," she said. "Do you want me to move in?"

"Lord no. I want Virna Khamitova, not a ball and chain. I picture an apartment above the river."

"I'd like that."

"You'll forgive me my moment with Pavel?"

"Who?"

Haberman felt another surge of strength go through him. He lifted Virna Khamitova's shapely hips and charged like a bull. Even as he ejaculated so fast, hard and long a star imploded somewhere deep in the back of his brain, they both heard a noise from downstairs, someone moving in Haberman's otherwise empty home.

"Stay where you are."

Haberman took the Pistolet Makarova—reloaded to capacity after the night's deployment against Pavel Dolgopolov—from the top drawer of the cabinet by the bed. He slipped into his Japanese robe and stepped quickly and silently through the house. His heart, it pleased him to find, beat strongly, but not with fear, only a sort of guileful anticipation. Whatever the witch had or hadn't done for him, he'd certainly found a renewed appreciation for the excitements of conflict. In a way he hoped, whoever this intruder was, they would warrant the use of the pistolet.

But it turned out to be no more than Donny Zap. Haberman saw the grunt was white as a sheet and losing hold of what looked like bloody rags pressed to his bloodied side.

"What on earth's happened to you?

"*Ho caduto...*"

"Speak English."

"Mr H, I ruin my own life... I make my own fall..."

And he did.

The Story of Donny Zap's Fall

The story begins just after the terrible Mr H, believing himself dead in a day, week or month, passes the majority of his quotidian business affairs to Hamid Nasser and Ronald Lundy. The pair call Donatello to come visit them at their club. He discovers a dingy laneway, strippers in the front room, a tiny casino at the back and waiting women upstairs. Plus a damp storeroom for troublemakers and non-payers to receive their punishments.

"Donny Zap, Donny Zap. How would you like the biggest bonus of your life?"

Nasser reaches for his pack of unfiltered Camels and flips the top, but instead of withdrawing a cigarette he slides out a neatly rolled notepaper. Splays it small and flat on the table to reveal a name and address.

"McCulloch. Harry McCulloch. Bastard works out at Jackson's Gym three nights of seven. Go see him this week."

"Is so urgent?"

"Want that bonus I mentioned?"

"I gotta do what?"

"We still want to be friendly with him, but we don't want him walking a few months."

"This one is police?"

"Not anymore."

"McCulloch. I know no one got this name. He done nuthin' to me."

"Yet he's earned himself two broken legs: you can take that as a fact."

"No." Donatello feels his skin twitching, this thing sounds so wrong. "You get someone else."

"We've got you."

"I don't need no trouble."

"How's family life?"

"Why you want to know?"

"Wouldn't you like to get yourself a nice family home?"

"Me and my wife and my baby boy, we got everything we want."

Yes, Donny Zap thinks, everything except the money and position he dreams of.

"Donatello, listen to me. I like you. Ronnie and me, we both like you. But okay, you drive a hard bargain." Nasser uses a blunt pencil to write a figure next to McCulloch's name. "How do you say 'double or nothing' in your language?"

And with the enormity of that figure Donny Zap's too blinded to see the beginnings of his sorrows.

"McCulloch's got red hair, curly, tight to the skull. And a fat moustache like this." Nasser traces it from under his nose down the sides of his mouth. "Drives a baby-shit-yellow soft top Mustang. You're not gonna miss it."

Donny Zap leaves that pathetic little club with a twitching irritation between the shoulder blades—and yet he'll do this thing.

Why?

Si chiama avidità. It's called greed.

❖

The next night he tells Candela his boss Mr Haberman needs him, so he takes their ugly little green and white Torana. It's got steering that pulls to the left and Lorenzo's bassinet still secured into the back. This is where the bassinet stays. Taking Lorenzo out remains Donny Zap's favourite thing, those hours he can spend alone with his boy, giving Candela a break, having his son to himself. He knows there's something special about his boy, though Donatello isn't so sure what that specialness is, or how it will reveal itself.

Time will tell; just look at who Lorenzo has for parents; just think about those two family lines.

Jackson's Gym is easy to find. After a slow reconnaissance, sure enough, there's a yellow beast of an American thing in the car park, soft top pulled up. Donny Zap counts one utility truck, three other cars and two motorcycles. McCulloch must be inside, lifting iron, and Donny Zap imagines a man big enough to give him trouble. All right. No problem. Good money never comes from easy jobs. He's resigned to what he needs to do.

Donatello parks the Torana three blocks away and walks tranquil streets back to the gym. Near the Mustang is a nice clump of mango trees fully grown, with fruit bats high in the branches. Though poor lighting illuminates the vehicles, among these heavy trunks Donatello stands in complete darkness. No one will spy him there and with a little luck no one will see him walk away either. Fifteen minutes pass, then thirty. A man emerges from the gym and drives away in the utility. A little later a kid with skinny legs but arms like a bodybuilder's climbs onto one of the motorcycles, a Kawasaki.

McCulloch makes his appearance ten minutes later. A large patch of sweat stains the front of his singlet, his red curly hair is plastered to his skull, and his Fu Manchu looks slightly ridiculous. Donny Zap blinks rapidly. This is the mark? McCulloch's far from well built. He's not even slightly muscular. There's a lazy pot belly and a small hunch to the man, as if he carries a weight on one shoulder.

Someone walks with McCulloch. They exchange a joke by the remaining motorcycle, and when it pulls away the rear tyre kicks up gravel, making McCulloch flinch.

Donny Zap lets himself out of the shadows. McCulloch receives a clubbing blow that knocks him straight to the ground. He's dragged under the trees, where Donny Zap wraps the man's right leg around his waist. At the snap, McCulloch's body tenses and goes into a spasm. With a guttural moan he's slightly awake, then his eyes widen as Donatello prepares his left.

"No, please… I'm recovering from—"

McCulloch's left knee goes and the man makes a gurgling noise, fingers not reaching down to either leg but tearing at his chest. Donatello pushes himself away. The shaking and gurgling intensifies and there's the sudden stench of *merda*.

What? Donny Zap asks himself. But this man McCulloch is limp as a fish.

This man McCulloch is one-hundred per cent dead.

And for that Nasser hands Donny Zap ten thousand dollars in denominations so small and grubby they must have been collected from a year's worth of entrance fees and gambling losses. Donatello knows homes in good suburbs are going for thirty to forty thousand, so in his hands he holds a wonderful future. He can move Candela and Zo from their tiny flat. Yet there's a problem: how will he explain this windfall when Candela believes implicitly his story of being a humble driver for a businessman of position?

He decides to hide the entire cache of cash in a canvas bag that he stuffs into a forgotten suitcase at the back of a closet. Donny Zap will think the problem through. Maybe he'll add more cash; after all, Nasser and Lundy, or the men they protect, will always have enemies. McCulloch must have done something very bad indeed; probably he'd been the filthiest, most corrupt cop alive—and these people breed like flies. More names will surely be written down onto more secret pieces of notepaper, and the little Zappavigna family's future will be assured.

However now there comes a compounding problem. Every day the newspapers say something new about the deceased, the late ex-Senior Detective Harry McCulloch. Journalists paint him a twenty-seven-year veteran who'd retired unwillingly due to a heart problem. Unwanted retirement found him writing a book about his experiences with the criminal underworld. Forget a seasoned detective's first-hand tales of robberies and murders, of crimes of passion and break-ins. He'd promised inside information about brown paper bags of money passed from criminals to police to politicians. In this book, the truth would out.

No one with any sense needs to be told the rest. One or some of the names that might appear in McCulloch's book hadn't liked the idea. Meanwhile, the police commissioner makes public statements that are variations on a regular theme:

"The murderer or murderers of this brave public servant, and, might I add, of one of my very best friends—Harry Mac—will not escape the long arm of the law or the full weight of our judiciary."

"Nope," Nasser assures an increasingly anxious Donny Zap, speaking one day on the telephone. "It was an upper echelon of the force who paid for your services, not me. You've got every penny of their money. The ones who talk loudest are the ones with the most to hide. Believe me, no one's looking into the McCulloch case."

At that moment Candela emerges from the kitchen. Donatello hangs up in the middle of Nasser's chuckle.

"We need butter and milk. If I go now I can catch the shop before it shuts."

"How's the boy?"

She looks down at Lorenzo in her arms. "Happy."

Still anxious, even afraid, Donatello passes the back of a finger along Zo's soft cheek and receives a nice murmur in response. It calms Donny Zap, that murmur, though Candela looks at Donatello without any sort of a smile. This marriage's ground is rough: he knows that. It's as if he and Candela have barely agreed on a thing since Zia Agata called them to this country. He notes how drawn her face is. So tired. Little Zo always feeds on the milk she produces as if there will be no tomorrow. Donny Zap would like to make his wife happy.

"Want a rest?"

"What do you mean?"

"I'll go to the shop." Donatello eases their baby from her arms. "This young man can come with me. And we won't hurry back."

In a minute the four door's steering is pulling against his hands as he drives off. Really, he shouldn't let Candela handle such a broken-down piece of *merda*. Maybe some of the ten thousand can go towards a car better and safer. His eyes have been filled by the sight of a motorcycle he'd seen one day in an expensive glass-walled showroom; too bad, his dream Ducati will have to wait. Better to make driving safer for all of them. What's the most trustworthy brand of car on the road these days?

Such are the thoughts occupying Donny Zap's mind as he heads towards the local shops, traffic so light it's as if half the city's already settled in for the coming evening. He'll park at the supermarket and push Lorenzo in his stroller, just walk him around for as long as they want, letting the baby enjoy the air. There'll be a playground somewhere. He'll cuddle his boy on a swing. Donatello glances into the rear-vision mirror. In the bassinet, Zo's out of view. Not only that, he's quiet, lulled to sleep by the rhythm of the ugly Torana's mostly-bald tyres on the road.

And it proves the one bit of luck still left in Donny Zap's life, the bassinet fixed into the back seat. Down so low, the baby is saved.

On the highway, speedometer uncomfortably nudging eighty, the rear window shatters and a small explosion of dust and rubber blows out from the dashboard to the left of the steering wheel. Donatello swerves the car as another popping explosion shatters the radio. He pulls the steering wheel hard to the right and the stupid thing fights him even as the car collects a short hail of sizzling slugs that strike everywhere but their intended mark.

147

The sedan ploughs off the road. With a crash of metal and glass it marries itself to a great timber power pole. Donny Zap lolls sideways, one bleeding hand grasping for the seat buckle, doing his best to get to Lorenzo.

———◆———

After the investigating officers leave him alone, at least for the while, Donny Zap digs the money out from its hiding place. Candela sees notes spilled onto the bed.

"How much is it?"

"Ten thousand."

"Where did it come from?"

"A job."

Her trembling tears at what could have happened to her baby begin to evaporate, though not for the joy of possessing such a substantial sum of money. Even Donny Zap understands it's for the opposite.

No need then to explain the finer details of the mission he'd been on. Candela doesn't even know of two men named Nasser and Lundy. But Mr Karl Haberman, yes.

"So he's some kind of criminal?"

Donny Zap nods.

"And so are you?"

"For you and our boy, I am."

The breath goes out of her. Candela stands holding Lorenzo in a way that suggests she will never let him go again. "Tell me the truth. Do you hurt people?"

"Sometimes."

"That money goes to the families of every person you've hurt. Do you promise?"

"I do."

"And this attack… It was some sort of payback for what you've done?"

"Revenge for a recent job."

"Worth all this money."

"Yes."

"And our baby's life."

Donatello doesn't answer that question.

"Does Haberman also run prostitution?"

"He does."

"Have you used these women?"

148

"Never. I protect them."

"You disgust me, Donatello."

"I do my best for you and Zo."

She's about to leave the room, but the moment's so raw that Donny Zap can see how Candela needs to empty her soul.

"Something's happening to you, Donatello. I've been watching you change. The man I married is long gone. Since we've come to this country you're a fool whose soul gets darker every day."

"Forgive me, Candela, please."

"I won't be near any of that and neither will Lorenzo."

"I'll change."

"What's to change?"

"Everything."

"No, only one thing: that I never see you again."

"Lorenzo needs his father."

"He doesn't need a monster. Get out."

———◆———

Though he does as he promised—or close enough, one 3:00am leaving a satchel containing exactly ten thousand dollars at the darkened back step of the McCulloch family home—the last element of their marriage collapses. The flat they used to live in is empty; so now is Donny Zap's life. In a sort of daze Donatello continues to drive for Mr H and take small jobs with Nasser and Lundy. Lundy hadn't lied. The investigation into Harry McCulloch's death goes nowhere. Similarly, there's no new attempt on Donny Zap's life. The entire situation has quickly cooled; Donny Zap might have ruined his family, but the rest of the world around him resumes its proper shape.

Except for one small fact Nasser keeps to himself.

The true friends of Harry McCulloch are definitely *not* cooled. A group of detectives honest to the bone yet brutal in their application of the law—their own—are champing at the bit. Which creates a greater problem for Hamid Nasser and Ronald Lundy, who'd passed these friends the killer's name and details in the first place.

Nasser and Lundy worry: *What if Donny Zap spills the beans before a shotgun blast blows his head off? We need to do something fast.*

Donatello doesn't understand he's the central integer in a looming equation of deceit. It's something he finally works out for himself after Nasser invites him to an unexpected Friday night job, the very bloody clean-up of someone named Dolgopolov, and the dumping of Dolgopolov's corpse over the side of Nasser's boat in a midnight-black, choppy Moreton Bay.

...and the Impossible Donny Zap

Careful to not get too much blood onto his patterned Japanese robe—a personal gift from the mamasan of a quite extraordinary sekukyabakura in Shinjuku—Haberman dragged the inert Donny Zap outside to the tiled terrace, depositing the grunt into a plastic poolside chair.

"You used your key?" Haberman nudged the chair with his foot. "Better give it back to me."

At no response he shook Donny Zap by the shoulder. The ugly Levantine's face was pale as death, which accentuated the jet-black hair and heavy eyebrows. One red-stained hand still loosely held a disgusting, bloody rag. His T-shirt and leather coat were wet.

With a few more nudges the boy lazily opened his eyes. Haberman wondered how close to death he was, and if Nasser would need to get rid of a second body after Pavel Dolgopolov's.

"I didn't hear your motorcycle."

"Couldn't ride no more, Mr H… Had to walk."

"Why's that?"

Incredibly, Donny Zap straightened, then pulled himself to his feet. There was a slight sway, but the boy had the constitution of an ox.

"Got a bullet, mister."

He shrugged out of his jacket and blood dripped. Haberman wondered if he'd ever feel any sympathy for this boy. After all, he really was loyal as a dog.

"Why did you come here?"

"Nowhere else to go."

Yes, loyal, and quite attached too. Haberman did feel a moment's sympathy.

"You were helping Nasser with the removal of a body?"

"Nasser and Lundy, yeah."

"And somehow you managed to catch a hole in your side?"

"We dump the body in the sea then Nasser he shoot me."

Nasser owned a good Pilothouse; they would have sailed out to the bay in it, weighting the corpse for the deep waters to swallow. But why this attack on the grunt?

"Let's see if we can't get you to live a little longer."

Haberman went to a cupboard inside and withdrew a handful of clean tea towels. He had Donny Zap press them to his side and follow him into the games room never used. The crisscross of fluorescent tubes over the smooth green of the billiards table were as bright as lights in an operating theatre. Haberman took two thick blankets redolent of camphor beads from a wooden storage trunk and folded them over the velvet, then he found the airtight container he wanted, untouched in years.

He passed Donny Zap a pillow and a bucket. "You'll lie on your back, but first put your shirt and those soiled cloths in here."

Starting to shake, the boy did, then bare-chested and breathing harder he lay flat over the velvet. Haberman started to use his collection of soft sponges to investigate what he was dealing with.

A bullet wound, the skin singed from a close-quarters firing. Yet the slug hadn't torn into the boy's organs and it had missed the ribs. Donatello had been very lucky. Haberman pulled on a pair of thin latex surgeon's gloves and irrigated the wound.

"Any numbness or tingling in your arm, say, or your leg?"

"Numb...yeah, like that."

"First the slug needs to come out and the area cleaned and disinfected. Then the stitching. No anaesthetic in this household so the procedure won't be pleasant."

"Gotta say thanks, mister."

"Let's see if you survive first. Wait there."

Haberman returned upstairs for his medicine box, another useful part of his life untouched in years. Virna had remained in bed, impatient and a little frightened.

"What's happening down there?"

"One waits for a nurse to show."

With minor help from Virna, Haberman cleaned, closed and taped gauze over the wound, marvelling at the grunt's constitution. A lesser man— any man—would have passed out cold, or screamed and kept screaming.

"I've used a simple suture. My touch should still be good enough that there'll be no necrosis of the flesh at the edges. I'll give you clean clothes and take you home in the morning. If an investigation arises, a taxi driver might recall you and your condition."

Donny Zap glanced at the bloodied lump on a china plate. The slug hadn't shattered and had come out intact.

"Infection will be the main concern. I'll check the wound in three days."

Haberman had to admit he'd enjoyed the surgical procedure, something he'd had the need to practice many times in the past. The distant past. Today, just as with the shooting of Dolgopolov, and indeed the raw *fucking* of the lovely Virna, playing the surgeon had thrilled his senses in a way he'd become quite unused to.

That witch has given me a second life—and something more.

She said I should devour this supposedly incredible girl she wants me to seek out. It would appear I am devouring life *itself.*

He was more than thrilled; Haberman was *enriched.*

Donny Zap eased himself off the billiards table. He pulled on a neat cotton shirt, an old one of Haberman's that Virna found in a bottom drawer. The grunt shook his head as if trying to shake off a weight, then pushed himself away and staggered through the downstairs rooms to the terrace and pool. The morning had turned itself into a lovely combination of sunlight and easy rain showers. Donny Zap, face upturned, caught the soft fall.

Haberman and Virna sheltered under an awning.

"So," Haberman said, "the incident?"

"Easy money for a cleanup, mister. Nasser and Lundy they call me for a man with half a head."

Haberman glanced at Virna; she didn't react.

"Midnight maybe in the boat we drive long, long way from the coast. I put the dead man in chains then he gone."

"So far so good."

"Nasser he say we stay on the water, drink beer. So we drinking. I tell Nasser and Lundy something I been working out in my mind."

"Oh dear, the sharing of independent reasoning while in a remote location. I believe I see what happens next."

"I tell Nasser that ex-detective he send me to hurt, Nasser must know this man gotta bad heart. So if I break his legs that heart gonna break too. So it gotta be true that Nasser he set me up. Truth is he want McCulloch dead and so he trick me to get this done."

"And of course Nasser responded to your accusation by drawing his pistol."

"He laugh and say I too dumb to work out the next part."

"Which is?"

"The real friends of McCulloch, the ones who don't pay for him to be dead, they want to know who killed him. Nasser and Lundy gotta protect themselves so they tell them my name knowen they gonna get me. But when they did try they miss."

"And so one Donatello Zappavigna Esquire is still around to spill the beans in a real investigation. Therefore Nasser pulled the trigger, intending to put you over the side to sleep with Dolgopolov and many others."

"Yeah."

"Yet here you are. What's the rest?"

"Nasser and Lundy dead. They double cross me but not only that, they nearly get my boy killed, and one more thing: because all this 'appen my wife she gone and she takes the baby with her."

"You've fallen from a great height, Donatello."

"That's what I say. *Ho caduto*."

Haberman kept his eyes fixed on the grunt. The story lacked something. While shot in the side, Donny Zap was claiming he'd managed to kill two very experienced men.

"Did you have a gun, or somehow wrested Nasser's away from him?"

The boy shook his head, and as he did something in him appeared to change, like a new form of misery. He started perspiring, droplets actually falling from his face to the tiled terrace.

Was the previous bloodless white of his face darkening? Indeed it was.

"Donatello, how did you turn the tables?"

Virna felt something as well; the air around them also was changing, becoming charged with—what? Some sort of invisible energy. An energy that emanated from the grunt. Haberman glanced at Virna and she moved closer to him, taking his arm.

"I asked you a question." Haberman composed himself, feeling Virna push her body even closer to his. "How did these two men die?"

"Mister…" Donatello groaned. "They dyen this way."

He held up his two hands. Haberman's jaw clenched.

Donny Zap's gaze flicked towards a sun that made raindrops glitter. His face was wet, but agonised, as if he wanted to absorb the goodness of the sky and couldn't.

"Zia Agata, she too old and gettin' sicker. And the sicker she get, the less she can stop me."

"What's that supposed to mean?"

"It mean the same for you too, Mr H. When her hand it not so strong, you gonna be back to where you was."

"What?"

"You think you gonna be strong forever? When she fall you fall too."

Haberman watched the boy's breath grow more laboured, nothing to do with being shot and repaired. Donny Zap was starting to hunch over. His body struggled with itself, as if in some inexplicable form of self-torture.

"Donatello—you've outstayed your welcome."

"Mr H…"

"You walked in. Take the same way out."

"…you and me…" Donny Zap moaned towards that sky "…we is already…"

"We're already what, boy?"

"Good and dead."

Haberman's insides quailed. Virna's body quivered against his.

"Get out of here."

And despite wanting to stand firm and strong Haberman stepped backwards; Virna came with him. They were against a wall, and from there they watched Donny Zap bend and crack joints.

And let out a howl.

Haberman's eyes were full and wide.

Oh god how Donny Zap howled.

He was a man yet no longer looked like a man. He was Donny Zap, and just about impossible.

Not the Past but Now

Show me the girl, show me the face of this girl and the place where she lives, Agata Rosso prayed, concentrating hard. Her candles flickered and if they did anything at all it was only to reflect Agata's past. She saw green meadows where horses, cows and sheep grazed, and the red house where she and Giancarlo once lived. Then the small flames were in front of her and she was home once again, having learned nothing.

Why show me the past when I need the now?

Exhausted by futility, the witch extinguished each candle. Celano guided her down the hallway to Giancarlo's bed at the back of the house.

"All right. Leave me alone."

The signora did. Agata dipped a sponge into the ceramic bowl Celano had prepared. Her husband's eyes followed the everyday ritual. Agata moistened his lips. She mumbled an apology, and the promise she repeated every day.

"You will walk again. You will be strong."

After the sponge bath she'd feed him, though he'd only take one or two spoonfuls of her creations. If the spirit guides would only speak properly—if the plan she believed in with her soul would come to pass—Giancarlo would raise himself from this bed and the two of them would walk into the future.

She'd hooked that horror Haberman, now she needed to give him information about how he could find their prize—but only the spirits could tell her where to send the man. Why did they play games? Did they really not know where she was?

God be with me or Lucifer guide my hands. I'll follow either one of you.

Giancarlo's mouth moved and his tongue licked her sponge, infused with lime and sugar. She watched his lined, grey mouth suck with less strength than that of a newborn baby at its mother's breast. She pictured little Zo feeding from Candela. The boy's wonderful eyes would gaze at his mother as the ecstasy of milk filled his body. That milk was his nutrition and power; one day that power would flow exactly where Agata needed it. She felt no remorse for this, just as she felt no remorse for what would happen to the girl the spirits promised her. The girl was the centre of the story and the baby with his wolf's heart an integral measure. The two of them combined—their hearts, their spirits, their blood—would make Agata and Giancarlo what they used to be.

And more.

So please, please show me her face.

A daily prayer.

Giancarlo made a slight cough at the back of his throat. Agata squeezed the sponge against his remaining teeth. He swallowed more juice. She glanced at the windows to her side and would have smiled if there'd been a smile left inside her. Rain. Soft drizzle pattering against the eaves.

Signora Celano returned with a cup of warm water and soap, and the cut-throat razor for shaving Giancarlo's face.

"The candles," Celano spoke with her usual deference. "Always the same?"

"I can't see her face."

"Maybe a name?"

Agata shook her head. Signora Celano hesitated a moment, trying to puzzle things out, to understand the clues. As always, and like Agata, she arrived nowhere new.

"They say she's a very powerful girl who wasn't here before."

"Yes," Agata Rosso agreed, looking away. The drizzle was welcome. Her garden would love the rain.

"Then," Signora Celano continued, "if she wasn't here before, she's come from somewhere else."

"That's what I'm thinking."

"A new arrival? Maybe a migrant?"

"I don't know."

"It's an imprecise science."

"It's not enough."

Giancarlo's tongue lay flat in his open mouth and his breath, though even enough, carried a putrid stench. Agata couldn't convince herself that her creations could keep him alive much longer. Every time she approached this room she feared his soul had finally sailed away.

"We can't keep waiting."

"Then what can we do?"

"After you're finished call Donatello. Tell him I want Haberman here. Today he gets to work."

Rain still drizzling, in the late afternoon Agata Rosso sat with new candles burning. The dolls were in their usual semi-circle, watching.

"Donatello and Mistah Hubbamante."

The pair followed Signora Celano at a distance from one another. To Agata an air of dislike was palpable, but only from Haberman to the boy. Donatello averted his eyes from her. At a glance Agata knew something was wrong.

"Why are you so miserable?"

Donatello's hand went to his right side. Agata pushed that hand away and pulled up his shirt. There was gauze. She tore it away to reveal a wound, freshly stitched.

"I got shot, Zia."

"Who operated on you?"

"Mr H."

"Wait here."

Agata left the living room and shuffled to the internal staircase leading down to her bricked-and-blocked-in cellar. She'd had the large, windowless and sound-proof room added more than two decades earlier: her retreat and solace, a place for experimentation and incantation. Now Agata rummaged through overcrowded shelves. She collected two jars of dried herbs, then opened the downstairs door to her back garden, vibrant and perfectly maintained. Its scents and colours alone were enough to lift flagging spirits. The drizzling rain did the rest. Using a knife she'd consecrated, Agata harvested a small quantity of lavender, thyme and rosemary, then bent her head in thanks for the gifts these botanicals possessed. She made a small offering in return: a half-bucket of fresh water and scoops of fresh organic fertiliser for the roots of the various herbs and plantings.

She returned to Donatello. Haberman sipped tea served by Celano, his displeasure barely hidden.

Singing a healing song Agata mixed her ingredients. She told Donatello to bow his head and imagine his body enclosed in light, to picture his wound mending. With one hand she smeared her fresh paste onto the stitching, which she saw was clean and precise.

She asked Haberman in English, "You studied medicine?"

"A humble amateur, fascinated now by your finishing touch."

Agata wiped her hands. Donatello tucked in his shirt.

"Madam, we need plain speaking."

Haberman stood from the armchair and crossed the room, moving lightly, the polar opposite of what he used to be.

"When sad Donatello came to me with a hole in his side, I discovered that the slug of a .38 fired at close range hadn't torn through his internal organs. It pierced his flesh but stopped well short. Then he told me he killed the man who shot him plus a second man present. Using his bare hands."

"So?"

"Might you explain how this boy resists a bullet, murders two men, then can make his way bleeding across an entire city for my help?"

To give a man renewed life, yet to suffer his derision. When she was done with his services she'd give Haberman the curse of the deadened tongue, so he'd know how worthless his utterances were, then prick his heart with a fine needle. She wondered if she could persuade Donatello to bury him alive.

"Mister, please," Donatello spoke up. "You no ask no more."

"Next he howled like a dog and almost was… something not really a man."

"Did he grow hair and bark?"

"No."

"Well?"

"He was…he was close to a more primal version of himself. I saw naked hunger and brutal strength, but also a young man in pain."

"Donatello attacked you?"

"He ran away. I thought I might never see him again—then this evening he's back, and quite himself. Incredible, no?"

"Donatello has the wolf in him. His father did and his father's father and now his child too."

"Beware the full moon?"

Agata clenched her few teeth together. She resumed her seat. "Enough talk."

The flames in the four candles barely danced. With the grey light and drizzle outside, and the four pairs of dolls' eyes giving witness, Agata Rosso felt just a little of her old self. Anger helped, kindling her authority. She needed to remember that despite her frailty she was a woman well trained; she was a witch with enchantments and pleasures to spare.

"I'm here for more about this mysterious girl, I assume?"

"Yes."

"You've promised someone extraordinary. I won't waste my time otherwise."

"You'll be more than satisfied." The witch curled her lip, barely hiding her disgust. "Then I'll grind her flesh, bones, skin and hair into paste and powder."

"The reason you'd do such a thing?"

"What's my profession?"

"So tell me—details. A name and a photograph."

"I can tell you she's young."

"How young?"

"She's not a baby, not a child and not a woman. I'm also certain her mother is dead."

"That's not something I'll be able to tell by looking at a girl. What distinguishing features?"

"Only one I'm sure of: power. In here." The witch tapped the side of her head. "She has such strength, and you'll see that. You might even feel it."

"These are useless generalities."

"She's new to this city. New to this country."

"New to our country, without a mother, maybe between twelve and seventeen or eighteen years of age. How could I possibly go wrong?" Haberman waited for a reply that Agata wouldn't give him. "Well, does she have a father or perhaps a teenage paramour?"

Agata again concentrated on the flames. Something, anything, needed to come. Please, *aiutami*, help me. Even Karl Haberman's dull wit was beginning to make her feel more despairing. She prayed in the order of the southern hemisphere's seasons:

"*Estate, primavera, inverno e autunno, fammi vedere.* Summer, spring, winter and autumn, let me see."

The dolls in their four seasons, ceramic eyes trained towards the candles' flames, helped Agata call the spirits. Their job: to add focus, to add concentration.

Fammi vedere. Fammi vedere. Show me. Show me.

Agata felt herself become a part of the pattering drizzle on her window-panes. Her eyes rolled back. At the same time her old heart filled with equal parts pleasure and horror. Because the girl, she felt her, really felt her, the very first time.

Dio mio, how I'll need to be careful.

She's more powerful than I imagined, even as an inexperienced child.

"Haberman, I see her learning. Books and knowledge."

"So she's in school, of course. Where?"

Instead of answering that Agata caught a glimpse of—

"Her skin isn't white."

The sudden vision of flesh and long limbs cost her everything. Agata slumped. She couldn't muster another ounce of energy. Her bristly chin wanted to fall to her chest.

"Donatello," she muttered, "get him out of here."

As the boy moved Haberman away her mind clouded over completely. The last she heard was that querulous voice, arrogant and arch:

"A non-white motherless schoolgirl, a revelation."

Then Donatello did his job and Agata slept where she was.

The Innocent One

He might have been making excuses for why he wasn't immediately going into Gavin Realty, but the reality of the job made Paul move more quickly into finding a school for Lía. He couldn't wait until the start of the next school year; she *would not* be alone on the property all the hours he was at work—dogs or no dogs.

The state schools nearby couldn't help but he found a Catholic girls' college right on their bus line. The principal, Sister Mary Sweetman, informed Paul that his daughter would need to sit a test to determine equivalency in her standard of schooling; things between Hong Kong and Australia were quite different.

"Let's have my assistant book a time. She'll send along a list of subject areas and topics we'll test. That will make things fairer for your daughter. And did you say it was Lía, with an accent over the 'í'? How lovely."

"When could she start?"

"All going well, we could have your child with us in a week or two."

The worry in this: Lía's classmates in Kowloon, how they'd turned against her; the once-loving missionary sisters of the New Hope School, how they'd bundled her out. And one more thing: Lía had become very quiet. She'd been this way since that night he'd locked himself in his room after being beaten up. Was it the awful state of his face that continued to plunge his daughter into silence? Paul didn't think so. What had Lía been doing that day? For her it had just been a simple visit to the State Library.

But what if this was only in Paul's mind?—him with the throbbing face and persistent ache in one temple, taking pain killers and drinking more whisky behind a locked door at night, already feeling guilty about upsetting the comfortable and steady life Lía had made for herself.

"I'm okay Dad. I'm just liking being alone."

When had she come into the kitchen? And when had he, for that matter? One minute he'd been lying in bed, next they were talking. Damn pills; maybe he should stop taking them. And whisky, he'd better think about getting rid of every drop.

"But is it the idea of school that's bothering you?"

"No."

Was she lying so as not to worry him?

He felt as if he was half dreaming. The conversation petered out as soon as it began, and he recalled how he'd watched Lía yesterday or the day before, or was it even this morning, sitting on a bench under one of the melaleuca trees ringing the house, both dogs with her. They seemed quieter as well, maybe sensing whatever was going on inside his daughter. Paul wondered if she was experiencing some particularly teenage sort of change; or maybe it was something about being a young, developing female that Paul didn't understand. Then again, the answer was probably very simple, the most obvious one: the new aura of negativity encircling Lía was all about her father taking active steps to find a housekeeper and gardener to come live with them.

"It's what we'll do."

"I'll make the walls of those maid's quarters fall in."

Wait—was she really telling him that, or was he in some kind of silly waking dream?

Sips of water, more painkillers. Trying to figure out why his headache only got worse. He must have come into the kitchen for the water and bottle of pills, because Lía was with him saying something else:

"Tomorrow I'll spend another day at the State Library."

"Ah, okay," he replied. Well, that was one good thing, wasn't it, that she wanted to do something off the property. "What are you after?"

My god how her face appeared to close up. She hesitated before speaking, as if she had to think about what to say.

"The school tests."

"What about them?"

"It's the mathematics."

Mathematics, Lía's Achille's heel. As much as he always tried to help her, it was just as she often said: for her, numbers didn't work.

"I could give you a day of refreshers."

"I'll find the text they're using. It'll be full of the right exercises."

This sounded much more like the version of Lía who gave him so much less to worry about. Paul moved to give her a hug yet he sensed even more of her hesitation, not wanting to be touched.

"Who am I?"

"Your mother and I told you all that."

"Where do I come from?"

"But I've told you everything I know."

Lía's face again seemed wan and worried; he watched her return to the sunshine and quiet of the day and her dogs, then he was back in his bed dreaming, only to come groggily awake to the burr of the telephone downstairs and the sight of Lía's adoption papers inexplicably pulled from the bottom drawer where he kept them, now scattered on the floor.

How? What happened?

◆————————————◆

She felt sunshine on her face and when she put her hands down to caress the dogs their breath was on her fingers, yet she'd moved to the barn housing the old tractors that had so interested Jake Minter, and reached for the thick wooden door handle.

The small boy's hand stopped her, first time they touched, and his great wounded eyes told her she didn't want to go in there. That touch, it was like a breath of air, neither hot nor cold, not warm yet not quite nothing either.

"You don't like it in there."

"But I need to know why I don't like it."

"You've been thinking about different things."

She had, it was true. For days after what happened at Mountford Lía wanted to forget herself, lose herself, find a way to go to a distant place and become someone new, then a different sort of feeling had started to preoccupy her.

Who am I?

Where do I come from?

The boy was no longer with her. Lía was in her father's bedroom, and as he remained crumpled in his bed she rummaged through his things until she found what she was after. She'd always known about this folder with papers to do with her, yet had never felt an overwhelming curiosity about it.

Until this new question grew in her mind:

WHAT am I?

She touched parchment and old documents. All written in Italian, the language of her birthright, a language she'd never learned beyond everyday words and a few basic phrases. Maybe that could change one day. It should. She'd claim that birthright. Here there was something called an *Atto di Nacsita.* Lía understood it was a birth certificate, her name and birth date on it. The certificate itself, however, had been endorsed in 1961, meaning she'd already have been two going on three years of age.

Of course, I was a foundling, so there was no proper birth certificate. My parents must have applied for one to be created. They had no real name, no real date of birth.

Here: Ospizio per L'Infanzia Abbandonata. *The hospital, maybe, or the place for abandoned children?*

The name Lía and my birthday created out of thin air.

Genitori: Incogniti.

Mother and father unknown.

There was a short hand-written note pinned to another document. That document was also something official, embossed with the wax stamp of a church or a chapel called *Santa Maria del Carmelo.*

Those are the Carmelite nuns of Sicily, Lía.

Ma? That's where you and Dad said you found me.

Lía didn't need to be able to read the language to see that Santa Maria del Carmelo was a nun's monastery by the river San Michele, which she knew was near the port city of Messina.

That looks like an affidavit written by the Mother Superior. And it's addressed to the authorities, and to Pope John, countersigned by the Archbishop of Messina.

No, you've never seen this before. I don't know who you are. You're not my mother.

But I am. And I can read that note in Italian even if the handwriting is difficult.

Then what does it say?

Lía felt the words go through her, in her mother's voice, the only details of her early life that could possibly be true.

I declare that the female child was discovered in the public wheel of our chapel's north wall. There was no information to accompany this infant, who was clean, wrapped in new clothes and examined to be in good health. As prescribed by the sacred law of our order we wrote to the archbishop with information we had taken such child into the care of the Holy Virgin of Carmel. Most blessed Archbishop Rizzo of Messina informed us we should name the child Innocentina della Santa Maria del

Carmelo. And so is she recorded.

That's my real name. Innocentina.

The Innocent One.

But Ma, after what I did, I'm more like an angel of death.

———◆———◆———

L ía was alone in the sunshine with her own words torturing her gut. Angel of death, so true.

And without a single friend, other than my dogs.

Teddy Quinn, I was mean to you.

She pictured him on that high branch in the Chinese elm, just a young man surveying a panorama he'd come to love, and yet, despite herself, whenever she pictured that moment Lía had to smile.

I'd be up there in that tree with you again, if things were different.

Dakota and Buster had moved into the shade. It might be midday. There was the trilling, low-pitched caw of a cockatoo. Then another and another. As she returned to herself from whatever these travels had been, Lía also heard the persistent burr of the telephone in the house.

———◆———◆———

S he climbed the staircase to get her father; the person on the line wanted to speak to him, and didn't sound very happy. Lía knew her father ought to have started work already but hadn't on account of his face. Two other days she'd spoken to someone from Gavin Realty, overhearing business-type talk about plans and land, plus his very unlikely story about an unfortunate encounter in a bar. Some stranger, some drunk, hadn't liked the look of his face and so had gone about rearranging it. Lía's father was supposed to start at the office just as soon as he was presentable.

This time, however, something sounded different.

Bleary-eyed, in rumpled clothes and with his hair awry, her father said, "Of course, tomorrow, ten a.m. Mike, I'll be there."

When he replaced the receiver he raised his eyes to Lía. "So how do I look?"

Dad, you better get your shit together.

Angel of Death, or Other Names

The next day, which was gloomy, rain coming, Lía's father dropped her in front of the State Library in town. He was on his way to Gavin Realty.

"Good luck with your maths."

The building was large, with an expansive reading room downstairs surrounded by shelves and stacks, and a higher mezzanine with more tables and chairs. Lía looked through the card system catalogues. It was so quiet a librarian with a name tag reading Mrs Oliver asked if she'd like some help.

"I'm looking for—" Lía tried to find a better way to say it, and didn't. "Angels of death, if you get what I mean?" And there was that strange term the ghost-boy had used: "Also, anything about a 'stone witch'."

"Is that a statue?"

"I'm not sure. Maybe it all has to do with witchcraft?" Lía found it hard to articulate what she really did want to investigate, and wondered how she could make certain it related to her. "Specifically in Italy, I think."

"School assignment?"

"Yes it is."

"Well, let's see."

Mrs Oliver was very direct yet softly spoken, and soon she had a pile of reference books on a private table for Lía. The entire reading room was almost empty; only a few other people were immersed in their own collections of research books, each at their own table. No one spoke or looked around much; Lía was by far the youngest person there. A head librarian stood at the front counter making notations in a ledger and another librarian picked up the odd discarded book, straightened an already straight chair. Lía thought this would have to be the safest place in the world to read about horrible things.

"Take all the notes you like, and the photocopier's over there if you need it. Five cents a page."

"Thank you."

"I'm thinking…" Mrs Oliver hesitated. "This one might be of use."

She opened one of the texts and thumbed to the contents page, which didn't list what she wanted, so she turned to the index at the back.

"The only Italian connection I can think of," Mrs Oliver said, pointing to the listing.

"*Benandanti?*" Lía read.

"You know the name?"

"No."

"Then read on."

Yet as soon as Mrs Oliver left Lía pushed that text aside and picked up another. The pressing topic on her mind: whatever angels of death were supposed to be.

Because isn't that what I was to Mrs Badger?

She studied a number of different books, sections of chapters, pages and paragraphs that appeared appropriate. The accumulated information made her realise her conception of the idea had been incorrect. She'd imagined some terrifying creature from antiquity, maybe vaguely Greek or Roman, with flowing black wings and a scythe to chop down the living.

Instead, Lía saw that many cultures believed in some variation of a kind of angel who brought peace to the soul. Not only that, this creature—in whatever form each superstition imagined it—was also meant to help the deceased make their journey into the afterlife. Lía noted down the many references to biblical stories, and to names such as Michael, Gabriel, Samael, Abaddon or Apollyon, then Azrael of the Qur'an, the Bodhisattvas of the Tibetan Book of the Dead, even Santa Muerte of Mexico. These weren't murderous monsters but loving guides to a better place.

So, she thought, you could even say these weren't angels of death but angels of peace.

As it had been for Mrs Badger, a soul released from a prison.

Lía put her pen down, becoming engrossed in other information. She read about the supernatural belief systems of different continents, countries and eras: there was China's long background in the occult and something called herbalism; native American culture's skin-walkers and the belief in the mystical as an everyday part of life. And so many more, wherever humans existed, from Icelandic sorcery and times of magic and fear to Aboriginal Australia's belief in the energies in the land and its landscapes.

She caught sight of another page in another book, with a drawing of Hansel and Gretel nibbling on their witch's gingerbread house. This chapter told her an idea called 'transference' featured in almost every spiritual belief system: the concept that eating human flesh might allow people to acquire the skills and traits of other individuals. At one end of the spectrum there was something like eating the legs of a fast runner in order to increase your own speed, and, at the other end, consuming the body and blood of Christ for divine enrichment.

European witches in particular were often accused of whisking away and eating desirable children in order to initiate themselves into the magical world and as part of specific rituals. The desirability of these children centred around many different qualities. Sometimes the younger and plumper they were the more coveted they would be. At other times, a child's very high intelligence, attractiveness or other positive personal qualities made them more valuable.

In this form of witchcraft, Lía continued to read, believers maintained that for the most effective transfer of physical and spiritual energy, the person being killed and eaten had to experience maximum torture and violence in the process—that way the victim's body would preserve the greatest amount of power for the witch to devour. Subjects were therefore not so much murdered as very slowly slaughtered. The longer and more excruciating the screams, the more effectively the spirit was magnified and trapped inside the body. Eating the eventual cadaver, combined with spells and incantations, allowed witches and their followers to absorb the greatest potency.

Lía closed the book, revolted. She didn't want to read any more. The few notes she'd scribbled and abandoned didn't tell her anything beyond the horrors of the human imagination. Steeling herself, she turned to the book with chapters about the *Benandanti*.

Those few individuals in the reading room with her had either left or were leaving. The very large space seemed to be emptying. Silent shadows crossed the floor, heeding the signs about the need to keep quiet. Lía didn't look around but instead concentrated on this particular textbook. She read that the word *Benandanti* translated as 'Good Walker' for a single

Benandante and 'Good Walkers' for the plural. She ran her fingertip down the page and over to the next, looking for more interesting information.

A new section told her the *Benandanti* were specific to a region to the northeast of Italy bordering Austria, Slovenia and the Adriatic Sea. The members of this cult were predominantly female. Their role in agrarian societies had been to act as good witches battling bad witches who brought ruin to peasant lives, and most especially to peasant crops and herds. Lía's heart skipped a beat when she came to a paragraph that described how in order to travel to the battles, a *Benandante* would send her spirit out of her body, usually at night. In the process she had to always lie flat on her back, otherwise her soul wouldn't be able to return. Such battles took place in the spirit realm and their outcomes determined whether the coming harvest would be plentiful, or if fire and pestilence might take hold of the fields. The other thing unique to good walkers was the way they were somehow associated with Livonian werewolves, and—

—and a larger shadow moved across the page and slid over Lía's hand before moving on. Curious, Lía turned her head to follow it, sensing the shadow cross the floor yet not quite seeing it disappear. Maybe people were moving about in the mezzanine above her; maybe it was lunch time? Yet all was quiet as ever. Even more so. The head librarian had left her post. There was no sign of Mrs Oliver. They might be in a tearoom eating sandwiches. Lía didn't wear a watch but the clock on the wall, she noticed now, had numerals but no hands, creating an oddly blank face. It had to be in the middle of being repaired.

But with the librarians absent, who'd stop someone simply walking out with a pile of books?

She didn't want to be so distracted; Lía felt in her clutch purse for coins and found a small handful of five cent pieces. She might as well photocopy these pages she was on and read them at home. Leaving the library now felt like a good idea; it was too empty and cold, and she had the impression that if she placed a hand on a wall she'd sense the spirits who were left to live in this place.

Lía noticed that the lightly dark down across the skin of her forearms had risen.

The photocopier was very loud, however there was no one in the empty space of the reading room to disturb. Lía copied one page and another, then stood a moment reading about another particularly Italian superstition.

This one was called *Malocchio*, the evil eye, revolving around an old idea that eyes emit rays in order to see, rather than that the eyes actually receive light. The evil eye that a witch or a very bad person could hurt someone with therefore worked when they used their powers to transmit curses through those rays.

Lía copied that page. The photocopier's loud rattle and the mechanical movement of its photoelectric light across glass didn't hide—

—the shapes and shadows of four very small people, but not, Lía thought, of children. These were only quick glances, yet she thought she saw the shadowed outlines of tiny women—almost doll-like—crossing somewhere in the mezzanine above. The photocopier stopped and Lía stared upward, her hand still holding an open text flat on the glass. With a prickling of the skin on her arms and an uncomfortable jangle at the nape of her neck, she thought she perceived shapes shift across a wall above, then drift toward the staircase coming down, then move to cover the front entrance in veils of black.

Lía backed away from the machine.

She wanted to go to the main counter and ring the bell. What if no one answered? She believed no one would. Somehow she was alone, completely alone. Every table was empty. Books had been abandoned. No librarian pushed a trolley collecting texts. Lía wanted to gather her things and run for the exit door but those shadows now curtained it in a sort of silky velvet. In her heart she understood this was a bad thing; those shadows, they shouldn't touch her, shouldn't even see her or find her. Lía backed further away, passing empty desks and chairs, moving into the stacks, those tall shelves holding musty books with all the history and thought of the world. The good and the bad of people and civilizations were contained in those tomes, and so she wanted to avoid the stacks as well, too much like dark tunnels now. Shadows continued to creep forward as if wanting to find and follow her.

But I'm alone; there's no one to help me; if I scream no one will come.

Now Lía was at the end of this long row. She edged herself around into the next and started to return the other way. When she crept to the start of this row of bookshelves she saw the vastly empty space of the reading room once again. Four shadows with nothing and no one creating them were stepping and stepping and stepping, tiny doll-like women or girls hunting for something Lía knew was herself. She was about to run down another tunnel of ancient books and try to find a different way

173

out when she saw what looked for all the world like a much larger, taller shadow extricate itself from the four, and this was a square-shouldered man, stepping steadily and slowly forward, with determination, looking, searching, wanting something.

The shadow-man raised his right hand and Lía perceived the unmistakeable shape of a gun.

The main exit had cleared. No shadowy veils, no velvety curtains. Lía ran with all her might toward it, crossing the open floor and scattering the pages she'd been unconsciously clutching in her hands. She wanted to scream for all the darkness of the world behind her—

—and struck a person entering the other way.

"Lía !"

"Teddy, what—"

He held her; held her by her shaking shoulders.

"This morning I rang the house. No answer. I took a chance you'd be studying here, like you said… But what's the matter?"

Every person in that place was back in their place; every eye was turned toward them. The clock had regained its hands and showed the time: 11:17. The head librarian glared unhappily from her position behind the front counter, pen poised over her ledger. Mrs Oliver was walking across the floor towards them, not so much annoyed as bewildered.

"Dear, are you all right? Your things, you've left them… These papers…"

She bent and picked several off the floor, but not all. Lía quickly rushed to pick up the rest, plus her bag, notepad and pens from the desk she'd been using.

"And this is a library," the head librarian spoke, stern as a headmistress. "Don't young people know enough to keep quiet?"

◆————————◆

In the passenger seat of the Stag, driving out of the city in the rain, Lía felt her shoulders still shaking.

"What do you want to do?"

"Take me all the way home."

"Do you think your dad will like that?"

"I don't care."

"What happened back there?"

"Nothing. It doesn't matter."

"You weren't in that library to study."

She wouldn't look at him. Lía chewed her bottom lip, distracted, wondering what those four small shadows were supposed to be, and the larger one, holding a gun. What could it all mean? Yet as soon as she asked herself the question she knew the answer: someone was looking for her, simple as that, as unmistakeable a fact as the downpour beading Teddy Quinn's windscreen. The wipers ticked rapidly.

Why was someone looking for me?

Because of what I am.

That made sense. She didn't need a disembodied voice to inform her. No ghost-boy's soulful eyes needed to make her see the truth.

And there was one more thing.

"Lía , why—"

"Listen," she interrupted him, "I want to ask you something."

"Good. Anything's better than keeping quiet."

"I want you to think a minute. Really think." Lía twisted her fingers together. "Why did you come to the library?"

"That's easy," he spoke, negotiating the wet traffic. "I won't pretend I understand how you did it, but I know you helped Nanny Viv. I wish she'd never got sick, but having her lying in that bed day after day and week after week was the cruellest thing ever."

"I stopped her heart."

She didn't need to glance at Teddy Quinn's profile to see how hard he had to swallow hard. After a moment he said, "Thank you."

"I don't want to be thanked." Silence fell between them once again, until Lía spoke. "You haven't answered me about the library."

"You've been on my mind. I keep thinking how you blamed me. How you were so angry. Maybe it was all my fault, I don't know, but I thought how alone that you maybe feel."

If I scream no one will come.

"It made me think something—"

When you need friends, you really need to call them.

"What did it make you think?"

"That maybe you could use a friend."

Lía thought she'd never be able to hold back another tear, yet as it happened once before, when she'd been in that giant elm and seen so much hurt in Teddy Quinn's eyes, a part of her wanted to reach out and touch his arm.

"Just take me home. I don't know what you're talking about."

Teddy didn't reply, except that he did. Lía heard him:

Jesus, but what can I do for this girl?

On an open road the Stag sped up as more rain pounded down.

Morning at the Blue Bird Café

Looked like it was going to rain, and Paul saw Lía hadn't brought an umbrella, but at the front of the State Library he didn't say anything about that.

"Good luck with the maths."

He was supposed to be at the office by ten, which was good, because he was early enough to first visit the Blue Bird Café. Two painkillers buzzed in his system and he was thinking he should go to a local doctor, that drilling sort of ache in his skull persisted so. More than that, there'd been that weird sort of disorientation: so many cut-up chats with Lía, and the way he'd scattered her adoption papers on the bedroom floor with absolutely no recollection of doing it.

At least the suit he was in looked good. His black leather shoes had a fresh coat of polish. His face; well, his face…

Mike Gavin wanted him in a meeting with a group of potential investors. Today Paul's job would be to describe Grandview in a local's terms, and outline how a new township would augment all that old-world character and natural habitat and not destroy it. In his mind Paul had a spiel ready, one that wasn't all bullshit and promises. It was still running through his head as he arrived at the café.

Federico had repaired the front door. Late breakfast service was busy. Paul couldn't see Candela working the floor and she wasn't sitting at a table with coffee and breakfast of her own. When he went to pay at the register Federico noticed him and came over, leaving three lemon meringue pies on a shiny counter.

"*Ciao*—Candela's friend."

"Yes."

"Your name is Paul."

"And you're Federico."

Paul received his change and left a tip. Federico studied the left side of Paul's face as three more people wanted to pay and leave.

"Bad stuff," Federico spoke *sotto voce*. "How many stitches?"

"Enough."

Paul noticed that Federico seemed to be doing more than studying the damage to his face; Paul felt himself being sized up.

"Candela's not working today?"

"You got a minute?"

"Sure."

Federico led Paul out of the café and down a few doors. Awnings protected them from the wet and rising gusts of wind.

"Is Candela all right?"

"More or less."

"What does that mean?"

"That bastard spoiled things for her." Federico shook his head. "Too much risk he'll come back for more."

"You fired her?"

"Never had to. Candela gave her notice. Now the woman needs a new job. A safe place. I met Donatello enough times. At first I thought he was okay, maybe a little quiet, but a good father. But then even I could see him getting darker. That's what Candela called it, you know the way she twists words? 'My 'usband he is darkening.'" Federico made an expression of disgust. "Separation. A baby."

"Where is she?"

"I suppose," Federico shrugged, "home."

"So why are you telling me all this?"

"She left something, in case you ever came looking for her."

"What?" Paul asked, feeling an unexpected rush.

The older man pulled aside his white smock and reached to his back pocket. He pulled out a very battered old wallet, his eyes friendly and very earnest.

"I need to ask you, *amico*. She's got that husband. You experienced it yourself." He held up his wallet. "So this is up to you. Someone smart might want to take a long walk in the opposite direction."

Paul raised his palm. Federico opened the wallet and gave him Candela's telephone number, in looping numerals carefully printed on a square of notepaper, a tiny bluebird drawn next to it.

◆━━━━━━◆

Paul walked up from the Gavin Realty car park. The receptionist at the front made a polite remark of sympathy about his face then sent him through to the offices. Things were already busy. Mike Gavin was at his desk with the door ajar. Three managers were in a quiet and very intense discussion with the boss, but Gavin sent them away as soon as he saw Paul.

"Dear lord, some idiot in a pub? I hope the cops are giving him hell."

Paul shifted uncomfortably, "Yes."

"What'll they charge him with?"

"I—I've preferred to leave things."

"You did report it," Mike Gavin frowned. "Right?"

Paul shook his head.

"What pub was it?"

"It wasn't actually a pub. It was a café. I don't want to make trouble for the owner."

Paul waited while Gavin gazed through a glassed half-wall at the open plan desks, mostly occupied.

"Tell me the story?"

"Let's talk about today's meeting."

"Tell me the story," Mike Gavin repeated, though not as a question.

"No."

Mike Gavin's gaze returned to Paul's face. Paul noticed he'd had a haircut recently: the style very short and trimmed, like a military buzz cut. In Gavin's eyes was something experienced and knowing.

"I used to box. Now I train youngsters, referee amateur fights. So I know what I'm looking at. You got done by someone not drunk at all. Someone who knew what he was doing. Look at your hands."

Paul moved them out of sight.

"Not a bruise on a knuckle, but your man was right-handed. That's why your left side's done. A drunk would have thrashed away. What caused this?"

"A misunderstanding."

"Problem over a woman?"

"I'm not answering that question," Paul replied, heat and anger rising.

"Someone attached, probably married."

"Bad things happen sometimes. I don't need to sit here and be interrogated."

"How about I told you to make sure you were always straight with me?"

"How about it's none of your business?"

"We're sitting in my business. I was about to introduce you to a classy group of people, owners of a bridal magazine and classical radio stations. And look at you, the guy I thought'd be my pitch man."

"Christ's sake."

"Lord's name," Mike Gavin warned. "Get out before they arrive."

Paul wasn't certain what he'd just heard.

"I told you my rules. Stay straight with me. So right here I'll be straight with you. You'll be paid from the moment we shook hands up to and including today. Go home and work out where lies and immorality have brought you."

"Are you crazy or something?"

If it was possible, Mike Gavin's eyes hardened even more.

Paul's face burned, his stitching and bruises inflamed. He stood and strode from the Gavin Realty office to its car park. The only good thing he knew about the morning was the drizzling rain, cool on his face.

❦

So he drives; he drives around. He finds a park in a green suburb and sits by the river, muddy and brown. He doesn't want to sit. So he takes a quick angry hike along a pathway by the riverbank, but the going becomes rough and muddy and he's in a suit and good shoes. Rain falls harder; anger and shame grow with it. Sheltering in his car the windscreen pearls and the world disappears. He starts up the Chrysler and drives through wet suburbs he doesn't recognise. He finds somewhere to eat but for no good reason sends a full plate of eggs back to the kitchen and ends up nibbling a corner of buttered toast someplace different. The coffee he drinks reminds him of muddy water. He should go home. He should go set Mike Gavin straight. A country hike with Lía and the dogs would do the world of good but she's at the library.

If only Anna were there; he'd give anything to talk to her.

Getting drunk would be nice too, but for the moment at least he's ruled that out.

At the top of Mt Coot-tha he stands at a lookout seeing a misted city he's not sure he loves or hates. The rain at least still feels good on his face, then he finds one other good thing in this day: a telephone number in his pocket.

A Witch at Work

In the room at the back of the house where Giancarlo Rosso lay, Donatello sat with his baby as his great-aunt checked the progress of his bullet wound. Donny Zap's recuperative powers and the witch's unguent were doing their good work; already he was fine.

Signora Celano finished up her morning task of preventing Giancarlo's bed sores. Three and sometimes even more times a day she forced his dead arms and legs into endless movements meant to keep the joints, ligaments and muscles as stretched and supple as possible. She turned him to one side, she turned him to the other. She massaged him thoroughly and lathered his body in creams and oils to keep his skin elastic. Of course she took his yellow water and cleaned his nappy, and bathed and shaved him. All this, yet never once had the old-man smell of him gone away—neither that, nor the putrid breath from his mouth, as if his insides rotted like old meat.

"Stay with him," Agata told her great-nephew, "until I'm finished with the morning's clients."

Yet again the witch had to marvel at the tenderness with which Donatello held his boy; not only that, but she knew how this baby was all Donatello, meaning the wolf line was in him. How did she know? Those extraordinary eyes, and when she was near the boy she felt the budding fire and rage that would grow as he grew, inescapable as time itself.

And so little Zo's life was going to be very, very useful.

"Are we ready?" she asked Celano.

"Everything."

Today's potion had been prepared: a recipe simple and direct. Celano had two granddaughters always willing to provide their menstrual blood, and plenty of it had been mixed with a set of other ingredients. The visitors arrived on the dot of the hour, wiping their feet politely and leaving their umbrellas in the foyer.

"Frau Neudorfer and daughter Fraulein Barbara."

Germans, that made a change. For a moment Agata worried the Neudorfers might not be all that superstitious, but in a moment she knew otherwise.

"My mother had the gift, but she's so long gone, Mrs Rosso." Frau Neudorfer spoke in an accent as broad as all of Australia. It was only Signora Celano's sense of the theatrical that had made her introduce them so. "She was blessed with visions and could even make predictions, but it's such a pity, I didn't inherit any of that and neither did my daughter."

"How old is this girl?"

"Eighteen in one month."

Barbara Neudorfer was so heavily pregnant she could barely make herself comfortable in her chair.

"So, Mrs Rosso, as I explained, what we need—"

Agata held up a dry finger. She already had a lock of the culprit's hair and a Polaroid photograph of him—a colourless, featureless, bland-as-water public service underling at least fifteen years older than the girl. Barbara, apparently, had met him at some sporting event. Barbara, apparently, hadn't known enough to keep her legs closed. Now this nothing of an individual wanted to marry her. The problem? The Neudorfers had too much money to want someone like that in the family and needed to persuade him to get out of the picture. So far he'd steadfastly refused; he might love the girl, he might actually want to be a father, or he might have understood there was a new world of wealth just waiting for him.

"But Mrs Rosso, he must go away and never come back."

"Exactly as you wish." Agata spoke as raspingly as she could. Clients preferred her that way; a witchy cackle fulfilled their nervous expectations. "He will not love your daughter, or the coming child, for very much longer."

"And if it's not a matter of love?"

"He will withdraw all the same."

"I was thinking of an accident. In a car...or crossing a street?"

The arrogance of the rich. It was always the moneyed ones who wanted death as a solution, murder ordered like a main course at an expensive restaurant.

"Be satisfied with what I give you."

"He mustn't pester Barbara anymore." Mrs Neudorfer sat back, her plump cheeks reddening. "Or have hopes."

Agata turned to the pregnant girl. "If you want him pestering you there's nothing I can do."

"I want him to go away."

"You need to want it with all your heart."

"With all my heart."

"Then let me pray."

They let her.

Agata Rosso's eyes now gazed into her four neatly arranged candles just as the eyes of her four dolls reflected the flickering flames. Today she believed there'd be no trouble; this thing with Barbara and the baby in her belly was straightforward. Agata's potion of virgin blood, powdered bone, garden herbs and the mucous of a frog's salivary sac, plus an incantation to the spirits, would do the job.

In moments the flames responded to Agata's prayer. In fact, it shocked her how today they were so alive: something was happening not quite as she'd intended. Mrs Neudorfer, a thoroughly unlikable woman, and Barbara, stupid as a stone, didn't interest them. At first Agata was confused, but now she understood. It was the fact of Donatello and Zo: their presence in this house completely engulfed the Neudorfers. The life force of the Zappavigna males—*wolf* males—utterly dominated these walls.

And so the spirits were drawn straight to them. Agata could only follow, and already she was moving from this place, from her chair, from the room.

There was no rain; no grey clouds; no sun or stars. The spirits in the four seasons bore her away. Agata was in the familiar guiding hands of *Estate, Primavera, Inverno* and *Autunno*, and where they helped her travel had nothing to do with buttery Barbara Neudorfer in the arms of that bland public servant; Agata found herself seeing Candela, so much in Donatello's thoughts and perhaps somewhere in the baby's pliant mind as well.

But is this the past or the future?

Candela was opening a door. Agata saw an individual in a navy suit with a white shirt dampened by rain, but she couldn't discern his face. Wife and mother were welcoming a man into her home.

A suit and shirt dampened by rain. It's raining outside.

This is now.

With a hacking cough Agata returned.

"What...what is it?" the mother asked.

Barbara, wide-eyed, grasped her mother's hand.

"Not today," the witch managed to croak, and this time the grating of her voice was perfectly real.

Immediately Signora Celano was in the room; it was her habit to always keep herself the other side of the door, an eternal vigilance. With polite yet firm urging she ushered the confused mother and frightened daughter out, telling them to return another day.

"But Agata, what did the spirits show you?"

"Where's Donatello?" Agata asked instead.

"Still with Giancarlo. And Zo in his arms, fast asleep."

Agata gathered her thoughts: Donatello, *povero scemo*. Donatello, you poor fool. To trust that no-good woman you still call your wife. You're a cuckold, do you know that? You wear the cuckold's horns.

"Leave me."

Agata took a long shaking breath. For Candela to welcome a man when she's still a wife, still suckling her baby.

"*Mille grazie, ragazze bellissime,*" Agata spoke to the dolls. "Thank you, beautiful girls."

The dolls' blank eyes, fixed to the flicker of the flames, wanted to know why they should be thanked.

It's our little wolf, little Zo. If the mother doesn't deserve to be a mother, then the baby stays with me. This information goes straight into Donatello's ear.

Is there anything that could be more perfect?

"Paolo, your face."

"I might need a bit more time before I'm presentable."

"But it improves. I will find a towel."

Candela led the few steps from the front door to her living room, what Paul saw was part of a combined kitchen. The flat was small and square. The building itself was square and ugly, a 1960s marvel of uninspired brickwork. His car was parked in the street out front. He'd rung the number on the notepaper, smiling at the bluebird. Candela didn't have a new job and was home. Lorenzo was with Donatello, one of their agreed days. She'd invited him over; Paul didn't have a clue what he was doing.

He saw a doorway into a bathroom and another door shut—the bedroom, he supposed. Coffee was percolating, giving off its aroma, and the mixed bunch of flowers on a side table had its own remarkable scent. Pictures were stuck to the walls, unframed old snaps, but what appeared to be a whole family history.

With the clean towel she gave him Paul took off his coat and dried his hair and face, careful with his left profile.

"You are dressed for work?"

"The fastest unemployment in history," and he told her the story.

"First your face and now this. I am a very bad piece of very bad news on you."

"Don't be silly." Paul liked the way her expression changed, something lighter in her eyes. "So who are these people?" he asked.

"Grandparents and generations." Candela showed him the pictures on the closest wall. "My mother when she was young. See how she stands with a bicycle? And my father plus his brothers."

The photographs were images of village life, all as rural as Paul's early life in Grandview but with a poverty so obvious and abject that was nothing at all like what he'd experienced. He noticed how in these pictures, even being faded black and whites, there were no folk as dark as Lía—of course that made sense. These pictures were from a life in the far north; Lía had been adopted from the far south.

"See this man with his bag? He has collected snails to sell. This one here has a sparrow he has caught. Someone with enough coins will have meat in their pot tonight. And these children, their dolls are made from rags. Buttons for eyes."

"Did you have one?"

"All of us. Our mothers sewed them and when we were older we have sewed them for others."

"So Agata Rosso's call sounded pretty good?"

"Even in a village like this we have the movie theatre. There we learn of better lives in other places. We see movie stars with lovely clothes and more money than it is possible to believe. The newsreels show us cities full of happy people. For the young a life in a new country is the dream we have all had. No one imagines it can go bad."

"Candela," Paul spoke, "it can still be really good."

"You think so?"

"I'm positive."

She hesitated a moment. He considered more of the photos.

"Let me guess, this one's your father?"

"An uncle. Here is my *papà* as a baby, always the youngest."

"Where are you?"

"Find me."

He did. The Candela he was looking at was maybe ten or twelve years of age, large eyes full of a child's innocence. Something moved in him to see her that way, something that reminded him of Lía, something that reminded him of Anna.

You see someone like that and you want to hold them. You want to tell them everything's all right. And if it isn't, you want to be the one who'll make everything better.

"Where are these men working?" In a distinct grouping of photographs men were inside some sort of dilapidated warehouse.

"All of them, a family business." She shrugged, looking a little embarrassed. "My father and my father's father they have made their professions in candle-making."

"Candela," he realised.

"No imagination at all."

He had to smile at that. "What's the family name?"

"Candiliere." She bowed her head, even more embarrassed. "Somewhere in some generation too far away, they have decided to take this name."

"Candela Candiliere. I've never heard a name quite so—so mellifluous."

"This means?"

"Musical."

Paul realised they'd moved closer to one another. He wanted to put a hand on her shoulder. The aroma of the brewing coffee, the scent of the flowers, they were nothing compared to her presence. Candela's skin had a kind of subtle perfume that didn't seem like perfume at all.

"I am still married," she said, her voice softer. "In this country the separation must be twelve months."

"Twelve months," Paul said, hesitating. "That's how long it's been since Anna."

"You loved her?"

"Yes."

"You still do."

He couldn't reply because it was true. He still did, and dreamed of her too.

"Paolo," Candela spoke, "it is too soon. Too soon for each of us. But can you know what?"

"What?"

"I am very lucky to find in you a friend."

It took a moment before a smile could come to his face, yet when it did he could see how much Candela liked it. That smile hurt his scar, the livid bruising, but when Candela leaned forward and kissed him there all pain seemed to evaporate. She took his hands.

And then he had to leave, and she let him, because in another moment they'd both let themselves go.

Virna Khamitova and George Bellman

Saturday evening, and Karl Haberman smiled at Virna Khamitova's arrival into his bedroom, her honey-blonde hair down, wearing a sort of hippie outfit that he found amusing. Her ensemble was a suede mini skirt to accentuate her long legs, white leather boots, a brightly patterned shirt with a braided waistcoat over it, and a very colourful Aztec sash as a headband knotted over her flowing hair. A throwback to the late 1960s or a '70s update, he didn't know which, though he knew it suited her. All manner of clothing suited Virna and so did its removal. She carried a very small suitcase and made him shift over from where he lay in his kimono, sipping a mint julep he'd made himself. She set the small case down on the other side of the bed.

"How do you like your new apartment?"

"Mr H," she said without a hint of a smile, "you're about to find out."

Virna took what she wanted from the suitcase without letting him see what it was, then disappeared into the adjoining bathroom. Haberman poured himself a third mint julep from the glass pitcher at his bedside.

Virna had meant her new outfit to be enchantingly transgressive, yet the moment she emerged in her schoolgirl's uniform—the skirt even shorter than the mini dress she'd been wearing, with a tight white blouse that barely contained her breasts, with little white socks, polished leather shoes and her hair parted down the middle and tied in twin braids—Haberman was struck by a leap of inspiration the complete opposite of what Virna had expected.

"Does this please you?"

"Nonpareil, my love. However something else would please me more."

"Anything," she purred, crawling across the bed towards him.

VENERO ARMANNO

"Why not demonstrate your culinary skills? Might you take yourself down-stairs and cook me a steak? I'd like it with potatoes and gravy. And also, if no bother, this pitcher of mint julep is done, so let's have another."

The look in Virna Khamitova's face told him that no one—Pavel Dolgo-polov, for instance—had ever had such blind gall as to order her to the kitchen.

"*Haberman*," Virna warned, yet she slid away, no fool, understanding the dulcet tones of the Haberman voice rarely reflected the Mr H inside.

———————◆———————

Well, it was Virna's schoolgirl outfit that lit the bulb over Haberman's head. He needed to speak with a man unlikely to be spending a Saturday night at home in his slippers. Haberman started with a telephone call to his accountant and sometime business manager Max Eureka, who definitely would be home in his slippers.

"Which of my ex-red-lights are more illegal than most these days?"

"You mean servicing homosexuals?"

"No, the underage inflection."

Where the sick Haberman of so recently would have gotten himself a driver, the thought of being confined to a vehicle with Donatello—after what he'd seen of the grunt, and still didn't like, much less understand—gave him a shiver. In the meantime Virna had created a dish of perplexing inedibility. The steak wasn't overcooked or undercooked, yet somehow managed to be both tough and tasteless. The potatoes and gravy looked worse than the muck the stone witch produced, but with none of her fragrance or flavour. He left Virna's dinner mostly untouched and told her to clean up, enjoying the flash of fury in her eyes. By the time he was ready to leave the kitchen remained a mess and she was in front of the television with her bare feet crossed on a teak coffee table. A self-created mint julep was in one hand. He liked the fact that she didn't pout. He appreciated the indignant, fixed tilt of her head, the simmering energy to her.

Now that was Virna Khamitova.

Max Eureka's information gave him four establishments to investigate. They'd know him at every place, of course, and each would be nervous about what had happened to Hassan Nasser and Ronald Lundy. The police were investigating, barely, and Haberman had received a quiet word that sooner rather than later he could expect to be interviewed. Police and newspaper reports hadn't yet revealed the details of what had been found on that Pilothouse boat, but Haberman had seen a headline, 'Massacre On

192

Pleasure Cruiser'.

Best to keep his mind on the night ahead.

In his early days Haberman had rarely carried a gun. Instead, as sort of insurance, he'd always kept on himself a simple, palm-sized box cutter. Before leaving he'd found one in a kitchen drawer. He wouldn't need it tonight, he was certain, yet something inside welcomed the return of the old Haberman. The younger Haberman.

At his first stop they hadn't seen his man in a month, but at the Lucky Tiger Golden Spa:

"Mr Bellman? Yes, he's here, sir."

In room number seven he discovered Bellman with three underage girls. Haberman waited as they quickly dressed and left. Bellman, hirsute as an ape, remained in the bed and covered his lower parts with a sheet, which was a mercy.

"I'm not guilty of anything, Mr H."

"We're all guilty of something, but for now I have a small request."

"Yes?"

"There's a girl I need to find. She's school age, new to this town and with skin a colour other than white. She has no mother but perhaps a father. She's so new to town, in fact, that I'm thinking she either is or will soon be a new enrolment in some local school. If that proved true, how long would it take a school inspector such as your good self to identify her?"

"I only cover public schools."

"Cover all schools. Private, religious, everything. Find a way."

"Well, there are precedents that would allow my jurisdiction to—"

"Lovely," Haberman cut him off. "Use whatever precedent makes you happy. Just make me a list of possibilities."

"But what you've described, it's so broad. Non-white means a thousand possibilities. Can't you tell me a little more, even what area she lives in?"

"That I don't know. But I'm told she's very powerful."

"A sportsperson?"

"More mentally or intellectually. Her eyes might be quite stunning."

"But how can I—?"

"We all learn to work within unfair parameters."

"Mr H, do you know how many schools you're talking about?"

"As many as the number of people who'd be fascinated by your nocturnal activities?"

"Wh-when would you like the information?"

"Tomorrow's Sunday, which I hope you'll make productive. The close of business Monday."

"But—"

Haberman left the room, then the building, happy to be out of that place and back inside the comforting interior of his Mercedes. Heavier rainfall blotted the windscreen. He ran the wipers. George Bellman might be able to help, or he might not, yet something else was on Haberman's mind now, a curious realisation: he'd felt no push or pull towards that massage parlour's young employees. His libido was high, like some super-charged battery, but the idea of the Golden Tiger's offerings, or even those of a place like Gorton's so far away in Berkeley Square, simply didn't entice him. Virna Khamitova was a stupendous gift, but his need, the real thing he yearned for, was now very, very specific.

Despite his antipathy towards her, Agata Rosso had created a new picture for his imagination: a girl somehow powerful, with dark skin and unmissable eyes.

On the Mercedes' steering wheel he found his hands had tightened, then he pulled the car away from the kerb.

A New School in a New Town

Teddy Quinn stood beside Mike Gavin with the staff gathered around. He wasn't lapping up the attention but wished instead that Lía hadn't put such a wall between the two of them. Maybe she'd never forgive him for taking her to Mountford; then again, when he'd dropped her home after whatever the hell it was that had shaken her up at the State Library, he thought he'd seen a softening in her eyes. If she'd been older, if she'd been any kind of woman he was used to, then he might at least have had a chance at understanding her mood.

She'd climbed out of his Stag into the rain, her dogs wet and gathering around her. Lía's father's car hadn't been there. Teddy had wanted to follow her into Rosso House, but no, she was just a sixteen-year-old kid, he needed to leave her alone. Probably he'd never see her again. The final nail in the coffin was when Teddy heard about what happened between Lía's dad and Mr Gavin: fired two minutes into his first day on the job. A disaster, that, in more ways than one, because it meant Teddy didn't have any sort of connection to Lía at all.

Well, gloomy it might be, but life went on; work marched on.

This stormy Monday morning, shaking rain from his hair, Teddy had gone to Mike Gavin's office. He presented his boss with not one but two signed contracts, sales he'd managed to close while other folk were still having their cereal or bacon and eggs.

Now Teddy faced the gathered retinue.

"So, everyone, persistence and determination has got our young Theodore to the top of the sales board one more time."

Mike Gavin, making a nice speech, and Teddy nodding on automatic. Despite the congratulations his thoughts were far away, still on Lía. No

195

connection left, yet for some reason he was experiencing a vivid recollection of a particular moment, of something he'd said to her:

When it comes to mathematics and mathematics alone, I'm a bit of a whiz. If you ever need any help…

"So, let's hear from the man of the moment."

"You solve a problem," Teddy said, as lightheaded as if he was drinking champagne instead of a 10:00am instant coffee, "by working through the items in brackets first."

"So that's the secret to success." Mike Gavin positively chuckled, personally passing around the Black Forest cherry torte he'd quickly ordered in for the occasion. "Now explain what the hell that's supposed to mean."

"It's easy as long as you don't forget that next you do the multiplications and the divisions, followed by additions and subtractions."

"If you want to move into the accounting department," Mike Gavin said to this kid not making a lick of sense, "you'll be wasting your God-given talent." He still chuckled, but leaned in to make sure there was no whiff of alcohol on Teddy's breath.

Teddy Quinn tried to hold himself together. His thoughts about Lía Munro were making him feel like a badly functioning fluorescent tube, blinking in and out of the Gavin Realty offices. Even he didn't quite know what he was talking about.

"Mr Gavin, I'm sorry…"

"Back to work everyone, take your cake with you, celebration's over. Teddy, you come with me. It's time we took a look at extending your sales territory."

Teddy Quinn's eyes moved to the rain falling outside as if that was where he preferred to be, then Mike Gavin had him by the shoulder.

* * *

Monday morning at the school and little wonder Lía couldn't concentrate. For days since the State Library she'd thought only about those shadows, whatever it was that might be searching for her, and now she was supposed to be interested in these sheets of paper and their questions. She would have liked to screw them up and throw them at the feet of Sister Mary Angela supervising her equivalency tests. Outside this small classroom, empty except for the two of them, she sensed hundreds of girls, normal classes were underway.

What's this school or any school got for someone who's killed an old woman? What am I supposed to say to girls whose secret hearts I can read more easily than these pages?

Lía had come to a sheet of maths problems, the stuff she remembered Teddy Quinn was supposed to be so good at.

Lía chewed the end of her pencil; Sister Angela passed her a sympathetic smile.

History, modern and ancient, had come first, then English. In the first hour of this test Lía had written easy paragraphs about Hammurabi's Code then a really quite informed treatise on the construction of the Berlin Wall, started August 1961. Next there'd been a full chapter from *To Kill a Mockingbird* to analyse. All straightforward, and if her mind wasn't wandering so, then sort of fun.

"Twenty minutes, dear," Sister Angela spoke, "then we're done."

The ghost-boy had told her that when she needed a friend she really needed to call. In that worst moment at the library, Teddy Quinn had been there. Then she'd read such a clear message in his mind, or maybe it was in his heart:

Jesus, but what can I do for this girl?

Lía concentrated on the page in front of her.

Okay Teddy, this stupid equation's as long as my arm. Where do I start?

Lía froze.

You solve a problem by working through the items in brackets first.

Her pencil didn't move.

He hears me.

The Story of Lily Cheung

*S*o you heard me, Teddy, when I needed your help. Does the word 'friend' have a better definition than that? I don't think so.

It's still Monday while I'm writing this letter, but late in the day, and the headmistress Sister Sweetman was already ringing by the time Dad and I got home from the test. She told him just how great I'd done, except for the mathematics. You were right there, Teddy, and I won't pretend I know how you were so ready to help me, but just before it was time to put my pencil down and hand over my answers, I scrubbed out everything you told me. I don't want to be a cheat; I don't want my life to be a cheat. In small ways and big ways I want to be true.

Whatever that might mean.

So Teddy what am I?

I still don't know.

Still, I want to explain whatever bits I can. I think you've earned that. You've earned it because you wanted to be a friend. You can't imagine what it means for me to be able to say something like that.

So let me tell you what's real, best I can.

It starts back in my old life, in Kowloon, and with a girl named Lily Cheung.

◆━━━━━━◆

*M*ostly in school I was good at all subjects except the one you already know about. Some sports were okay too. Outside of school my mother encouraged me to read books and learn to draw and paint, and I loved all of that. She tried me on the piano as well but I didn't have the ear or the touch. I'm one of those people who can't get enough music while not having the slightest aptitude for making music. My mother was a natural, though, and she was interested in just about everything. That's what I'll always remember about her, this sort of constant curiosity. For a long time she was a sociologist. Her field was child development. She loved children and she loved me. It was

199

as simple as that and I was as lucky as that.

Dr Anna Munro née Mosca, my ma.

My father worked hard in his business but he was never distant. When he came home late he usually opened my door. He wasn't supposed to wake me but mostly he did, and we'd have a little chat about the day and what I'd done. It was just a normal sort of life and there was nothing to it. Hong Kong was my home and I never thought I should be anywhere else. My parents were my parents and even if I didn't look a thing like them and people stared when we were in the street I learned not to let it bother me. We were who we were and that was fine—right up until Ma got sick and went downhill.

It happened so fast I never had time to understand one thing before the next thing came along. It was horrible for her. She must have felt like she was on a roller coaster that always ended up going down. Nothing came slowly—her dying was a rush. There were operations. Ma's hands lost their steadiness. Our piano stopped being played. She had to give up work and if I ever found her crying I knew it wasn't for herself but for the children she couldn't help any more.

Soon she was in hospital for longer stays and then came the last stay and I spent every hour possible with her. The more she faded the more I started to feel strange inside, and it never helped that step by step and day by day my father started to carry this new stink on his breath. I knew what it was and you probably do too.

The connection I had with your grandmother in Mountford? My ma lying in her hospital room was the first time I felt something like that, us not talking but me feeling like I could see or feel what was going on in her mind. It wasn't direct like a conversation. Instead I felt the love she had for me and for my dad and the memories she had of growing up. That was really strong in her, life on her farm so long ago, and that made me feel like maybe I needed this mysterious place called Grandview for myself. Later, when Dad decided we'd move back to Australia, I kept aiming this thought at him: Grandview. *And that's how it worked out.*

Ma died when I was alone with her in her hospital room. My dad was there that afternoon but we'd been sitting so long he decided to go get himself an instant coffee and a drink and some chocolates for me. He came back and Ma was gone. She and I were holding hands. One moment I felt my mother and the next moment her body was as empty as a table or a chair. The room was empty too; what I mean is, she wasn't there anymore. I lost my mother and she went somewhere else. In those days I never imagined there could be anything different. To be alive is to be alive and to be dead is to be dead. Now I know that some people get stuck in between.

That wasn't my ma, and of course it's not Mrs Badger anymore either.

So that left me and my father, and a nice housekeeper he ended up employing named

Mrs Wu. And this is where I get to Lily Cheung.

Lily was a nice girl in my class. We liked each other and sometimes went to the movies. We listened to records. One day she kissed me on the mouth but it didn't mean anything because afterwards we just giggled and never even spoke about it. After Ma died I went back to classes and things were mostly the same. Until, I don't know why, another girl in our class had money stolen from the purse she had in her schoolbag. It was a lot of money because she was supposed to go into town and put a deposit on her family's holiday travel tickets, and Lily Cheung pointed her finger at me and said, "There's the person who stole your money."

Everyone believed her because why wouldn't they?

I had no idea why Lily would accuse me of something so awful and I begged her to go tell everyone the truth. When we were absolutely alone with no one to overhear she said: "You're Miss Misery Eyes and you bring everyone down."

"Misery Eyes?"

"Miss Misery Eyes! You don't even know that's what we've been calling you?"

It was less than a month since Ma died and Lily was probably right, I probably was miserable in my eyes and everywhere else too, but why should a friend hate me for that?

Then maybe I understood just a bit.

Lily stole that money and she chose the easiest and most obvious scapegoat. I'd only vaguely noticed that the other girls, while sort of sympathetic, hadn't really kept themselves close to me since Ma died. It never crossed my mind they found me a downer. It never occurred to me that maybe their schoolgirlish spirits didn't have room for someone so depressed. I actually had to sit down and figure it out. That's when I realised I had no friends except for one, Lily, and in fact I had exactly zero.

What happened next was like seeing all those scattered images and thoughts from my mother's mind. I was thinking about Lily Cheung and just like that I saw a picture of her father strapping her naked back with his belt, and her mother turning the other way, and this happening just about all the days of Lily's life. She'd never told me about any of that, and I would never have guessed.

That girl's purse with her family's money for a holiday? I saw that Lily would use it to escape Kowloon for the Chinese mainland. She wanted to lose herself in some big teeming city. All that came to me without any effort at all, and so did the image of a tree with rotted roots right at the edge of our biggest sportsground. Turns out it was the place where Lily had hidden the fat roll of notes. She meant to collect it after the last bell, when everyone was gone and the school grounds were quiet.

What Lily didn't count on was me, normally quiet me, seeing red.

I heard I was going to get called to the headmistress's office, and at that moment I *felt like everything about the last year had come to a head. Lily was in a huddle with some other girls and I shoved her hard. Instantly there was a crowd. The words that made me hang myself came straight out of my own mouth. I told everyone where to go to find the money because of where Lily hid it.*

Lily went crazy and screamed things at me I won't write down here. I'll just stick with the one she spat again and again: "Miss Misery Eyes!"

I retaliated with everything I'd seen about her father and his belt and her mother with her back turned. Lily looked like she'd been stripped naked. She tried to shut me up with her long fingernails. I stepped backwards once, twice, three times, but now Lily was hysterical. She managed to grab me and tore off my collar. I pulled her hair and she raked my cheek.

Then her long fingernails were trying to get at my eyes.

Stop it now, Lily, stop!

But it didn't come out in words.

Lily made this wet growly gasp like a fish bone got caught in her throat. She let go of me and froze where she was, standing crooked. Her face turned pink then red. Veins stood out in her forehead and neck. The extra-big circle of excited girls saw Lily's eyes bugging out. She kept making a strangulated choking sound and urine gushed down her stockinged legs, so much of it coming that it was like she hadn't peed in days. Then, bang, she dropped like she'd been shot in the head.

Lily Cheung, dead. Lily Cheung spontaneously expired right in front of us. That's what everyone thought. That's what I thought. One girl screamed. One girl cried. One girl ran away fast as she could.

There were the smarter do-gooders who performed things they'd learned in first-aid classes. More quick-thinkers dashed to the sick bay for our two full-time nurses. Another contingent took off for the main building to call the principal and the higher-ups.

No one touched me. No one came close. If anything, girls backed away.

A trio of teachers hauled me away. The deputy kept me in her office while the headmistress tried to figure out what happened. It all took forever. There was an ambulance for Lily, and questions and explanations that didn't include me. All this time I wondered if Lily was dead, but I wasn't crying. Instead I felt a sort of coldness, even an air of something like superiority. Just look what I'd done; look what I could do.

Those feelings crumbled when the headmistress finally strode in with the stolen money, personally collected from that rotted tree root.

"I've spoken to your father. He's on his way."

Then two hard questions.

"Why did you steal this money?"

"What did you do to Lily?"

Later when my dad was bundling me out through the school gates I heard something new, and so did he, from the girls gathered at the iron gates and along the fences. It was a nasty singsong:

Miss X-Ray Eyes.

Miss X-Ray Eyes.

Miss X-Ray Eyes.

My coldness was well and truly gone. I blubbered like a baby, "But what if Lily's dead?"

"Nonsense. It's schoolgirl histrionics. I'm sure there's not a thing wrong with her."

Except that when we'd been fighting in the schoolyard I'd pictured grabbing Lily by the throat and choking the life out of her, and the feel of that, somewhere in my head, had been thrilling and beautiful.

The next day at assembly it was announced that after her overnight stay in hospital Lily had been released. Some girls had already heard that Lily swore she'd never set foot again in the Good Hope Girls' School. Soon it was the same for me.

Teachers heard my new name, 'Miss X-Ray Eyes', and I think some of them even believed it. Whatever the case I was branded a thief and a liar, and in the principal's office my father and I were informed that I was no longer welcome in this place. That night we looked at each other and in the exact same moment knew our lives in Kowloon, in Hong Kong itself, was over.

The one good thing? We had somewhere to go. A country where my school record wouldn't follow. Dad called it Home and if Ma was alive she would have as well.

But I was already thinking something, Teddy.

Maybe home's the one thing I'll never have, and you know what? I'm thinking it again.

———◆———

Lía stopped there.

She hadn't thought to write so much. Her bedroom was quiet except for the sound of rain well and truly settling in. Her dogs were with her but weren't asleep.

Lía glanced at the pages but didn't reread them. If there was a better way to finish she couldn't find it. So she slid her letter into a large-size envelope and wrote Teddy Quinn's name on the front. There were stamps downstairs. Lía knew Teddy's telephone number but not his address. Well, tomorrow or the next day she'd post it to Gavin Realty.

Just as she was about to seal the envelope she saw her photocopied pages from the State Library. *Benandanti*, *malocchio*; maybe there'd be something in that to interest Teddy. She added the pages to the envelope then left it on her study desk.

As she did both Buster and Dakota jumped to their feet, ears pricked. Buster of course started barking and barking at the sound of a strange car arriving.

Possible Means
of Escape

Lía was keeping Buster quiet in her room, and Candela sat in the kitchen with Lorenzo in her arms. Her eyes were faraway but tears hadn't streaked her cheeks.

"So what has happened," Candela spoke, "Agata Rosso knows you have come to my flat."

Paul studied the seriousness of her face before he said, "How would she know that?"

"One way or another way. It doesn't matter. Of course she does not know who you are. She only knows of a man, and this she tells to Donatello, and of course to Donatello this is the end of the world."

"What happened?" Paul asked, quietly pulling a chair up so that he could sit beside her.

"What I have learned about Agata is that she fears Donatello will lose his son. I do not trust this woman. She has never had her own children. I believe she wants him to herself."

"But what did your husband do?"

"The typical. He comes to my flat like a hurricane. *Who is this man? What am I doing with him? Wasn't one beating enough, or is it someone else, you whore?* He demands now he must have Zo all the time. He breaks things."

"You managed to get rid of him?"

"For that day."

"You could have come straight here."

Candela made herself breathe evenly. Paul didn't move. Zo's eyes were heavy but didn't quite close.

"He gives me one more chance. One more chance to come back to him. This morning he is at my door demanding the right answer. I give him the wrong one, still believing that somewhere inside that stupid head he can be reasonable."

Candela pushed heavy locks of her hair from her neck. Paul saw finger marks deep in the skin, deep in the flesh. She slid the shoulder of her dress down to reveal her long back. Marked the same way, and so dark.

Paul went to the sink and poured a glass of water, which he set on the table before her.

"Candela," he said, keeping the loathing that made him want to scream out of his voice, "it's time for the police."

"I made this telephone call. I am transferred to a detective. This man has not helped me before, he has helped Donatello. He and his friends and all their friends are in the circle with Haberman. So I put the telephone receiver down without speaking." Again Candela evened her breathing, now considering Zo. Paul saw how much strength her baby gave her—or how much strength she would have for him. "I try to imagine where I can run."

"What do you need?"

"First, I am so sorry—"

"I'm glad you're here. So just tell me."

"I was not sure... I could not convince myself until I was driving far away from my flat..."

"Convince yourself about what?"

"Something I have been thinking, imagining. Donatello does not know this, but when we separated I have applied for Lorenzo's passport. It is hidden. Mine is hidden also, to make sure he can never steal it and trap me."

"Wait, you mean you want to leave the country?"

"Yes."

"That's more trouble."

"The divorce court is more than a half-year away and even the lawyer knows the truth. Donatello will never live by agreements. In this case it is not enough to wait for the law. And it is not enough to get in my car and drive away from this city."

"You'd be a fugitive. And wouldn't he know where to find you?"

"I will not go home or anywhere he can follow me. I have friends in the north of Spain and Donatello does not know them, friends before the courting and marriage. I will start there but always keep going. Until I find a small corner of the world where he can never find us. I will raise Zo and make a new life."

Paul tried to think this through. Candela met his eyes.

"So," he said, "you've already started."

As if relieved by his response Candela sipped from the glass of water, her hand almost but not quite steady. Paul knew she was more than justified but her plan would shift the law from her side to Donatello's; she'd indeed be a fugitive, kidnapping a man's son. Yet there was no way he'd try to stop her. What she wanted wasn't impossible, but she'd need to move fast. If he was going to help her, so would he.

"Where are these passports hidden?"

"At my flat. I am so stupid."

"You're shaken up. You can't think of everything. But it's not safe to go back there. Stay this evening. We'll go first thing in the morning and pick them up with whatever else you need. Like you said, no one knows me, no one knows about the connection to this house. You'll be safe here. Is your passport in your married name?"

"It is."

"Would you be listed at the airport, Customs, to stop you from travelling?"

"If Donatello starts to suspect, maybe yes…but not yet."

"Good."

"Paolo, my friends, we studied together at the university. Two couples from Spain who returned to Spain after finishing degrees at the University of Milano, where we all were. We had interests together, things Donatello doesn't care about. They are still in Spain and have said that if it was ever needed, they will send money—"

"Forget it. Money transfers take time, which you don't have. I'll cover it for now. You'll get air tickets tomorrow for the first flights available. If you're sure."

"I am sure."

"Then that'll beat any authorities getting involved."

"What do you mean?"

"Well, I'm no expert in something like this, but if we get you and Lorenzo one-way tickets, paid cash, then there are no tell-tale cheques and less of a trail."

"How can you think of all this?" She almost managed to smile.

"Consider it my revenge on your husband for my face."

"Paolo, I will get your money to you one day, but you understand I will never come back?"

"That's okay."

"Why?"

"I like Spain. I like Spain a lot."

He wanted to touch her hand; maybe she wanted him to. What seemed more important was this plan and making it work. That, and the way Candela held her baby. Wasn't that the real thing? For now he was a helper and a helper only—maybe one day something more, but that sort of a day could only be far, far in the future.

Now he needed to go upstairs and find a way to explain all this to Lía. Introduce her to their unexpected guests. And tell her, promise her, his drinking was forever done.

Before he could move, Lorenzo reached for Paul as if only now realizing there was someone with his mother. The baby's eyes were bright and brightening still. Zo twisted hard in Candela's arms.

So Paul took her baby and cradled him; it reminded him of the first time he held that beautiful, abandoned baby he and Anna would name Lía, all those years ago.

"If Donatello could see this he would kill you."

The guy wants to kill me already, so what's the difference?

Zo's head went to Paul's shoulder; the palm of Paul's hand was on his back.

Donatello's Dream

In another wet evening he went again to Candela's flat, wishing he'd never laid a finger on her, ready to beg forgiveness—yet when there was no answer at her door he felt his blood howl and he kicked his way in. That ugly small place, he tore it apart, and himself he tore apart with it, then his misery and rage ate him alive and he needed to collapse and sleep, and with that sleep came a dream.

In this dream he was no longer a man shouting at his woman that she should return home with their baby. Instead he was an animal running through thick woodlands, running as hard as he could because he knew what was after him.

This time it's men carrying the things he fears most. Not guns. There are no guns.

It's axes.

If they catch him and bind him these ignorant villagers will give him a trial, the type where it won't matter what he confesses or doesn't confess; the procedure he'll face is inscribed in Law. He'll be tied to a wheel and hot pincers will be used to tear off his flesh; an executioner will break his arms and legs with the flat of an axe; then he'll be beheaded and dragged away in two pieces.

So is a man-wolf dealt with.

There's even worse, of course. For the Law decrees that if the man-wolf has a wife and children they must also suffer. The unnatural beast's entire family will be tied to wooden posts and burned alive, with the man-wolf's headless corpse staked between them.

So is the Dark dealt with.

Then run and run, Donatello, don't stop, not until you find yourself a safe cave to hide in, and if you have to sleep, do it, but always with one eye open.

◆━━━━━━━◆

Donatello Zappavigna woke with his temples throbbing hard, his body curled into a ball inside a dark, enclosed space. He felt drained and exhausted, and remained perfectly still, expecting to discover that he'd secreted himself inside a cave, maybe deep in some forest. Through the pulsing ache in his skull he listened for sound, for movement, trying to picture where he was and who might be near. Dull splinters of light gleamed through the cracks around him. Had villagers trapped and caught him in the night, tied him with rope and shoved him into a hole? Maybe. Naked fear made him tremble. Donatello held his knees close to his chest, Haberman's stitches still pinching.

Wait, that wound was made by Nasser's pistol. Not the blow of an axe.

Dove sono adesso? Where am I now?

There were no villagers; there was no woodland he'd run through; no axes were raised over his head. He'd come to Candela's flat and like a fool and a coward in Candela's flat he was hiding.

With a gasp of comprehension Donatello pushed the makeshift barricade with one hand. The curled mattress from Candela's bed slid a few inches along the floor. He kicked out with his feet. Pillows and a chair fell backwards. What had he been thinking? Lost in some kind of dream or nightmare of being hunted he'd created his own little cave.

And *caro Gesù*, look at this disgrace, because not only had he made a child's fortress, but he'd fouled himself too.

Or a man-wolf had marked his territory, the odour was so strong.

The transformation. It had happened right in this flat. He'd torn the man part of himself to pieces, then he'd torn Candela's flat apart.

His clothes, they were in shreds.

Morning, and Candela hadn't returned.

All this rage for nothing. He hadn't achieved a thing. His wife and baby must still be with that man Zia Agata had seen. The next problem, then: how to track them down? Staggering to the bathroom Donatello splashed his face and the back of his neck. A nylon stocking hung off a rail, mocking him. He felt the ache of being away from his boy. Which pain was worse, the one in his head or this dreadful separation from his boy?

Donatello tried to shake away the clouds that wouldn't let him think straight. He leaned where he was at the bathroom sink. If he found the

English then wouldn't he also find Candela and Lorenzo? That made sense. So how to hunt down a man whose name you don't even know?

The question seemed insoluble. It made his temples pound. He needed to sleep properly; he needed cold fruit and chilled drinks for the dry dirt of his throat; he needed an answer.

Donatello raised a fist and smashed it into the bathroom mirror, then regarded himself in a hundred shards. How, how, how to find the English? Well, wait... The Blue Bird Café was where he'd been sitting so nicely with Candela, so maybe the boss would know something. Yes, that was the way. First Donatello needed to get rid of this awful stench clinging to him like a dead body; he needed to lay himself down and draw strength from sleep. Later in the day he'd get his answer from Federico, and something else too: he'd have the man cook him one of his famous fat-rimmed steaks, this one served sizzling, bloody and thick. Then he'd take him by the neck and make him say everything he knew.

Donatello nodded to his thousand reflections, the fingers of his right hand curling.

So they might take a neck. Not Federico's.

Candela's.

Dio mio. He saw it again.

Donatello's hands on his wife; his fist against the mother of his boy.

What has he done?

Skull needing to crack in two, Donatello backs away from the mirror, stumbling out of the disaster of the flat as if to run and run yet again.

Candela's door, smashed open. Here in broken bits and pieces Paul saw the grim facts of her life. Everywhere things were shattered, overturned and torn; then there was that pungent wet stain in the bedroom, like something from a marsh or fresh animal spoor.

Candela lifted a corner of the carpet: the passports were underneath. She collected everything she needed and took family photographs from the wall. Paul waited, holding Zo, worrying for the sound of heavy footsteps up the stairwell.

"Wait. One more thing."

They'd nearly been out of there. She returned to open a drawer and retrieve something Paul didn't recognise.

"Lorenzo's baptism candle."

Wrapped in cellophane and tied with a gold bow, the candle was long and white. Like any other candle, but embossed with a red crucifix and with Lorenzo's name engraved along the side.

"New life," Candela spoke, meaning her candle.

"After the bank, travel agency and shops," Paul told her.

She half-smiled; she understood.

Candela had a small suitcase, a shoulder bag and a handbag, more than enough.

A Long Tuesday
Evening (i)

During the day, using George Bellman's list, Haberman visited a dozen schools in the guise of William Monk—supposedly a freelance investigative journalist researching the new-world experiences of migrant children. George Bellman's authority as a school inspector meant Haberman was welcomed into classrooms where the correct young female arrivals had recently enrolled. More difficult for Bellman had been the task of determining, at a distance, skin colour, and who had mothers and who didn't. There'd been a mass of possibilities to get through. To these faces of differing shades Haberman asked polite yet penetrating questions, making every pretence of noting their responses in the journal he carried.

But how to find the one said to be so extraordinary? Haberman imagined her eyes would shine like specks of gold among a creek's sediment and gravel.

"If you believe you have gifts, would you explain these to me?"

One girl liked very much to read; one thought she could sing; Haberman watched a fifteen-year-old swing a tennis racquet with an expertise to warm any future financial sponsor's heart. Nothing hearkened to anything the witch had told him.

In certain instances 'William Monk' was invited to peruse home-country school records. Haberman saw a plethora of middling grades. Pathetic. Then, at a school he visited after lunch, Papua New Guinean twins had given Haberman a flutter of hope, they looked so dark and so exotic.

"Your lives must have been very different in your country. Was there sorcery and witchcraft?"

One sister nodded enthusiastically and took his hand, curious and innocent. The other reached for the colours in his tie. The teacher supervising in the room with him cleared her throat.

"Tell me about these practices."

"Women who are witches are burned because the elders say so."

"What of your own mother?"

The teacher cleared her throat again, more loudly, increasingly discomfited.

"Mami's a cleaner for the school."

"Has your mami taught you to cast wicked spells?"

Quickly escorted to the wet footpath outside Haberman thought the twins didn't fit Agata Rosso's information anyway. He asked himself: But how will I be sure? At the final school on the list Haberman discovered the young student in question was enrolled but wouldn't start until the new year.

His stomach grumbled. After a different type of search, that is, for a decent restaurant, Haberman sat down to a dinner he wouldn't hurry through. He ordered a carafe of red wine and stewed over this preposterous chase. As he flicked with irritation through the pages George Bellman had given him, he noticed that this last girl's home address had been provided; Bellman must have discovered she wouldn't be at her new school yet.

After Haberman emptied the carafe and savoured a *Rémy Martin* cognac, he decided not to slide into another wasted day. This girl's grades were meant to be very high, plus she professed an interest in fencing and chess.

Promising, or yet another blind alley?

⸻

Evening at a featureless front door, shaking the rain from his hat, Haberman surveyed a property in need of mowing, its bushes and shrubbery neglected. The house was old and bent and when he knocked he heard a dog bark inside. *Wonderful,* he thought, *why not end this day with jaws clamped to my ankle?*

A black man in his mid-thirties opened the door, standing barefoot in long trousers and a white Bonds singlet. He needed a shave and a haircut.

"Yes?"

The man listened to Haberman's story with an expression that revealed a contempt not only for Haberman, but the world in general.

"So you're a journalist and you want to hear about my daughter's experiences." The man spoke with a Londoner's accent. "Experiences in transferring from one racist education system to another."

"If this is your characterisation, then indeed I do. The school sent me here as young Lashana's enrolled but hasn't started."

"Then how's she supposed to tell you about experiences she hasn't even had yet?"

"Though you already speak of racism, sir."

"My observation. What's yours?"

"Might Lashana be home?" Haberman countered. "It would be so much easier to put a few questions to her direct, Mr Okonedo, then leave you to your evening."

At that moment the barking dog revealed itself in the corridor behind Okonedo. It wasn't barking per se, it was yapping. A tiny terrier, more balls than brains. A small voice called, "Come back, Delroy," and the dog skittered away, sharp nails on a hardwood floor.

Okonedo clearly didn't like the fact that Haberman heard that voice.

"You've got three seconds to go away, whoever you are—"

"William Monk. Call me Bill," Haberman spoke as he slid his hand into his trouser pocket. His fingers touched the boxcutter he'd re-habituated himself into carrying.

"—because bollocks you're a journalist. And bollocks that school told you our home address. I'm a journalist."

Haberman imagined the gush of arterial blood from the man's carotid, but there were the deaths of Nasser, Lundy and even Harry McCulloch to consider. Friendly investigating police had their limits, and Haberman wasn't certain he could get away with a death in this house. His damn Mercedes, parked right out front.

"My press card, Mr Okonedo," he said, presenting one of the many fake IDs he'd maintained over the years. "And the authority signed by the local school inspector."

Okonedo looked at the press card, then the letter. "George Bellman. I'll be contacting him."

"A deeply cautious man like your good self. He'll welcome your call."

"What's that?"

Haberman opened his journal. "Notes from interviews at a dozen schools."

"Well, look, all right. But make it quick."

From somewhere around the corner came the sound of a television. The girl Lashana must be in the next room, with her terrier. There was no mention of other siblings on Bellman's list and Okonedo seemed the only adult there; perhaps there really was no mother.

Could I have found her?

Okonedo led Haberman down the short corridor into a bare living room. A small girl and her dog were curled together on a couch watching some kind of comedic animation. Flowerpots seemed to be dancing and singing. Around the room, indeed everywhere, packing boxes were strewn. The Okonedos were certainly new arrivals.

"Lashana, this gentleman wants to ask you a few things."

Okonedo didn't leave them. He remained standing very close to Haberman. In his singlet his arms and biceps looked veined and muscled. Haberman kept one hand in his pocket, gripping the boxcutter and now edging the flat, sharp blade out two notches.

At a pinch maybe he *could* get away with a killing.

"Hello, Lashana," Haberman said, "and your friend Delwin."

"This is Delroy."

"A pretty dog."

"Daddy, who's this man?"

"A journalist, baby, like me. He wants to know what you think about coming here and going to a new school."

She cuddled the terrier, which rubbed the white fur of its face into the crook of Lashana's arm. And Lashana herself? Thirteen years of age, according to Bellman's information. Was this the extraordinary teenager the witch had promised him? Lashana might have excelled in science, physics, history, and of course there was that interest in fencing and the manoeuvres of the chess board, but she was so young and, Haberman saw, almost completely under-developed.

Still, he couldn't help thinking about the possibilities.

"Go ahead," Okonedo said, minimal patience eroding.

"Apologies, I was just thinking what extraordinary eyes your daughter has. Are they green?"

"Yes."

"And a high brow signifies great intelligence."

"Lashana, drag yourself away from the television a minute."

Now she looked at Haberman, her face set into a small mirror of her father's irritation.

"If you could just tell me a few things, dear, then I'll be on my way. What are you looking forward to at your new school?"

Her eyes flicked towards her father in an expression of *Do-I-have-to?*

Her father gave her a quick nod.

"Nothing," Lashana said. "I didn't miss home when we arrived, but I do now. This isn't home. This is some stupid country."

"What makes you say that?"

"Outside," she said.

"The flora and fauna, or the weather?"

"The children in this street. And at the park. Most of them go to that stupid school I'm supposed to join. Whenever I think about that place I want to make its walls fall down and its roof smash to pieces."

"Lashana, for God's sake, I've warned you about that sort of talk. Now be polite to Mr—whatever his name is."

"Why so much anger, dear?"

"My name isn't 'dear'. No one here likes my name. No one says it right. Kids make fun of me and the things they say are awful. They're all white. I made a boy's face bleed for what he called me."

"How did you do that?"

"I picked up a rock and hit him."

"That was a mess," Okonedo said wearily.

"This thing you said about making the school's walls fall down... You really imagine something like that?"

"And make it burn up like in a fireplace." She fixed her gaze on Haberman. "I'm going to close my eyes and make it happen. You just wait."

For moments he was held by that gaze. Haberman simply couldn't pull away. Then he pretended to scrawl some notes. By now his heart was beating so fast it actually frightened him. The girl's eyes, so pretty, yet my god how they contained such a blaze of fury. Lashana was just a child, and tiny, but inside her was something so angry it was—just the word the witch used—*powerful*.

"Look, that's enough," Okonedo told him. "Scratch Lashana off your list. I'm getting my daughter professional help, that's why she's not started yet."

Even if she wasn't the one the witch had promised him, someone special was right before him. Not quite what he'd imagined, not quite what he'd dreamed of, but definitely food for the new and fertile thoughts that had planted themselves in Haberman's head. Not to mention his seething loins.

To take her, to make her his own, to devour her.

Well, what effort would it be? Silence the father, crack the dog's neck, and enjoy the privacy of this downbeat home. No need to ask for the witch's pleasure—she'd make him wait for his reward until she said he deserved it.

I always deserve it, you stupid woman.

And if this child really is your special one, I won't leave you enough to squeeze into an eyedropper. How will you like that?

There was a hurrying footfall—several hurrying footfalls, very tiny— and a toddler appeared in a doorway carrying in one hand a large plastic spoon, mouth smeared with food, wearing a nappy and nothing else. This small thing's head was a mass of even greater curls than the girl's, skin the darkest chocolate.

Haberman watched the toddler fall forwards, hit its face and lie on the floor, where it started to cry.

"There you are," Okonedo said, hurrying forwards.

"Danny doesn't cry much." Lashana looked at Haberman again. "Except when Mother's out."

"You have a mother?"

"Don't you?"

In Okonedo's arms, Danny stopped crying, looking at the stranger with his wet mouth a perfect O. Here was another set of very green eyes—yet in a moment, as the child's expression changed from hurt to happy surprise, what these eyes projected was the polar opposite of Lashana's. The girl was all vexation and wrath; this toddler was like a vessel for pure delight.

And for Haberman it was as if the very brightness in little Danny's eyes forced him awake from a dream. A dream of the very darkest flavour.

A thirteen-year-old girl, a baby boy, and their father. Most likely I'd cut the throat of the mother as well, if she made an inopportune arrival from wherever she'd gone.

A wave of nausea passed through him, his dinner, wine and cognac repeating like toxic substances. Haberman clicked the boxcutter's blade to its safety position and withdrew his hand from his pocket. His legs had started to tremble.

For one small moment, perhaps in the green happy mirror of Danny's eyes, he'd seen himself covered in blood, rutting on a screaming child. Not a Haberman renewed, but a Haberman inexplicable even to himself. In his mind he cursed the crone whose bidding he should never have attempted:

So this is where your influence brings me?

He found himself outside the house now, back on a weedy, cracked pathway. The Okonedo door closed behind him. Haberman faced the dark suburban street, his mind made up.

Explain yourself properly, witch, or to hell with you.

He looked at his watch, the hands moving to seven p.m.

A Long Tuesday
Evening (ii)

In the travel agency office it was almost seven by the time Candela was able to sign the papers required. The machinations of trying to get everything organised had taken the entire day; however Mrs Kessleman, owner of Wonder Travel, had stayed back to see her through.

Paul handed her the cash amount in full—and finally that was that. Tomorrow morning Candela and Lorenzo would be on a BA flight with two stops, Sydney and London, before landing at Charles de Gaulle Airport. Paris was a ruse for anyone wanting to trace Candela's ultimate destination. Train fares from Paris to San Sebastian were organised; these tickets didn't need names on them. Once in San Sebastian mother and baby would take bus connections into Catalonia, where local bus and rail would help them disappear.

Mrs Kessleman gave Candela her itinerary and two plastic wallets of travel tickets, one for flights, one for the Spanish railway system. Then, in the street with rain running through the gutters, Candela sheltered Lorenzo's head, clutched the two plastic wallets instead of immediately slipping them into her purse, and turned her face up to the sky, eyes open, lips parted.

◆———————————◆

At the same time, in the Blue Bird Café, Donny Zap was refreshed, eating his way through a huge slab of steak. And, yes indeed, it was served just as bloody as he'd told Federico it needed to be. He'd slept the entire day away, just about comatose, exhaustion at the draining fury of his own body having left him sore in the head and limp all over. Yet the replenishment of sleep was a tonic even better than Zia Agata's creations.

Donatello had arrived after closing time, knocking on the repaired front glass until Federico came to investigate from where he'd been cleaning and prepping for the next day.

"I need one of your steaks."

Federico knew better than to argue. Nervous, he'd invited Donatello to sit, switching on several lights, then had returned to the kitchen and got the gas on. Better to satisfy a madman than to enrage him, correct?

Belly full, Donny Zap waited while Federico delivered him a hot cup of espresso and started to collect the cutlery and dinner plate, wiped clean with white bread.

"Where is my wife?"

"You know Candela doesn't work here anymore."

"Sit down."

Slowly and unhappily Federico did.

"So you won't let my wife work for you."

They spoke in a sort of middle ground of their home country's language. Italian, but inflected by the Friulian dialect in Donatello's case, and a Calabrian dialect for Federico.

"She felt it was better to move on."

"Why is that?"

"The work here is very hard…"

"You think my wife is lazy?"

"She was the best."

"Does Candela have another job?"

"I don't know."

"Tell me about the man who was here with her."

"You hurt a total stranger."

"This total stranger has a name. What is it?"

Federico shook his head. "How would I know?"

"Because you do."

"Donatello, if I did know I'd tell you. But I'm only the owner. Whatever the staff do—"

Donatello flung the scalding contents of his espresso cup into Federico's face. Federico screeched. He tried to jump up and wipe his face with his hands, yet in a fluid motion Donatello had Federico by both wrists and now held him where he was.

"His name."

Almost half Federico's face had turned red, blood rushing to the surface

222

of the skin. Coffee dripped from his chin to the table. If Donatello had thrown that espresso higher it might have poached an eye.

"Paul... I don't know the rest." Federico couldn't withhold a sob of pain. "Paul. Australian."

"Where does the English—?" Donatello stopped and corrected himself. "Does the Australian live near?"

"I need—cold water, ice, please..."

"Tell me and I'll be on my way."

"I don't know where he lives—"

Donatello let go with his right hand, lifting it as a fist.

"—but where he works," Federico cowered, "his job, it's near."

"Where?"

"Real estate... A real estate office. It's a few streets away. Gavin-something, that's all Candela ever told me. But it's too late now. You go there tomorrow morning, maybe you'll see him."

"What else do you know?"

"Nothing, I swear. I swear on my children—"

Donatello delivered him a quick, short blow to the chin. "Never swear on your children."

He let go and Federico, rocked, held his burned face, stumbling in the direction of the kitchen. Donatello thought a moment, then got moving.

<hr />

And so he prowled, prowled until he found the right place: Gavin-something was a small building called Gavin Realty.

Federico had been wrong about one thing at least. It wasn't too late. Many lights were on, inside and out, people working past normal closing time. Donatello counted eleven vehicles in the parking lot. He should storm into that building and drag the Australian Paul out, yet he knew he wouldn't be able to stop people calling for help. Then the police would get involved. Those uniformed monkeys might be in the palm of Mr H's hand, but a scene and complaints would cause too many problems.

Especially when Donatello wanted things finished and closed tonight.

So as the streets of this busy little suburb slowly emptied he kept his eyes fixed on Gavin Realty's glass doors and windows. Every now and then he saw silhouettes moving about inside. The wait reminded him of being outside Jackson's Gym, anticipating McCulloch's exit. When the Australian Paul emerged Donatello would follow him to the car park and beat the truth out of him. Or he might tail him home. There, he was certain, he'd find Candela and his beautiful boy.

If by chance the Australian didn't appear tonight, then Donatello would be back first thing in the morning. He'd have that *fottuto bastardo*—that fucking bastard—bleeding before he downed his first coffee.

Finally, people were exiting; they must have had some task to do as a group. Several people walked along the footpaths, maybe to public transport. The car park started to empty. None of these faces belonged to the Australian, Donatello was careful to make certain. He paced back and forth the length of a long, concealing shadow. Soon only one vehicle remained. Donatello waited another fifteen then twenty minutes. The car stayed where it was, a silver Jaguar, so sleek and special it seemed to shine with diamonds.

If this car was the Australian's, he was a rich man. Donatello's head started to burn. His throat turned dry.

Candela, tu sei mia felicità.

Lorenzo, non posso vivere senza voi.

Andiamo. Let's go.

———

Donatello crossed the street and took the front steps. Through the glass doors he saw things were mostly dark, yet there were glimmers of light inside. A high chair at a reception desk was empty; all the other chairs and desks he saw were also empty. He pushed the door; it wasn't yet locked for the night. There was no bell to announce an arrival. When he sniffed the air, among the many lingering scents—potted plants, the remnants of cheap cologne, ink, very feminine perfumes—he sensed the stale perspiration of a long day.

And the Australian?

Donatello stepped further into what to him was a vast alien space, an open plan office. No shadows moved.

Devoted late-night worker, where are you?

He spied this person in a separate office, its door ajar. Even in his ignorance of how offices and businesses worked Donatello guessed this had to be the boss, or close enough. So the Australian owned this place?

The man working at his desk looked up sharply and barked a surprised, "Hello?" Just as quickly he rose to his feet, though Donatello didn't note a great deal of fear. There was something far tougher here; this was not another Federico, and it wasn't the Australian.

"Everyone's gone home," this boss said.

"You is here."

"There's no money in these offices."

"I no want money."

"What are you, some dago?" When Donatello didn't reply this boss spoke in a friendlier tone. Donatello sensed the lie it was: "How can I help you, friend?"

"You have man name of Paul."

"What's that supposed to mean?"

Donatello took a step forwards.

"Wait, let me guess."

He did stop, preferring that this man should speak.

"So, you—you're after Paul Munro. You're the one who had the altercation with him, right?"

"What is this thing?"

"Fight. You bashed him up."

Donatello nodded once.

"And now you're back for more? Well son, that's finished. There'll be no quarrels in this place. So turn around and go home."

"Where he is?"

"That's up to Paul."

"Where he live?"

"Friend, there's only one thing you need to understand. Paul Munro doesn't work here. He won't be back, you got that? It means you're drawing a blank."

Donatello turned his head to look at the filing cabinets lining the walls. The tags on each drawer didn't mean much to him. In his peripheral vision he of course noted how this boss intended to still be the boss. The man's right hand edged down to a desk drawer. His mistake, Donatello knew, was that he'd stood straight up. The man was very tall, the drawer was just a little too far out of reach, and that gave him away.

"You got gun?"

The boss quickly reached the remaining six inches. His fingers touched the drawer's handle, yet even as they did Donatello was on him. Two heavy bodies crashed into a corner of the office, walls shaking. Struggling hard, the type to fight and never give an inch—all this Donatello sensed—the boss spat, "You piece of shit, go fuck yourse—" and died gurgling, feet kicking more and more feebly as Donatello held him down.

So quick this thing that could come over him, just as it had that night with Nasser and Lundy. No different last night when the beast in Donatello destroyed Candela's flat. Now he breathed hard, rocked by his own capacities, bringing himself back to some sort of sanity. If Zia Agata had been stronger this would never have happened; when she'd called Donatello to this country she'd promised to make sure it never would again. For a time it had been so, until her own frailties overtook her.

Yet maybe he was wrong to think of it as a curse. It might be his blessing. The blessing of who he was, and of who Zo would one day be.

How can it be wrong, to be so strong?

The boss's blood was on his face and his hands, his T-shirt and leather jacket. Donatello refused to look at the strong-featured face draining of colour. He closed his eyes and repeated the name he'd heard—Paul Munro Paul Munro Paul Munro—then achingly found his feet. This boss's desk was crowded with papers, graphs and folders. There was that dizzying array of filing cabinets. Everything in this place of business dealings appeared overwhelming. Donatello gritted his teeth, ready to tear through it all.

Wait, the animal won't help you this time.

He forced himself to understand the tags on the various drawers. *Sales Ladders & Targets; Account Invoices; Marketing and Publicity; Contracts & Correspondence.* But what made men and women want to fill their heads with such babble? How could they live with their brains more important than their hands, fluorescent lights and typewriters more important than sun and dirt?

Annual Reports; Government & Qangos; Staff & Staffing; Position Descriptions; Telephony & Technical.

The stuff was incomprehensible. Donatello's confidence wavered. He had yet another murder to accompany those of Nasser and Lundy. Sooner or later he'd be called to account; money could only perform so many miracles. He'd already started to realise that he'd need to leave Zia Agata and Mr H behind, and travel far—he'd do it with both Candela and his boy, or with his boy alone.

The way it had to be.

So, Paul Munro Paul Munro Paul Munro.

Donatello slid into the boss's very deep armchair and surveyed the jigsaw puzzle of papers, the in-tray and out-tray.

And right in front of him was his answer, signed in blue ink by a man named Michael Walter Gavin, a cheque written out to Paul Munro Esq. A sheet of paper was attached to the cheque and on the back was a telephone number followed by a jumble of words. It was some kind of description of Paul Munro's job. Donatello understood the one word in big print: *Dismissed.*

At the bottom of the page was Paul Munro's home address.

Donatello's eyes widened. His consciousness actually seemed to waver, as if he blinked from this realm into the next.

Come è possibile? How is it possible?

Donatello left everything the way it was. This cheque and page he didn't need; his heart raced, and he felt an elation matched only by his happiness at understanding how the world of people and spirits could work to bring all problems to their solution—just as Zia Agata always promised him.

We have no map, so we pray for our answers.

We travel thousands of miles, and return to our start.

The universe is alive, and it knows we're here.

He left the squat building behind and found his Ducati, parked safely in a dark lane behind a closed grocery store. At a roar Donny Zap started for a place he knew so well, the red house in the country.

The Rider in the Night

It wasn't so late but after a few bites of dinner alone in the kitchen Lía wanted to go to her room. Her father plus the woman and baby visiting hadn't been home until late; now they were in the living room. As she crept to the staircase in the downstairs hall with Dakota and Buster following, Lía heard her father speaking softly with the woman. Her name was Candela, the baby Lorenzo, and both of them had been here at Rosso House the first time Lía and her father had come to see it. Lía wondered about that, and the connection; had her father and this woman made one that day? Was Lía really so blind?

And of course she'd at least learned one thing: what happened to her father's face had to do with Candela. So he'd got in the way of a husband who was angry with his wife? Well, just look at that wife. Lía thought her stunning.

Then, either her shadow or the dogs gave her away.

"Lía, why don't you come in here?"

Candela was in an armchair as Lorenzo suckled at her breast. Lía's father's chair was turned politely to the side. He kept his gaze elsewhere. Lía was glad for the cup of tea he held; the previous night she'd seen him empty all his whisky bottles into the sink. And later that night the woman and her little one had slept in one of the spare bedrooms. First thing in the morning they'd all gone out. So far Lía hadn't had much to do with these guests; she wasn't even sure how she felt about them.

Or about this woman, married, with a baby, her father's little mystery.

"Maybe you will help me?" Candela asked, looking up without a smile.

Lía made the dogs put aside their curiosity about the strangers and go lie down in their usual spots. "What can I do?"

"Have you helped a baby to burp?"

"I don't think so."

"Then come here."

Candela lifted Lorenzo—little Zo, she'd been told—up to her. Lía felt the awkwardness of taking him into her arms. She saw his mother cover her breast and wet nipple with her bra and then her blouse. For a moment Lía couldn't help wondering if one day she'd feed a baby of her own. She didn't know if the answer was yes or no, or which of those she wanted. Lorenzo's body, sated with milk, was warm against her chest. How did a baby's head resting on her shoulder give such immediate solace?

At the same time Candela stood and guided Lía's hand to pat the baby's back.

"Like this, and he will like it too."

In a moment Zo produced a cracking burp big enough to make everyone smile.

"Can I keep holding him?"

"He wants it."

Lía sat facing Candela, and just as they were about to speak Buster walked over. Lía, her father and Candela watched the dog rasp his tongue against Lorenzo's bare heels. Lorenzo kicked his feet with giggling pleasure.

"Okay, that's enough," Lía's father said, rising and taking Buster by the collar. "He might think he's looking at dessert."

He led Buster to his corner and made him lie down, however as soon as he moved away Buster rose to his feet, tail wagging, to once again stand in front of the baby. Lía could tell Candela wasn't afraid of what the dog might do, but she thought there was something indecipherable in the woman's expression, as if Buster's attention actually meant something to her.

"Buster, go away or else."

At Lía's father's warning the dog chose a halfway path: he laid himself at Lía's feet, eyeline never wavering. Dakota's breath, meanwhile, rumbled as she went to sleep. Then Lía felt Zo reach a hand into her hair and tug with his fist.

"This means he likes you."

There was something so odd to holding this baby, so small and warm and yet so vibrant. He was like some soft motor, quietly pulsating with life, sensual and gentle yet promising to roar. Instinctively, she held him closer.

What is it about you, Zo?

Lía felt Candela's eyes on her, slightly questioning, slightly unnerving. So she cleared her throat:

"Are you really travelling somewhere?"

"In the morning. Thank you for letting us stay."

"Where are you going?"

"The world is very big," Candela spoke, which created an uncomfortable silence.

Lía tried not to frown, wondering what sort of secret needed to be added to her father's little mystery. She was about to speak again, but the awkward silence of the room was broken by the household's relentlessly vigilant sentinels.

Buster jolted upright. At the same time Dakota came awake, ears twitching fast. Moments passed as Lía, her father and Candela stared in curiosity at the dogs, then, as one, they heard the growing sound in the distance. Behind the steady patter of the rain, howls came on the wind.

"A few wild dogs in the area," Lía's father spoke. "Harmless, unless you happen to be a hare or a deer."

Candela stood and took Lorenzo back into her arms. She carried him to the living room's windows. After watching the wet night a moment, she said, "Could we close these?"

The cries drifted closer, then there was something extra, the hum of an approaching engine—which quickly became a violent roar.

Now Candela backed right away from the windows.

Lía and her father took her place. The howling of dogs was drowned by that echoing engine, then a coming searchlight cut a white diagonal swathe through the falling rain. They saw it was the headlight of a motorcycle that had roared up the driveway and into the courtyard. The bike raced on with higher and higher revs. The rider circled the house, destroying grass and gardens as he went, two thick tyres spitting up flowers and great clods of dirt and mud. Lía saw long circular scars gouged into the property, illuminated by the motorcycle's headlight, then she turned her head to father.

No more than a minute had passed.

"Lía, stay here, I'm locking the front and back doors."

He disappeared quickly, as if he understood what was happening, and maybe even why. Alone at the window Lía saw the motorcycle disappear, making one more quick circumnavigation of the house. When it reappeared, maybe fifteen to twenty dogs ran as a pack with it. Lía had to physically restrain Dakota and Buster by their collars.

Her father returned. From behind Lía heard Candela ask, "Do you have a pistol?" and as he shut the living room's doors and locked them at both ends her father replied, "Of course not."

To Lía it felt as if her years had dropped away. Sixteen? She was six years of age, if that, wanting to run and hide.

How about being interested and not scared? Not this time.

Her father put his arm around her as they stood at the window, needing to see what was going on. Candela was in a far corner of the living room, her body turned in as if to protect her baby.

The rider cut the engine and the pack dogs stopped around him. They panted in groups, some with their snouts upturned making their howling cry into the rain. Lía watched the stranger kick his motorcycle onto its stand. The headlight kept burning and the motorcycle's hot metal ticked.

He was in full leather. His wet helmet glistened, the visor down and beaded with droplets. When the rider slipped off that full-face helmet it revealed a hard, angular face. Short black hair against the '70s trend, his leather all black and silver to match the bike. When he looked towards the quarter moon he blinked at the rain and made the sign of the cross, then lifted a tiny crucifix from around his neck and kissed it.

"Paolo," Candela spoke, "this is with me. Please hold Lorenzo."

"Stay where you are." The sheer hostility in his voice was something Lía had never heard before.

The rider pushed himself off his motorcycle and strode toward the windows, helmet swinging from one hand. The dogs crowded with him. The sight of them took Lía's breath away; then she realised she hadn't needed to quieten her own dogs since the motorcycle had stopped. They no longer barked and when she looked down they stood by her, silent, doing nothing.

As if they were in thrall to the man outside.

"The police are on their way," her father called. "And if you're stupid enough to keep coming I've got a shotgun."

The rider smiled up towards the voice.

"Lía, I need to stay where I am. Go use the telephone. Ring triple zero and tell the police to get here as fast as they can."

She didn't hesitate, but as she moved to unlock one of the living room's doors for the telephone in the hallway they all heard something new.

"Wait," her father breathed. Lía's hand was on the doorknob and she moved her ear close to the timber. He asked, "Is it?

Lía nodded.

Inside Rosso House, on the wooden floors around both sides of the living room, there was the unmistakeable tick-tick of many paws walking slowly and carefully; it sounded like they were stalking—stalking their way to a locked room from which there was no way out.

"Lots of windows," Lía whispered, "lots of windows are open down here."

She returned to her father. The rider and his dogs had stopped maybe ten metres from the windows. Lía saw the man gaze up and around the front of the house, then smile. He stepped back, then hurled his helmet at something above them. There was a crash and a crack. The helmet thudded to the wet grass, a broken piece of white porcelain falling next to it.

"What's that?"

"The outside telephone connection," her father told her, then drew several breaths. "Turn out the lights."

As she did her father pulled the windows shut and bolted them down. There were no shutters.

"Go stand with Candela."

Lía didn't. Even though she was afraid she needed to know what was happening.

The living room was shadowed but the moon through the rain and the motorcycle's headlight were bright enough. The rider came closer. Now all that separated them were panes of glass and ancient timber frames. The rider was doused in the rain. Unblinkingly he watched Lía and her father watching him.

"Send my wife and my baby and I go."

They didn't reply.

He started to climb the side of the house, grasping the window frame—which let him see into the room, its darkness not enough:

"Candela!"

The rider punched a gloved fist through a lower pane. It exploded inwards. Lía and her father jumped back. He smashed another and another, more glass shattering. The excitement set off every dog, both inside and out. The pack with the rider howled; the dogs outside the living room doors whined and scratched at the timbers; Buster and Dakota went so crazy Lía wanted to cover her ears.

The room had become a cacophony of noise and now the baby was crying.

The rider reached through the broken panes and pulled away timber framing. Two large crisscrosses of wood broke away. He snapped more framework and Lía's dogs leaped for his hands, the instinct to defend greater than whatever had silenced them before.

Lía's father grabbed a standing lamp and smashed it across one gloved hand. Pieces of metal, plastic and the shattering bulb sprayed across the room. Dakota and Buster scurried back as her father picked up a wooden chair and crashed it against both the rider's grasping hands. The man tore blindly at the frames, his face twisted with rage. His pack was maddened with him, howls and barks resounding from outside and both sides of the living room's doors.

Lía heard the clawing become more frenzied; and in the night she saw mangy dogs, big ones, small ones, dogs that snarled, dogs that hid behind other dogs, dogs that stared wide-eyed and some that only had one eye, all with their master in leather.

Lía heard:

Must be thirty of the bastards!

What'll we do?

Shoot!

And Lía did. Her body stiffened, eyes fixed on the attacking rider.

At the broken glass and splintered frames he managed to pull the lasts shreds of timber aside and clamber up, yet then he froze.

The new grimace in his face wasn't for fury; a shudder travelled through his body. At the same time his dogs backed away. The scraping at the living room's doors died off. Dakota and Buster quietened, the baby too. There was a dead silence in the house; silence only broken by a choking, gurgling deep in the rider's throat. His eyes started to bulge, reddening, doubling in size. Lía saw the tiny veins, capillaries thickening. He was trapped right there, like a great spider in a broken window, and Lía kept him where he was; she'd keep him there until she was finished what she was doing.

So she concentrated all the more.

A hum grew and circled the room. Lía's father was watching the rider, spellbound and confused by whatever was happening, but now he tried to follow that hum. It intensified and became something like the moan of an over-amplified bass guitar playing a static note. Lía's father, she vaguely understood, would feel that deep in his chest, his bones. So would the woman and her baby. Lía, meanwhile, felt nothing, only a power that grew and grew and a thrilling satisfaction that grew with it.

Lily Cheung was nothing; Mrs Baxter was a match easily whispered out; *but you, I'm going to make your body of blood explode.*

Her focus shifted from the rider's throat and chest to his entire being. As if run through by a great knife he let out a cry and his grip on the window's pieces gave; he fell away. The bass note was now a keening shriek that pierced the eardrums and shook the walls.

Lía felt her own blood rising; she felt her power a sort of electric ecstasy.

Candela was at her side. Lía felt her rigid, curled hand being taken, though gently, gently. Candela turned her. The baby in Candela's arms had bright shining eyes. Smiling behind those eyes was a small promise; all can be well.

Lorenzo stretched out his hands. He wanted Lía. Lía, inside herself, wanted Lorenzo. The rest was nothing, nothing at all.

So she took him.

He was warm and reassuring.

They all turned to watch the scene outside. Now it all seemed so irrelevant, an anti-climax of something that hadn't been much at all.

The rider was dragging himself away across the freshly dug up grass and vast patches of mud. As he went, his dogs, to the very last one, cowered in silence.

You've done so well, Lía. You're far stronger than Donatello. He's the father of the baby you're holding. You did well to stop him, but even better to stop yourself. Now watch him run away with his dogs, because to hurt or kill isn't you.

Candela eased Lorenzo from her grasp.

Lía's father stepped forward and took his daughter's hand.

She thought:

To hurt or kill isn't me?

I'm so many things, you can't imagine.

And the room tilted. Her father's arms had her before she could fall.

The Real Mr H

He strode the wet, fragrant, peony-lined pathway to the witch's door, his blood still up and that discreet *Magia Bianca* sign only infuriating him more. Endless minutes after the buzz of the electric bell Signora Celano appeared.

"Mistah Hubbamante, is late."

"Where is she?"

"You go home, come back tomorrow."

Haberman pushed his way through, looking for Agata Rosso. He passed the tiny waiting room, the lounge room where he was usually received, and rooms with doors always closed that he now flung open to reveal dust and disarray. What a dump this place was, home to bitter old age and impossible dreams. The kitchen, nothing, then a staircase—where did that lead? There was a secluded add-on to the back rooms, with wood floors and cheap aluminium-framed windows. Music played, a voice singing a cappella.

For a moment it threw him, how pretty it was, the beauty in that song.

Celano tried to pull him away. Haberman shook her off with an uncharacteristic growl. He followed the song into the room and found the witch bathing the exposed, mottled skin of some geriatric. Of course, this had to be the husband, a man once dead, returned to life, by her.

Allegedly.

"Witch," Haberman called.

"Ssh," Celano tried to quieten him.

Agata Rosso remained intent on her task, which she performed with a tenderness Haberman didn't want to acknowledge. And there was something else Haberman didn't want to acknowledge; it was the small wonder of the witch's voice, so sweet, yet produced by a throat all gristle and sandpaper. He'd mistaken such perfect music for a radio or record. So Agata Rosso sang to her husband in the voice of a girl—of a maiden, Haberman thought—while at the same time she caressed his aged flesh with a sponge and cloth.

Haberman smelled lilac, perhaps lavender, and heard words he couldn't understand.

"La morte non è la fine dell'amore
Le tombe sono anche luoghi d'amore
Prega l'amante, l'amante che è morto
Pace e ricordi degli antichi fiori."

The simplest line in that quatrain, he could make an educated stab at it: *Non è la morte la fin de l'amore*. Death is not the end of love.

The witch fell silent then spoke without looking his way. Her voice had returned to that detested croak: "My husband will walk again, Haberman."

"I nearly killed an entire family."

"Maybe you'll cry?"

"Just get out here."

Haberman withdrew to the familiarity of the lounge room, though he glanced with renewed disgust at the gewgaws and knickknacks, the artless decor and religious-cum-pagan artefacts, and of course at the dolls.

Stiff and obviously sore, the witch soon entered the room. Her face was more wizened than ever, much closer to the stone she was supposed to resemble. The smell about her wasn't of lilac or lavender; she carried a whiff of her own decomposition. Purple slippers scuffed along threadbare rugs leeched of colour. She wouldn't be rushed, and used wooden matches to light long slender candles in front of each doll.

Haberman sat beside a doll he decided to call Miss Fire, for her richly auburn hair. Opposite him, then, was a Miss Sun, hair golden, of course. Then Miss Earth in heavy black tresses, and Miss Water, wearing an aqua, hand-stitched frock, eyes startlingly blue.

"What do they see?" he asked, not bothering to keep the contempt from his voice.

"What I ask them to."

"It appears they have nothing to say."

"They will."

The witch's gaze might have been weary but he saw no acquiescence in it.

"Well?" she asked.

"I'm wondering what you think you've done to me. This evening I was close to snuffing out three lives."

"Your passions must have been inflamed."

"By a child of thirteen."

"Is she…" The witch's eyes darted to his face, searching for the truth. "…Is she the one I need?"

"Extraordinary as she seems, no."

"Then why are you here to waste my time?"

"To tell you I understand I've been blinded by your tricks and sleight of hand. I've ingested your muck and I find myself changed. So I have a question: why should I want to possess a child and slaughter her family?"

"Am I the person to ask?"

"I shot a man in the back of the head when I could just as easily have achieved my objective some quieter way."

"You enjoyed it, didn't you?"

Haberman took her in. "Why did I?"

"Because this is the real you, Mr H."

"No, the men in the past, that was business. And a child… That's madness. You've performed some act of mesmerism on me. This is your influence."

"I can't nurture a weed that hasn't already found its root."

"What's that supposed to mean?"

"These feelings are in you, Haberman. You've wanted them and dreamed them your entire life. I've given your desires the chance to see daylight, that's all."

"It's not me."

"Look how you tremble, Haberman."

"I'm not trembling."

"Look how fear makes you the imitation of a man."

"I'm not afraid of you."

"You're a dog that denies it should eat meat, Haberman. A fish that doubts it should swim. Your blindness is perfect. I adore it. You're my most valuable fool."

"My god, a penny-witch playing with candles—"

"Which reveal so much. Will I tell you some of the things my candles let me see, Mr H?"

"Forget it, no more lies."

"I've seen a lovely bedroom. A suite, you like to call it. Not in this country but across the ocean. I've seen a bloated toad fill himself with platters of food and bottles of drink and think himself a king. I've seen him preside over a roomful of angels. Naked and with wings! Now he thinks himself a god. For the right money these angels perform unspeakable acts, they even bleed if the money is good. Yet they see this toad for what he is, they whisper to one another about the skin that flakes from his skull, and how his great belly stops his prick from piercing them. They laugh that they perform for a castrato, and that's you, Haberman, that's you."

My god, what was she doing? This was another trick, because even as Haberman stares into her face, into that rotted mouth with its rotted gums—

He *hurts* the angels. He pounds, he bites, he slaps and he pinches. He places a wad of extra money down and raises a cat-o'-nine-tails while behind him two young women point at his wobbling arse and do their best not to laugh.

Haberman needed to grip the arms of this comfortable chair he was in.

Now the witch sighed, unmoved and pitiless. "Get out," she spoke. "Get out and do my work."

"There's no more work for you. This is over," Haberman said through gritted teeth. "My answer is no."

His eyes moved to the knots in the joints of her gnarled hands; the protruding Adam's apple in a dead-skin throat. Damn the authorities. Damn the consequences. Why not do what she said and let his most base desire free? Why not enjoy the mindless act of choking her to death? Why not use his boxcutter blade across Celano's throat?

"Haberman," the stone witch started, reading him thoroughly. "When I die, don't you?"

He went to his feet. If he couldn't choke the witch he could do something else. He reached for Miss Fire and picked her up by her hair; he smashed her to the floor. The doll's head cracked. He stamped down with his heel and her pretty face split in two, revealing air.

The stone witch's eyes opened wide; her mouth opened wide as if she must scream.

Instead, out of that mouth came a force that made his chest burn.

From her eyes came a power he couldn't defend himself against. A flame flared around his heart, his lungs. With a cry Haberman lunged for her witch's throat but she seared him all the more.

◆————————◆

And now cottony purple slippers shuffle behind a doggedly crawling Haberman.

In the corner of his mind still capable of rational thought he knows the witch is enjoying his struggle along these varnished timber floorboards, the patterned runner. He knows she's laughing at the way his bulging eyes are so fixed upon the doorway ahead.

He steals a panicked glance over his shoulder. The witch looms, cold-blooded as Mother Death; the tub Celano walks beside her mistress. Behind them he almost believes he sees a stiff-legged troupe: the four dolls of the four elements.

No, there are only three, for Miss Fire's head is broken. Miss Sun pokes out a long pink tongue, pulling up her pretty dress to reveal a bald plastic pubis. Perspiration salts Haberman's eyes; salt and pain makes him weep.

The door ahead, the great world past it, let me out.

"Look at you, Haberman, are you a cockroach?"

Yes, a broken cockroach, with its futile scratching at the ground, dragging itself inch by inch. Has a cockroach ever prayed so?

The wet evening and night air, please oh please let me have them.

Yet the fire the witch has put inside his chest is killing him, and she enjoys every moment of it.

"You say I'm weak, Haberman, but look how easily I deal with you."

No, he won't look and he won't listen. If he can make it to the door then he can make it outside. His lovely Mercedes will whisk him away. He'll never come back. He crawls more doggedly and refuses to give in. He'll crawl even if his heart bursts, if every organ implodes. Anything to be away from this woman, this crone—

This witch.

Then there's a crashing sound right ahead of him. The front door is inexplicably shaking and jolting.

Good god, now what?

The door rattles. The thing vibrates to a relentless banging. Hinges expand and screws threaten to pop. Haberman understands: something is throwing itself against that door.

One monster wants out, another wants in.

A resounding blow against the timber makes Haberman cower. Glass flies and the door bursts inwards. Screws and splinters of wood scatter. Out of the wet and wind a thing comes crashing through. It heaves, drags itself, then drops with a thud onto the hallway floor in front of Haberman's disbelieving head.

"*Tenerlo*." The stone witch's sharp command. "Hold him."

Haberman shies away as Signora Celano's stout frame stands over him, just before her heavy foot presses down against his neck. He's pinned like the broken piece of house roach he is.

On the floor ahead of him—Donatello's mad eyes. There's dried foam around the boy's mouth. Dried bits of vomit and spittle.

"*Ho trovato la cagna*." Donny Zap's voice is hoarse and strained. "I found the bitch."

The witch stops, but her face comes alive.

"What's her name?"

Donatello shakes his tortured head: he doesn't know.

"Where is she?"

"With Candela...and they...and they..."

"What?"

"They at the old house." His voice shakes. "The red house..."

Haberman sees the shock of recognition. The old witch stands perfectly still. Donatello's words have frozen her into a block of dumbfounded ice.

Then she starts to mutter.

"They kept showing me...my old home...the land, the pastures, forests, the house. *My* house. I thought they were telling me to forget the past, that it was all an anchor...so of course I sold it..."

The sound she makes is a soft, coughing laugh, full of bitterness.

"So old, too old. Too blind to see the truth in front of my eyes. My darlings were giving me my answer, and I didn't know..."

Donatello tries to raise himself onto all fours, but whatever's happened to him, it's taken a toll Haberman can't understand. He realises the burning inside his chest has subsided. The witch can't divide her attention. Haberman still thinks of escape, assesses his chances.

The witch speaks to Donatello: "And she did this to you?"

"Zia, she too strong, too strong..."

The effort of trying to get himself up is too great. The boy's head drops and his body slumps. Donatello's face is flat and wet on the floor.

Signora Celano's foot comes off Haberman's neck as she scurries to help the boy. Then the witch herself blocks his way, standing in front of the remnants of the door.

"This is the end, Haberman. I can tell you where you need to go."

Haberman perceives fat drops of his own perspiration falling to the rug between his hands. He's looking up at the witch, silently imploring her to let him escape, to forget she ever heard his name.

"So one small service, little dog?"

There'll be no escape. There'll only be more pain. And even as he struggles to find his answer, in his mind something else grows dull, ugly and inevitable:

A girl so extraordinary, for him to have.

As if losing his consciousness into the consciousness of someone else—the real Mr H always looming at his shoulder—Haberman nods wet-eyed, acquiescing completely.

A Night in Three Parts (i)

There was no easy answer to the things that had happened and no way to find that answer tonight. So until morning came, and they all got out of there Lía's father stayed in the living room with Buster, and Lía shared the spare room where Candela had already slept a night with Lorenzo.

They believed one thing at least: a man who'd had to drag himself to his motorcycle and ride away slumped over the front wouldn't be returning quickly. He'd looked for all the world like someone lucky to be alive, and, as for his dogs, there wasn't a single bark or whine left in the rain-filled night.

Still, Lía's father wouldn't relax until Candela was on her way to the airport and he was on his way to the police—for police it had to be, there was no other way.

"How do you feel now?" he'd asked Lía as he'd settled her under warm blankets on a mattress moved into the spare room. Dakota came to lie down beside her.

"Just tired. I want to sleep."

"Then that's what you're doing."

Her father had been himself, yet terse, full of questions she knew he didn't like and that for the rest of this one night, at least, he'd keep bottled in.

"You know we'll talk in the morning?"

"Yes, Dad."

Thing was, Lía wanted to. Finally she'd tell him everything—even about Mrs Badger, even if it made her own father hate her or be afraid of her. For now, though there was dawn to wait for, and sleep to try and find, yet she kept thinking of how she'd brought Candela's husband to the brink of death and would have gone further. She would have killed him and she would have enjoyed it; was that another truth she'd share with her father?

"You're not asleep?"

She heard Candela move from the bed where Lorenzo was wrapped up. She came to sit on the floor beside her. Dakota woke briefly and rested her head on Candela's thigh. Lía felt the touch of Candela's hand on her face, so much like her mother's touch.

Maybe even too much.

"You have heard the hammering?"

"Yes."

"That is the broken windows, now blocked."

"Will my father be all right?"

"All I have done is bring trouble. Tomorrow I will be gone. I want to tell you I am very sorry."

Lía hesitated, then said, "Maybe you could stay?"

"If it was possible… I would like to know your father. He is a good man, and he loves you so much. But he doesn't know what you are, Lía."

"How do you know about me?"

"The first day we have met it was shining from you. Your light made me feel warm, but it has also frightened me."

Lía knew it now for certain: *Not your ma* was here.

"Now for a secret, but it stays between us for tonight at least. All right?"

Lía nodded.

"Since eight years of age I have a little bit of what is inside you. Sometimes I feel what other people feel, or see what they see. My mother has tried to teach me about this. She had a bigger gift. Mine is small."

"But what does it make you do?"

"Nothing. Or to be careful of other people."

"Why?"

"To know too much about how people think, to see inside them, it drives you mad."

"I don't like to get close to people. Not since my mother died."

"And so this house in the middle of nothing suits you."

"Yes."

"But if we want to live in the world we must allow the dark and the light of people to touch us. If we cannot find a way to do this then we are too lonely—and we become sorry to be alive."

"You got married."

"I met a man with his own troubles. I thought I could help keep quiet this thing inside him. For some time this was true and we were happy. Now I know he cannot be controlled."

"What is he?"

Shaded by darkness, Lía saw a sad smile on Candela's lips.

"You have seen it tonight. I think you already know."

"Those wild dogs followed him—"

Lía stopped. She thought of Lorenzo in her arms, the way he'd felt to her.

"What about your baby?"

"I will never let him be like his father." Candela thought a moment longer, and Lía knew this was something she must have reflected on over many weeks and months: "But if there was no Donatello in my life there would be no Lorenzo, so I cannot be unhappy. Like every mother my love for my baby is for everything he is, and so if some of Zo's spirit comes from his father then some of my love must stay with that man. Do you understand?"

"You stopped me hurting him."

Candela gave a small nod, then she caressed Lía's hair.

"Now this is enough. I know what has happened has made you tired."

"But what should I do?"

Candela took Lía's hands as if to return her some strength. "Why would it matter what I say? Your life is for you to find. But I hope one day you will discover how much love there is in the world."

"There's my father."

"And that starts to show you what I say is true."

"Starts?"

"He will not be the only one."

"Can I ask you one more thing?"

Candela nodded.

"Why did you speak to me, I mean, in my mind?"

"You did not need me to learn how to travel, but I think I have helped you to not be afraid of this."

"So, if you're like me," Lía tried not to hesitate, "do you feel them?"

Candela knew what she meant.

"From the moment I have come to this place I sense there are children. I clean and they follow me. I put Zo down and they look at him. I sing and maybe, just maybe they smile. They do not hurt anyone and never will, but they need to be free."

"Why are they here?"

Candela shook her head. She didn't know. "Maybe they want to tell you."

"They don't say very much."

"Then let them be." Candela's caress moved to the sleeping Dakota. "Like this lovely dog, if they are asleep, let them be."

But they aren't asleep, Lía thought. *They're standing in the hall right now.*

A Night in Three
Parts (ii)

Candela's breathing was soft and regular. Lorenzo didn't make a sound. Despite a fatigue she'd never known before, Lía couldn't sleep.

She sat up and needed to steady herself for dizziness. Dakota shifted and snuffled. Lía soothed Dakota's head, but as Lía slipped from under the warmth of the covers the dog wanted to be with her. They went together into the bathroom. Lía silently closed the door and switched on the light. Dakota investigated this strange room, then made herself at home on the cold tiles. At the mirror Lía looked into her own eyes.

If I could give Mrs Badger what she wanted, and can stop a man with a beast inside him, then how far can I go?

Her reflection didn't have an answer; she looked perfectly the same as always, no happier or sadder. Lía told herself she should be too tired to be worrying about this. In a few days her mind would be clearer and things would make better sense. There was one thing that needed thinking out, though: Donatello on his motorcycle with those dogs following, he'd come here for Candela and Lorenzo, he hadn't come for Lía. Then what did that vision in the State Library mean, of shadows searching for her and a man raising a pistol?

Lía leaned at the sink, as drained as an over-used battery. All thought felt too much to deal with. Yet she still wouldn't return to bed.

This thing inside, could she raise it again?

Lía straightened her spine and once more considered her eyes. She tried to rekindle the anger she'd felt, the hatred, but there really was nothing at all. What had been so natural and unforced against Donatello didn't even seem a part of her.

She was spent; might as well try to convince herself to flap her arms and fly around the house. She gazed at the things in this cold bathroom. A toothbrush and toothpaste, some deodorant, a much-used hairbrush.

Okay hairbrush, move a little. Shake, vibrate. Or, come on, melt like hot chocolate.

The thing sat there untroubled, a hairbrush doing just what a hairbrush should do. Lía told the toilet to flush itself; the hot water faucet to turn on; her toothbrush to do a dance in its cup and for the soap to slide off its holder and wriggle across the floor.

There was a small yelp.

Lía spun around. Dakota was curled in on herself the way she liked to rest and sleep, but her head was up, tensed, and her eyes were wounded and questioning. In fact she was looking at Lía as if she'd been kicked in the ribs and didn't understand why. Lía fell to her knees beside her, hugging the dog, holding her close and very hard.

"Oh my god, oh my god," she whispered, "I'm so sorry…"

She caressed Dakota's head. In a moment Dakota was licking her face. *But how did I hurt you? How did I do it?*

Chastened, shaking still, Lía led Dakota back to the bedroom. On the mattress she cuddled up close with her dog. Dakota didn't seem to suffer any ongoing ill effects. She seemed as contented as always.

Lía lay with her and wished for daylight to break, but the night wasn't over, and sometimes daylight can seem like it stubbornly refuses to come.

A Night in Three Parts (iii)

The digital clock's red numerals—3:47—floated in the darkness. The children had returned. They crowded the doorway with their shadows missing and they were led by the small ghost-boy. Lía felt herself enter a different space, a netherworld between two states of existence.

She went with them, led by that boy who didn't know his name, the one Lía always felt closest to. She followed him and the four others followed her, perfectly ordinary children, two abreast, in two rows. Though none of them smiled she knew they liked her. Lía still couldn't imagine why that should be.

Downstairs, they passed into the living room. Despite the hour her father stood at the windows and Buster sat at his side, ready for anything.

Her father didn't hear her or feel her; Buster's ears didn't twitch. Though her father had boarded up the destroyed set of windows with sheets of timber panelling, he'd left a small open space. It was ready to be sealed with another board leaning against the wall; the gap was so he could keep watch. He'd told Candela he didn't have a gun, which was true. What he did keep close was a claw hammer, and beside that a short iron bar plus a mattock with a pickaxe head.

"You won't need them. He's not coming back."

His hand stayed close to all three.

Lía noticed he had a Thermos with him. She knew it didn't hold any alcohol. There would never be alcohol again for him; she saw this perfectly. She also felt how weary and spent her father was, how he needed to close his eyes. He refused to do it, his mind clouded with misgivings about waiting until morning to leave Rosso House. Force of will and adrenalin kept him awake; plus confusion still churning. That confusion wasn't quite for the man who'd come, or the howling dogs the rider had brought with him. Instead her father's mind was on his daughter, his girl Lía, and this inexplicable thing he couldn't deny she'd done.

"I confuse you, Dad, and that hurts you. I'm sorry. I'll explain it the best I can, promise. For now why don't you sit down and close your eyes?"

She felt his resistance; he wouldn't let everyone go unprotected, even for a moment.

Lía wouldn't follow the children until her father accepted her thoughts.

Slowly, as if coming to the decision himself, he had to. She watched him step back and settle into a lounge chair. He didn't need to make himself comfortable. He closed his eyes. He slept.

It was the mistake that changed all their lives.

◆━━━━━━━━◆

Then Lía was with the children out into the still-dark morning. Rain had lifted but the ground and air remained very damp. Mist hung above them and a wet mushy carpet of red bougainvillea flowers welcomed Lía to the three large, desolate timber sheds one paddock back from the red house.

None of these sheds had power and for safety's sake Lía's father still kept each bolted shut, but none of that mattered because now she was in the largest shed with the children, and in the dusty dark they weren't alone.

"You didn't want me to come in here."

The ghost-boy's eyes said it was time for answers to come.

With a start Lía recognised the situation: time had reversed to the day she'd come into this barn and her father had been talking to Jake Minter, the man who ran the slashers.

"You shouldn't come in here," her father said.

"I tied the dogs up so they wouldn't."

Her eyes had been fixed on the machinery, machinery that had made her heart pound with apprehension.

"Let me... Just let me stay here a bit."

That was Jake Minter talking. So they'd left Jake Minter alone.

Now the scene continued from that point because the children wanted Lía to watch Mr Minter's face as he ran his hands over the dusty, rusted mechanical parts. So maybe Mr Minter was the bad thing she'd sensed in this shed? Yet the children gathered with him as he bent his head and his tears fell fat and heavy to the dirt. Lía felt the children's sympathy, plus the way they would have wept with him if they could.

Which sent Lía travelling on her own into a sunlit opening in the middle of thick woodlands, and Jake Minter was there but time was being very tricky indeed. It was him, but as a muscular teenager not a heavy-set man, without a bushy black beard or that wild curling hair.

Lía knew without having to think about it that his father rode and drove the backhoe. The thing sputtered with a strong smell of burning petrol and oil, and the great machine lurched and swung and crunched its gears as it excavated a hole among the trees. Watching what was happening were two men around the same age as Jake Minter's father, plus someone completely different, a woman in a bright, straight sun-coloured dress. She was young and radiant and her hair and skin caught the light.

"This means no more," the first man shouted over the grinding machinery, his body long, hard and lean in rough farming clothes. "It's your promise, Mrs Rosso, your promise, or goddamn it nothing'll protect you—or any of us. You understand?"

The second man didn't speak. He was another farmer for certain, maybe not quite as long and lean as the first man, but his arms and face were just as sunburned, his hair sparse and sandy. The skin around his eyes was very wrinkled, probably from a lifetime's squinting into the sun, and they were filled with a sadness Lía recognised at a glance. That sadness was like the blackest form of misery; it ate his insides down to his soul. Watching him, being somehow drawn to him, Lía felt his blackness want to spread into her—and now she had to resist; she had to resist or risk falling into the same hopelessness.

There was one more thing about this man. His eyes so hooded, and so grey in colour, they made her think she knew him.

How? Had she met him somewhere in modern-day Grandview?

The woman, young Mrs Rosso, waited until the hole was dug and the driver reversed away, the backhoe's engine clattering to a halt. Jake Minter's father climbed down and ran a rag around the dirt and perspiration of his forehead. They all stood there considering the fresh hole he'd made: Jake Minter and his father, the two farmers, and Mrs Rosso.

"This is evil pure and simple." It was Jake Minter's father speaking now, his voice gruff and dispirited. "You never promised nothing like this. And nothing's worth the price. Whatever you do or don't do from this day forwards, there's no one left in this community's gonna help you. Your husband's dead, so why don't you move on? You're no farmer. You've got no place here."

"You'll be seeing my husband in a few days."

Slowly the others looked at one another.

Mrs Rosso, Lía thought, had the strangest expression. It held a summer breeze. The smallest hint of her smile made Lía imagine the scents of meadows in bloom.

"Mrs Rosso—you're crazy, crazy as they come," Jake Minter's father spoke again. "And whatever you decide, be sure you'll never catch me on this godforsaken property one more time. You can do what you like with that information."

"In my language we say '*va bene*', Mr Minter, which means 'all right'. If that's what you want, why would I argue? And you, Mr Egan," she continued, addressing the first man who'd spoken. "I hope you won't mind the good crops and stock you've been blessed with returning to drought."

She looked at the sky, at the sun. Three men and one boy followed her gaze. They squinted against the harsh light. Mrs Rosso didn't. Instead there was a clarity to her eyes that wanted to take Lía's breath away.

"We know your country doesn't do favours for anyone. It's been my business to help you with that, but if you don't want it anymore—" She made a small sigh. "I won't think of any of you as ungrateful. Maybe only a little spoiled."

"It's you who's done the spoiling," the one she'd called Mr Egan said, bitterness barely restrained. "Spoiled us in our hearts and our very souls."

"Though you haven't minded reaping your rewards."

"We're taking to our church again. None of us, to a man, woman or child should ever have turned our backs on those doors. That's where you've sent us. All of us will be praying for our children—and forgiveness for what we've done." His hurt, yet pitiless eyes were on her. "Maybe you've had a spell on us and maybe that spell's simple greed. But that boy there," he said, nodding with disgust towards a wrapped pile of rags lying among long weeds, "that boy there's the last straw. It's over."

"Is it, Mr Egan?"

"It is."

"How many years of drought, do you think, before it isn't?"

Mr Egan looked away, across fields shimmering in a suffocating heat haze.

Mrs Rosso turned to the one who hadn't yet spoken, the man with grey eyes. "So quiet?"

It was clear to Lía that here was an individual unused to speaking, a man truly of few words.

"Egan's right," he muttered, "every word." Then his voice was stronger. "I'm calling it right now. My family, we'll sell up, clear out. The war took my twins. Now this entire countryside's covered in our sins." He made the sign of the cross. "I've got the one boy left and I'm making sure he never knows it or why."

Mrs Rosso stepped away from all of them.

Jake Minter's father said, "Help me," and he and his son went to the bundle of rags. Young Jake couldn't restrain himself; with a wary hand he reached to that part of the rags covering the small body's face, and uncovered it, and curiosity made him look into death itself.

Which Lía did as well—and through a boy's hollowed eyes she saw the nightmare vision of dogs being hunted and shot, and of a very handsome man collapsing to a forest's ground cover with three bloody holes torn into his white shirt. She smelled gun smoke and wafting cordite, heard the dying cries of dogs, then smelled the new scent in this boy's nostrils— rosemary and basil, fennel and marjoram, and other things so familiar, even if he couldn't name them. And she saw what the boy saw, Mrs Rosso naked and smiling prettily, in her outstretched hand a knife.

The backhoe was rattling again and Jake Minter's father had finished refilling that hole—that fresh grave. He added a mountain of extra dirt and forest debris, then without goodbyes father and son rode the machine away across the green paddocks, a thin exhaust trail of smoke following them. Lía observed that smoke against the stark blue, and it gave her a bearing; she saw the familiar rooftops of Rosso House, her own future home, so close.

Mr Egan and the second man didn't speak. They looked at the woman as if for a final word or promise. She gave neither. Instead Lía felt the way anticipation of something great filled Agata Rosso's soul, but Lía had no idea what that great thing might be.

Mrs Rosso left the men where they were. They looked at one another and might have thought of shaking hands, but didn't. Each walked off in his separate direction.

Lía was back in the shed watching bushy-haired and bushy-bearded Jake Minter weep while trying not to. In a moment he was gone and only the children remained, then Lía was alone with one small boy.

He watched her with the same sad eyes as always.

"Your name is Giacomo Mosca, but everyone called you Little Jack. My mother used to tell me everything she remembered about you. Do you know what that means? You're my uncle."

And even though that made sense it wasn't until Lía returned to her mattress, with an arm across Dakota, and the morning sun rising past the trees outside the bedroom's windows, that the next bit of sense fell into place.

She blinked languidly for the heaviness of a sleep which wasn't sleep, and thought of the quiet second farmer's sad grey eyes and why they'd seemed so familiar—and of course now she knew: those were her father's eyes and the man her father's father.

Lía's own grandfather, true, and in her travel she'd seen the moment Henry Munro had become a man of the land no more, and, in his heart, barely a man at all.

The Unmistakeable Squirming of the Belly

Jesus Christ, the late Henry Munro's only remaining son thought, *I've been dreaming of my father, and my brothers too, Bill and Jimmy. Funny how the idea of them stays in my mind when I can barely picture them anymore. How long since I dug out an old photo album or lit a candle in a church for them?*

Candles, Candela, a baptism candle with a red cross and a little baby's name embossed into it. All good things to think about.

Paul stretched and yawned. His hand fell onto Buster's head, the dog still by his side.

Wait, what am I doing?

Paul's eyes opened, and the idea of the best sleep he'd had in a year vanished.

The claw hammer, iron bar and mattock were as close at hand as the dog, but had he really let himself fall asleep? Paul shoved himself out of the lounge chair. Through the gap in the boarded-up window he saw the sun up high. A warm fresh breeze was blowing through. Dammit but he was supposed to get everyone out of here first light, if not before. How could he have gone so wrong?

Paul's belly squirmed. Candela's Toyota was still parked outside. She needed to get her stuff into that car and get going. He and Lía would be out of here too, a few belongings in the Chrysler as they headed for some motel. They wouldn't come back to this place until the police got involved and could reassure them that returning home was going to be okay.

All of this, and he'd let himself fall asleep.

Shaking out the clouds in his head Paul took the internal staircase two steps at a time.

Candela was checking the passports and paperwork, probably for the tenth time. Lía was with her, holding the baby.

"It's almost seven-thirty," he told Candela, coming into this spare room without knocking. "You should have been on your way."

"We thought you needed to sleep."

Paul looked at his daughter, concern and irritation combining, but he didn't reply. The exhaustion in her face was easy to recognise. It was Lía who needed that sleep, not him. He'd take her to a doctor today, just to make sure everything was okay. Yet again his belly squirmed.

"Okay, let's go."

Lía said to Candela, "I'll take Zo?"

"Yes, outside, his last chance of sunlight until these long flights."

She left the room, the baby happy in her arms, and Paul collected Candela's small suitcase. Candela had her shoulder bag, which seemed to hold the types of things a mother with a baby would need.

"You'll leave your car at the airport?"

"Donatello can find it one day, or it can be towed away never to be seen again." She stopped him from leading the way out. "Paolo, I owe you everything."

"Nothing. Absolutely nothing."

"It is a debt," she said, and the way she touched the bruised and scarred side of his face said how sorry she was. "One day you must collect it."

"Come on," Paul spoke more gently, wishing he could hold her, wanting more than anything that he didn't have to say goodbye to her. "It's time for you to disappear."

<hr />

Lía was waiting, then she saw her father and Candela emerge from the back of the house. She felt an ache in her heart for needing to say goodbye to Candela, and to little Zo of course. Maybe mostly for little Zo. She wondered if one day she and her father, or maybe even Lía on her own, might visit Candela and Lorenzo wherever they'd make a home. By then she'd be older; the baby would be so much bigger. Running, talking, and if enough time passed Lorenzo would be a small boy, or even older again.

Though there were heavy clouds brewing on the horizon, she kept him in the warm sunlight of this new day. She tried not to think about last night, or the children, or the ghost-boy, her uncle Little Jack Mosca.

Lía held Lorenzo closer; the ache in her heart said she'd never see or hold Lorenzo as a baby again.

Candela's sedan was parked away from the driveway and courtyard. It was on grass in the shade of one of the property's largest Chinese elms. Dakota and Buster were nosing around it. They'd been investigating all around the house, sniffing everywhere because of the motorcycle, nostrils flaring at the scents of so many dogs.

Lía looked around. The morning was heavy with humidity and the gardens and grass surrounding Rosso House were gouged and churned. There was a hum of insects.

She took Lorenzo's hand and held it in her own. Her hand completely enclosed his. Standing like this Lía felt more than the warm touch of a baby's flesh; instead she was conscious of a deeper part of him. She sensed a soul that was of course just as strong and real as her own. And maybe that was all Lía could know about life and death and the things in between. Lía had a soul; this baby had a soul. She was a soul when she travelled so far from her body, and as that entity she was free. Come the moment of death it might be the same for everyone; the deepest part of themselves travels away, and that's that. Yet some stayed. Some remained trapped—floating— in a liminal space between life and eternity.

Why?

Her only answer was a picture of Rosso House and its children, the little ones who wanted her to set them free.

To let them escape, just as Candela and her boy were about to do.

She watched her father stride to the Toyota. Candela opened the boot. They put her things in then Candela opened a back door for Lorenzo to be placed into the travelling bassinet. Lía took him to her and watched Lorenzo kick as his mother gently lay him down.

At least I've got the dogs, Lía thought. I hope Dad will let them come with us wherever it is we're going to hole up.

Candela straightened. There was colour in her cheeks and her car keys were in her hand. Her eyes were on Lía's father.

Lía found herself more moved than she might have expected.

The quiet lethargy of the day allowed sounds to carry from near and far, though Lía didn't hear anything.

Of course, Buster and Dakota did.

Beware of Dogs, and More

Haberman drove up the steep country hillside. He'd been considering a more surreptitious entrance then decided that a direct approach might be less threatening. If there was any truth to what Donatello said about the previous evening's events this family could have called in the authorities. At the very least they'd be on their guard. It might even have been smarter to wait a week or two—however the witch had been impatient. Of course, now that he'd acquiesced so completely Haberman himself wanted things moving.

Meaning he wanted this mythical girl plus her mythical promise.

If this morning suspicions were raised Haberman had with him a set of business cards made up years back. Just as he'd been able to present himself as William Monk with a press card, today he had another handy accreditation: Ray Harrison, Real Estate Agent. What could be a better cover in this godforsaken outer region where *For Sale* and *Sold* signs dotted the countryside?

Just as he possessed a different name for this visit, he'd also brought something more useful than a simple boxcutter. Nestled inside a smooth calf-hide holster in his left armpit was that somewhat exotic specimen of a semi-automatic, his eight-round Makarova. It had been given to him by an inveterate gambler, once a member of the Russian Army. The repayment of a debt had been slow in coming; the pistolet had been the Russian's down payment. Eventually the debt was paid. Haberman kept the gun anyway.

The Mercedes reached the top of the acute rise. There was a latched gate with a sign:

Beware of Dogs

and

Please Shut the Gate

He set the handbrake and opened the long, wide gate. After he drove through he didn't stop to shut it after him, imagining an exit that might need to be fast and unimpeded. Then two damnable mutts were worrying at the Mercedes, barking in a way that invited a shot each in the head. They accompanied Haberman all the way to what he saw was a great old red house, and a circular courtyard. Just past that courtyard he observed a white Ford Chrysler, a Toyota parked further back beneath some kind of huge tree, and three figures. Continuing slowly, Haberman turned the 450SEL so that it pointed back down the drive. He also made sure the Mercedes blocked that drive.

The dogs now barked at his door. As he carefully opened it they backed away, though not very far. Haberman straightened his blazer and waved politely.

"Hello," he called.

"Wait there!" the man in the group called back.

"They're lovely puppies—they won't eat me?"

"Who are you?"

"Ray Harrison of Ray Harrison Real Estate. Interested in your wonderful property."

There was no immediate reply. Haberman risked taking a few steps forward. He wanted to get a closer look at these people: looked like a man, a woman, and someone else behind them. The Toyota was no less than that cheap piece of trash Donatello had purchased after his even cheaper Torana had been shot up, crashed and wrecked.

So that woman there had to be the grunt's estranged wife, whom as per his own rules Haberman had never met. Poor Donatello had been correct about one thing at least: his beloved did indeed dally with the gentleman of this house. Haberman could have laughed at the persistent vagaries of the human heart. Instead he manufactured a broad smile, making a production of expansively taking in the red brick home, the rolling paddocks and fields, the forest and the cloud-shrouded mountains in the distance.

There was a whistle from the group and the two dogs started to leave him, moving back across the courtyard, though they remained very alert to his presence. The owner of this house, according to Donatello, was one Paul Munro. So over there was Munro, Candela—and what of the girl who'd just about turned the grunt to blood and bone?

It had to be her stepping out from where she'd been standing behind the other two. It was difficult to tell at this distance, but at first sight his heart beat faster.

Lean and long, dark skin, dark gold hair.

It's you it's you it's you.

Haberman maintained his smile. He braved a few more steps forward and saw the way the others spoke among themselves, probably working out what to do with this unexpected visitor.

"We're not interested. Clear the driveway—we're on our way out."

"Of course, Mr Munro! But a word before I go?"

Haberman felt longing and hunger inside, raw as the morning's stark sunshine. He had no doubt whatsoever that this was her, the girl the witch had waited for, the girl Haberman was promised.

Not rushing, careful not to upset this pair of dogs. As he came closer he saw the girl's skin was a sort of light umber. Sunlight revealed long strands of cinnamon tints in her hair. To Haberman these looked like gold thread. Where once his heart had burned with the witch's tortures it now filled with desire. The mask of affable kindness grew more difficult to maintain; he'd never felt a disguise so thin, or a time when his true self was so eager to surface.

"I told you, we're not interested." The man, Paul Munro, turned to help Donatello's wife into the driver's seat of the car. The door slammed. The girl, his daughter, was staring at Haberman across the short distance. Paul Munro shouted again, this time in a far harsher voice: "Get in your car and get the fuck off this property. Do it now!"

Haberman glanced toward the great house. His feeling was that no one else waited inside. He noted the vast expanse of ruined, gouged grass and drying mud. He still wanted to approach these people with caution, yet he was beginning to lean toward sliding his hand to his holster.

Then things happened in a rush.

There were more dogs, different ones from the black and the brown pets who'd greeted him. These were mangy beasts in a pack, maybe eight or ten, stalking down out of a thick wood further back.

Immediately they sensed their presence, the black and the brown bolted towards that pack. The girl called out; the man called too; there was no stopping this fray.

Donatello. Goddamn him but this had to be Donatello's doing, still wanting his wife and baby.

Haberman made up his mind. There was no need for further subterfuge. He reached into his blazer and withdrew the pistol, striding forwards with it held straight out in front of him, intercepting Paul Munro who seemed about to run to the dogs.

"Stay where you are. You in the car get out."

"Start the car and go," Paul Munro ordered her.

Haberman twitched the Makarova a little to the right and fired a shot through the back windscreen, creating a shattered hole. Candela behind the wheel flung her hands to her ears. Haberman stood his ground.

As the booming echo died, and the snarling, screeching cries of dogs in crisis reached a crescendo, he spoke again.

"Please get out of the car, Candela. It would appear your husband is here."

Donatello's wife wasn't important. Haberman only watched her from the corner of his eye. Instead he made certain to keep Paul Munro and his daughter in plain view. He was aware that the grunt's wife didn't reach for the ignition key, though she didn't emerge from her car either. Haberman pointed the pistolet in Paul Munro's face and cautiously approached the depressingly bargain-basement Toyota. With one hand he opened the driver's door.

"Should I put a slug into a man's head over a woman's recalcitrance?"

Candela emerged. He waved her away from the car toward the other two. He saw her eyes gaze fearfully towards the back seat; *Ah, her baby kicking in a bassinet, not crying even for the shattering boom of a pistol shot.*

"What do you want?" Munro asked.

"I'm taking your daughter."

It was too much. Munro lunged at him. Haberman had expected a dose of mad heroics. He side-stepped and pistol-whipped the man's face, a sharp crack. He observed how that face had already known other trouble. Bruising and scars; Donatello's touch, no doubt.

Bleeding from the way a line had been opened across one cheek, dazed as well, and even with the pistol's dark muzzle pointed at him, Munro moved in front of his daughter. The girl appeared almost completely frozen; whether in surprise or fright Haberman couldn't tell. Her eyes were wide, not transfixed on Haberman but the gun in his hand. He'd expected something from her as well—some incredible act that proved her exceptionality—and might have been disappointed if he'd given this some thought.

The dogs had broken apart. There was a vicious, snarling standoff. The black and the brown backed away and circled as the pack appeared to circle them. Something in that was bringing the girl to life. Yes, she longed to save her dogs, Haberman could see that, but he sensed her growing need to protect her father and Donatello's wife.

Things become interesting, Haberman reflected.

Gun trained on the three, he took an involuntary step back as the girl moved slowly around her father; it was as if she was now ready to confront Haberman.

He kept the Makarova steady. "What's your name, girl?"

"Shut up! You don't talk to her!"

Like an admirable father Paul Munro again pushed his body right in front of his daughter's.

Haberman pulled the trigger twice, but the impact of the first slug, just below Paul Munro's collar bone, spun the man in a powerful half-pirouette, making the second slug miss and ricochet off the hard bark of a distant tree trunk.

He noted that some of the dogs reared back at the sharp loud shocks, and the screams from the girl and the woman, yet they didn't run. Instead the shots set off yet another attack. Crazed with blood and fear and excitement, the pack dogs tore into the black and brown.

The twin retorts returned as soft echoes from faraway forests. Haberman turned the gun towards Donatello's wife, this lovely young woman named Candela. A wife—an ex-wife, really—and mother. Yet mightn't it be better to lose all witnesses?

"Don't hurt her," the girl spoke. "I'll do what you want."

For the moment Haberman resisted the urge to squeeze the trigger. Shoot the wife, then have to deal with mad Donatello? Maybe not such a good idea after all.

Immediately the woman turned and opened her Toyota's back door, scooping up her baby.

Paul Munro just like a father; this Candela just like a mother.

And the girl, just like a loving daughter.

Because she'd fallen to her knees beside her father, holding his face, his hands, half-blubbering over him in a way that made Haberman want to turn away. Blood from the hole in the man's chest looked worse for the white of his shirt. Paul Munro lay on the grass gasping rapidly. The hole steamed and bubbled. He stared at Haberman as if he might still find the strength to stop him. Or make a supplication.

"…don't hurt… don't hurt…"

Something in all this filled Haberman with revulsion. The bravery of a man, the motherly love of a woman, a daughter's devotion to both her father and her pets. Better to end this display and move on; Haberman would give Munro a bullet to the skull, drag the girl away, and leave Candela and the baby to Donatello—wherever the stupid grunt was hiding.

The girl understood what Haberman was about to do. With a scream of "No!" she covered her father's already dying body with her own.

"Remove yourself." Haberman aimed the Makarova at Paul Munro's hairline. "A splinter of skull might blind you."

She darted a look up at him.

By god, Haberman thought. Look at the green of those eyes and their wrathful terror. Better watch out, witch, this girl will bite you.

A clear shot; he'd do it.

Yet, instead of immediately firing, Haberman felt himself compelled to again look at the girl. He did, and found a surprising warmth in her gaze, warmth and perhaps even a special sort of understanding, one that carried a message. The message was for him.

Haberman slowly lowered his aim. The message was that he should not point the pistol at that man but instead raise the muzzle to his own temple. There he was free to squeeze the trigger.

Why would I want to do that?

Because I say so.

Now the girl stood from her father's side, both hands red with the wash of his blood. She faced Haberman. Before he was quite aware of what he was doing, and of how far he was going, or for what reason, the small metal circle of the still-hot muzzle, redolent of bitter-sweet cordite, pressed itself to his right temple.

His index finger started its soothing pressure.

The melee of dogs was over. The pack had vanished like air. Only the brown dog was standing; the black was in the grass. With amazement, Haberman observed the ragged thing, body rent and torn, stumble along, trembling and shaking, and come to the girl's left side. The dog pointed its bloodied snout to the sky and the blood-stained fur of its neck rippled to a wail.

Here, Haberman understood, was the music to accompany Haberman's death.

The girl's eyes were now the colour of silver, and that silver was a beacon cutting into the corners of wretched Haberman's mind.

The trigger, squeeze it to the point of no return. Hurry.

There was a blur of motion from the trees. It plunged across the green. The brown dog was tossed aside. Something struck the girl a brutal blow, knocking her sideways and to the grass, then that same blur passed and struck the woman Candela. Haberman heard the sickeningly solid thud of her head striking the side of her sedan. She slid, nerveless, to the ground, unmoving by a rear tyre.

All of it so quick, a single heartbeat.

And the woman's baby?

Paul Munro remained struggling and bleeding where he was; the girl lay crumpled; Donatello's wife didn't move—and yet here was the most impressive thing of all: the frayed and torn brown dog was now utterly humbled. It lay flat and submissive, almost in supplication.

Why?

Maybe for the beauty of this new thing with them.

A man-wolf, carefully holding the baby to his matted chest. The baby yawned and made a small cough. Haberman's right hand dropped, still holding the pistolet, which he wouldn't use. The man-wolf turned towards him. Haberman had never imagined a being so terrifying and magnificent. A work of art, a primal divinity. No longer Donatello giving a madman's imitation of some animal, but the pure beast itself.

There was no foul stench; he smelled of earth and sky.

Of forests and rain.

Of snow and blood.

And those eyes, even as he held his baby, were all torture and sorrow.

The man-wolf put his head back and howled. The blue sky swallowed that cry and wanted more. Haberman covered his ears at the long tone, so lost and forlorn, yet so thrilling too. The creature's pelt was black, pure black, with a dense layer of soft fur topped by longer hairs now standing upright. His mane and the tip of his short tail were darker still, dark to the point of a most glossy velvet, and the facial hair didn't act to hide the boy but instead accentuated the tormented features captured within it.

Now Haberman understood: Donatello's angular face, his long torso and short arms, such features made sense. For this thing stood on two legs, and now there was another blur of motion and beast and baby were gone.

The brown remained in its submission. Haberman saw how this dog quivered. His own limbs shook as well.

Then he forced himself to move, to slide the handgun into its holster. He crouched over the girl. Hair covered her eyes and thin strings of blood made spider-web beads to the grass beneath her face. Haberman used his handkerchief to dab that blood away. Then he gathered her up.

The glazing eyes of her father no longer looked at him, or her, but at wisps of cloud.

Haberman carried the girl. At the Mercedes he first considered the passenger seat, then the back seat, but instead opened the trunk, clean and spacious. He deposited her inside and locked the lid. Nothing would describe this day so Haberman kept his mind empty.

His body, however, already thrummed for touching her.

He turned the key and drove the Mercedes to the open gate. No dog followed. Haberman paused at the top of the rise, rolling down his window to listen to distant sounds. A cry pealed out into the hills. Or it emerged from those hills.

Haberman drove on.

The howling still came.

Then We'll All Go

Sometimes Paul Munro understood his situation clearly. Often he didn't. Worst dream ever. Worst drunk ever. *But didn't I swear that off?*

One minute he's sharing a couch with Anna watching the baby they've struggled and waited and dreamed to adopt now crawl across a rug with an earnest look of determination in her face, next he's walking through the rooms of Rosso House thinking how great it is that his daughter feels so at home here.

Somewhere in between he's standing with his father and mother at the remembrance ceremony for Jimmy and Bill, their bodies never recovered from the HMAS Sydney's sinking. Next he's holding Lía's hand as he walks her home from a good day at school, clear as anything, first day of a new year at *Good Hope* in Kowloon.

Then a sensation of deep sleep, which Paul tries to fight. He turns his head and for a moment gets some focus. What does he see? The blurred image of Rosso House looming over him, but what did Lía call it?

Stately Munro Home.

That's a good one.

And inside their home's the telephone, a lifeline he needs to reach.

❖————◆————❖

Somewhere along the infinite stretch between the front door and the grassy plain where he's lying, Paul tries to sit up and can't quite do it. He knows Buster, ragged and still bleeding, was with him for some time before scurrying away. And Candela, beautiful Candela, she's in a British Airways jet with Zo in her arms, right?

Be safe, both of you. Maybe we'll meet again one day. What do they say? Godspeed.

Wait, wasn't there something not very godly at all to this day? Yes, that stranger, a well-dressed man, bald, raising a pistol.

Panic makes Paul try to call out for Lía yet he can't make the slightest sound. So he exerts himself beyond physical limits by crawling backwards using his elbows, feeling his dead heels dragging to the front edifice of Munro Home. There he peers upwards again. Now he sees the shining gold of a setting sun. He closes his eyes a moment, or he thinks it's a moment, only to reopen them to an almost total darkness in the sky. Not just darkness, but the clouds that have brooded since early morning.

There's a thunderstorm ready to blow through.

Get yourself inside, he tells himself. *Man, you're in trouble and you need that telephone.*

Paul's managed to drag himself to the short set of bricked steps leading into the front portico, then he's struggled himself up every awkward step all the way to the front door. Which is shut of course, and probably locked, too. With even more frustration he realises he just can't get to his feet to find out. So much time has passed since the stranger came onto the property, and now there's this rising, howling wind to presage a storm. Paul uses the last of his strength to prop himself with his back against the door frame. He slaps weakly at the door with the palm of his hand.

Let me in, he says, or imagines he does.

Then Buster's returned, looking a fright. He has burrs and weeds caught in the now dried blood of his coat. Where's the other dog? Buster's caught what might have once been a chicken, or maybe a duck. Paul's blurred vision makes him vaguely aware of the dog eating through to the gizzards. He hears that wet snuffling before his head drops and he sleeps some more. What wakes him is Buster nuzzling close, licking his face.

No, the stupid dog's lapping at the fresh blood in Paul's shirt.

He'd scream if he could. If he had a voice. He tries to strike the dog's muzzle but now can't even lift his hand. Buster rests back on his haunches and those pretty brown eyes appear pitiless.

Let me into this house, Paul's mind races. *Someone let me the hell in.*

Brilliant white veins crack the velvet black, ground rumbling. *Jesus, you swelter like mad in the heat of the day and you wilt with your crops, then come the evening there's a storm with pounding rain to make you shiver with cold, but also makes you give thanks.* Life in the country; the farmer's lot on the land. So rain pelts down hard and heavy and Buster scurries off again. Paul's protected by the portico's tiled roof, though its sides are open.

Then, what's this?

Children emerge from Rosso House, drifting right through that heavy, closed front door. One, two, three, four of them. Nice looking kids, could have been friends to Lía if things had worked out that way. They gather around Paul, curious, the dead looking at the living soon to be dead.

And here's one more kid. Recognition flickers in the clouded depths of Paul's mind.

Wait, isn't he Anna's brother?

All these decades later Paul would recognise young Giacomo Mosca anywhere. Out of nowhere, from the depths of despair, Paul feels excitement mounting.

Hey Jack, it's me. It's Paulie. Yes, right here. And you want to hear something funny? We became brothers-in-law when I married your little sister. We're family you and me.

Little Jack stands with the other children, then there's one more of this group that Paul recognises. He can't quite put his finger on the second boy's name, but he's a son from hard-faced Mr Egan's big clan. Somehow Paul understands the Egan boy wants to go find his dad and his farm and all his brothers and sisters. He wants to return to them—and these other kids, they all want to return to their families as well.

Paul knows the Egans are right where they've always been, still on their big dairy farm, but he thinks better of giving the other children this news: *Sorry, your families sold up and moved out a long time ago, just like mine.*

But Little Jack, you remember me, right?

Sure, Paulie. Do you want to come with me?

I do, but remember my brothers? They're not here yet.

Well, maybe we'll stay until you're ready.

That'd be good. Stay close, okay?

Okay.

So Jack and the others wait with him, but it's as if there's so much more than Paul's bloodied body keeping them. In fact, Paul gains the distinct impression these kids *can't* leave, no matter what they might want.

Paul has a new thought, and it's like a prayer out of nowhere:

Dear Billy and Jim, I'm waiting for you.

And don't think I've forgotten you either, my Anna. I'll wait to see your beautiful face here with me.

Then I'll go.
Then we'll all go.

———◆————————————◆———

Teddy Quinn hadn't seen or spoken to Lía since that day he drove her home from the library. Then there'd been that curious scene at work, with poor Mike Gavin trying to get him to say something great about being top of the sales ladder and Teddy mumbling bits and pieces about mathematics. Almost as if he was reaching out to help Lía, or she was reaching out to him.

He'd called the house once to see how the school test went but her dad Paul answered the telephone; it had been as awkward a phone call as Teddy could imagine. The tone of her father's voice made things very clear: he wasn't happy about being instantly fired by Teddy's boss, and why might Teddy be ringing his sixteen-year-old daughter anyway?

"Lía's doing well and she'll go to a great school." A significant pause before: "Soon she'll be making friends her own age."

Teddy had burned with shame; how could he explain that he only wanted to make sure she was okay? That she would always be okay.

Thing was, he could honestly say he didn't want a thing in return.

I guess that means I just want to be your friend, Lía.

Well, it was probably far too late to try to tell Lía anything. Far too late and far too confusing, especially on this Wednesday evening, Teddy home now, weary and drained after a day of shocks and interviews with police and detectives.

Who'd believe something like this could happen, and to Mike Gavin of all people? Cause of death wasn't talked about but everyone in the office knew there'd been a lot of blood. On the footpath outside Gavin Realty Teddy's co-workers had been in stunned tears, some sobbing uncontrollably. After Nancy the receptionist found Mr Gavin, police had come and had quickly corralled all the employees outside. They'd taken names and details—so many details that a number of initial conversations with plainclothes detectives had essentially already taken place.

"Theodore Quinn. What can you tell us about Mr Gavin?"

"What sort of a boss was he?"

"Do you have an access key?"

"A number of your colleagues have mentioned you were the boss's favourite. Did the age difference make you like a son?"

"What can you tell us about any people he disliked?"

"Any deals gone sour, Mr Quinn?"

"You're a pretty ambitious young guy, right?"

The effect of all this made Teddy want to do two things. The first was to hit the booze, which he did with a long draught of cold beer. The second was an overwhelming desire to see Lía, no matter what her father might say. He couldn't think of anyone else he wanted to talk to—but when Roxanne rang, hearing endless reports on the radio, she told him she was coming straight over.

Teddy drank some more and tried to get interested in the cracking storm outside. He couldn't; not Mr Gavin or Roxanne but Lía kept coming to mind. How bloody weird. He stood at his covered balcony and felt the bracing whip of cold spray against his face. Teddy could almost imagine Lía somewhere inside that storm. And the wind and rain, why did they sound like they masked Lía's voice?

Help me.

Teddy, please help me.

Shaking his head, feeling too much the effects of the beer, Teddy slid shut the verandah's doors, doing his best to silence the elements. In the centre of his flat he stood thinking. Or maybe it wasn't so much thinking as listening. Was the girl really crying out for him? Was this just one more extraordinary thing she could do?

Teddy trembled.

It was for the horror of what happened to Mr Gavin, and for the sound of a voice that couldn't be there. So he went to the telephone and from memory dialled the Munro's number. Maybe there'd have to be another awkward conversation with Paul Munro, but now Teddy didn't care. He waited, listening to the ring-tone's burr, his heart—curiously—beating fast, but the call died, no answer.

They've gone out. Okay, good. Probably fed up with the boring black of country nights, gone to take in a mid-week movie or something.

Was he convincing himself of this?

Not sure. Just not sure.

Just about a relief, then, when Roxanne let herself in with her key. Bedraggled by rain, she had a heavy bag over one shoulder. Wet shoes left a trail in the carpet into the kitchen. She unloaded her bag: she'd brought him a ceramic pot of something that smelled good plus a bottle of red wine. Then she took Teddy's hand and led him to the couch.

"What a horrible, horrible thing."

"Yes…"

"Is what they're saying true? Really, it's murder?"

"And so much blood—"

His shoulders shuddered and he felt himself weep against the silky satin of Roxanne's blouse. It scared him how he couldn't stop; simply could not stop.

"This is awful," Roxanne caressed his hair, "but you're alright. You know that don't you? Everything's fine with you, Teddy, and things'll work out." She let him rest where he was against her. "And I was making a chicken casserole for my housemates but now it's for you."

There was something in the way Roxanne Mortensen held him, something in the way she was so uncharacteristically caring, that it was as if he didn't know her at all.

"But I think—" He needed to clear his throat. "I've got this crazy feeling someone needs me."

"Lots of people from your office, right? I can believe it."

"Tonight…"

"No, tonight's just for you. In the morning you go give all the help you can."

"I think I—"

"You think nothing, Theodore Quinn," Roxanne spoke, now pulling away. "Let me get this dinner ready. You open that bottle. We are staying right here. *You* are going to be looked after."

Teddy wiped his eyes and his cheeks, trying to understand the expression in Roxanne's face.

He said, "What's—?"

"Teddy," Roxanne spoke quickly, interrupting him, her voice a hundred times gentler than he'd heard it before. Then she shook her head.

"What?"

"Just one thing I want you to hear: you are not a shit."

But what he really wanted to hear? That voice in the wind and rain. It didn't matter that the sliding door to the balcony plus all the windows were closed tight. The voice had petered out. It simply wasn't there anymore. Lía wasn't there anymore, like he'd imagined the whole thing.

"Okay," he heard himself say. "For tonight I'll stay."

"Of course you will."

"Then in the morning I'll go."

Roxanne gave him a small smile, yet a new chill ran deep into Teddy's belly, out of nowhere. It was as if he'd heard a sort of echo:

Then we'll all go.

A Witch's Vault

Beneath the witch's home, this solid room within concrete walls was substantial and carefully constructed, a place for genuine secrets. Haberman hadn't been down here before; what he saw was a veritable vault, the type of place perfect for magic and evil combined.

Agata Rosso's jars and canisters, containers and smoky bottles, filled every available gap and corner. Some were glass, some porcelain, some plastic, some large, many very small. He recognised the sorts of olive, jam, marmalade and condiment jars she'd sent him, full of her potions. Shelves were overfilled with dried flowers and dried fruit and dried other things. Such as animals with small, pinched and wizened faces. Or snake skins laid out in rows of variable length. He thought he perceived a bowl of snails; a bowl of talons; a dish of hard, beady eyes. There were rough-hewn wooden tables and side tables, and all together there was a scent and a smell of no one thing in particular: herbs and flowers, must and mildew, spice and earth and blood leached together.

So he'd accepted it all as true: Agata Rosso toyed with equal parts good and evil. For pay she might perform the former; today it was definitely the latter, and of the oldest form imaginable. What he himself had done to men had always been, in its way, honest. Perfectly reasonable as well—but this tonight? It possessed a different and far darker complexion.

For the time being he'd stay in the background and observe the crone's plan unfold, which wasn't easy when the hairs at the back of his neck and along his arms raised themselves in excitement. That excitement wanted to be freed, for the fact of the girl and the way she was strung unconscious at the centre of this cold chamber.

"Tell me your name, child," Haberman had asked her. Then, to those glinting eyes refusing: "I haven't hurt you, have I?"

"You…you shot my father… Where is he?"

"No tears, Miss Munro. Tell me your first name and we'll proceed. We won't have any secrets, that's a promise."

"Lía."

"Lía. Miss Lía Munro. And I am Karl Haberman, your servant."

"You said a different name."

"Life's a game we play with many names and faces and things we pretend to each other. But the games have ended and we meet in complete honesty. How old are you, sweetheart?"

"Sixteen."

No Lashana Okonedo here, but all the things I've imagined, encapsulated in a single word.

Haberman had delivered Miss Lía Munro to the witch and the witch had immediately and with great agitation applied a compress to the girl's nostrils and mouth, holding it there hard until the girl, trying not to breathe, simply had to.

"She stays asleep until I need her," Agata Rosso commanded, as if Haberman had been foolish to bring her to the house awake. Well, maybe she had a point. Haberman wouldn't easily forget the overpowering urge to pull the pistolet's trigger and blow his brains out.

Now Lía hung by her wrists in a scene of medieval torture—or, more appropriately, because of the knives arrayed on a table, the ancient and not so-ancient Chinese practice of slicing a victim to death.

This procedure, he knew, hadn't been formally banned in that country until 1905. For Haberman had investigated this particular means of torture and execution many decades back, when he'd first considered his options for maintaining order over his little fiefdom of massage parlours, gambling dens and weekly cash payments. The ancient Chinese penchant for expert torture had been of great interest. He knew that in the Ming Dynasty the cuts carefully applied before the victim was allowed to die could number into the thousands. The ceremony would follow a laid-out pattern of stages, sometimes over a period of days. Always the objective was to inflict as much cruelty and humiliation as possible.

The witch obviously had something similar in mind, tortures decreed for Lía Munro and to be delivered, of course, by heartless Haberman himself. Did he feel any pity for the girl, shackled by chains which were in turn strung from the thick timber beams above her slumped head? The answer was that he felt as much pity as he would for the cow slaughtered for its finest cuts of meat, or the big game hunted in an African veldt. So tonight Haberman's excitement was the thing: his coming pleasure the one and only consideration.

He watched the full dead weight of Lía Munro's young body taken solely by her wrists and shoulders. Her hands had darkened, suffused with blood, and the girl's chin was on her chest, lovely face covered by that extraordinary hair. Beneath her nerveless feet was something perfect in its practical efficacy: a blue children's wading pool, five-feet square. It had a galvanised metal frame and a heavy duty, laminated plastic liner.

Signora Celano left the room at something the witch told her. Haberman didn't understand the words except for Donatello's name and the mention of her husband Giancarlo. Celano took the staircase into the main part of the house. Haberman heard movement on the floorboards above then the signora was back. She handed the baby Lorenzo—stolen away from the Munro house—to the witch. Agata nursed that baby as uncomfortably as Haberman himself might have done.

Soon Celano returned a second time, this time awkwardly manoeuvring a small cot into this crowded vault. She positioned it a little out of the way, on the floor by Agata Rosso's omnipresent dolls. In this light three were ready to come to life but the auburn-haired fourth, that poor miss of the terribly cracked skull, looked positively cadaverous. Then Donatello was descending, and he carried the good-as-dead Giancarlo Rosso. He laid the man onto the cot and set him straight. Tonight Giancarlo's wizened body was bare-chested and bare-footed, yet he wore long trousers as if half-dressed for going out.

Donatello took his baby from the witch and made to leave, glancing at the hanging girl then quickly turning his head away. He headed for the staircase but the witch spoke to him sharply; she wanted him to stay. Donatello clearly said something along the lines that he would not. His great-aunt's tongue was even sharper. Donatello Zappavigna sat himself glowering in a corner.

How curious, Haberman reflected. Why would the witch want this boy and his baby present? At least—thank the lord—there was nothing of the man-wolf to Donny Zap this evening. All the same, Haberman kept his distance; his desire to interact with Donatello was exactly zero.

Outside there was persistent wind and rain, though the thunder had passed. With typical mockery Haberman had been moved to ask, "You've raised the elements to complement your proceedings?" and a corner of the witch's mouth had twitched with annoyance.

Night had come and Agata Rosso worked at a whetstone, bringing a final gleam to the blade of a small paring knife. Her worktable was busy with many knives. Alongside that assortment were hacksaws and a power drill. The witch had explained her objectives. She told Haberman that the greater Lía Munro's screams the greater the effect of the next part: from her flesh and blood, from her viscera and organs, from the ground ligaments and bone of this innocent, even from her skin, teeth and hair, Agata Rosso would create the concoctions that would raise Giancarlo Rosso.

This miracle she vowed would be true.

Celano took down bunches of dried herbs, wizened animal feet, and what might have been weeds. A twin set of hot plates warmed juices inside two pots. Meanwhile the crone began to sing to her task, to her ingredients. Her voice was quavering and ugly; there was no pretty melody for this ceremony.

Celano had been making, of all things, tea. She poured a cup for Donny Zap, then, unseen by the boy, poured something quite different for Haberman.

"What is it?"

"Mr Hubbamente," she leaned in, whispering as if he should be privy to a secret, "yours is jasmine."

Obviously in a hurry to get himself and his baby out of there, Donny Zap slurped his tea. Celano lifted Lorenzo away from his father's lap, little feet kicking. Almost simultaneously the grunt's hands twitched, his face twisted, and he dropped the teacup. Parts of him buckled.

Haberman watched Donatello fall sideways from his chair and crash to the cold hard floor.

◆————————◆

The witch now uncorked a green bottle and inverted it into a ceramic bowl. She took a dried bunch of rosemary and set it alight over a flame. This she also placed into the bowl. In moments a smoky, pleasant scent started to rise. She went to the slumped girl and let tendrils of smoke drift into her nostrils.

Which made Lía's fingers quiver and her back arch. Her knees straightened, feet taking the weight away from what must be screamingly aching wrists, arms and shoulders. She coughed and let out a series of low moans. Even though she blinked rapidly her features remained dull and slack; at first she offered no resistance, then tried to struggle away from the smoke. By a fistful of hair the witch kept the girl's face over the fumes.

Haberman observed Lía's eyes open fully; she began to comprehend her position and with greater effort strained away from the smoke. The witch struck her hard in the solar plexus. The girl gasped and the fumes completed whatever their work was supposed to be. In a moment Haberman understood what that was: on the one hand Lía was awake, but on the other hand her resistance had waned.

He remembered how easily this girl's voice had entered his mind, persuading him to raise his pistol to his temple. This thing about her was real; she did have power or powers that transcended the most extraordinary human attributes—and Agata Rosso, always sly, had now conquered it.

But as long as Lía's not too controlled.

Because more important than anything Agata Rosso wants is the pleasure in my blood against the screams that will accompany the shedding of yours, child.

The Ceremony (i)

Lía's eyes were on the baby in Celano's arms. She wanted to speak but when she tried she coughed with smoke deep in her lungs. Then her gaze found Haberman.

"Is my father dead?" came as a whispery wheeze.

"One would expect so."

Her teeth clenched, tears welled, and her lips trembled, yet the rest of her body didn't respond.

"Look at me, not him," the witch spoke sharply, and when Lía did: "Do you know who I am?"

It took her a moment. "From Rosso House…"

"Where my spirits tried to tell me I could find you." The witch considered the girl. "Who visits in your dreams?"

"No one."

"Wolves and spirits?"

"No one."

"Where do you travel?"

"Nowhere."

"How far do you go?"

"I stay in bed."

"Don't try to be brave," the witch spoke without a hint of sympathy. "You've come to your end, girl."

Lía's attention moved from the witch's face to her chest. Haberman saw her try to concentrate hard. *Now*, he wondered, *will she be able to make a witch's heart burn?*

The answer was that she couldn't. There was no reaction from Agata Rosso. Lía let out a gasp as if she'd already used up what little strength she'd had left. Focus appeared to melt from her eyes. That smoke really did have an effect; again Haberman had to admit it, the witch was shrewd.

"One more time: do you travel very far?"

"I…I don't know what—"

"You have no idea of yourself at all, do you?" The witch once again pulled Lía's head up by her hair, forcing their gaze to meet. "The colour of your skin and eyes, the shape of your nose and mouth, the texture of your hair. Your long body. You don't understand how far your roots go or the distance they've travelled. I can see an African savannah inside you just as easily as I sense the spices of Morocco. Where were you born?"

"Just let me go."

"Do you know anything about your roots?"

Lía shook her head.

Agata Rosso looked more deeply into the girl's green eyes.

"Ah," she nodded, "I see you very clearly, girl."

"What?"

"Your father was a man like a wolf. Your mother was one of us."

"What does that mean?"

"I see the *Benandante* line in you. Like me, like my mother and my spiritual sisters, like all of us. Our line changed over generations because of our love for the wolves who once helped us. That love created something new, and so we travelled away from our roots and spread through Europe. No more helping others; we learned the best magic is to help ourselves."

"I don't understand."

"Girl, you're the child of an animal father and a miraculous mother, and that's what makes you so special."

"I'm not special."

"With you I'll make wonderful magic tonight." The witch started to turn away, her usually grey cheeks actually enlivened with a rising pink.

"Wait, please tell me…just one thing."

"What is it?"

"Why is that woman holding Lorenzo?"

"Isn't he an equal part of what we'll do?"

"Please…no. I saw the children and what you did to them. Why not… why not let the baby go?"

The witch shook her head. Lía kept watching dumbfounded, almost completely unable to comprehend what this hating woman might mean.

Then she gathered the spit in her mouth and spat in Agata Rosso's face. The crone used a lace handkerchief from her sleeve to wipe her cheek clean. She returned to the wooden table holding all the knives.

"Her clothes, Haberman, then when I tell you use the small knife for the first incision. Whenever the child faints, we wait. I want her to know at least another morning, maybe another evening as well." The witch glanced again at Lía. "I think we'll achieve that quite easily. The girl is strong."

"Wait," Lía spoke. "I'm begging…please, the baby."

Celano placed Lorenzo onto the cleared space of the wide wooden tabletop in front of Agata Rosso, then pulled off his small cotton shirt and nappy. Zo lay looking up, hands opening and closing. Haberman took the paring knife. The witch took up a cleaver.

The sight of the cleaver in that wizened hand made a moment of something like revulsion twist inside Haberman's belly.

"You really must include a baby?"

"He'll go straight away. That's the best I can do. Celano will render his remains as we continue with the girl."

Well, ugly it might be, Haberman told himself, but this was the witch's business. For a moment he wondered how that great grunt Donny Zap would react when he discovered his own son's fate. Then Haberman noted the way Celano remained so close to Donatello's slumped body, an axe she'd collected from a corner now held loosely in her hands. With her rounded shoulders and powerful arms, how long would it take her to, say, behead the boy?

Well, well, the ruthlessness in this room certainly eclipses anything I've ever done.

"Stop thinking," the witch told him. Her eyes met his, hard and unyielding.

Yes, enough thinking. I'm Haberman finally freed.

He approached Lía Munro. Her eyes were different now—wet and wide, silently pleading less for her own life than for that of one small boy. Haberman set himself before the girl and found the place where he'd start to cut away her clothes.

With no effort at all he slashed downwards.

The Ceremony (ii)

As the rain kept coming down Candela raised her dripping head from an increasing pool of mud. A morning's sunshine had changed into this bleak wet night. The promise of a British Airways flight was a million miles away.

She was beside a rear wheel of her sedan. Above her prone body two doors hung open. Candela pushed to her knees then pulled herself upright. Rain and mud had soaked her through and such a powerful feeling of nausea travelled from the side of her head to her belly that she threw up where she was. Then she could only squint through one eye; there was a pulse of pain in her skull.

None of it important; Candela saw the baby carrier in the back seat was empty.

Cry tomorrow. Move. Find your baby.

Every stumbling step forward brought her closer to falling yet again. Candela held her head, distended above her left ear, the swelling the size of her palm.

Donatello. Only Donatello could deliver such agony.

She had piecemeal details of what had happened. That expensive-looking dark car —a Mercedes?—had arrived; there were dogs out of nowhere; a horrible man and a gun. She whirled around to see that shattered bullet hole in the back windscreen. Then she again felt the crushing split-second of her head striking the side of her car.

It was a perfect enough picture now: a picture of Donatello, and how he'd come for Zo.

Candela continued to the house, yet stopped at the sight of a dog on its side in the wet glistening grass. Jet black—Lía's dog, the one called

Dakota. Candela moved on. Closer to the house she perceived yet another dark shape. Rain in her face and the swell of one eye made her peer in uncertainty. The shape was inside the portico, a slumped silhouette pressed up against the front door.

She ran.

The portico's light was off, operated by a switch inside the house, but Candela took the steps and had all the light she needed. A dull series of sobs made her chest want to split in two.

She fell to her knees beside Paolo. His hands were cold. The opaque emptiness of his eyes made shudders travel all the way through her body. Even so, knowing all was lost, Candela tried to find a pulse at his wrist, then in his throat. Below Paolo's collar bone a round, ragged hole had created a great stain of blood that soaked his entire shirt.

Paolo, I'm sorry, I have to go find my baby.

Yet she remained there kneeling, weeping. She leaned down and embraced that still, dead body.

You didn't deserve this. You didn't deserve to die because of me.

A hatred for Donatello rose up in her throat, a hatred more intense than anything she'd known before. The words she'd used to Lía —*some of my love must stay with that man*—she couldn't believe them anymore. And now this animal, this monster Donatello, has their baby.

My baby.

Mine.

Candela took Paolo's bloodless face in her hands and kissed his lips. If there was the slightest chance of it, then she wanted to let him know.

You were a good man, Paolo. I love the man you were.

Candela pushed away, found her feet, and tried the front door. It was locked. Again doused by rain she hurried around the side of the house. The back door was ajar and the screen door was on its latch. Even if instinct told her no one was inside she needed to search every room. Mightn't Lorenzo have somehow been left behind? Or maybe Lía?

She stood listening. There was the rain and nothing else. Lía's second dog, the brown, wasn't here either. She checked through the house floor to floor, turning on lights as she went.

Nothing and no one.

Then Candela snatched up the telephone receiver. It was dead; Donatello, of course.

She replaced the receiver. She needed to slow down and empty her mind of panic and fear. Agata Rosso's old home only appeared to be empty; the spirits of children were present, glowing like starlight through clouds. She didn't know who they were or how many remained here, but, as always, she felt no anger or hatred from them, only a vast empty longing to be set free. Even so, Candela had never offered her help. She hadn't wanted to have anything to do with these lingering dead, just as she'd never wanted anything to do with the gifts her mother had assured her she possessed.

What's bred in the bone will come out in the flesh, Candela's mother would say, *so don't deny what you are*. Candela *had* denied it, over and over, and had feared it too. The world of witchcraft and superstition was something she'd fought against, yet fate had led her to marry her wolf, and so in all things her mother hadn't lied.

She turned as if to address the walls: "Will you help me?"

Yes.

A new chill spread the full length of her spine, and even as she felt that chill and told herself not to, that immediate answer out of the cold air told Candela what she needed to do.

So through the rain she hurried back to the sedan, though it wasn't to drive away. Candela opened the boot and unsnapped her small suitcase. Among the soft clothing she felt around until she found what she wanted: Lorenzo's baptismal candle. Keeping it wrapped and dry under her shirt she returned to the empty kitchen.

Which wasn't empty at all.

A box of safety matches was by the gas stove. She turned off the overhead light and the light in the hallway, then in the pressing dark she lit the candle's wick. She dripped wax onto a small dessert plate. Instinct told her she needed to hurry. Zo was somewhere with Donatello, and she sensed more death close by, moving and spreading like an ugly shadow.

Candela set the candle straight in the puddle of wax. All this and more her mother had insisted on teaching her.

Now she addressed the sputtering flame.

In itself the flame was nothing, only a small keyhole into the powers of her mind. The spirits in this house—like all spirits—were instruments to intensify the experience. You can't do anything completely on your own, her mother had tutored her. When the spirits are with you truly, their strength will give you what you need. Candela had even seen Agata Rosso do the same thing, lighting candles and studying their flames with those strange dolls of the four seasons always close by, intensifying her visions and travels.

There was one thing Candela refused to do, even now. She wouldn't speak any of the pagan words taught her by rote. Instead she had her own, simple and direct, learned in school and church:

"*Ave, o Maria, piena di grazia, il Signore è con te. Tu sei benedetta fra le donne e benedetto è il frutto del tuo seno—*"

As she sat at the table in the dark, praying to the flame of Zo's baptismal candle, spirits came to stand behind her shoulders. She felt them; she wouldn't turn to see.

"*Gesù Santa Maria, Madre di Dio, prega per noi peccatori, adesso e nell'ora della nostra morte.*" Candela paused, concentrating, then spoke her real prayer: "Show me where my baby is and tell me how to find him."

She felt a surge inside her soul and now she knew it was five children standing with her. Then, sucked into a vortex of black, an infinite universe of nothing, she travelled.

She didn't see anything.

There was no Lorenzo.

It was as if Candela was looking left with her eyes shut, looking right but with a great shadow blinding her. She was moving in circles when she needed to make a straight line.

A voice:

Help me.

Teddy, please help me.

The voice seemed too far off, as if struggling in a vacuum.

That cry and that name drifted somewhere out of reach. Candela thought, *No, that name's useless. It doesn't mean anything. Spirits hear me: I want only Zo. Spirits understand me: take me straight to my baby.*

Help me.

Teddy, please help me.

Dio mio, but now Candela understood. The spirits were pushing her to Lía. There had to be a reason. She gave herself over to their will. The darkness melted away. It was as if she now opened her eyes to a new world, and in a moment Candela understood what Lía was facing, what was happening to her, and why she cried out.

Close your eyes from what's in front of you and come see me. You're not alone. Stop telling yourself that you are. Lía, listen to me.

Candela felt the girl running and running and running.

You can't run, you're stuck where you are. Lía, come find me.

Something's happened to my father. This man, this Haberman, he shot him. My father could be dying... Don't you understand? I need help. Maybe Teddy can help me...

Stop. Force yourself to calm down. You need to be brave. No one's coming to help you. But I'm here. Trust me.

Candela can feel the girl wracked with the sobs of terror: No, no, no.

Trust me. Be strong. Travel.

But this Haberman...my father's alone... Teddy, go find my father. Teddy, go help him...

Stop trying to find this person. Concentrate.

And now Haberman, with a knife, to cut off my clothes—

Stop looking at him.

I've read about what people like this used to do. They kill others because they want their strength. That's what—

I've got something to help you. Something I learned from my mother. It's a spell. But you have to believe in it, Lía, you have to give this spell everything you've got. Your all. And I won't lie to you, the price is very high. This is a spell that can save you, but it takes just as much as it gives.

I don't care. Anything.

Good, then listen: there are three questions.

What questions?

Three questions that once asked and answered, don't allow a way to turn back. Understand what I'm telling you, Lía. There'll be no turning back ever again.

Who do I ask?

No, these questions have to be asked of you. Your job is to make Haberman pose these questions to you. And you can only answer with absolute truth.

How do you know this?

My mother taught me, and my mother's mother taught her, and Lía—

Yes?

—I believe your mother would have taught it to you, if things had been different.

Are you my sister?

No. But a long way back we all started from the same people.

There was a silence so bleak Candela thought she'd lost the girl, or that

Haberman had plunged the blade into Lía's heart and she was already gone. If that was the case, how would this candle and these children help her find Lorenzo?

Then Candela felt the girl more clearly than ever:

All right. Please tell me the questions, Candela.

The Harmony

Her clothes were in pieces at her feet and Lía wouldn't let herself look at this hellhole one more time. Instead, she felt she could fight the numbing clouds of the witch's smoke and really stare into this man's eyes— eyes that she now understood could only pretend to be alive, because of the death inside him.

This thing called Karl Haberman wanted to burn with some kind of ecstatic life. Well, he never would, no matter what steps he took, because there was nothing inside him to burn.

So I'll put these questions inside you instead.

Lía concentrated on the hidden deep of Karl Haberman's thoughts.

You've got three things to ask me.

Haberman was so close Lía was aware of the pores of his skin, the texture of the lines of his face. The fakery of him, a man to drain your soul. Perfectly kind and courtly on the outside yet a pit on the inside. A true imposter.

Not only that, but Lía saw that what he would do to her he'd repeat many times over with so many more. The things he'd done to his enemies and the things he'd spent his life paying young girls and women to accept were nothing, nothing at all.

The true Karl Haberman moved the tip of the blade beneath her chin.

Mr Haberman. Mr Haberman. You've got three things to ask me.

His fever longed to consume her; Lía wouldn't let herself falter, even though a different part of her mind wanted to scream and scream and scream.

Haberman, listen to me. There are—

She did falter.

VENERO ARMANNO

This man was a rock, a wall, and she was too, too weak. The strength that had made her repel the rider and even make Haberman turn his gun on himself was gone. Maybe her father was gone too. Again she could only think of one person to call out for.

Teddy, if you really are a friend, please help, and if you can't find me, then go to my Dad.

Her voice was too weak. In the ether she couldn't make herself heard. There was no thread to Teddy Quinn, there was no connection to anyone—

Stop doubting yourself. Stop doubting me. Be brave. Make Haberman ask the three questions.

It was Candela, firm and strong, and now Lía understood that just as Candela wanted to help her the children of Rosso House were helping Candela.

So Lía wasn't alone; so Candela wasn't alone either; they were all there together, facing a monster named Karl Haberman, and behind him, a witch with no heart.

Now Lía made sure they spoke as one.

Mr Haberman, listen very carefully and listen very hard. You've got three things to ask me.

———◆———

The point of the blade was under the girl's chin. As the first bright droplet of blood stained his finger there was a breath by his ear.

The girl's gaze had steadied. It didn't plead and neither did she react to the pain of the incision. The calm intensity of Lía Munro's stare was both unnerving and all the more exciting—but this thing, this breath by his ear, it was a thin wisp of breeze whispering something that travelled further inside his head.

You've got three things to ask me.

Haberman held the blade very still. Without a doubt this was the girl's voice. Yet again she was proving how unique she was; in spite of the stupefying smoke Lía had a trick up her sleeve. As if he'd let himself fall for something so obvious. Lía could make all the sweet nothings in his ear she wanted. In fact, wasn't it so much better that she pushed back against him? What hunter chooses to shoot a sleeping prey?

So come on, girl, let's see your mettle.

It came again, yet in a different way, as *two* voices now, combining to create a nice harmony.

294

Mr Haberman, you've got three things to ask me.

Then there were even more voices; he enjoyed a lovely chorus. Did he hear children?

Mr Haberman, Mr Haberman. You have three things to ask.

It should have been maddening, these sentences in his skull, however the harmony of voices created a melodious secret.

Which was completely unlike the witch's sour croak:

"Don't waste time, Haberman."

"Amuse yourself with that wriggling infant and wait for me," he spoke, then glanced behind to see the witch slightly lower the cleaver.

"Lía," he leaned in, studying her green eyes, "the black door is calling you."

You've got three things to ask me.

Haberman shook his head; he didn't.

Are you so sure, Mr Haberman?

Well, he couldn't quite deny the itching niggle that harmony inspired somewhere at the back of his mind. *Maybe*, Haberman wondered, *maybe the idea's quite reasonable. Maybe it's my idea after all, and not hers. There might be things worth asking this extraordinary girl, so why rush through these moments only to please a foul witch?*

Three questions? Indeed, he saw them now.

The paring knife's sharp tip remained where it was, creating further droplets to colour his hand. He put his lips to Lía's cheek and asked the first.

She waited, then replied, *Yes.*

Haberman moved his lips to her ear. He asked the second question.

Lía spoke to him in a soft breath: *Yes.*

"*Haberman.*" The witch's caustic snarl.

Haberman put his mouth against the girl's and pressed the blade. Her body shuddered and the droplets fell fatter.

"*Hurry up.*"

Intruding against the lovely song was Agata Rosso's infuriating voice, something for any sane person to detest—and of course it wasn't only the witch Haberman detested, it was all of them there. Let this decrepit audience hang. May Celano rot and Giancarlo Rosso die, and Donatello sleep an eternity. They could all burn in the place they belonged, for Haberman was beginning to understand he had one job and one job only, and its name was Lía Munro.

He asked his final question, the simplest and most direct.

Despite the pain she must be in, Lía's breath was full of a countryside's perfect summer. It was the sort of breath that would only ever answer his question with a most wonderful:

Yes.

Three affirmations spoken by the girl and at that third Haberman felt Lía Munro break through his barriers.

She entered him so completely as to immediately deliver something impossible: a view of a squirming evil that was his own abundance of corruption. His was a monstrous self, created by a blancmange of deceit and brutality, of the love for material gain multiplied by unvarnished greed. Of the need to inflict pain entwined with the overwhelming desire for physical pleasure. In the Haberman head mocking justifications for rapes and murders competed with self-serving congratulations at his corruption of a hundred, a thousand weaker souls. There was no honesty in his heart or soul, there was no room for selflessness or heroism. The Haberman hell allowed no understanding or desire for even the slightest moments of good in the world.

And all of it was a fire, the howling holocaust of Haberman meeting his own demolished soul, naked. He shrieked inside a void; he begged succour of a yawning hollow; he felt himself tumble towards hollow eternity.

Until Lía found his hand.

"What are you doing, Haberman?"

The paring knife, red-stained, now on the floor at his feet.

He turned, hot tears running from his eyes.

The witch slapped her shining cleaver onto the wooden table. The sharp clatter startled Lorenzo and made him cry. Behind her Signora Celano's little mouth was a straight line of determination. Still holding the axe, lifting it as if ready to take off Haberman's hands, she came forwards with belligerent little steps.

Haberman wouldn't fight that squat beast off. He reached into his coat and drew the pistolet.

The confined space made one shot resound a deafening thunder. Signora Celano fell backwards, taking with her a chair, a side table and various pots. A hole beneath one cheek emitted blood and a tendril of smoke. Her fat knees trembled. Haberman went to stand over her and shot again, into the wide serious brow. Her eyes were spider-web-cracked like a smashed windscreen.

A small fire kindled itself in his chest, a familiar sensation.

It was familiar from those days spent so close to death's door—yet how weak it was. The witch stood at the table with the baby bawling and kicking on its back, and she was trying to set Haberman's heart on fire, make it burst like an overfilled balloon.

There was no fire, only a small heat that soon faded. The more she tried, the more she concentrated, the more this ugly witch's features drained of the last of their juice.

My god, Haberman reflected, *how she really did need this girl and poor infant to feed her. She's weak. She'll never know strength again.* And, at the same time, the witch seemed to come to an understanding of her own incapacity.

She uttered his name as an entreaty: "Haberman."

Will I die if she dies?

You won't, Mr Haberman, because I'm with you. I'll look after you now—as promised.

"Don't—" Agata Rosso gasped, "—don't believe her."

He stared at the way her exhausted features made her more than ever a witch carved from stone.

Then she spoke one more word—"Please"—and Haberman saw the sum of her plans and the sum of her dreams replaced by the sum of her fears, and so he shot once then twice, and as the witch lay twisting on the ground he used the last of the handgun's eight. In the confined space of this vault, the painful echoes resonated and lingered. When silence finally came even the baby was stunned, wide-eyed and quiet.

"Mr Haberman…"

He was distracted instead by the dolls. Why didn't he have a second magazine to shoot each through the head, followed by that man on his cot? Haberman stood over Giancarlo Rosso. The eyes moved in a body that was dead.

A spike or one of these blades, I'll drive it into him.

"…Mr Haberman…forget him. Please…"

He moved back towards the girl.

"Get me down…and the baby, make him safe…"

Lía's voice gave out. She'd already fallen into a dead-slump, head hanging forwards, feet slipped from beneath her. Her hair was over her face and her wrists and shoulders once again took her weight.

Haberman had no more sense of any harmony, of nothing sweet being whispered into his skull—and there was no further feeling of his bleak eternity. Instead he felt curiously whole; almost contented; attached to Lía Munro as if by a leash, yet the sensation was entirely agreeable.

A pocket in Celano's apron held the required key. He dug it out then snapped open the small padlock holding Lía's chains together. He noticed a startling thing. Even as Haberman freed the girl's wrists and arms, and held her so she wouldn't fall, he saw how wizened and mottled her skin had become.

For the effort of what she'd just done?

He carried her out of the plastic pool and placed her on the floor. As she breathed he smelled earth and decay. There was no more summer inside her. He moved grey, stringy hair aside to reveal a face the mirror of the witch Agata Rosso's. Stunned, Haberman sat with Lía, trying to understand. Her ordeal and what she'd willed to happen—the cost of it was clear.

And of course there were her three questions:

"Can you save me, Lía?"

"Yes."

"Will you change me?"

"Yes."

"And will you let me serve you forever?"

"Yes."

And so from this moment forward I'll live and die for her in whatever she'll have me do.

Now that the former Karl Haberman is dead.

He needed to get her out of there. Agata Rosso rested in a pool dark and red, yet Haberman perceived the faintest glow around the shrivelled corpse. It was a subtle, almost transparent light. He regarded the bare bulbs, he searched the ceilings and walls. There were no windows. He simply couldn't pinpoint the source of this glow. Something so mysterious and strange didn't bode well; yes indeed, he'd take Lía Munro away fast.

One thing remained, however. It was about Donatello's child, Lorenzo, and what Lía had managed to gasp:

"…and the baby, make him safe…"

So he'd do that of course, but how? Most natural would be to return the baby to his mother, but Haberman had no idea where she'd now be. Then was the father the right person to have Lorenzo?

No he was not.

Haberman went to the table and picked the baby up, held him for the first time. In fact Haberman couldn't remember when he'd previously held a baby. The sensation was—interesting. And then there was the way Lorenzo looked at him, as if with understanding. Haberman shook his head; nothing in this vault was simple; and nothing in this vault felt over and done with.

As if to underscore the thought Donatello Zappavigna started to stir from where he remained face-flat on the floor. Still holding the baby, Haberman glanced at the staircase, then at Lía's prone body. His pistolet was empty; he was trapped. Haberman didn't have enough time to get the baby and Lía away, and he had nothing to protect them from Donatello.

The grunt's fingers stretched and curled. Haberman retreated. Donatello pushed himself to his knees, and, blinking, saw the blood and splatters of human bone and viscera. His eyes fell on Haberman and the bundle he held, and did not shift as he slowly and deliberately found his feet. It was as if the grunt understood what had happened; he also appeared to comprehend the meaning in the way Haberman held Lorenzo away from him.

Donatello staggered with a first step, then gathered himself and came forward. Haberman's arms wrapped more protectively around the boy.

Silence.

A wolf's eyes met a very different Haberman's.

Haberman wouldn't let himself yield.

With a glowering threat, the wolf looked away to Lía helpless on the floor.

Another silent moment passed. The colour in the grunt's face deepened.

Haberman understood the unsubtle meaning.

Donatello extended his hands.

Haberman let the boy be taken.

A father kissed his son's brow, then without a word he carried him up the internal staircase, steps soon lumbering and creaking in the floorboards above.

Haberman rushed to Lía's side. By god was that his first failure for her? Or was the boy now in his best safe place?

Whatever the case, Haberman would never, ever, fail her. Picking up her limp body now, holding her, the sensation was—

—beautiful.

A word he'd never understood.

He carried her from the house.

The night was fresh, rain gone, clouds scudding under a quiet moon. Haberman lay Lía on the soft leather of his vehicle's back seats, then turned the Mercedes to follow the running clouds.

The Children Are Air

The kitchen remained in darkness, the candle had burned itself out. Candela raised her head from where she'd slumped. She'd helped Lía but the effort left her feeling that the blood had been sucked from her veins.

Candela could no longer feel the girl. And there was nothing of Lorenzo, the most frustrating thing of all.

With jittery hands she reached for the candle to light it yet again, but the thing had melted down, becoming one flat puddle that overflowed the dessert plate.

She refused to cry. She refused to give up hope. Candela felt around for the box of matches. She struck one and tried to relight the tiny stub of the wick. It flared and went out. She tried again and again with the same result. When she stood it was so quick and harsh that her chair clattered backwards. She found the wall switch and in the obscene glare there was nothing to see. The side of her head felt horribly swollen; one eye had closed completely. *To hell with that and to hell with this house.*

She pushed herself outside to sodden ground. The rainfall was gone. Wisps of cloud crossed an arc of moon. The wind was now warm.

Her car waited with two doors still open. The key would be in the ignition. The only thing Candela could think was to drive to the witch's house. Donatello might be there or she might find some clue. Signora Celano usually knew everything; she might say where Donatello had taken Lorenzo.

Yet her panic increased. What would stop Donatello spiriting her baby away? He might have already taken him somewhere Candela couldn't find them. Soon it might be them travelling to some new country.

Please don't do it, Donatello. I swear I'll come back and live with you as your wife if you'll just put my baby in my arms.

An empty prayer that only wasted time. *Then think. What did your mother try so hard to teach you?*

The spirits, I'm supposed to ask the spirits to help focus my mind. But there are no spirits, the children have gone, haven't they?

Candela looked around at the dark night, at the vast silhouette of Rosso House.

She sensed something waiting for her. It couldn't be Paul, but what if she'd been too anxious, in too much of a hurry and he was still somehow alive? She might have missed some incredible subtlety to his breathing, or to a pulse barely perceptible. Candela returned to the portico. Paul was there exactly as before. She kneeled beside him and touched his cold hands and face once again.

Are you still trying to help me?

He wasn't.

She laid his hands down and stepped away.

But the children...

They were gathered by Paul as if to give comfort, or friendship, or maybe even the help he'd need for leaving. Candela saw them now, the first time, passing her as they left Paul, and the portico, and Rosso House, to gather on the wet spreading field of grass past the circular courtyard. There were three girls and two boys. One of the boys was much smaller than the others. They'd all stood behind Candela in the dark kitchen and through the candle had helped her find Lía, but not Lorenzo.

"Why not?" she asked out loud. "Why not?"

The smaller boy turned his face towards her.

But we did.

What?

We did.

Candela wanted to argue. She wanted to tell him he was lying, that they all were such hateful little monsters—then it was as if Candela finally reached past her own boundaries, boundaries she'd set herself as a girl no older than this ethereal child—and where she'd only been seeing Lía, of course Lía had seen a far wider view: of a large horrible room overcrowded with witching elements, and with dolls, and with Signora Celano, Giancarlo on a cot, Donatello crumpled on the floor, the hating man with his fine clothes and bald skull, and then of course Agata.

The picture made Candela gasp. Agata, and on a table in front of her,

Lorenzo, naked and with a cleaver held over him.

"What happened to him? Where's my baby?"

They knew the answer. She could read it in them.

The boy turned to consider the distant forests. The four others followed his lead. They all raised their hands and pointed past the southern reaches of the property.

"Why? Why there?"

The children replied by letting her see a new image, of a beast carrying a baby, pushing through thickets of trees, bare feet running beside a swiftly moving creek, surrounded by wooded hills—his new home.

Candela swoons for the intensity of this vision, and the children are air, each now free to travel to whatever their next place might be, no witch left to hold them in Halfway. They're gone and Candela senses their absence, and the great yawning vacancy of Rosso House behind her, and she can either believe she's gone mad or get in her car and hurry.

The Pleasure of
Obedience

He opened his eyes to the dawning glow of his bedroom, then slowly and carefully extricated himself from between the sheets. He let Roxanne sleep on—he wanted her to sleep on. His thoughts remained full of someone else.

Teddy Quinn slipped into a light cotton dressing robe and eased the bedroom door shut behind him. He went to the living room's sliding doors to take in whatever sort of day might be coming. It looked promising out there, yet a weight of melancholy rested on his shoulders. Roxanne's chicken casserole and bottle of red wine, not to mention Roxanne herself, hadn't quite taken his mind off what had happened to Mr Gavin. Roxanne couldn't know yet another problem bothered him; half-waking dreams of a girl named Lía.

He addressed the blue sky past his glass doors and small balcony:

Lía, are you all right?

Teddy put his fists to his temples. There were things in his head that weren't questions at all:

Help me.

Teddy, please help me.

And then there was this one, clear as the sound of a church bell on a quiet suburban Sunday morning:

Teddy, go find my father. Teddy, go help him…

Yet he hadn't done a bloody thing.

Not even six-thirty; Teddy Quinn dialled the Munro's number anyway. Something told him that just as there'd been no answer last night, the same would be repeated now. In fact the line was a dead burr, and what gripped his belly was greater and deeper than fear, it was an overwhelming sense of dread, of bad things having already happened.

Roxanne opened the bedroom door, emerging wrapped in a white bed-sheet. She squinted hard, sleepy eyes tortured by daylight.

"So early?"

Teddy kissed the top of Roxanne's tousled hair. She had to follow him back into the bedroom, where he dressed in jeans, a t-shirt, an old leather bomber jacket and sneakers.

"No work?"

"Not today." His voice, even to himself, was surprisingly husky. "And not again."

"Huh?"

"I'm sick of being a salesman."

"But that's what you are."

"I'm sick of everything I'm doing. Or not doing. Anyway, I have to go."

"So you're sick of me too, right?"

"No," Teddy spoke, and to his surprise it was the truth.

"Then what do you want to do?"

There was a second piece of truth, but he couldn't quite articulate it. Teddy didn't know what he wanted to do, or what would come next, but he was certain he would find that out at Rosso House.

◆━━━━━━━━━◆

Haberman watched as Lía Munro slept in his bed, bad dreams making this young girl with the old face grimace and twist. She was disagreeable to look at and gave off the mildewed odour of age, yet for hour after hour Haberman lay on the floor beside her.

He'd dressed Lía in a few of the more decent clothes Virna Khamitova had left in this room, and when he'd observed her nakedness he hadn't felt revulsion, nor any attraction, only the overpowering need to protect. Meanwhile, a part of his mind—some essence perhaps of the old Haberman—always wanted to go downstairs to check the late-night television and radio news. If murders were being talked about, what connections might police detectives eventually make? And if a net closed around Haberman, what would that mean for his devotion to the girl?

Well, he'd die before leaving her, and he wholeheartedly believed she would do the same for him.

That was the bond they'd made.

Lía continued to sleep unsoundly; Haberman wished he had some of Agata's muck to feed her. Twice he tried to make her sip a few drops of water, pressing a glass to her grey lips, but he might as well have forced a drink into one of the dead witch's dolls. So he let her be. His job was to stay where he was. Occasionally he checked his half-dozen neat stitches in the wrinkled skin below her jaw, a procedure he'd completed in spite of the girl's unquiet slumber.

And now he wondered if she might not be having nightmares after all. There were mysteries inside her he'd never understand. What if she was already fighting this premature aging? He prayed for a miracle overnight, one that would allow her to come awake as a lovely sixteen-year old girl once again. He prayed this only for her good self, of course, not for any need of his own. Whatever she would be, old or young, dry as a bone or full of the lush bloom of youth, Lía Munro was his guiding star; to her he'd always gaze.

In the hours after dawn his heart leaped to see Lía's eyes slowly open. Immediately Haberman stood from the covers and pillow he'd thrown onto the floor and moved to sit at her bedside. The girl's eyes were dull and heavy-lidded in a one-hundred-year-old face.

"Where am I?"

"In a safe place. This is where I live."

"I need to find my father. Please take me home."

"Of course."

She didn't quite have Agata Rosso's aged croak, but she did sound deeply weary. That weariness was reflected in the way he needed to help her sit up.

"If you could, some water, maybe something to eat."

"Give me a few moments."

He'd give her more than that. The girl had a completely new life to comprehend. So he took his time in the kitchen and when he returned the ensuite bathroom's door was shut, a tap running. He'd offer her the bath, bathing salts, shampoo, whatever she needed. Several minutes later the door opened and Lía shuffled back into the room. She sat on a chair in the corner of the room.

"You've been crying."

"It doesn't matter."

He passed her the glass of water. She needed both hands to hold it steady, taking tiny sips.

"Am I wearing your wife's clothes?"

"No wife, I'm pleased to say."

Haberman observed Lía as she tried to eat the sandwich he'd made her. His heart ached for the girl, a new sort of feeling, to be so concerned for another's well-being.

He said, "And so you hate me?"

"Isn't that the least of what you deserve?"

"I might have experienced something of a sea-change."

"Nothing reverses the things you've done."

"Yes," he said, "but one looks ahead, not behind."

She didn't like so easy an answer, and even as he said it a sense of shame enveloped him. Her contempt was barely restrained; well, he must certainly try harder. He'd earn the terms of their pact by showing Lía Munro that no sacrifice would be too great, if it would please her. Yet, at the same time, a small voice inside himself asked:

Just how much has this girl changed? She doesn't sound at all like a sixteen-year-old. In fact, doesn't she sound a little like the witch now dead?

Haberman had to admit it: this revelation actually shook him. Was she a new stone witch?

"Other than to be taken home," he said, "please tell me what you need."

"I don't know that yet." She couldn't eat more than a small corner of the sandwich and pushed the plate aside. "Let's go."

"First a shower or bath, perhaps allow me to find you more appropriate clothes?"

She shook her head, then she looked straight at him. "This sea-change of yours, how permanent is it?"

The question surprised him. Surprised him because the answer was so self-evident.

"It lasts forever, of course."

She contemplated him.

"We'll see."

Haberman felt the pain of her doubt, a loyal hound rebuffed by the hand of its master—though when Lía spoke, "Take me home, Haberman," the new sense of command in her voice filled him with a satisfaction most astonishing: no less than the sensual pleasure of obedience.

A Crying Forest

At the very end of a twisting and very muddy lane that had gone on for-ever, only to face an impenetrable wall of trees, the Toyota rested at a sideways angle in a wet ditch, its driver's door wide.

From there she'd hiked all the way through the night, flashlight from the car's glovebox in hand, Candela calling out in rough country. Sometimes slivers of moonlight helped her; often the moon disappeared, obstructed by heavy branches or thick forest canopies. Through an initial nature reserve she'd stumbled into open paddocks with horses still and silent as noble statues, then found her way across plains and vast tracts of scrub and rock. When she found herself back in bushland it was either part of the same reserve or something new altogether—she couldn't tell and it didn't matter. Candela would cry her baby's name wherever she was. In a section wet and thick as the most ancient rainforest she discovered a long gulley and a winding creek that ran deep with water, then flowed into a pretty pond bordered by broken, captured branches—a nice natural dam. The water glittered. She heard the cries and croaks of toads. Her flashlight's beam searched the surface of the water and the crannies of old broken branches that had fallen into it, then the furthest banks for Lorenzo's body. Mightn't he have been washed down to this point?

There was nothing, relief overcoming her.

Candela then climbed a long and slippery earth bank for higher ground. Overhanging vegetation sponged her face. She tripped over reeds and roots; she stepped over logs and avoided vast seas of lantana. Sometimes she sloshed through mud, sometimes coursing water. She pulled away leeches, fattening on her skin. There was the occasional mound left by a horse and smaller piles left by deer, kangaroos, wallabies and other mammals she couldn't name. She was lost in this dark world of scrub and bush and hardwood trees: there was ironbark, tallowwood, spotted gum and yellow stringybark, all illuminated into hulking shapes, or spectral beings, by her light.

And still nothing.

Yet Candela believed the children. They said Lorenzo was somewhere here and so here he had to be. She would never let herself stop crying Zo's name, no matter what. Morning would have to come soon, then it would be easier to find her way, to keep going.

She went into deeper valleys—Lorenzo! Lorenzo!—she climbed greater hills and ridges—Zo! Zo!—she walked into and across the deepest creek of all, dappling water carrying his name far along into silent, thickening bushland. The water, when she drank, needed spitting out, sour as brine. She felt thirst and hunger, then forgot them, falling too many times to count. She was always tripping, slipping, stumbling, but kept moving on.

Now she had no idea where she was. The trees and scrub thickened. She'd lose a trail, find another, then be completely encircled by moonlit forest. It was better when she could see the moon and stars above; worse when the world was enclosed in stifling vegetation. There was the devastation of some fire here, very wet woodlands there. A smell of ash plus the scents of trees and myrtle in what she'd now made into her very own crying forest.

Stop your weeping, it's useless. Call Lorenzo's name, that's your only job.

Candela collapsed between immensely tall hoop pines, and even as she fought off the urge to sleep two brothers found her.

Twins.

It felt like the deepest part of the night. The flashlight flickered its last moments and moonlight cast greater shadows; the pair, lanky and fair, walked out of inky black into an open patch where Candela saw them very clearly. They were mirrors of one another. Unnerved, Candela crawled away as fast as she could, scuttling like a field mouse. She sheltered by the trunk of a thick rosewood, and even as she did she kept repeating Lorenzo's name.

"Lorenzo? No, we don't know him. Do you know Paul?"

"Paul... Paolo... You mean Paul Munro?..."

She had to be talking to herself, a mad woman with mad hair and her mind gone running away. There was no one in this dark with her, yet in this dark here these young men were.

"Paul Munro," the first said, "that's the one."

"We've come to see him," continued the second, "but damned if we can find our way."

"My baby, do you know where my baby is?"

"He's our baby brother."

"Lorenzo!" she suddenly cried.

"Paulie!" the twins shouted together, laughing at their adventure.

———

By dawn she's fallen again, this time with her body a weight her legs didn't want to carry. How far has she gone? How many hundreds of scratches and insect bites has she collected in a single night? Sitting, leaning sideways against the exposed roots of a tree she can't name, she breathes hard and holds her side from a tumble maybe an hour back, down a slope of harsh scree. Blood on her scraped hands, more blood from her cheek. She remembers the throbbing lump at her head, given her by Donatello. She wishes she could open her swollen eye. Though what does pain matter? Her clothes are torn. Her hair's a bird's nest. More leeches are attached to her and she's lost her shoes.

Lorenzo, Lorenzo.

Softly, softly she speaks his name as she picks herself up. Then she takes a deep breath and wails that name into the hills and valleys as if for the very last time—as if a baby might finally prick up his ears and come find the arms of the mother calling.

As if to demand he return from the dark where he's gone.

Or to break the will of stones and trees and wild scrub.

Plus pastures full of light and timid deer running.

As if to summon a dog pack lost, looking for a home.

Or to awaken the heart of a wolf; yes, a mother wailing as if to break the heart of a wolf who's been freed from the hold of a witch, and who now wonders what it is he might really be.

A cry so forlorn as to make this man-wolf wonder: Do I even have a man's heart left inside me, one that can still break?

For a last moment, maybe the answer's *yes*.

———

Later Candela wakes in a bed of long wet grass and leaves, her face protected from the sun by an overhang of heavily laden branches. It's as if she's still in a dream because she's curled up beside a fragrant patchwork of wildflower, their colours yellow and violet-purple. More than that, nestled in her arms is a warm thing. He's naked and smells of wet fur. His hair is matted as if he's been licked and licked by great tongues.

He kicks his dirty feet and yawns.

His eyes are emerald.

She cries; she cries and opens the remnants of her shirt. Zo feeds happily and hungrily on what's left of her; she thanks God and Heaven and Angels, and the children too. Pure happiness brings her back to life; happiness tells her she still has a soul and her husband Donatello must as well. She wishes this same sort of undiluted happiness on Lorenzo forever, on Lía wherever she is, on Paul with his good heart, on every person and every creature no matter where they are or what they might be.

Then, with her baby, Candela laughs and cries and pulls him close so they might both sleep a little.

In his small yet determined way Lorenzo makes it clear he doesn't want this. Now fed, he instead wants his mother on her feet, moving. The light in his eyes and the furrowing of his brow conveys this to her. Well, Candela tells herself, a mother should always understand what her baby needs, maybe even what he's thinking.

So she finds her feet. With spit on her fingertips she wipes dirt from his cheeks; her baby, meanwhile, is interested in something past the thickest, most obstructing line of trees.

Candela carries him into the trees and picks her way around the trunks of twenty, maybe thirty ancient hoop pines. There's an unexpected clearing—a clearing that exposes a gulley and an open, rolling landscape. There's a running creek and a huge Chinese elm just made for the climbing feet of children. She knows this place; she's been here before.

Candela gathers her strength and climbs the hill.

To see what's in the distance, though not too far.

Look where we've come. It's Rosso House.

Little Zo makes a happy gurgling and puts a fist into Candela's hair, tugging it as if not to play but to pull her forward.

Meanwhile the wolf watches Candela and her baby walk across grass-land toward a house he knows well—or might have known well, in the once-upon-a-time of a thing called Donatello Zappavigna. He's silent and tense, this wolf, almost certain now of what he really is, and what he won't be again. His mind is doing something he doesn't quite understand: words and sentences are being replaced by images; thinking and reasoning become sense impressions; logical thoughts and illogical desires fade into instinct and need.

The man in him is darkening.

The man in the wolf is going.

And something better has grown.

In the last moments of thinking like a man he wonders what this thing called a man really is. Two-legged and slow, weak yet cruel, using something he calls love as a way to feed his desires and to sometimes feed the needs in others.

The wolf feels the very different need of a growling belly. He feels the growling in the bellies of his friends too, and so he calls them, not with useless names like Donny Zap or Mr H or Agata Rosso; he simply flattens his ears and bares his teeth and raises his tail, signs of dominance they understand.

And so he summons his friends the dogs, the long-lost, scattered, hungry, frightened dogs, and this new one too, the brown all jittery, and he leads them away, back into the forest, far from the hill and the red house, to rove through brush and scrub and find a narrow mountain ridge, and soon a kill—a young meaty doe.

So in this spot marked with blood and fur and bone they'll feed and sleep and play, waiting for the fall of night, when they'll move on together in search of some beautifully reddening moon.

In the Rooms of the Red House

A sort of snake cunning remained ingrained in his soul, he couldn't deny that, though he thought this might prove an attribute most useful in the service of the new Lía Munro. For even as the Mercedes approached the circular driveway of Rosso House, Haberman felt a familiar wariness descend, no matter how perfectly his disposition and outlook had changed. He hadn't expected to see a sports car, so garishly scarlet, parked close to yesterday's white Chrysler; he was happy he'd slipped the reloaded Makarova into the soft holster beneath today's brown linen blazer.

"Do you know this vehicle?"

"It belongs to Teddy Quinn."

"Who is he and why might he be here?"

"Be quiet Mr Haberman."

And so he was quiet, yet with senses attuned for anything that might be a danger to Lía Munro or that might threaten to come between them. Haberman's fingers itched to hold the pistolet; the skin across his scalp prickled for the eyes that must already be upon them.

The girl shuffled as a one-hundred-year-old, Haberman helping her by her thin right arm.

"But where's my father?"

"No doubt the visitor carried him inside."

"Or he made his own way."

Haberman made no comment about that, or about the sad desperation in her aged features. He let Lía investigate where she wanted, slow as a snail, seeking out her father's body until she spied the very obvious remains of her black dog, lying in grass. It hurt Haberman to know how the girl trembled, then he helped her kneel so she could wrap her arms around the mutilated corpse; the flies didn't bother her.

When he could make her move again Haberman kept his face averted. Too many shadows of pain were in that old face, yet now he felt little guilt or sorrow at the events and consequences of the previous day; the perpetrator was a man of the past; the Karl Haberman of today and the future was a completely different individual.

Wasn't he?

Haberman kept himself aware of everything surrounding them. The quiet was unnatural, even in this place of death.

"I'm not sure if the gentleman you refer to as Teddy Quinn is alone inside, but the fact he hasn't emerged speaks volumes."

"He might think I need saving."

"Do you also think this?"

"I don't need to be saved from you, Mr Haberman, but from what's happened to me, yes."

"Still," he said, and reached under his coat.

"Stop it."

He did.

"Your stupid gun. Take it out and empty it and drop it in the grass."

Haberman should do as she commanded, of course, yet why did he hesitate? It was as if beside his snake-cunning something else was too-well entrenched: the obstinate desire to be only himself.

"You refuse?"

"I apologise, but the answer is yes." He withdrew his hand, but without the gun, "My intention is only to protect you."

"You protect yourself."

"I understand your suspicion, but even you must admit that you seem quite afraid."

"I am."

"Of me?"

"Of what's inside the house. You won't need your gun for that."

"Meaning?"

"Mr Haberman, what I want more than anything is to go inside that house and find my father safe and well. I'm very afraid I won't."

"He did sustain a mortal wound."

He saw her grit her teeth, then Lía spoke with the stone witch's brittleness returned to her voice:

"Just help me."

Haberman guided her around the side and to the back door of silent Rosso House, fingers again itching for the Makarova.

Teddy Quinn didn't tremble. He waited barely breathing, holding himself still and straight in a dark corner of the hallway just outside the kitchen. He wasn't afraid. In fact he experienced the sort of dead calm that only comes with certainty: when they went into the kitchen and stepped into the hall, Lía and that man would walk right past him.

From upstairs, cowering at a curtain, he'd had glimpses of the two. The bedraggled, scratched and insect-bitten woman who'd arrived at the house with her baby had leaned beside him, also watching, though her vision was terribly impaired by that one black and swollen eye.

With an accent she'd whispered: "This is the man who has shot Paulo. His name is Haberman"

"And Lía's with him. Why would he be back?"

Together they'd watched them move with aching slowness around the green grounds, the man holding Lía by the arm. There seemed to be no coercion in that touch; instead it was as if he assisted her. But had she been hurt somehow? What was wrong with Lía? The man, that Haberman, actually helped her to kneel so she could hug what was left of the black dog.

God, but she must be hurt, Lía looked so odd, so strange. So not herself. For long moments Teddy wasn't even certain it *was* Lía. Her hair appeared so different: was it the colour of steel? And her face, from this distance, like a Halloween mask or something.

Yet it was her.

With the baby nestled close the woman told him, "This man Haberman will have a gun."

"You're sure he did this to Paul?"

Then, involuntarily, they'd both glanced toward the covered body in the bed. When she'd nodded, the apprehension in Teddy Quinn's gut changed to something more useful, something full of—how could he think of it, what was the right word?—*determination*. It might have been the shocks of the morning that scared him straight: Teddy arrived at Rosso House to discover Lía's dog Dakota torn apart, then to find Paul Munro propped dead at the front door. The hole in his chest, the grey face, the dried blood in his shirt, the flies—Teddy had left him there to tear through the place searching for Lía, crying out her name. When he didn't find her, he'd hurried to call for an ambulance and police, but the telephone was dead, useless. Then he'd checked outside and found the broken junction box.

What had happened here?

He needed to hurry off the property and find the nearest public telephone or drive over to the nearest home. Yet he hadn't wanted to leave Paul so alone in that cold portico, grey-faced, attracting ever more flies and insects.

And something else had been on Teddy's mind:

When he'd gone through Rosso House in his futile search for Lía he'd seen a large envelope on her study desk, addressed to him at Gavin Realty, waiting—he supposed—to be mailed. Nervous and shaking, he'd returned to the room, then sitting at the edge of her small single bed he read through what she'd written:

So you heard me, Teddy, when I needed your help. Does the word 'friend' have a better definition than that? I don't think so.

He read about Lily Cheung; he read about Miss Misery Eyes becoming Miss X-Ray eyes; he even read about Nanny Viv—then there were the pages photocopied from text books at the library, and he tried to understand information about evil witches and their love for wolves, and spells called the evil eye.

All this had made him return to the portico and Paul Munro; all this made him scan the property and the blue distance; all this together made him feel he was waiting for something more—and so he carried the dead man inside, and up the staircase, and to the main bedroom at the front of the house. Teddy had laid the body down thinking: *There's more to this, there's more to Lía Munro, and everything I'm looking at feels unresolved.*

So what's going to happen, now that I've disturbed a crime scene and I've covered this poor man with a blanket?

To answer him, a woman who'd been through her own sort of hell, by the look of her, had arrived with her baby.

Who are you?

How did you get here?

Him to her and her to him.

First thing this morning Teddy Quinn had believed that in Rosso House he'd find his destiny, now here it was, coming as quiet footfalls in the kitchen, no voices.

H e gripped the short, heavy duty crowbar quickly snatched from one of the downstairs rooms Lía's father had been renovating.

A small grey thing emerged through the kitchen doorway, passing right before him and stumbling on a carpet runner. The man with her—Haberman—well-dressed and with a shining skull, immediately reached forward to assist.

Against that gleaming skull Teddy cracked the top flat of the crowbar with all his might. The man thudded hard to the floor. Teddy stared, amazed at what he'd done. The man didn't twitch or move in any way.

The small grey thing turned. Teddy dropped the crowbar and stepped into the light. The moment was over and so was his calm. Teddy stood wide-eyed, even breathless for what he'd just done.

And wide-eyed, even breathless, for what he was seeing: *My god. My god my god.*

"Teddy—you came," this thing that might be Lía spoke.

"I think...I think I heard you. But—"

He couldn't finish the sentence, not faced with this utterly changed Lía Munro. He could see this was her; he perceived the girl in the crone; and yet, and yet...

"Did you help my father?"

He nodded, nodded hard, stupid, useless tears now springing to his eyes.

"I...I put him upstairs. And, and, there's a woman. A woman called Candela."

"Alone?"

"With a baby."

Teddy Quinn felt his conscious mind must detach itself from his head and evaporate like mist, yet this news, he saw, was good. Ancient Lía Munro wanted to be helped up the staircase. The way she moved, the way she was, it made a horrible squirming in Teddy's belly.

Reading that letter, this wasn't what I expected.

Then Teddy Quinn pushed all misgivings aside.

Whatever you need, Lía .

Her quavering hand, thin, mottled and wrinkled, found his bicep.

L ía wasn't certain she'd make it to the top of the staircase. Her breath was laboured; every step a trial greater than the step before. In the short period since this change had come she'd learned new things about life—that is to say, about life near its inevitable end. The increasing shadow over the senses, a dimming perception of the world outside her own head, her eyes perceiving far less than she was used to and her ears blunting the sounds of the natural world—all of this she now understood.

And so it must have been for her mother, and for Mrs Badger too. Even for Agata Rosso, with her mad intention to be young and strong again.

To have Father Death so present at your shoulder; to count the last beats left in your heart; yet to want Life more than anything.

No, to want to see my father more than anything.

At the top floor Lía tried to quicken her pace, but her hips hurt, her joints ached, and her knees begged her to sit down. She forced herself on, guided by Teddy.

By my friend, Teddy Quinn.

The bedroom door was shut and locked.

"I told her to keep it that way." Teddy tapped. "It's me, it's okay."

The sound of the key in the old lock, the door opening, and there was Candela. At first the expression in Candela's face reflected the hag she saw; and Lía of course saw what Donatello had done to Candela. They held one another. Lía's shoulders shuddered and she felt her frail bones wracked by the sobs she now couldn't stop.

Candela didn't weep. Candela spoke soothing words. Lía felt the long caresses of Candela's hand along her steel-wire hair.

She seemed almost happy.

"Everything will be good," Candela tried to ease away. "Now wipe your tears. Don't let him see you crying."

Lía tried to do as she was told. She wiped her face with the back of one hand. Even that small movement created stabs of aching pain, but when Candela stepped aside Lía's dimmed eyes filled with the sight of a baby, a baby whose bright eyes, in turn, seemed to fill with the sight of her.

This baby resting in the arms of a man who was sitting up in his bed, bare-chested, one round scar beneath his collar bone.

Little Zo held by Lía's father.

"I see it happen." The wonder in Candela's voice was as nothing against what Lía felt. "It happens in seconds, so without pain and drama it is like a dream. After your friend has gone downstairs Lorenzo wants to go to Paolo. He kicks and struggles for him. So I have laid him on his chest. Soon Paolo moves and takes the blanket from his face. He sits up and is concerned for what Donatello has done to me. I take off his shirt so awful with blood but underneath when I clean his skin there is a hole fixed and healed."

As Candela spoke Paul Munro kept watching his daughter. Now he put out a hand. They didn't speak. As she took shuffling steps forwards Lía felt her heart lift. He would be seeing her as she now was, of course, and he must be horrified, but that reaching hand, it was happiness and hope combined.

Once again Teddy Quinn helped her. For a moment Lía glanced at him as if for an explanation of how all this was happening, but in a moment Lía understood her father was already holding the explanation, and Agata Rosso had provided its first clue, even though the witch hadn't quite understood the real extent of what she'd been saying:

Girl, you're the child of an animal father and a miraculous mother, and that's what makes you so special.

So Lorenzo—Lía tried to speak to him, mind to mind—*little Zo, you're the child of a father a wolf and a mother who carries miracles, and that's made you more special than any of us could have dreamed.*

Lía watched Zo's eyes so deep and serious. Agata Rosso would have destroyed the world and everything in it for the one chance to give herself and her Giancarlo new life. Here, Zo had provided that life to Lía's father without being asked and with no price attached.

How?

Because he feels, and he feels me:

Mr Haberman, what I want more than anything is to go inside that house and find my father safe and well.

And why?

Maybe for the love around him.

———

His snake cunning might have failed him downstairs, but now he came ever-so-silently up the staircase, then he was through the doorway holding his bleeding skull, with the Russian Makarova drawn and pointing in their faces. He looked at Lía with all the fawning need of a dog kicked by its master; then at these others in this bedroom, including Paul Munro sitting up in his bed, holding a baby.

For moments Haberman held steady, not moving, instinct allowing the threat of the gun to do all the talking required. Gently he'd take Lía by the arm and lead her out and away from these people.

And if it's her desire that she should stay?

I serve and obey you, Lía Munro, and so nothing and no one must come between us. If the pistolet needs to speak four times in order to silence those gathered here in this room, including a little one, then let it be so.

Wait.

What am I seeing?

In the tense silence Karl Haberman received a dawning vision of a man still a monster, no matter his promises of change. In earlier times such a monster might have been chased by villagers with torches and axes, to be set alight in a field or strung up by the heels until his miserable life faded away. Today such a thing might be damned forever to live a life behind iron bars, or even fall under a hail of law enforcers' bullets.

Why these images, and who forces them on me?

Not my new stone witch, she's too loyal, and far too reduced.

Haberman's eyes moved: this young man of the garish vehicle; Donatello's wife; Paul Munro.

Which of you is playing these games?

Haberman stumbles.

Wait. It doesn't matter.

His hand loses its tight grip on the Makarova. His hand drops to his side.

It doesn't matter because when I look into the twinkling eyes of this baby boy, I see he wants me to pick him up and hold him.

The pistolet makes a quiet thud onto the bedroom's carpet. Haberman comes forward. The mother, Candela, starts, yet Haberman sees how Lía reassures her.

Yes, all is well, all is well, he also thinks toward that mother. *I'm a man with little experience of babies about to do what he should have done many times in his life.*

Hold one close.

At the bedside, with great care he takes the child. Everyone in this room can see how little Zo comes to Haberman willingly and warmly; *maybe,* Haberman reflects, *I should have made time—or given the space in my heart—to make a few of my own, sons and daughters never born that I could have filled with appreciation for the world rather than to learn how one can crush its people and bleed them dry.*

Haberman feels Life against his chest and so Lorenzo wants Life back.

It's for Lía, isn't it?

Haberman feels the heavy beating of his own heart. Lorenzo must swallow that beating, and so demands it.

Take it, it's yours.

This little thing wants Haberman's hand in Lía's.

So he reaches out and Lía puts her hand in his. Her palm is warm; his has turned dead-cold. Haberman gazes at her and would like to brush a lock of grey hair from Lía's deeply lined forehead. He wants to carry the memory of that wiry and brittle hair, even if it is the quality of steel wool, with him forever. And remember her green eyes too, which even though they sag with age, and never looked at him with love, reflect intelligence and determination.

She may, or may not, be a new stone witch, but—

I'm sorry for the evils I've done. I apologise for the hurt I've put into your heart.

Haberman feels the last of himself going, conscious thought disappearing, all of Karl Haberman turning to ether.

I'm sorry because I lo—

And he feels his life, the powerful beating of his heart, going into Lía Munro.

No more a stone witch to anyone's eye, but a girl, a glorious girl.

Epilogue

Wolf

The glow emanating from the old witch Agata Rosso darkened and darkened again, as if spoiled by the air it met. Slowly it spread like a stain over the dolls and the wrinkled body of Giancarlo Rosso. In time Giancarlo Rosso's irregular flicker of a heartbeat steadied and started to worry at the translucent skin near his sternum. It wouldn't be strong, this body, because what the dead witch had to offer wasn't much. He'd remain old and weary until some fuller miracle, if it ever came, but for now at least he'll walk, he'll function.

Giancarlo blinks mucus from his eyes.

Gentle hands reach down.

His muses, but only three. There's blonde Soleil; yellow-haired Primavera; black Martina, for coming wars. And no flame-haired Malvolia, which makes his soul burn.

"*Aiutami.*" Help me.

They help their wolf to stand.

And will continue to help him, now and to the day he can create the world he dreams.